FATED TO BE FREE.

A Novel.

BY JEAN INGELOW,

AUTHOR OF "OFF THE SKELLIGS," "STUDIES FOR STORIES," "MOPSA, THE FAIRY," ETC.

BOSTON:
ROBERTS BROTHERS.
1875.

Cambridge:
Press of John Wilson & Son.

AUTHOR'S PREFACE TO THE AMERICAN EDITION.

When authors attempt to explain such of their works as should explain themselves, it makes the case no better that they can say they do it on express invitation. And yet, though I think so, I am about to give some little account of two stories of mine which are connected together, — "Off the Skelligs," and "Fated to be Free."

I am told that they are peculiar; and I feel that they must be so, for most stories of human life are, or at least aim at being, works of art, — selections of interesting portions of life, and fitting incidents, put together and presented as a picture is; and I have not aimed at producing a work of art at all, but a piece of nature. I have attempted to beguile my readers into something like a sense of reality; to make them fancy that they were reading the unskilful chronicle of things that really occurred, rather than some invented story as interesting as I knew how to make it.

It seemed to me difficult to write, at least in prose, an artistic story; but easy to come nearer to life than most stories do.

Thus, after presenting a remarkable child, it seemed proper to let him (through the force of circumstance) fall away into a very commonplace man. It seemed proper indeed to crowd the pages with children, for in real life they run all over; the world is covered thickly with the prints of their little footsteps, though, as a rule, books written for grown-up people are kept almost clear of them. It seemed proper also to make the more important and interesting events of life fall at rather a later age than is commonly chosen, and also to make the more important and interesting persons not extremely young; for, in fact, almost all the noblest and finest men and the loveliest and sweetest women of real life are considerably older than the vast majority of heroes and heroines in the world of fiction.

I have also let some of the same characters play a part in both stories, though the last opens long before the first, and runs on after it is finished. It is by this latter device that I have chiefly hoped to give to each the air of a family history, and thus excite curiosity and invite investigation; the small portion known to a young girl being told by her from her own point of view and mingled into her own life and love, and the larger narrative taking a different point of view and giving both events and motives.

But in general, while describing the actions and setting down the words, I have left the reader to judge my people; for I think many writers must feel as I do, that, if characters are at all true to life, there is just as much uncertainty as to how far they are to blame in any course that they may have taken as there is in the case of our actual living contemporaries.

But why then, you may ask, do I write this preface, which must, if nothing else had done so, destroy any such sense of truth and reality?

Why, my American friends, because I am told that a great many of you are pleased to wish for some explanation. I am sure you more than deserve of me some efforts to please you. I seldom have an opportunity of saying how truly I think so; and besides, even if I had declined to give it, I know very well that for all my pains you would still have never been beguiled into the least faith as to the reality of these two stories!

LONDON, June, 1875.

CONTENTS.

CHAPTER I.

A WATCHER OF LILIES.

"Unto whom all hearts be open, all desires known, and from whom no secrets are hid."—*Collect, English Communion Service.*

IN one of the south-western counties of England, some years ago, and in a deep, well-wooded valley where men made perry and cider, wandered little and read less, there was a hamlet with neither farm nor cottage in it, that had not stood two hundred and fifty years, and just beyond there was a church nearly double that age, and there were the mighty wrecks of two great oak-trees, said to be more ancient still.

Between them, winding like a long red rut, went the narrow road, and was so deeply cut into the soil that a horseman passing down it could see nothing of its bordering fields; but about fifty yards from the first great oak the land suddenly dipped, and showed on the left a steep cup-like glen, choked with trees, and only divided from the road by a few dilapidated stakes and palings, and a wooden gate, orange with the rust of lichens, and held together with ropes and bands.

A carriage-drive was visible on the other side of the gate, but its boundaries were half obliterated by the grass and weeds that had grown over it, and as it wound down into the glen it was lost among the trees. Nature, before it has been touched by man, is almost always beautiful, strong, and cheerful in man's eyes; but nature, when he has once given it his culture and then forsaken it, has usually an air of sorrow and helplessness. He has made it live the more by laying his hand upon it, and touching it with his life. It has come to relish of his humanity, and it is so flavoured with his thoughts, and ordered and permeated by his spirit, that if the stimulus of his presence is withdrawn it cannot for a long while do without him, and live for itself as fully and as well as it did before.

There was nothing to prevent a stranger from entering this place, and if he did so, its meaning very soon took hold of him; he perceived that he had walked into the world of some who were courting oblivion, steeping themselves in solitude, tempting their very woods to encroach upon them, and so swathe them as in a mantle of secrecy which might cover their misfortunes, and win forgetfulness both for their faults and for their decline.

The glen was about three hundred yards across, and the trees which crowded it, and overflowed its steep side encroaching over the flat ground beyond, were chiefly maples and sycamores. Every sunbeam that shot in served to show its desolation. The place was encumbered with fallen branches, tangled brushwood, dead ferns; and wherever the little stream had spread itself there was a boggy hollow, rank with bulrushes, and glorious with the starry marsh marigold. But here and there dead trees stood upright, gaunt and white in their places, great swathes of bark hanging loose from their limbs, while crowds of young saplings, sickly for want of space and light, thrust up their heads towards the sunshine, and were tied together and cumbered in their struggle by climbing ropes of ivy, and long banners of the wild black vine.

The ring of woodland was not deep, the domain was soon traversed, and then stepping out into a space covered with rank meadow grass, one might see the house which should have been its heart.

It was a wide, old, red brick mansion, with many

irregular windows, no pane in which was more than two inches square. One end of it was deeply embedded in an orchard of pear and apple trees, but its front was exposed, and over the door might be seen the date of its building. The roof was high and sloping, and in its centre rose a high stack of brick chimneys, which had almost the effect of a tower, while under the eaves, at regular intervals, were thrust out grotesque heads, with short spouts protruding from their mouths. Some of these had fallen on the paving-flags below, and no one had taken them up. No one ever looked out of those front windows, or appeared to notice how fast the fruit-trees by the house, and the forest-trees from the glen, were reaching out their arms and sending forth their young saplings towards it, as if to close it in and swallow it up.

So still it looked with its closed shutters, that what slight evidence there was of its really being inhabited appeared only to make it yet more strange and alone; for these were a gaunt, feeble, old dog, who paced up and down the flags as if keeping guard, and a brass handle on the oaken door, which was so highly polished that it glittered and shone in the light.

But there was a great deal of life and company up aloft, for a tribe of blue pigeons had their home among those eaves and chimneys, and they walked daintily up the steep roof with their small red feet while they uttered their plaintive call to their young.

It was a strange fancy that prompted the cleaning of this door-handle. "I mun keep it bright," the old woman would say who did it, "in case anybody should come to call." No one but herself ever opened the door, nobody within cared that she should bestow this trouble. Nobody, for more than fifty years, ever had "come to call," and yet, partly because the feigning of such a possibility seemed to connect her still with her fellows of the work-a-day world, and partly because the young master, her foster-brother, whom she deeply loved, had last been seen by her with this door-handle in his hand, she faithfully continued every day to begin her light tasks by rubbing it, and while so doing she would often call to mind the early spring twilight she had opened her eyes in so long ago, and heard creaking footsteps passing down the stairs; and then how she had heard the great bolt of the door withdrawn, and had sprung out of bed, and peering through her casement had seen him close it after him, and with his young brother steal away among the ghostly white pear-trees, never to return.

"And I didn't give it a thought that they could be after aught worse than rook-shooting," she would murmur, "for all I heard a sort of a sobbing on the stairs. It was hard on poor old Madam though, never to take any leave of her; but all her life has been hard for that matter, poor innocent old critter. Well, well, I hope it's not a sin to wish 'em happy, spite of that bad action; and as for her, she's had her troubles in this world, as all the parish is ready to testify, and no doubt but what that will be considered to her in the world to come."

All the parish was always ready to testify that poor old Madam had had a sight o' troubles. All the parish took a certain awful pleasure in relating them; it was a sort of distinction to have among them such an unfortunate woman and mother, so that the very shepherds' and ditchers' wives plumed themselves upon it over those in the next parish, where the old Squire and his wife had never lost one of their many children, or had any trouble "to speak of." "For there was no call to count his eldest son's running off with a dairymaid, it being well beknown," they would observe with severity, "that his mother never would let e'er a one of the young madams as were suitable to marry him come nigh the house."

The dairymaid belonged to their parish, and so afforded them another ground of triumph over their rivals. "Besides," they would say, "wasn't their own church parson—old parson Green that everybody swore by—wasn't he distinctly heard to say to the young man's father, 'that he might ha' been expected to do wus'? They didn't see, for their parts, that aught but good had come of it neither; but as for poor old Madam, anybody might see that no good ever came nigh her. We must submit ourselves to the Almighty's will," they would add with reverence. They couldn't tell why He had afflicted her, but they prayed Him to be merciful to her in her latter end.

It was in old parson Green's time, the man they all swore by, that they talked thus; but when parson Craik came, they learned some new words, and instead of accepting trouble with the religious acquiescence of the ignorant, they began to wonder and doubt, and presently to offend their rivals by their fine language. "Mysterious, indeed," they would say, "is the ways of Providence."

In the meantime the poor old woman who for so many years was the object of their speculations and their sympathy, lived in all quietness and humbleness at one end of her long house, and on fine Sundays edified the congregation by coming to church. Not, however, on foot; her great age made that too much an exertion for her. She was drawn by her one old man-servant in a chair on wheels, her granddaughter and her grandson's widow walking beside her, and her little great-grandson, Peter, who was supposed to be her heir, bringing up the rear.

Old Madam Melcombe, as the villagers called her. She had a large frame, but it was a good deal bowed down; her face was wrinkled, and her blue eyes had the peculiar dimness of extreme old age, yet those who noticed her closely might detect a remarkable shrewdness in her face; her faculties were not only perfect, but she loved to save money, and still retained a high value for, and a firm grip of, her possessions. The land she left waste was, notwithstanding, precious to her. She had tied up her gate that her old friends might understand, after her eldest son's death, that she could not be tortured by their presence and their sympathy; but she was known sometimes by her grand-daughters to enlarge on the goodness of the land thereabouts, and to express a hope that when Peter's guardians came into power, they would bring it under the plough again. She went to church by a little footpath, and always conducted herself with great decorum, though, twice or thrice during the reading of the lessons, she had startled the congregation by standing up with a scared expression of countenance, and looking about her while she leaned on her high staff as if she thought some one had called her; but she was in her ninety-fifth year, and this circumstance, together with the love and pity felt for her, would easily have excused far greater eccentricities.

She had felt very keenly the desertion of her second and her fourth sons, who had run away from home when the elder was barely eighteen, and without previous quarrel or unkindness so far as was known; nor was it believed that they had ever come to see her since, or sought her forgiveness. Her eldest son, while still in the flower of his age, had died by his own hand; her youngest son had died in the West Indies, of fever; and the third, the only one who remained with her, had never been either a comfort or a credit to his family: he had but lately died, leaving a son and a daughter. Of these, the daughter was with her grandmother, and the son was just dead, having left an only child, his heir.

At one end of the house, as had been said, was an orchard, at the other was a large garden. If the desolate appearance of the house was likely to raise oppressive feelings in a stranger's mind, how much more this garden! It was a large oblong piece of ground, the walls of which enclosed the western end of the house completely. One of them ran parallel with the front, and a massive oaken door somewhat relieved its flat monotony; but this door afforded no ingress, it was bolted and barred from within.

The garden was that special portion of her inheritance on which the ancient owner rested her eyes; morning, noon, and evening she would sit gazing on its green fishpond, all overgrown with duckweed, on the lawn now fast being encroached on by shrubbery, and on the bed of lilies which from year to year spread and flourished.

But she never entered it, nor did any one else.

That end of the house had but four windows on the ground floor, and these were all strongly barred with iron, the places they lighted consisting of kitchen, offices, and a cider store-room. Above these on the first-floor were three pleasant rooms overlooking the garden, and opening on to a wooden gallery or verandah, at each end of which was an alcove of an old-fashioned and substantial description.

The gallery was roofed above, had a heavy oaken balustrade, and being fully ten feet wide afforded a convenient place in which the lonely old lady could take exercise, for, excepting on Sunday, she was scarcely ever known to leave her own premises. There also her little great-grandson Peter first learned to walk, and as she slowly passed from one alcove to the other, resting in each when she reached it, he would take hold of her high staff and totter beside her, always bestowing on her as much as he could of his company, and early showing a preference for her over his aunt and even over his mother.

Up and down the gallery this strange pair would move together, and as she went she gazed frequently over the gay wilderness below, and if she sat long in one of the alcoves, she would peer out at its little window always on the same scene; a scene in the winter of hopeless neglect and desolation. Dead leaves, dead dry stalks of foxgloves and mullens, broken branches, and an arbour with trellised roof, borne down by the weight of the vine.

But in spring and summer the place was gorgeous in parts with a confused tangle of plants and shrubs in flower. Persian lilacs, syringas, labernums made thickets here and there and covered their heads with bloom. Passion flowers trailed their long tendrils all over the gallery, and masses of snow-white clematis towered in many of the trees.

All distinction between pathway and border had long since been obliterated, the eyes wandered over a carpet of starred and spangled greenery. Tall white gladiolas shot up above it, and spires of fox-gloves and rockets, while all about them and among the rose-trees, climbed the morning glory and the briony vine.

Stretching in front of the ruined arbour was a lawn, and along one edge of it under the wall, grew a bed of lilies, lilies of the valley, so sweet in their season, that sometimes the old lady's grand-daughters would affirm that a waft of their breath had reached them as they sat up in the gallery at work.

It was towards this spot that Madam Melcombe looked. Here her unquiet face was frequently turned, from her first early entrance into the gallery, till sunset, when she would sit in one of the alcoves in hot weather. She gave no reason for this watch, but a kindly and reverent reserve protected her from questions. It was felt that the place was sacred to some recollection of her youth, when her young children were about her, before the cruel desertion of two, the ceaseless quarrels of other two, and the tragic death of one of them, had darkened her days.

The one door in the wall being fastened, and the ground-floor at that end of the house having none but barred windows, it follows that the only entrance to the garden was now from this gallery. There was, indeed, a flight of steps leading down from it, but there was a gate at the top of them, and this gate was locked.

On the day of her eldest son's funeral, his stricken mother had locked it. Perhaps she scarcely knew at first that the time would never come when she should find courage again to open it; but she took away the key to satisfy some present distressful fancy, and those about her respected her desire that the place should not be entered. They did not doubt that there was some pathetic reason for this desire, but none was evident, for her son had gone down to his death in a secluded and now all but inaccessible part of the glen, where, turning from its first direction, it sunk deeper still, and was divided by red rocks from its more shallow opening.

A useless watch at best was hers, still of the terrace, and the arbour, and the bed of lilies; but as she got yet deeper down into the vale of years, those about her sometimes hoped that she had forgotten the sorrowful reason, whatever it might be, that drew her eyes incessantly towards them. She began even to express a kind of pleasure in the gradual encroachments of the lovely plants. Once she had said, "It is my hope, when I am gone, as none of you will ever disturb them."

Whatever visions of a happy youth, whatever mournful recollections of the sports of her own children, might belong to them, those now with her knew not of them, but they thought that her long and pathetic watch had at last become more a habit with her than any conscious recalling of the past, and they hoped it might be so.

The one sitting-room used by the family opened into the gallery, and was a good deal darkened by its roof. On one side of it was Peter's nursery, on the other his great-grandmother's chamber, and no other part of the house was open excepting some kitchen offices, and two or three bedrooms in the roof. The servants consisted of a nurse (herself an old woman), who sat nearly all day in the parlour, because her far more aged mistress required much attendance, a grey-headed housemaid, a cook, and a man, the husband of this last. His chief business was to groom the one horse of the establishment, and ride on it to the nearest town for meat, grocery, and other marketings.

The floor of the parlour was oak, which had once been polished; all the furniture was to the last degree quaint and old fashioned; the two large windows opened like double doors upon the gallery, and were shaded by curtains of Madras chintz. The chairs, which were inconveniently heavy, were also covered with chintz; it was frilled round them like a petticoat, and was just short enough to show their hideous club-feet. Over the chimney-piece was a frame, and something in it said to be a picture. Peter, when a very little child, used to call it "a picture of the dark," for it seemed to be nothing but an expanse of deep brown, with a spot of some lighter hue in one corner. He wished, he said, that they had put a piece of moon in to show how dark that country was. The old nurse, however, had her theories about this patch; she would have it that it was somewhat in the shape of a jacket; she thought it likely that the picture represented a hunt, and said she supposed the foremost horseman in his red coat was watering his horse in a pond. Peter and the nurse had argued together on this subject many times before the old lady was appealed to, but when they once chanced to ask her about the picture, she affirmed that the patch was a lobster, and that a sort of ring which seemed faintly to encircle it was the edge of a plate. In short, she declared that this was a Dutch picture of still life, and that in Peter's time, when he came to have it cleaned, it would prove to be worth money.

"And when will it be my time?" asked little Peter innocently.

"Hold your tongue, child!" whispered his mother;

"it won't be your time till your poor dear grandmother's in heaven."

"I don't want her to go to heaven yet," said Peter in a plaintive tone (for he regarded her as much the best possession he had), and, raising his voice, he complained to her as to one threatening to injure him, "Grandmother, you don't want to go to heaven just yet, do you?"

"Lor bless the child!" exclaimed old Madam Melcombe, a good deal startled.

"No, don't," continued Peter in a persuasive tone; "stop here, but let me clean the picture, because I want to see that lobster."

"Now I tell you what," answered his great-grandmother rather sharply, "if you was to go and play in the gallery, it would be a deal better than arguing with me." So Peter departed to his play, and forgot the lobster for a little while.

But Peter was not destined that evening to please his great-grandmother, for he had no sooner got well into the spirit of his play in the gallery than he began to sing. "I'm a coward at songs," she would sometimes say; "and if it wasn't for the dear birds, I could wish there was no music in the world."

Her feeling was the same which has been beautifully described by Gassendi, who, writing in Latin, expresses himself thus:—

"He preferred also the music of birds to the human voice or to musical instruments, not because he derived no pleasure from these last, but because, after hearing music from the human voice, there remained a certain sustained agitation, disturbing attention and sleep; while the risings and fallings, the tones and changes and sounds and concords, pass and repass through the fancy; whereas nothing of the sort can be left after the warbling of birds, who, as they are not open to our imitation, cannot move the faculty of imagination within us." (Gassendi, in *Vita Peireskii.*)

In the garden was plenty of music of the sort that Madam Melcombe still loved. Peter could not shout in his play without disturbing the storm-cock as he sat up aloft singing a love-song to his wife. As for the little birds, blackcaps haunted almost every bush, and the timid white-throat brooded there in peace over her half-transparent eggs.

So no one ever sang in old Madam Melcombe's presence unless Peter forgot himself, and vexed his mother by chanting out snatches of songs that he had caught up from the village children. Mrs. Peter Melcombe formed for herself few theories; she was a woman dull of feeling and slow of thought; she knew as a fact that her aged relative could not bear music. So, as a matter of duty and self-interest, she stopped her child's little voice when she could, and if he asked, "Why does grandmother cry when I sing?" she would answer, "Nobody knows," for she had not reflected how those to whom music is always welcome must have neither an empty heart nor a remorseful conscience, nor keen recollections, nor a foreboding soul.

Peter was a good little boy enough; he was tolerably well tamed by the constant presence of old age and, with the restraints it brought upon him, and having less imagination than falls to the lot of most children, he was the more affected by his position. When he strayed into a field of wheat, and there was waving and whispering above his head, it was not all one to him, as if he had been lost in some old-world forest, where uncouth creatures dwelt, and castles and caverns might be encountered before the stile. He could not see the great world out of the parlour window, and understand and almost inherit another world beyond the hills; as to the moon, the child's silver heaven, he never saw something marvellous and mild sitting up there and smiling to him to come.

But he was happy, and instead of the wide-open

eyes of a child fed to the full with the wonders about him and within him, his eyes were shaded constantly by their light lashes; he enjoyed his play, but he blinked when day was at the full; and all his observations concerned realities. Some story had reached him about a ghost which had been seen in that immediate neighbourhood.

"Who cooks his dinner for him?" inquired the child.

"He has no dinner," answered the old housemaid.

"I don't want to see him, then," said the little winking, blinking philosopher; "he might ask me for some of mine."

But that was a height of prudence that he could not reach often, and he several times annoyed his mother and alarmed his aunt by asking questions about this ghost.

Laura Melcombe, Peter's aunt, acted as his governess, and took a certain pride and pleasure in his young intelligence. It was well that she had something real to interest her, for her character was in strong contrast to her nephew's. She lived mainly in an ideal world, and her life was fed by what she fetched up from the clod or down from the clouds. Chiefly by the former. She was "of imagination all compact;" but that is a very unlucky case where there is weak judgment, little or no keenness of observation, a treacherous memory, and a boundless longing for the good things of life. Of all gifts, imagination, being the greatest, is least worth having, unless it is well backed either by moral culture or by other intellectual qualities. It is the crown of all thoughts and powers; but you cannot wear a crown becomingly if you have no head (worth mentioning) to put it on.

Miss Laura Melcombe thought most of the young farmers in the neighbourhood were in love with her. Accordingly, at church or at the market-town, where she occasionally went on shopping expeditions, she gave herself such airs as she considered suitable for a lady who must gently, though graciously, repel all hopeless aspirations. She was one of those people to whom a compliment is absolute poison. The first man who casually chanced to say something to her in her early youth, which announced to her that he thought her lovely, changed her thoughts about herself for ever after. First, she accepted his compliment as his sincere and fervent conviction. Secondly, she never doubted that he expressed his continuous belief, not his feeling of the moment. Thirdly, she regarded beauty in her case as thenceforward an established fact, and not this one man's opinion. Fourthly, she spent some restless months in persuading herself that to admire must needs be to love, and she longed in vain to see him "come forward." Then some other casual acquaintance paid her a compliment, and she went through the same experience on his account, persuading herself that her first admirer could not afford to marry; and this state of things had now gone on for several years.

CHAPTER II.

THE LESSON.

"Or those eighteen on whom the tower in Siloam fell, think ye . . . ."

MANY and many an hour had Peter spent, when he was a very little boy, in gazing through the heavy banister-like railings of the gallery; and, as he grew older, in pensively leaning upon them, and longing in vain to get into the forbidden Paradise of the garden. The gallery floor being about twelve feet from the ground he could see the whole place from it. Oh the stores of nests that it must contain! the beautiful sharp sticks for arrows! the capital elder shoots, full of pith! how he longed to get at them for making pop-guns! Sometimes, when the pink hawthorns were in flower, or the guelder-roses, he would throw a ball at one of them just to see what showers of bloom would come down; and then what a commotion such an event would make among the birds! what chattering and chirping, and screaming and fluttering! But the experiment was rather a costly one, for the ball once thrown there was no getting it back again, it must lie and rot till the seams burst open, and birds picked the wool out for their nests.

Sometimes Peter would get a hook tied to the end of a long string, and amuse himself with what he called fishing, that is to say, he would throw out his line, and try to get it tangled in the slight branches of some shrub, and draw it up, with a few of the flowers attached; but with all his fishing he never got up anything worth having: the utmost being a torn cabbage-rose, and two or three shattered peonies, leaf and root and all.

It is melancholy to think how much valuable property was engulphed in this untrodden waste, how many shuttlecocks, hit a little too hard, had toppled over and settled on some flowery clump, in full view of, but out of reach for ever of their unfortunate possessor; how many marbles had bounded over and leaped into the green abyss; how many bits of slate-pencil, humming-tops, little ships made of walnut-shells, and other most precious articles, had been lost there to human ken, and now lay hidden and mouldering away!

Sometimes when Peter had lost anything of more than common value, he would complain to his aunt, or his mother, and hint a humble wish that he could get it again. On such occasions his mother would remark, with a languid sigh, that it certainly did seem a pity such a fine piece of land should lie waste; but if Peter followed up the conversation by declaring that he could easily climb over the gate and get down into the garden if he might, he was immediately met by such stern rebukes from all parties, and such fervent assurances that if he ever dared to do such a thing he should certainly be sent to school, that he grew to the age of seven years with two deep impressions on his mind; first, that it would be very wicked to go down into the garden; second, that it would be very dreadful to be sent to school.

One very fine hot day in July Madam Melcombe had caused a table to be set in the gallery, that she might enjoy her early tea in the open air. Peter and the rest of the party were with her, and after a long silence he turned towards her and said, "Grandmother, there are no ghosts in our house, are there?"

"Ne'er a one," exclaimed the nurse with zealous promptitude, "they don't come to houses where *good folks live.*"

"I wish they would," said Peter, thoughtfully, "I want to see one."

"What does he say?" asked the great-grandmother. The nurse repeated Peter's audacious remark; whereupon Madam Melcombe said briskly and sharply, "Hold your tongue, child, and eat your bread and milk like a Christian; you're spilling it on the floor."

"But I wish they would," repeated Peter softly; and finishing his bread and milk, he said his grace; and his fishing-rod being near at hand, he leaned his elbows on the balustrade, threw his line, and began to play at his favourite game.

"I think," he said, presently turning to his aunt, "I think, aunt, I shall call the garden the 'field of the cloth of gold;' it's so covered with marigolds just now that it looks quite yellow. Henry's tent shall be the arbour, and I'll have the French king's down in this corner."

On hearing this, his mother slightly elevated her eyebrows, she had no notion what he was alluding to; but his grandmother, who seemed to have been made rather restless and uneasy by his remarks about ghosts, evidently regarded this talk as something more of the same sort, and said to her granddaughter, "I wish, Laura, you wouldn't let him read such a quantity of fairy tales and heathenish nonsense—'field o' the cloth o' gold, indeed!' Who ever heard of such a thing!"

"He has only been reading the 'History of England,' grandmother," said Peter's aunt.

"I hadn't read anything out of that book for such a long time," said Peter; "my Bible-lesson to-day made me remember it. About that other field, you know, grandmother."

"Come, that's something like," said old Madam

Melcombe. "Stand up now, and let me hear your Bible-lesson."

"But, grandmother," Peter inquired, "I may call this the 'field of the cloth of gold,' mayn't I?"

"O dear me, call it anything you like," she replied; "but don't stand in that way to say your task to me; put your feet together now, and fold your hands, and hold your head up. To think that you're the child's aunt, Laura, she continued fretfully, and should take no more heed to his manners. Now you just look straight at me, Peter, and begin."

The child sighed: the constraint of his attitude perhaps made him feel melancholy. He ventured to cast one glance at his fishing-rod, and at the garden, then looking straight at his great-grandmother, he began in a sweet and serious tone of voice to repeat his lesson from the twenty-seventh chapter of St. Matthew's Gospel, the third to the tenth verse.

3. "*Then Judas, which had betrayed him, when he saw that he was condemned, repented himself, and brought again the thirty pieces of silver to the chief priests and elders,*

4. "*Saying, I have sinned in that I have betrayed the innocent blood. And they said, What is that to us? see thou to that.*

5. "*And he cast down the pieces of silver in the temple, and departed, and went and hanged himself.*

6. "*And the chief priests took the silver pieces, and said, It is not lawful for to put them into the treasury, because it is the price of blood.*

7. "*And they took counsel, and bought with them the potter's field, to bury strangers in.*

8. "*Wherefore that field was called, The field of blood unto this day.*

9. "*Then was fulfilled that which was spoken by Jeremy the prophet, saying, And they took the thirty pieces of silver, the price of him that was valued, whom they of the children of Israel did value,*

10. "*And gave them for the potter's field, as the Lord appointed me.*"

What was this!—standing upright again, as she had done several times in the church—was she listening? It scarcely appeared that she was; she took first one hand from her staff, and looked earnestly at it, and then she took the other, and with wide-open eyes examined that also.

"O cruel, cruel," thought Peter's mother, when Peter had repeated a verse or two, "why did not Laura prevent this, she who knew what the child's lesson was?" and she sat cold and trembling, with an anguish of pity; but she felt that now it was too late to stop her boy, he must go on to the end. As to the nurse, she sitting there still, with her work on her knees, felt as if every word rose up and struck her on the face. He was slowly, pensively, and O so calmly, describing to the poor mother the manner of her son's death.

"That will do, master Peter," she exclaimed, the moment he had finished; and she snatched his hand and led him away, telling him to go and play in the orchard.

Peter was not destitute of gratitude, and as he made his exit, he thought, what a good thing it was that he did not say his lesson to his grandmother every day.

When the nurse turned again she observed that Madam Melcombe had tottered a step or two forward: her grand-daughter, and her grandson's widow were supporting her. One of them called to her to fetch some cordial, and this seemed to disturb the poor old woman, for she presently said slowly, and as if it caused her a great effort to speak,—

"What are they gone for? and what are you doing?"

"We're holding you up, grandmother; you tremble, dear; you can hardly stand. Won't you sit down?"

"Won't I what?" she repeated. "I don't hear;"

and she began to move with their help and that of her staff to the balustrade.

The old fancy; the constant fancy; gazing at the bed of lilies, and talking to herself as, with her trembling hand to her brow, she peered out towards the arbour. They were words of no particular significance that she said; but just as the nurse came back bringing her a cordial, she turned round and repeated them distinctly, and with a solemnity that was almost awful.

"They all helped to dig it; and they know they did."

Words that appeared to be so far from the tragical recollection which must have first caused this disturbance in her poor mind; but her grand-daughter thought proper to make her some kind of answer.

"Did they, grandmother?" she said in a soothing tone, "and a very good thing too."

She stopped short, for upon the aged face fell suddenly such a look of affright, such renewed intelligence seemed to peer out of the dim eyes, and such defiance with their scrutiny, that for the moment she was very much alarmed.

"She's not quite herself. Oh, I hope she's not going to have a stroke!" was her thought.

"What have I been a saying?" inquired Madam Melcombe.

"You said it was a good thing they dug the lily bed," answered her grand-daughter.

"And nothing else?"

"No, ma'am, no," answered the nurse; "and if you had, what would it signify?"

Madam Melcombe let them settle her in her chair and give her her cordial, then she said—

"Folks are oft-times known to talk wild in their age. I thought I might be losing my wits; might have said something."

"Dear grandmother, don't laugh!" exclaimed her

grandson's widow; "and don't look so strange. Lose your wits! you never will, not you. We shall have you a little longer yet, please God, and bright and sensible to the last."

"Folks are oft-times known to talk wild in their age," repeated Madam Melcombe; and during the rest of that evening she continued silent and lost in thought.

The next morning, after a late breakfast, her family observed that there was still a difference in her manner. She was not quite herself, they thought, and they were confirmed in their opinion when she demanded of her grand-daughter and her grandson's widow, that a heavy old-fashioned bureau should be opened for her, and that she should be left alone. "I don't know as I shall be spared much longer," said the meek nonogenarian, "and I've made up my mind to write a letter to my sons."

"*My sons!*" When they heard this they were startled almost as they might have been if she had had no sons, for neither of them had ever heard her mention their names. Nothing, in fact, was known concerning them in that house, excepting that what portion of success and happiness had been allotted to the family seemed all to have fallen to their share.

They were vastly unpopular in the hamlet. Not that any but the very old people remembered the day when they had first been missing, or what an extraordinary effect their behaviour had produced on their mother; but that the new generation had taken up her cause—the new parson also—and that the story being still often told had lost nothing in the narration.

Parson Craik had always been poor old Madam's champion since his coming among them. He had taken pains to ascertain the facts from the oldest hedger's old wife, and when first he heard her tell how she had opened her door at dawn to let in her husband, during the great gale that was rocking the orchard trees and filling the air with whirls of blossom, that came down like a thick fall of snow, he made an observation which was felt at the time to have an edifying power in it, and which was incorporated with the story ever after. "And when I telled him how the grete stack of chimneys fell not half-an-hour after, over the very place where they had passed, and how they were in such a hurry to be off that they jumped the edge for fear us should stop them or speak to them. Then says Parson Craik to me, sitting as it might be there, and I a sitting opposite (for I'd given him the big chair), says he to me, 'My friend, we must lay our hands on our mouths when we hear of the afflictions of the righteous. And yet man,' says he, 'man, when he hears of such heartless actions, can but feel that it would have been a just judgment on them, if the wind had been ordained in the hauling of those chimneys down, to fling 'em on their undutiful heads.'"

Poor Madam Melcombe, her eldest son, whose heir she was, had caused the stack of chimneys to be built up again; but she was never the same woman from that day, and she had never seen those sons again (so far as was known), or been reconciled to them. And now she had desired to be left alone, and had expressly said, "I've made up my mind to write a letter to my sons."

So she was left alone and undertook, with trembling hands and dimmed eyes, her unwonted task. She wrote a letter which, if those about her could have seen it, would certainly have affected their feelings, and would perhaps have made them think more highly yet of her meek forgiving nature, for she neither blamed her sons nor reminded them of what they had done; but rather seemed to offer a strange kind of apology for troubling them, and to give a reason for doing so that was stranger still.

THE LETTER.

"SON DANIEL AND SON AUGUSTUS,—This comes from your poor unfortunate mother that has never troubled you these many, many years, and hoping you and your families are better than I am at present, son Daniel and you son Augustus; and my desire is both of you, that now you will not deny your poor mother to come and see her, but will, on receipt of this, come as soon as may be, for it's about my funeral that I want to speak, and my time is very short, and I was never used to much writing.

"If you don't come, in particular you, son Daniel, you will break your poor mother's heart.

"And so no more at present from her that never said an unkind word to you.

"ELIZABETH MELCOMBE."

This letter was addressed to the elder son, went through the village post-office, and when its direction was seen, such interest was excited and so much curiosity, that half the women in the hamlet had been allowed to take a look at its cover before it was sent away.

Perhaps Madam Melcombe herself, when she sat expecting these long-lost sons to appear, was scarcely more agitated or more excited than were the people in that sequestered place. A good many cottagers were hanging about or looking out of the windows when they alighted, and going into the small inn called for spirits and water. It was known outside at once what they had asked for. No wonder they wanted some Dutch courage to take them into her presence, was the general thought.

Several little boys had gathered in front of the door longing, and yet dreading, to get a sight of them. Some inhabitants would have liked to hiss, but lacked unanimity or courage, nobody wanted to begin. Some would have liked to speak, but had not considered beforehand what to say.

The brothers came out, the children fell back; but one little fellow, a child five years old, with a sort of holy necessity upon him (as was supposed) to give his testimony, threw a very little bit of soft dirt at the legs of one of them.

This action was not noticed; and before the other little urchins had found time for aught more fruitful than regret that they had not done likewise, the gentlemen got into their post-chaise, and were driven to the old mansion.

And their mother?

She was quite alone, sitting in all state and expectation, in one of the alcoves, while the deep shadow of the house fell distinct and well defined over the wilderness of a garden.

Her senses were more acute than usual. She was grasping her long staff, and already wearying for them, when she heard the sound of wheels, and presently after a foot in her parlour, and the nurse appeared with two cards on a tray.

Mr. Mortimer, Mr. Augustus Mortimer. This formal introduction flurried Madam Melcombe a little. "The gentlemen are coming," the nurse almost whispered; and then she withdrew, and shutting the glass-doors behind her, left this mother to meet with these sons.

Whatever anxiety, whatever sensations of maternal affection might have been stirring within her, it is certain that her first feeling was one of intense surprise. The well-remembered faces that she had cherished now for much more than half a century—the tall, beautiful youth—the fine boy, almost a child, that had gone off with him, could they be now before her? She was not at all oblivious of the flight of time; she did not forget that the eldest of these sons was scarcely nineteen years younger than herself; yet she had made no defined picture of their present faces in her mind, and it was not without a troubled sense of wonder that she rose and saw coming on towards her two majestic old men, with hair as white as snow.

Her first words were simple and hesitating. She immediately knew them from one another.

"Son Dan'el," she said, turning to the taller, "I expect this is you;" and she shifted her staff to her left hand while he took the right; and then the other old man, coming up, stooped, and kissed her on the forehead.

Madam Melcombe shed a few tears. Both her sons looked disturbed, and very ill at ease. She sat down again, and they sat opposite to her. Then there was such a long, awkward pause, and her poor hand trembled so much, that at last, as if in order to give her time to feel more at ease, her younger son began to talk to her of her grand-daughter who lived with her, and of her little great-grandson, Peter Melcombe. He hoped, he said with gravity, that they were well.

There seemed to be nothing else that either of them could think of to say; and presently, helped by the rest their words gave her, Madam Melcombe recovered her self-possession.

"Son Dan'el," she said, "my time must be short now; and I have sent for you and your brother to ask a favour of you. I could not lie easy in my grave," she continued, "if I thought there would be nobody of all my children to *follow me.* I have none but poor Peter's daughter and grandson here now, and I hope you and Augustus and your sons will come to my funeral. I hope you'll promise me faithfully, both of you, that you'll certainly come and follow me to the grave."

A silence followed. The disappointment of both the sons was evident.

They had hoped, the younger remarked, that she might have had something else to say.

No, she had not, she answered. Where would be the good of that? They had written to her often enough about that.

And then she went on to repeat her request. There was nothing she would not do for them, nothing, if they would but promise to come.

"So be it," replied the elder; "but then, you must make me a promise, mother, in your turn."

"It isn't the land?" she inquired with humble hesitation. "I should be agreeable to that."

"No, God forbid! What you have to promise me is, that if I come to your funeral, you will make such a will that not one acre of the land or one shilling you possess shall ever come to me or mine."

"And," said the other promptly, "I make the same promise, on the same condition."

Then there was another pause, deeper and more intense than the first. The old mother's face passed through many changes, always with an air of cogitation and trouble; and the old sons watched her in such a suspense of all movement, that it seemed as if they scarcely breathed.

"You sent your cards in," she said as if with sudden recollection, "to remind me that you'd kept your father's name?"

"Nothing will ever induce either of us to change it," was the answer.

"You're very hard on me, son Dan'el," she said at last; "for you know you was always my favourite son."

A touching thing to say to such an old man; but there was no reply.

"And I never took any pride in Peter," she continued, "he was that undutiful; and his grandson's a mere child."

Still no reply.

"I was in hopes, if I could get speech of you, I should find you'd got reasonable with age, Dan'el;

for God knows you was as innocent of it as the babe unborn."

Old Daniel Mortimer sighed deeply. They had been parted nearly sixty years, but their last words and their first words had been on the same subject; and it was as fresh in the minds of both as if only a few days had intervened between them. Still it seemed he could find nothing to say, and she, rousing up, cried out passionately,—

"Would you have had me denounce my own flesh and blood?"

"No, madam, no," answered the younger.

She noticed the different appellation instantly, and turning on him, said, with vigour and asperity,—

"And you, Augustus, that I hear is rich, and has settled all your daughters well, and got a son of your own, *you* might know a parent's feelings. It's ill done of you to encourage Dan'el in his obstinacy."

Then, seeing that her words did not produce the slightest effect, she threw her lace apron over her head, and pressing her wrinkled hands against her face, gave way to silent tears.

"I'm a poor miserable old woman," she presently cried; "and if there's to be nobody but that child and the tenants to follow me to the grave, it'll be the death of me to know it, I'm sure it will."

With an air of indescribable depression, the elder son then repeated the same promise he had given before, and added the same condition.

The younger followed his example, and thereupon humbly taking down the lace from her face, and mechanically smoothing it over her aged knees, she gave the promise required of her, and placed her hand on a prayer-book which was lying on the small table beside her, as if to add emphasis and solemnity to her words.

CHAPTER III.

GOLD, THE INCORRUPTIBLE WITNESS.

Accipe Hoc.

AFTER she had received the promise she desired from her sons—a promise burdened with so strange a condition—Madam Melcombe seemed to lose all the keenness and energy she had displayed at first.

She had desired above all things that honour should be shown to her in her death; her mind often occupied itself with strange interest and pertinacity on the details of her funeral. All her wishes respecting it had long been known to her granddaughters, but her eldest surviving son had never been mentioned by name to them. She always spoke of him as "the chief mourner."

Suddenly, however, it appeared to have occurred to her that he might not be present at it, after all. Everything must be risked to ascertain this. She must write, she must entreat his presence. But when he and his brother sent in their cards she, for the first time in her life, perceived that all she had done was useless. She saw the whole meaning of the situation; for this estate had come to her through the failure of heirs male to her father, and it was the provision of his will that she and her heirs should take back his name—the name of Melcombe.

She knew well that these two sons had always retained their father's name; but when they sent it in to her, she instinctively perceived their meaning. They were calling her attention to the fact, and she was sure now that they never meant to change it.

She had not behaved kindly or justly to her grandson's widow, for people had called little Peter her heir, and she had not contradicted them. But she had never made a will; and she secretly hoped that at the last something would occur to prevent her doing so.

Everything was absolutely in her own power, to leave as she pleased; but a half superstitious feeling prompted her to wait. She wished her eldest surviving son to inherit the estate; but sad reflection seemed to assure her that if it simply lapsed to him as heir-at-law, he would think that next thing to receiving it through a dispensation of Providence; and she was such an unhappy mother, that she had reason to suppose he might prefer that to a direct bequest from her. So she left the kindly women who shared her seclusion entirely unprovided for, and the long services of her old domestics unrewarded, in order to flatter the supposed prejudices of this unknown son, who was destined now to show her how little he cared for all her forethought, and all her respect for his possible wishes.

This was now over. She felt that she was foiled. She sat, leaning her chin on the top of her staff, not able to find anything more to say; and every moment they spent together, the mother and sons became more painfully embarrassed, more restless and more restrained.

In the meanwhile Peter's mother and aunt, just as unconscious that his heirship had ever been a doubt, as that it had been secured to him then and there, sat waiting below, dressed in their best, to receive these visitors, and press them to partake of a handsome collation that had been prepared by their mother's order, and was now spread for them with unwonted state and profusion in the best parlour.

This large room had not been used for forty years; but as it was always kept with closed shutters, excepting on those days when it received a thorough and careful cleaning, the furniture was less faded than might have been expected, and the old leather-backed chairs, ebony cabinets, and quaint mirrors leaning out from the walls, looked almost as fresh as ever.

"Only let me get speech of them," the mother had thought, "and all may yet come right between us; for it's a long time ago, a weary while since we parted, and they ought to find it easier to forget than I do!" Then she had charged her grand-daughter, when the lunch was ready, to ring a bell, and she would send them down. "Or even, mayhap, I may come down myself," she had added, "leaning on the arm of my son."

So the bell was rung, and Laura and Mrs. Peter Melcombe waited for the grandmother and her guests with no little trepidation.

They had not intended to be cordial. Their notion of their own part in this interview was that they should be able to show a certain courteous coldness, a certain calm gravity in their demeanour towards these two uncles, but neither of them knew much of the world or of herself. They no sooner saw the majestic old men come in without their mother than Laura, feeling herself blush down to her very finger tips, retreated into the background, and Mrs. Peter Melcombe, suddenly finding that she had forgotten what she had intended to say, could scarcely collect enough composure to answer the gentle courtesy of their rather distant greeting.

A sort of urban polish struck her country sense, making her feel at once that she was a rustic, and that they belonged to a wider and more cultivated world. She felt herself at a disadvantage, and was angry with herself that it should be so, in that house of all places in the world, where she had every right to hold up her head, and they had surely reason to be ashamed of themselves.

Peter was the only person present who was at ease; the unwonted joy of finding himself in the "great parlour" had excited him. He had been wandering about examining the china vases and admiring the little rainbows which sunshine struck out from the cut-glass borders of the mirrors.

He was very well pleased to include the two great-uncles among the new and interesting objects about him. He came up when called by one of them, answered a few simple questions with childlike docility, and made his mother more sure than before that these dignified old men were treating him, her sister-in-law, and herself, with a certain pathetic gentleness that was almost condescension.

Indeed, both the ladies perceived this, but they also saw that they could not play the part their old relation had assigned to them. Such a handsome collation as it was too, but each, after accepting a biscuit and a glass of cider (the very finest cider and more than ten years old), rose as if to take leave. One patted Peter on the head, and the other ordered the chaise. Neither Laura nor Mrs. Peter Melcombe could find courage to press them to eat, though their secluded lives and old-fashioned manners would have made them quite capable of doing so if they had felt at ease. They looked at one another as the two grand old men withdrew, and their first words were of the disappointment the grandmother would feel when she heard that they had hardly eaten anything at all.

Madam Melcombe, however, asked no questions. She was found by them when Mr. Mortimer and his brother had withdrawn sitting in her favourite alcove with her chin resting upon her staff. She was deep in thought, and excepting that she watched the chaise drearily as it wound down among the apple and pear trees and was lost to sight, she did not appear to be thinking of her sons. Nor did she mention them again, excepting with reference to her funeral.

"He's a fine man," she remarked in a querulous tone; "he'll look grand in his cloak and scarf when he stands over my grave with his hat off; and I think (though Dan'el, you understand is to be chief-mourner) that he and his brother had better follow me side by side, and their two sons after them."

How little Laura and Mrs. Peter Melcombe had ever thought about these old men, or supposed that they were frequently present to the mother's mind. And yet now there seemed to be evidence that this was the case.

Two or three guarded questions asked the next day brought answers which showed her to be better acquainted with their circumstances than she commonly admitted. She had always possessed a portrait in oils of her son Daniel. It had been painted before he left home, and kept him always living as a beautiful fair-haired youth in her recollection. She took pains to acquaint herself with his affairs, though she never opened her lips concerning them to those about her.

His first marriage had been disastrous. His wife had deserted him, leaving him with one child only, a daughter. Upon the death of this poor woman many years afterwards, he had married a widow whose third husband he was, yet who was still young, scarcely so old as his daughter.

Concerning this lady and her children the poor old mother-in-law continually cogitated, having a common little photographic likeness of her in which she tried to find the wifely love and contentment and all the other endearing qualities she had heard of. For at rare intervals one or other of her sons would write to her, and then she always perceived that the second Mrs. Daniel Mortimer made her husband happy. She would be told from time to time that he was much attached to young Brandon, the son of her first marriage, and that from her three daughters by her second marriage he constantly received the love and deference due to a father.

But this cherished wife had now died also, and had left Daniel Mortimer with one son, a fine youth already past childhood.

Old Madam Melcombe's heart went into mourning for her daughter-in-law whom she had never seen. None but the husband, whose idol she was, lamented her longer and more. Only fifty miles off, but so remote in her seclusion, so shut away, so forgotten; perhaps Mrs. Daniel Mortimer did not think once in a season of her husband's mother; but every day the old woman had thought of her as a consoler and a delight, and when her favourite son retired she soon took out the photograph again and looked sadly at those features that he had held so dear.

But she did not speak much of either son, only repeating from time to time, "He's a fine man; they're fine men, both of them. They'll look grand in their scarves and cloaks at my funeral."

It was not ordained, however, that the funeral should take place yet awhile.

The summer flushed into autumn, then the apples and pears dropped and were wasted in the garden, even the red-streak apples, that in all the cider country are so highly prized. Then snow came and covered all.

Madam Melcombe had been heard to say that she liked her garden best in winter. She could wish to leave it for good when it was lapped up under a thick fall of snow. Yet she saw the snow melt again and the leaves break forth, and at last she saw the first pale-green spires shoot up out of the bed of lilies.

But the longest life must end at last, the best little boys will sometimes be disobedient.

It appears strange to put these things together; but if they had anything to do with one another, Peter did not know it.

He knew and felt one day that he had been a naughty boy, very naughty, for in fact he had got down into the garden, but he also knew that he had not found the top he went to look for, and that his grandmother had taken from him what he did find.

This punishment he deserved; he had it and no other. It came about in this wise.

It was a sweet April day, almost the last of the month. All the cherry-trees were in full flower; the pear-trees were coming out, and the young thickets in the garden were bending low with lilac-blossom, but Peter was miserable.

He was leaning his arms over the balustrade, and the great red peonies and loose anemones were staring up at him so that he could see down into their central folds; but what is April, and what is a half-holiday, and what indeed is life itself when one has lost perhaps the most excellent top that boy ever spun, and the loudest hummer? And then he had taken such care of it. Never but once, only this once, had he spun it in the gallery at all, and yet this once of all misfortunes it had rolled its last circle out so far that the balustrade had struck it, and in the leap of its rebound it had sprung over.

At first he felt as if he should like to cry. Then a wild and daring thought came and shook at the very doors of his heart. What if he climbed over the gate and got down, and, finding his top, brought it up so quickly that no one would ever know?

His mother and aunt were gone out for a walk; his great-grandmother and the nurse were nodding one on each side of the fire. It was only three o'clock, and yet they had dined, and they were never known to rouse themselves up for at least half an hour at that time of day.

He took one turn along the gallery again, peeped in at the parlour window, then in a great hurry he yielded to the temptation, climbed over the wooden gate, got down the rotten old steps, and in two minutes was up to his neck in a mass of tangled blossoms. Then he began to feel that passion of deep delight which is born of adventure and curiosity. He quite forgot his top: indeed, there was no chance of finding it. He began to wade about, and got deeper and deeper in. Sometimes quite over-canopied, he burrowed his way half smothered with flowers; sometimes emerging, he cast back a stealthy glance to the gallery.

At last he had passed across the lawn, arrived almost at the very end of the garden, and down among the broken trellis-work of the arbour three nests of the yellow-hammer were visible at the same time. He did not know which to lay hands on first. He thought he had never been so happy in his life, or so much afraid.

But time pressed. He knew now that he should certainly climb over that gate again, though for the present he did not dare to stay; and stooping, almost creeping, over the open lawn and the bed of lilies, he began to work his way homeward by the wall, and through old borders where the thickest trees and shrubs had always grown.

At last, after pushing on for a little distance, he paused to rest in a clump of fir-trees, one of which had been dead for so many years that all its twigs and smaller boughs had decayed and dropped to the ground. Only the large branches, gaunt and skeleton-like, were left standing, and in a fork between two of these and quite within his reach, in a lump of soft felt, or perhaps beaver, he noticed something that glittered. Peter drew it away from the soft material it was lying among, and looked at it. It was a sort of gold band—perhaps it was gold lace, for it was flexible—he had often heard of gold lace, but had not seen any. As he drew it away something else that depended from a morsel of the lump of rag fell away from it, and dropped at his feet. It might have been some sort of badge or ornament, but it was not perfect, though it still glittered, for it had threads of gold wrought in it. "This is almost in the shape of an anchor," said Peter, as he wrapped the gold band round it, "and I think it must have been lost here for ages; perhaps ever since that old uncle Mortimer that I saw was a little boy."

So then with the piece of gold band wrapped round his hand he began to press on, and if he had not stopped to mark the places where two or three more nests were, he would have been quicker still.

On and on, how dangerously delightful his adventure had been! What would become of him if he could not get down to-morrow?

On and on, his heart beat with exultation; he was close to the steps and he had not been discovered; he was close to the top of them and had not been discovered; he was just about to climb over when he heard a cry that rang in his ears long after, a sharp, piercing cry, and turning he saw his great-grandmother in her cloak and hood standing in the entrance of the alcove, and reaching out her hands as if she wanted to come and meet him, but could not stir.

"Peter! Peter! Peter!" she cried, and her voice seemed to echo all over the place.

Peter tumbled over the gate as fast as he possibly could; and as she still cried, he ran to her at the top of his speed.

All in a moment she seemed to become quite still, and though she trembled as she seized him, she did not scold him at all; while he mumbled out, "I only just went down for a very little while. I only wanted just to look for my top; I didn't take any of the nests," he continued, mentioning the most valuable things he had been amongst, according to his own opinion.

His grandmother had let go his hand and raised herself upright; her eyes were on the bit of gold band. "What's that?" she said faintly.

"It's nothing particular," said Peter, unwinding it slowly from his hand, and humbly giving it up. "It's nothing but a little sort of a gold band and an ornament that I found stuck in a tree." Then Peter, observing by her silence how high his misdemeanour had been, began to sob a little, and then to make a few excuses, and then to say he hoped his grandmother would forgive him.

No answer.

"I wish I hadn't done it," he next said. He felt that he could not say more than that, and he looked up at her. She was not regarding him at all, not attending to what he had said, her face was very white, she was clutching the bit of gold lace in her hand, and her wide-open eyes were staring at something above his head.

"Peter! Peter! Peter!" she cried again, in a strangely sharp and ringing voice. It seemed as if she would fall, and Peter caught hold of her arm and held her, while the thought darted through his mind, that perhaps she had called him at first because she was ill, and wanted him to hold her, not because she had observed his visit to the garden. He felt sure she could hardly stand, and he was very much frightened, but in a moment the nurse, having heard her cry, came running out, and between them they guided her to her chair in the alcove.

"I'm very sorry, grandmother," Peter sobbed, "and really, really I didn't take any nests or lilies or anything at all, but only that bit of stuff. I'll never do it again."

As he spoke he saw his mother and aunt coming up with looks of grief and awe, and on looking into his grandmother's face he beheld, child that he was, a strange shadow passing over it, the shadow of death, and he instinctively knew what it was.

"Can't you move poor grandmother out of the sun?" he sobbed. "Oh do! I know she doesn't like it to shine in her eyes."

"Hush! hush!" his mother presently found voice enough to say amid her tears. "What can it signify?"

After that Peter cried very heartily because everybody else did, but in a little while when his grandmother had been able to drink some cordial, and while they were rubbing her cold hands, she opened her eyes, and then he thought perhaps she was going to get better. Oh, how earnestly he hoped might be so!

But there was no getting better for Madam Melcombe. She sat very still for some minutes, and looked like one newly awakened and very much amazed, then, to the great surprise of those about her, she rose without any aid, and stood holding by her high staff, while, with a slightly distraught air, she bowed to them, first one and then another.

"Well, I thank you for all your kindness, my dears," she said, "all your kindness. I may as well go to them now; they've been waiting for me a long time. Good Lord!" she exclaimed, lifting up her eyes, "Good Lord! what a meeting it will be!"

Then she sank down into her chair again, and in a moment was gone.

CHAPTER IV.

SWARMS OF CHILDREN.

"As our hope is that this our sister doth."—*Burial Service.*

AND now was to take place that ceremony to which Madam Melcombe's thoughts had so often been directed. She had tried to arrange that it should be imposing, and imposing indeed it was, but not by virtue of the profusion of the refreshment, not by the presence of the best hearse from the county town, the best mourning coaches, the grandest plumes, but by the unsolicited attendance of a great company of people come together to do homage to a life distinguished by its misfortunes, its patience, and its charities.

She had never been able to think of herself as taking part in that ceremony unconsciously; her orders had always been given as if by one who felt that if things were meanly done she should know it; but in taking care that refreshments should be provided for all the funeral attendants, she little thought that the whole parish, men and women, were to follow her, and most of them in tears. But it was so. The tenants had been invited; they walked after her in scarf and band, two and two, and after them, in such mourning as they could afford, came all the people, and pressed on in a procession that seemed to the real mourners almost endless, to look down upon her coffin and obtain a place near her grave.

It was out of doors, and all nature was in white.

Round the churchyard pear-trees grew, and leaned their laden branches over its walls. Pear-trees, apple-trees, and cherries filled the valley and crowded one another up all the hills. Mr. Craik's voice, as he stood at the grave, also in white, was heard that quiet afternoon far and near. It was remarked on all sides how impressively he read, and there were plenty to be edified by the solemn words who had never heard his voice before, for many people had walked over from neighbouring parishes, and stood in groups at respectful distances.

All looked at the stranger-sons; they stood side by side, awe-struck, motionless, depressed. The old do not easily shed tears, but there was something in the demeanour of both these old men that was felt to tell of no common emotion. One of them seemed unable to look down into the grave at all, he kept his eyes and his face lifted up. The other, as little Peter stood crying by his side, put his hand down and let it rest on the child's uncovered head, as if to quiet and comfort him.

This little, half-unconscious action gave great umbrage to some of the spectators. "Hadn't the dear child allers been the biggest comfort to his grandmother, and why indeed wasn't he to cry as much as ever he liked? He had nothing to reproach himself with, and if he had had his rights, he would have been made chief mourner. Those that stood next the corpse had never been any comfort or pleasure to her, but that dear child had walked beside her to church ever since he had been old enough to go there himself."

"And so those were Daniel and Augustus Mortimer's sons. Very fine young gentlemen too, one of them not over young, neither; he looked at least thirty. Well, very mysterious were the ways of Providence! Poor Cuthbert Melcombe, the eldest son, had left neither chick nor child; no more had poor Griffith, the youngest. As for Peter, to be sure he had left children, but then he was gone himself. And these that had behaved so bad to their blessed mother were all she had to stand by her grave. It was very mysterious, but she was at rest now, and would never feel their undutifulness any more."

It was about four o'clock on that summer-like afternoon that the mourners came home from the funeral. The ladies for the sake of quiet retired with Peter to their rooms in the roof; the Mortimers, after partaking of a slight repast in the great parlour, stepped out and began to pace up and down before the house to refresh their spirits with a little air.

The will had been read in the morning, before the funeral took place. Valentine Mortimer and John Mortimer, the two grandsons, were both present. Valentine being a mere boy, barely eighteen, may well have been excused if he did not notice anything peculiar in the demeanour of the two old men; did not notice, as John Mortimer did, the restless excitement of both, and how they appeared to be sustaining and encouraging one another, and yet, when the important sentence came which left them without so much as a shilling, how bravely and soberly they took it, without the least betrayal of mortified feeling, without any change of countenance or even of attitude.

Valentine had often heard his father say that he had no expectations from his mother, that he was quite sure the property never would come to him. He had believed this, and excepting that he found the preamble of the will solemn and the reading impressive, he did not take any special interest in it.

Every shilling and every acre were left to little Peter Melcombe, his mother being appointed his sole guardian till he reached the age of twelve years, and a request being added that her dear son Daniel would see to the repairing of the house, and the setting in order of the garden and woodland.

"And yet not a shilling left to either of them," thought John. "I always fancied there was some estrangement—felt sure of it; but if my father and uncle were so far friendly with their mother that she could ask this favour, how odd that she leaves nothing, not so much as a remembrance, to either of them! The eldest son, by all accounts, was a very violent, overbearing man; I've heard my father say as much; but he has been dead so long that, if there was any estrangement on his account, they must have made it up long ago."

And now the funeral was over. John Mortimer, taking the youth with him, was walking about among the pear-trees close to the garden-wall, and the two old brothers, who appeared to have a dislike to being separated, even for a moment, were leisurely walking on, and in silence looking about them.

"I should like to get into the garden," said John Mortimer; "here's a door."

"But it's locked," remarked Valentine, "and Mrs. Peter Melcombe told me yesterday that none of them ever walked in it."

"Ah, indeed!" said John carelessly—he was far from giving a literal meaning to the information. "It looks a rotten old thing," he continued; "the key is in the house, no doubt, but I don't want to have the trouble of going in to ask for it."

"Perhaps it's not locked," said Valentine; "perhaps it only wants a push."

John and Valentine were standing among some cherry-trees, which, being thickly laden with their blossom, screened them from observation as far as the windows of the now opened house were concerned. John did push, and when the door creaked he pushed again, and the rotten old lock yielded, came away from the lintel, and as the two old fathers turned, they were just in time to see their sons disappear through the doorway and walk into the garden. With a troubled glance at one another, and an effort not to appear in haste, the fathers followed them.

"Can't we get them away?" exclaimed Mr. Mortimer; "can't we tell them to come out?"

"Certainly not, certainly not, brother," answered old Augustus, in a reassuring tone. "You'll not say a word to dissuade them from going wherever they please."

"No," said the other, in a nervous, hesitating manner. "You're quite right, Augustus; you always are."

"Is it not a strange place?" exclaimed John, as they walked forward and looked about them. "It seems to me that really and truly they never do enter it."

"Well, I told you so," answered Valentine. "It is on account of the eldest son. Miss Melcombe told me that he was a very eccentric character, and for many years before his death he made gardening his one occupation. He never suffered any one but himself to garden here, not even so much as to mow the grass. After he was dead the poor old grandmother locked it up. She didn't like any one else to meddle with it."

"Why, he was dead before I was born," exclaimed John, "and I am two-and-thirty. Poor soul! and she never got over that misfortune, then, in all those years. There's a grand pear-tree! lots of rotten fruit lying under it—and what a fine apple-tree! Is this of the celebrated 'redstreak' variety, I wonder, that Phillips praises so in his poem on cider."

"A poem on cider!"

"Yes, I tell you, a poem on cider, and as long as 'Paradise Lost.' It has some very fine passages in it, and has actually been translated into Italian. I picked up a copy of it at Verona when I was a boy, and learned a good deal of it by heart, by way of helping myself with the language. I remember some of it to this day:—

> 'Voi, donne, e Cavalier del bel paese
> A cui propizio il ciel tanto concesse
> Di bene, udite il mio cantare,' &c., &c.

I wonder, now, whether this is a redstreak."

As their sons talked thus the two fathers approached, and gravely looked on at this scene of riotous and yet lovely desolation. Nests with eggs in them adorned every little bush, vines having broken the trellis ran far along the ground. John, remembering that the place must have painful thoughts connected with their dead brother for his father and uncle, continued to talk to Valentine, and did not address either of them: and whatever they may have felt they did not say a word; but Valentine presently observed the bed of lilies, and he and John moved on together, the two fathers following.

They outwalked their fathers, and Valentine, stooping over the bed, gathered two or three of the lovely flowers.

"The poor old grandmother!" he observed. "Miss Melcombe told me she loved to watch this bed of lilies, and said only a few days ago, that she could wish they might never be disturbed."

He turned—both the old men stood stock still behind him, looking down on the lily-bed. Valentine repeated what Miss Melcombe had told him. "So no doubt, papa, you'll give orders that it shall not be touched, as you are going to have all the place put in order."

"Yes, yes, certainly my boy—certainly he will," said Uncle Augustus, answering for his brother.

Valentine was not gifted with at all more feeling or sentiment than usually falls to the lot of a youth of his age, but a sort of compunction visited him at that moment to think how soon they all, alive and well, had invaded the poor old woman's locked and guarded sanctuary! He stooped to gather another lily, and offered the flowers to his father. Old Daniel looked at the lilies, but his unready hand did not move forward to take them; in fact, it seemed that he slightly shrank back. With an instantaneous flash of surprise Valentine felt rather than thought, "If you were dead, father, I would not decline to touch what you had loved." But in the meantime his uncle had put forth a hand and received them. "And yet," thought Valentine, "I know father must have felt that old lady's death. Why, when he was in the mourning-coach he actually cried." And so thinking, as he walked back to the garden-door with John Mortimer, he paused to let John pass first; and chancing to turn his head for one instant, he saw his uncle stoop and jerk those lilies under a clump of lilac bushes, where they were hidden. Before either of the old men had noticed that he had turned, Valentine was walking with his cousin outside, but an uneasy sensation of surprise and suspicion haunted him. He could not listen to John Mortimer's talk, and when the rest of the party had gone back to the house, he lingered behind, returned to the garden, and, stooping down for an instant, saw that it was as he had supposed; there, under the lilac bushes, were lying those gathered lilies.

So he went back to the house. The two grandsons were to return home that afternoon; the two sons were going to remain for a few days, that the wishes of the deceased might have prompt attention, as regarded the setting of the place in order. They were to sleep at the inn in the hamlet, by their own desire, that, as they said, they might not give trouble.

When Valentine entered the great parlour, his cousin was talking to Peter's mother, and in the presence of his father and uncle he was inviting her to let the boy come and stay awhile with his children shortly.

Mrs. Peter Melcombe hesitated, and observed that her dear child had never been away from her in his life, and was very shy.

"No wonder," quoth John Mortimer; "but I have several jolly little boys and girls at home; they would soon cure him of that."

Mrs. Peter Melcombe seemed pleased. She had taken a great fancy to the good-looking young widower; she remarked that Peter had never been used to playing with other children—she was half-afraid he would get hurt; but as Mr. Mortimer was so kind she would risk it.

"Poor little beggar!" said John Mortimer to his father, as they all walked to the inn together; "those two women will mope that boy into his grave if they don't look out."

"No, John," exclaimed his uncle, "I hope you really don't think so."

John, in spite of his youth, had some experience. He had already filled his house with little Mortimers. There were seven of them—some of the largest pattern, and with the finest appetites possible. So his opinion carried weight, and was at the same time worth nothing, for as his children had never but once had anything the matter with them, his general view of childhood was that if it had plenty to eat, a large garden to play in, and leave to go out in all weathers, it was sure to prosper, as in fact the little Mortimers did. They brought themselves up (with a certain amount of interference from their governess) in a high state of health and good-humour, and with no quarrelling to speak of, while the amount of sleep they got out of their little beds, the rapid skill with which they wore down their shoes, and the quantity of rice milk and roast meat they could consume, were a wonder to the matrons round.

"I see nothing special the matter with him," continued John Mortimer; "but one cannot help pitying a child that has no companions and no liberty. I thought I should like to plunge him for a little while into the sweet waters of real child-life, and let him learn to shout and stamp and dig and climb, as my little urchins do."

"But his mother is a poor, faded, fat creature," observed Valentine. "You'll see she won't let that boy go. You can no more get her to do a sensible thing than you can dry your face with a wet towel."

"Gently, sir, gently," said his father, not liking

this attempt at a joke on a day which had begun so solemnly.

So Mr. John Mortimer presently departed, taking his handsome young cousin with him, and the old men, with heavy steps and depressed countenances, went into the inn and began anxiously to talk over the various repairs that would be wanted, and all that would have to be done in the garden and the grounds.

In the meantime it was known in the neighbourhood that parson Craik was going to preach a funeral sermon for poor old Madam the very next Sunday morning, and an edifying description of her death passed from mouth to mouth—how she had called her little great-grandson, Peter, to her as the child was playing near, probably that she might give him her blessing—how, when the nurse came running out, she had seen her looking most earnestly at him, but evidently not able to say a word. Afterwards, she had a little revived and had risen and beautifully expressed her gratitude to all about her for their long kindness and attention, and then, how, piously lifting up her hands and eyes, she had told them that she was now going to meet with those that she had loved and lost. "O Lord!" she had exclaimed, "what a meeting that will be!" and thereupon she had departed without a sigh.

For several days after this Mr. Mortimer and his brother went about the business left to them to do. They sent for an architect, and put the house into his hands to be thoroughly repaired. Mrs. Peter Melcombe was desirous not to leave it, and this they arranged to allow, giving orders that the apartments which the family had always occupied should remain untouched till the rest of the house was finished and ready for her. They also had the garden-door repaired to give her ingress, and the gallery-gate taken away. These same sons who for so many years had never come near their mother, seemed now very anxious to attend to her every wish ; scarcely a shrub was cut down in the garden excepting in the presence of one of them, and when Mrs. Peter Melcombe especially begged that the grandmother's wish respecting the bed of lilies might be attended to, Mr. Mortimer, with evident emotion, gave orders to the gardener that it should not be touched.

And then Sunday came, and with it a trial that the two sons had not expected. It was announced by the churchwarden to the family, first to the ladies at the hall, and then to the gentlemen at the inn, that Mr. Craik was going to preach a funeral sermon. He did not wish, he said, to take them by surprise —he felt that they would wish to know. In his secret soul he believed that the old men would not come to hear it—he hoped they would not, because their absence would enable him more freely to speak of the misfortunes of the deceased.

But they did come. The manner of their coming was thought by the congregation to be an acknowledgment that they felt their fault. They did not look any one in the face; but with brows bent down, and eyes on the ground, they went to the places given them in the family pew, and when morning prayers were over and the text was given out, as still as stones they sat and listened.

"Let me die the death of the righteous, and let my last end be like his."

The sermon was more full of eulogy than was in good taste, but the ladies of the family did not find it so ; they wept passionately—so did many of the congregation, but the two sons, though their hands might plainly be seen to tremble, maintained a deep, distressed immobility, and because it was neither right to upbraid them to their faces, nor to judge them publicly, a piece of the sermon which concerned Madam Melcombe's sorrow, caused by their desertion, was mercifully left out.

That was the last the people saw of the brothers;

they went away almost before it was light on Monday morning, and for a long time after, their faces, their words, and their every attitude, remained the talk of the place.

In the meantime, John Mortimer and Valentine had a very pleasant little excursion. As soon as they were out of the presence of their fathers, they naturally threw off any unusual gravity of demeanour, for though suitable to a solemn funeral, this might well pass away with it, as their grandmother had been a total stranger to them.

John hired horses, and they rode about the country together to see the rosy apple orchards; they inspected an old Roman town, then they went and looked at some fine ruins, and otherwise they enjoyed themselves for three days; for John had plenty of money, and Valentine was far from suspecting that not many months before his own father had dispossessed him, with himself, of an ample fortune and a good inheritance. He had always been brought up to understand that his father was not well off, and that he would have to work for his place in the world. John's place was made already—lucky for him! Lucky for Valentine, too, for John was very liberal to his young relative, and had taken him about with him more than once before.

So the first few days after the reading of that will were passed by Valentine in very good spirits, and with much self-gratulation on things in general. John invited him to stay at his house till his father came home, and Valentine accepting, they reached their station, and John was at once received into the bosom of his family, that is to say, he was pushed and pulled with difficulty into a very large carriage so excessively full of young Mortimers that it was perfectly impossible to add Valentine also.

"What did you bring them all for?" said John, falling foul of the servants in a momentary fit of impatience, while they sat smiling all over him.

"Well, sir, they were all inside the carriage and out of it ready, before even we put the horses to. We didn't know which to pull out," answered the coachman, grinning.

John Mortimer's house was only reached by a country lane; and to all appearances (though it was situated but two miles from the small town of Wigfield), it was buried in the depths of the country. It was a thoroughly unreasonable house, appearing outside to be more than half of it roof, the stables being so arranged as to seem almost imposing in comparison with it.

These stables ran down at right angles with the house, their windows and doors below, being on the further side. But a story had been added which was made of long wooden shingles, and one of these shingles having been removed to admit light and air, you might very often see seven round faces in a row looking out there, for the opening overlooked every window in the front of the house without exception. The long loft, which was called "parliament," and had been annexed by the children, admitted of their sending down cheerful greetings to their grandfather and other friends; and it was interesting, particularly when there was company to dinner, to watch their father sitting at the head of the table, and to see the dishes handed round.

The inside of the house was peculiar also. There was a very fine hall in the centre, and a really beautiful old oak staircase wound round it, being adorned with carving, and having a fine old fireplace on one of the landings. This hall was the only good room in the house: on the right of it were the kitchens and the kitchen offices, on its left was the dining-room, which was a thoroughfare to the drawing-room, and through that again you reached a pleasant library; John Mortimer's own particular den or smoking room being beyond again. All these rooms had thorough lights excepting the last, and in fine weather every one entered them, back or front, from the garden.

Up-stairs there were a great many bedrooms, and not one good one: most of them had sloping roofs. Then there was a long school-room, with a little staircase of its own. You could make a good deal of noise in that room, and not be heard beyond it; but this circumstance is no particular advantage, if your father has no nerves at all, and scarcely observes whether there is a noise or not.

John and Valentine Mortimer had a cheerful dinner, and after that a riotous game at romps with the children. It was four days since the funeral; it had now passed into the background of their thoughts, and they concerned themselves very little further with the will of old Madam Melcombe; for it must not be supposed that they knew much about her—not half as much, in fact, as every man, woman, and child knew round about the place where her house was situated.

They knew she had had a large family of sons, and that their father and uncle had left home early in life —had been *sent away*, was their thought, or would have been if the question had ever been raised so as to lead them to think about it.

They were sent to Wigfield, which was about sixty miles from their home. Here they had an old second cousin, of whom they always spoke with great respect and affection. He took Augustus into his bank, and not only became as fond of him as if he had been his son, but eventually left him half of what he possessed. Daniel went into a lawyer's office, and got on very well; but he was not at all rich, and had always let his son know, that though there was an estate in the family, it never could come to him. John having also been told this, had not doubted that there must have been a family quarrel at some time or other; but in his own mind he never placed it very far back, but always fancied it must be connected with his uncle's first marriage, which was a highly imprudent and very miserable one.

Whatever it had arisen from, his father had evidently taken part with his uncle; but old Augustus never mentioned the subject. John was aware that he wrote to his mother once a year, but she never answered. This might be, John thought, on account of her great age and her infirmities; and that very evening he began to dismiss the subject from his mind, being aided by the circumstance that he was himself the only son of a very rich and loving father, so that anything the mother might have left to her second surviving son was not a matter of the slightest importance to her grandson, or ever likely to be.

CHAPTER V.

OF A FINE MAN AND SOME FOOLISH WOMEN.

"For life is like unto a winter's day,
Some break their fast and so depart away;
Others stay dinner, then depart full fed;
The longest age but sups, and goes to bed."

ANON.

MR. JOHN MORTIMER, as has before been said, was the father of seven children. It may now be added that he had been a widower one year and a half.

Since the death of his wife he had been his own master, and, so far as he cared to be, the master of his household.

This had not been the case previously: his wife had ruled over him and his children, and had been happy on the whole, though any woman whose house, containing four sitting-rooms only, finds that they are all thoroughfares, and feels that one of the deepest joys of life is that of giving dinner-parties, and better ones than her neighbours, must be held to have a grievance—a grievance against architects, which no one but an architect can cure.

And yet old Augustus, in generously presenting this house, roof and all, to his son, had said, "And, my dears, both of you, beware of bricks and mortar. I have no doubt, John, when you are settled, that you and Janie will find defects in your house. My experience is that all houses have defects; but my opinion is, that it is better to pull a house down, and build a new one, than to try to remedy them."

Mr. Augustus Mortimer had tried building, rebuilding, and altering houses more than once; and his daughter-in-law knew that he would be seriously vexed if she disregarded his advice.

Of course if it had been John himself that had objected, the thing would have been done in spite of that; but his father must be considered, she knew, for in fact everything depended on him.

John had been married the day he came of age. His father had wished it greatly: he thought it a fine thing for a man to marry early, if he could afford it. The bride wished it also, but the person who wished it most of all was her mother, who managed to make John think he wished it too, and so, with a certain moderation of feeling, he did; and if things had not been made so exceedingly easy for him, he might have attained almost to fervour on the occasion.

As it was, being young for his years, as well as in fact, he had hardly forgotten to pride himself on having a house of his own, and reached the dignified age of twenty-two, when Mrs. John Mortimer, presenting him with a son, made a man of him in a day, and threw his boyish thoughts into the background. To his own astonishment, he found himself greatly pleased with his heir. His father was pleased also, and wrote to the young mother something uncommonly like a letter of thanks, at the same time presenting her with a carriage and horses.

The next year, perhaps in order to deserve an equally valuable gift (which she obtained), she presented her husband with twin daughters; and was rather pleased than otherwise to find that he was glad, and that he admired and loved his children.

Mrs. John Mortimer felt a decided preference for her husband over any other young man; she liked him, besides which he had been a most desirable match for her in point of circumstances; but when her first child was born to her she knew, for the first time in her life, what it was to feel a real and warm affection. She loved her baby; she may have been said, without exaggeration, to have loved him very much; she had thenceforward no time to attend to John, but she always ruled over his household beautifully, made his friends welcome, and endeared herself to her father-in-law by keeping the most perfect accounts, never persuading John into any kind of extravagance, and always receiving hints from headquarters with the greatest deference.

The only defect her father-in-law had, in her opinion, was that he was so inconveniently religious; his religion was inconvenient not only in degree but in kind. It troubled her peace to come in contact with states of mind very far removed not only from what she felt, but what she wished to feel. If John's father had set before her anything that she and John could do, or any opinion that they might hold, she thought she should have been able to please him, for she considered herself quite inclined to do her duty by her church and her soul in a serious and sensible manner; but to take delight in religion, to add the love of the unseen Father to the fear and reverence that she wanted to cultivate, was something that it alarmed her to think of.

It was all very well to read of it in the Bible, because that concerned a by-gone day, or even to hear a clergyman preach of it, this belonged to his office; but when this old man, with his white beard, talked to her and her husband just as David had talked in some of his psalms, she was afraid, and found his aspiration worse to her than any amount of exhortation could have been.

What so impossible to thought as such a longing for intercourse with the awful and the remote—"With my soul have I desired thee in the night;" "My soul is athirst for God;" no, not so, says the listener who stands without—I will come to his house and make obeisance, but let me withdraw soon again from his presence, and dwell undaunted among my peers.

There is, indeed, nothing concerning which people more fully feel that they cannot away with it than another man's aspiration.

And her husband liked it. He was not afraid, as she was, of the old man's prayers, though he fully believed they would be answered.

He tried to be loyal to the light he walked in, and his father rested in a trust concerning him and his, which had almost the assurance of possession.

She also, in the course of a few years, came to believe that she must ere long be drawn into a light which as yet had not risen. She feared it less, but never reached the point of wishing to see it shine.

At varying intervals, Mrs. John Mortimer presented her husband with another lovely and healthy infant, and she also, in her turn, received a gift from her father-in-law, together with the letter of thanks.

In the meantime her husband grew. He became first manly, more manly than the average man, as is often the case with those who have an unusually long boyhood. Then by culture and travel he developed the resources of a keenly observant and very thoughtful mind. Then his love for his children made a naturally sweet temper sweeter still, and in the course of a very few years he had so completely left his wife behind, that it never occurred to him to think of her as a companion for his inner life. He liked her; she never nagged; he considered her an excellent housekeeper; in fact, they were mutually pleased with one another; their cases were equal; both often thought they might have been worse off, and neither regretted with any keenness what they had never known.

Sometimes, having much sweetness of nature, it would chance that John Mortimer's love for his children would overflow in his wife's direction, on which, as if to recall him to himself, she would say, not coldly, but sensibly, "Don't be silly, John dear." But if he expressed gratitude on her account, as he sometimes did when she had an infant of a few days old in her arms, if his soul appeared to draw nearer to her then, and he inclined to talk of deeper and wider things than they commonly spoke of, she was always distinctly aggrieved. A tear perhaps would twinkle in her eye. She was affected by his relief after anxiety, and his gratitude for her safety; but she did not like to feel affected, and brought him back to the common level of their lives as soon as possible.

So they lived together in peace and prosperity till they had seven children, and then, one fine autumn, Mrs. John Mortimer persuaded her father-in-law to do up the house, so far as papering and painting were concerned. She then persuaded John to take a tour, and went herself to the sea-side with her children.

From this journey she did not return. Their father had but just gone quite out of her reach when the children took scarlet fever, and she summoned their grandfather to her aid. In this, her first great anxiety and trouble, for some of them were extremely ill, all that she had found most oppressive in his character appeared to suit her. He pleased and satisfied her; but the children were hardly better, so that he had time to consider what it was that surprised him in her, when she fell ill herself, and before her husband reached home had died in his father's arms.

All the children recovered. John Mortimer took them home, and for the first six months after her death he was miserably disconsolate. It was not because they had been happy, but because they had been so very comfortable. He aggravated himself into thinking that he could have loved her more if he had only known how soon he should lose her; he looked at all their fine healthy joyous children, and grieved to think that now they were his only.

But the time came when he knew that he could have loved her much more if she would have let him; and when he had found out that, womankind in general went down somewhat in his opinion. He made up his mind, as he thought, that he would not marry again; but this, he knew in his secret heart, was less for her sake than for his own.

Then, being of an ardently affectionate nature, and having now no one to restrain it, he began to study his children with more anxious care, and consider their well-being with all his might.

The children of middle-aged people seem occasionally to come into the world ready tamed. With a certain old-fashioned primness, they step sedately through the paths of childhood. So good, so easy to manage, so—uninteresting?

The children of the very young have sometimes an extra allowance of their father's youth in their blood. At any rate the little Mortimers had.

Their joy was ecstatic, their play was fervent, and as hard as any work. They seemed month by month to be crowding up to their father, in point of stature, and when he and they all went about the garden together, some would be treading on his heels, the select two who had hold of his arms would be shouting in his ears, and the others, dancing in front, were generally treading on his toes, in their desire to get as near as possible and inform him of all the wonderful things that were taking place in this new and remarkable world.

Into this family the lonely little heir of the Melcombes was shortly invited to come for awhile, but for some trivial reason his mother declined the invitation, at the same time expressing her hope that Mr. Mortimer would kindly renew it some other time.

It was not convenient to John Mortimer to invite the boy again for a long time—so long that his mother bitterly repented not having accepted the first invitation. She had an aunt living at Dartmouth, and whenever her boy was invited by John Mortimer, she meant to bring him herself, giving out that she was on her way to visit that relative.

Who knew what might happen?

Mr. John Mortimer was a fine man, tall, broad-shouldered, and substantial-looking, though not at all stout. His perfect health and teeth as white as milk made him look even younger than he was. His countenance, without being decidedly handsome, was fine and very agreeable. His hair was light, of the Saxon hue, and his complexion was fair.

Thus he had many advantages; but Mrs. Peter Melcombe felt that as the mother of a child so richly endowed, and as the possessor of eight hundred a year in order that he might be suitably brought up, she was a desirable match also. She did not mean the boy to cost her much for several years to come, and till he came of age (if he lived) she had that handsome old house to live in. Old Augustus Mortimer, on the other hand, was very rich, she knew; he was a banker and his only son was his partner. Sure to inherit his banking business and probably heir to his land.

Mrs. Peter Melcombe had some handsome and becoming raiment made, and waited with impatience; for in addition to Mr. John Mortimer's worldly advantages she found him attractive.

So did some other people. John Mortimer's troubles on that head began very soon after the sending of his first invitation to Mrs. Melcombe, when the excellent elderly lady who taught the little Mortimers (and in a great measure kept his house) let him know that she could no longer do justice to them. They got on so fast, they had such spirits, they were so active and so big, that she felt she could not cope with them. Moreover, the three eldest were exceptionally clever, and the noise made by the whole tribe fatigued her.

John sent his eldest boy to school, promised her masters to help her, and an assistant governess, but she would not stay, and with her went for a time much of the comfort of that house.

Mr. Mortimer easily got another governess—a very pretty young lady who did not, after a little while, take much interest in the children, but certainly did take an interest in him. She was always contriving to meet him—in the hall, on the stairs, in the garden. Then she looked at him at church, and put him so out of countenance and enraged him, and made him feel so ridiculous, that one day he took himself off to the Continent, and kept away till she was gone.

Having managed that business, he got another governess, and she let him alone, and the children too, for they completely got the better of her; used to make her romp with them, and sometimes went so far as to lock her into the schoolroom. It was not till this lady had taken her leave and another had been found that Mr. John Mortimer repeated his invitation to little Peter Melcombe. His mother brought him, and according to the programme she had laid down, got herself invited to stay a few days.

She had no trouble about it. Mr. John Mortimer no sooner saw Mrs. Melcombe than he expressed a hospitable, almost a fervent hope, that she could stay a week with him.

Of course Mrs. Melcombe accepted the invitation, and he was very sociable and pleasant; but she thought the governess (a very grand lady indeed) took upon herself more than beseemed her, and smiled at her very scornfully when she ventured to say sweet things to John Mortimer on her own great love for children, and on the charms of his children in particular.

Peter was excessively happy. His mother's happiness in the visit was soon over. She shortly found out that an elderly Scotch lady, one Miss Christie Grant, an aunt of the late Mrs. Daniel Mortimer, was to come in a few days and pay a long visit, and she shrewdly suspected that the attractive widower being afraid to remain alone in his own house, made arrangements to have female visitors to protect him, and hence the invitation to her. But she had to leave Peter at the end of the week. and which of the two ladies when they parted hated the other most it might be difficult to determine.

It cannot be said with truth that Peter regretted his mother's departure. The quantity of mischief he was taught (of a not very heinous description) by two sweet little imps of boys younger than himself, kept him in a constant state of joyous excitement. His grandmother having now been dead a year and a quarter, his mourning had been discarded, and his mother had been very impressive in her cautions to him not to spoil his new clothes, but before he had been staying with his young friends a fortnight he was much damaged in his outer man, as indeed he was also in his youthful heart, for the smallest of all the Mortimers—a lovely little child about three years old—took entire possession of it; and when he was not up a tree with the boys in a daring hunt after bergamy pears, or wading barefoot in a shallow stream at the bottom of the garden catching water-beetles, caddis-worms, and other small cattle for a freshwater aquarium, he was generally carrying this child about the garden pickaback, or otherwise obeying her little behests, and assuring her of his unalterable love.

Poor little Peter! After staying fully six weeks with the Mortimers his time came to be taken home again, and his mother, who spent two days with them on her way northwards, bore him off to the railway, accompanied by the host and most of his children. Then he suddenly began to feel the full meaning of the misfortune that had fallen on him, and he burst into wailings and tears. His tiny love had promised to marry him when she was grown up; his two little friends had given him some sticklebacks, packed in wet moss; they were now in his pockets, as were also some water-beetles in a paper bag; the crown of his cap was full of silkworms carefully wrapped in mulberry leaves; but all these treasures could not avail to comfort him for loss of the sweet companionship he had enjoyed—for the apples he had crunched in the big dog's kennel when hiding with another little imp from the nurse—for the common possession they had enjoyed of some young rats dug out of the bank of the stream, and more than all, for the tender confidences there had been between them as to the endless pranks they spent their lives in, and all the mischief they had done or that they aspired to do.

John Mortimer having a keen sympathy with childhood, felt rue at heart for the poor little blinking, sobbing fellow; but to invite him again might be to have his mother also, so he let him go, handing in from his third daughter's arms to the young heir a wretched little blind puppy and a small bottle of milk to feed it with on the way.

If anything could comfort a boy, this precious article could. So the Mortimer boys thought. So in fact it proved. As the train moved off they heard the sobs of Peter and the yelping of the puppy, but before they reached their happy home he had begun to nurse the little beast in his arms, and derive consolation from watching its movements and keeping it warm.

CHAPTER VI.

THE SHADOW OF A SHADE.

"The world would lose its finest joys
Without its little girls and boys;
Their careless glee and simple ruth,
And innocence and trust and truth;
Ah! what would your poor poet do
Without such little folk as you?"

LOCKER.

"WELL, anyhow," observed Mr. Nicholas Swan, the gardener, when the children came home and told him how Peter had cried—"anyhow, there's one less on you now to run over my borders. He was as meek as Moses, that child was, when first he came, but you soon made him as audacious as any of you."

"So they did, Nicholas dear," said one of the twins, a tall, dark-haired child.

"Oh, it's Nicholas *dear*, is it, Miss Barbara? Well, now, what next?"

"Why, the key of the fruit-house—we want the key."

"Key, indeed! Now, there's where it is. Make a wry path through your fields, and still you'll walk in it! I never ought to ha' got in the habit of lending you that key. What's the good of a key if a man can never keep it in his pocket? When I lived up at Mr. Daniel Mortimer's, the children never had my key—never."

"Well, come with us, then, and give us out the pears yourself. We won't take one."

Nicholas, with a twin on each side, and the other children bringing up the rear, was now walked off to the fruit-house, grumbling as he went.

"I left Mr. Mortimer's, I did, because I couldn't stand the children; and now the world's a deal fuller of 'em than it was then. No, Miss Gladys, I'm not a-going any faster; I wouldn't run, if it was ever so. When the contrac' was signed of my wages, it was never wrote down that I had to run at any time."

And having now reached the fruit-house, he was just pulling out his big key, when something almost like shame showed itself in his ruddy face, as a decided and somewhat mocking voice addressed him.

"Well, Nicholas, I'm just amazed at ye! I've lived upward of sixty years in this island, Scotland and England both, and never did I see a man got over so by children in my life! Talking of my niece's children, are ye—Mrs. Daniel Mortimer's? I wonder at ye—they were just nothing to these."

Here Mr. Swan, having unlocked the door, dived into the fruit-house, and occupied himself for some moments in recovering his self-possession and making his selection; then emerging with an armful of pears, he shouted after Miss Christie Grant, who had got a good way down the walk by this time.

"I don't deny, ma'am, that these air aggravating now and then, but anyhow they haven't painted my palings pink and my door pea-green."

Miss Christie returned. She seldom took the part of any children, excepting for the sake of argument or for family reasons; and she felt at that moment that the Daniel Mortimers were related to her, and that these, though they called her "aunt," were not.

"Ye should remember," she observed, with severity, "that ye had already left your house when they painted it."

"Remember it!" exclaimed the gardener, straightening himself; "ay, ay, I remember it—coming along the lane that my garden sloped down to, so that every inch of it could be seen. It had been all raked over, and there, just out of the ground, growing up in mustard-and-cress letters as long as my arm, I saw '*This genteel residence to let, lately occupied by N. Swan, Esq.*' I took my hob-nailed boots to them last words, and I promise you I made the mustard-and-cress fly."

"Well, ye see," observed Miss Christie, who was perfectly serious, "there is great truth in your saying that those children did too much as they pleased; but ye must consider that Mr. Mortimer didn't like to touch any of them, because they were not his own."

"That's just it, ma'am, and Mrs. Mortimer didn't like to touch any of them because they *were her own;* so between the two they got to be, I don't say as bad as these, but—" Here he shook his head, and leaning his back to the fruit-house door, began diligently to peel the fruit for an assembly, silent, because eating. "As for Master Giles," he went on, more to torment the old lady than to disparage the gentleman in question, "before ever he went to school, he chalked a picture that he called my arms on the tool house-door, three turnips as natural as life, and a mad kind of bird flourishing its wings about, that he said was a swan displayed. Underneath, for a *morter*, was wrote, 'All our geese air swans.' Now what do you call that for ten years old?"

"Well, well," said Aunt Christie, "that's nearly twenty years ago."

Then the fruit being all finished, N. Swan, Esq., shut up his clasp-knife, and the story being also finished, his audience ran away, excepting Miss Christie, to whom he said—

"But I was fond of those children, you'll understand, though they were powerful plagues."

"Swan," said the old lady, "ye'll never be respectit by children. You're just what ye often call yourself, *soft.*"

"And what's the good of being rough with 'em, ma'am? I can no more make 'em sober and sensible than I could straighten out their bushes of curly hair. No, not though I was to take my best rake to it. They're powerful plagues, bless 'em! but so far as I can see, we're in this world mainly to bring them forrard in it. I remember when my Joey was a very little chap, he was playing by me with a tin sword that he was proud of. I was sticking peas in my own garden, and a great hulking sergeant came by, and stopped a minute to ask his road. 'Don't you be afraid of me,' says Joey, very kind. 'I won't hurt 'e.' That man laughed, but the water stood in his eyes. He'd lost such a one, he said. Children air expensive, but it's very cutting to lose 'em. I've never seen any of the Mortimers in that trouble yet, though."

"And you've been many a long year with them too," observed Miss Christie.

"Ay, ma'am. Some folks air allers for change, but I've known when I was well off and they've known when they were well off." Mr. Swan said this in a somewhat pragmatical tone, and continued, "There's nothing but a long course of just dealing and respect o' both sides as can buy such digging as this here family gets out of my spade."

"Very true," said Miss Christie, who did not appear to see anything peculiar in this self-eulogy.

"But some folks forget," continued Mr. Swan, "that transplanted trees won't grow the first year, and others want too much for their money, and too good of its kind; but fair and softly, thinks I; you can't buy five shillings with threepence-halfpenny in any shop that I ever heerd of; and when you've earned half-a-crown you can't be paid it in gold."

The next morning, while Peter sat at breakfast revolving in his mind the delights he had lost, and wondering what Janie and Bertie and Hugh and Nancy were about, these staunch little friends of his were unconsciously doing the greatest damage to his future prospects—to their most important part, as he understood them, namely, his chance of coming to see the Mortimers again.

Miss Christie Grant always presided over the school-room breakfast, and John Mortimer, unless he had other visitors, breakfasted alone, generally coming down just after his children's meal was over, and having a selection of them with him morning by morning.

On this occasion, just as he came down, his children darted out of the window, exclaiming, "Oh, there's Mr. Brandon down the garden—Mr. Brandon's come."

John walked to the window, and looked out with a certain scrutinising interest; for it was but a few weeks since a somewhat important visitor had left old Daniel Mortimer's house—one concerning whom the neighbourhood had decided that she certainly ought to become Mrs. Giles Brandon, and that it would be an odd thing if Mr. Brandon did not think so. If he did, there was every appearance that she did not, for she had gone away all but engaged to his young brother Valentine.

"He looks dull, decidedly dull, since Miss Graham left them," soliloquised John Mortimer. "I thought so the last time I saw him, and now I am sure of it. Poor fellow," he continued with a half smile. "I can hardly fancy him a lover, but, if he does care for that graceful little sea-nymph, it is hard on him that such a shallow-pated boy as Valentine should stand in his light;" and he stepped out to meet his guest, who was advancing in the midst of the children, while at the same time they shouted up at the open school-room window that Nancy must come down directly and see her godfather.

The grand lady-governess looked out in a becoming morning costume.

"A fine young man," she remarked to Miss Christie Grant.

"Yes, that's my oldest nephew, St. George they call him. Giles Brandon is his name, but his mother aye disliked the name of Giles, thought it was only fit for a ploughman. So she called him St. George, and that's what he is now, and will be."

Miss Christie Grant said this with a certain severity of manner, but she hardly knew how to combine a snubbing to the lady for her betrayal of interest in all the bachelors round, with her desire to boast of this relative. So she presently went on in a more agreeable tone. "His mother married Mr. Daniel Mortimer; he is an excellent young man. Has no debts and has been a great traveller. In short a year and a half ago he was shipwrecked, and as nearly lost his life as possible. He was picked up by Captain Graham, whose grand-daughter (no, I think Miss Graham is the old gentleman's niece) has been staying this summer with Mr. Daniel Mortimer. Mr. Brandon, ye'll understand, is only half-brother to Valentine Mortimer, whom ye frequently see."

Valentine was too young to interest the grand lady, but when by a combined carelessness of manner with judicious questioning she had discovered that the so-called St. George had a moderate independence, and prospects besides, she felt a longing wish to carry down little Anastasia herself to see her godfather, and was hardly restrained from doing so by that sense of propriety which never forsook her. In the mean time Brandon passed out of view into the room where breakfast was spread and the little Anastasia, so named because her birth had taken place on Easter day, was brought down smiling in her sister Barbara's arms.

Peter's little love, a fair and dimpled creature, was forthwith accommodated with a chair close to her godfather, while the twins withdrew to practise their duets, and more viands were placed on the table.

The children then began to wait on their father and his guest, and during a short conversation which ensued concerning Mrs. Peter Melcombe and her boy, they were quite silent, till a pause took place and the little Anastasia lifted up her small voice and distinguished herself by saying—

"Fader, Peter's dot a dhost in his darden."

"Got a ghost!" exclaimed John Mortimer, with a look of dismay; for ghosts were the last things he wished his children to hear anything about.

"Yes," said the youngest boy Hugh, "he says he's going to be rather a grand gentleman when he's grown up, but he wishes he hadn't got a ghost."

"Then why doesn't he sell it, Huey?" asked the guest with perfect gravity.

The little fellow opened his blue eyes wider. "I don't think you know what ghosts are," he remarked.

"Oh yes, I do," answered Brandon. "I've often read about them. Some people think a good deal of them, but I never could see the fun of having them myself, and," he continued, "I never noticed any about your premises, John."

"No," answered John Mortimer, following his lead; "they would be no use for the children to play with."

"Do they scratch, then?" inquired the little Anastasia.

"No, my beauty bright, but I'm told they only wake up when it's too dark for children to play."

"Peter's ghost doesn't," observed Master Bertram. "He came in the morning."

"Did he steal anything?" inquired Brandon, still desirous, it seemed, to throw dirt at the great idea.

"Oh no, he didn't steal," said the other little boy, "that's not what they're for."

"What did he say then?"

"He gave a deep sigh, but he didn't say *nothink.*"

"Ghosts," said Bertie, following up his brother's speech as one who had full information—"ghosts are not birds, they don't come to lay eggs for you, or to be of any use at all. They come for you to be afraid of. Didn't you know that, father?"

John was too much vexed to answer, and Peter's chance from that moment of ever entering those doors again was not worth a rush.

"But you needn't mind, father dear," said Janie, the eldest child present, "Peter's ghost won't come here. It doesn't belong to 'grand,' or to any of us. Its name was Melcombe, and it came from the sea, that they might know it was dead." John and Brandon looked at one another. The information was far too circumstantial to be forgotten by the children, who continued their confidences now without any more irreverent interruptions. "Mrs. Melcombe gave Peter four half-crowns to give to nurse, and he had to say 'Thank you, nurse, for your kindness to me;' but nurse wasn't kind, she didn't like Peter, and she slapped him several times."

"And Mrs. Melcombe gave some more shillings to Maria," said Bertie.

"Like the garden slug," observed Brandon, "leaving a trail of silver behind her."

The said Maria, who was their little nursemaid, now came in to fetch away the children.

"Isn't this provoking," exclaimed John Mortimer, when they were gone. "I had no notion that child had been neglected and left to pick up these pernicious superstitions, though I never liked his mother from the first moment I set my eyes on her."

"Why did you ask her to stay at your house then?" said Brandon, laughing.

"Giles, you know as well as I do."

Thereupon, having finished their breakfast, they set forth to walk to the town, arguing together on some subject that interested them till they reached the bank.

Behind it, in a comfortable room fitted up with library tables, leather chairs, and cases for books and papers, sat old Augustus Mortimer. "Grand," as he was always called by his descendants, that being easier to say than his full title of grandfather; and if

John Mortimer had not taken Brandon into this room to see him, the talk about the ghost might have faded away altogether from the mind of the latter.

As it was, Grand asked after the little ones, and Brandon, standing on the rug and looking down on the fine stern features and white head, began to give him a graphic account of what little Peter Melcombe had been teaching them, John Mortimer, while he unlocked his desk and sorted out certain papers, now and then adding a touch or two in mimicry of his children's little voices.

Old Augustus said nothing, but Brandon, to his great surprise, noticed that as the narrative went on it produced a marked effect upon him; he listened with suppressed eagerness, and then with a cogitative air as if he was turning the thing over in his mind.

The conclusion of the story, how Janie had said the name of the ghost was Melcombe, John Mortimer related, for Brandon by that time was keenly alive to the certainty that they were disturbing the old man much.

A short silence followed. John was still arranging his papers, then his father said deliberately,—

"This is the first hint I ever received of any presence being supposed to haunt the place."

The ghost itself had never produced the slightest effect on John Mortimer. All he thought of was the consequence of the tale on the minds of his children.

"I shall take care that little monkey does not come here again in a hurry," he remarked, at the same time proceeding to mend a quill pen; his father watching him rather keenly, Brandon thought, from under his bushy, white eyebrows.

"Now, of all men," thought Brandon, "I never could have supposed that Grand was superstitious. I don't believe he is either; what does it mean?" and as there was still silence, he became so certain that Grand would fain ask some more questions but did not like to do so, that he said, in a careless tone,

"That was all the children told us;" and thereupon, being satisfied and willing to change the subject, as Brandon thought, the old man said,—

"Does my brother dine at home to-day, St. George?"

"Yes, uncle; shall I tell him you will come over to dinner?"

"Well, my dear fellow, if you are sure it will be convenient to have me—it is a good while since I saw him—so you may."

"He will be delighted; shall I tell him you will stay the night?"

"Yes."

"Well done, father," said John, looking up. "I am glad you are getting over the notion that you cannot sleep away from home. I'll come over to breakfast, St. George, and drive my father in."

"Do," said Brandon, taking his leave; and as he walked to the railway that was to take him home, he could not help still pondering on the effect produced by the mention of the ghost. He little supposed, however, that the ghost was at the bottom of this visit to his stepfather; but it was.

CHAPTER VII.

AN OLD MAN DIGS A WELL.

"And travel finishes the fool."
GAY.

MRS. PETER MELCOMBE, all unconscious of the unfavourable impression her son had made on his late host, continued to think a good deal of the agreeable widower. She made Peter write from time to time to little Janie Mortimer and report the progress of the puppy, at the same time taking care to mention his dear mamma in a manner that she thought would be advantageous.

It cost Peter a world of trouble to copy and recopy these epistles till his mother was satisfied with them; but she always told him that he would not be remembered so well or invited again unless he wrote; and this was true.

His little friends wrote in reply, but by no means such carefully-worded letters; they also favoured him with shoals of Christmas cards and showers of valentines, but his letters never got beyond the schoolroom; and if John Mortimer's keen eyes had ever fallen on them, it would have availed nothing. He would have discovered at once that they were not the child's sole production, and would have been all the more decided not to invite him again.

When first Mrs. Melcombe came home she perceived a certain change in Laura, who was hardly able to attend to Peter's lessons, and had fits of elation that seemed to alternate with a curious kind of shame. Mrs. Peter Melcombe did not doubt that Laura fancied she had got another lover, but she was so tired of Laura's lovers that she determined to take no notice; and if Laura had anything to say, to make her say it without assistance. It seemed to her so right and natural and proper that she should wish to marry again herself, and so ridiculous of Laura to fancy that she wished to marry also.

On Valentine's day, however, Laura had a letter, flushed high, and while trying to look careless actually almost wept for joy; for the moment Mrs. Melcombe was thrown off her guard, and she asked a question.

Laura, in triumph, handed the valentine to her sister-in-law. "It's strange," she said tremulously, "very strange; but what is a woman to do when she is the object of such a passion?"

It was a common piece of paper with two coloured figures on it taking hands and smiling; underneath, in a clear and careful hand, was written—

"What would he give, your lover true,
Just for one little sight of you?
"J. S."

"J. S.?" said Mrs. Melcombe, in a questioning tone.

"It's Joseph, dear," replied Laura, hanging down her head and smiling.

Joseph was the head plumber who had been employed about the now finished house, and Mrs. Melcombe's dismay was great when she found that Joseph, having discovered how the young lady thought he was in love with her, was actually taking up the part of a lover, she dreaded to think what might occur in consequence. Joseph was a very clever young workman, of excellent character, and Laura was intolerably foolish and to the last degree credulous.

If the young man had been the greatest scamp and villain, but in her own rank of life, it would have been nothing to compare with this, in the eyes of Mrs. Melcombe, or indeed in most people's eyes. She turned pale, and felt that she was a stricken woman.

She was not well educated herself, and she had not been accustomed to society, but she aspired to better things. The house was just finished, she had written to Mr. Mortimer to tell him so. She thought of giving a house-warming; for several of the families round, whose fathers and mothers had been kept at arms' length by old Madam Melcombe till their children almost forgot that there was such a person, had now begun kindly to call on the lonely ladies, and express a wish to see something of them.

Also she had been rubbing up her boarding-school French, and hoped to take a trip to Paris, for she wanted to give herself and her son all the advantages that could be got with money. She knew there was something provincial about herself and her sister-in-law, as there had been about the old grandmother; and indeed about all the Melcombes. She wished to rise; and oh what should she do, how could she ever get over it, if Laura married the plumber?

Her distress was such that she took the only course which could have availed her—she was silent.

"I was afraid, dear, you might, you would, you must think it very imprudent," said Laura, a little struck by this silence; "but what is to be done? Amelia, he's dying for me."

Still Mrs. Melcombe was silent.

"He told me himself, that if I wouldn't have him it would drive him to drink."

"Laura!" exclaimed Mrs. Melcombe with vehemence, "it's not credible that you can take up with a lout who courts you in such fashion as that. O Laura!" she exclaimed in such distress as to give real pathos to her manner, "I little thought to see this day, I could not have believed it of you;" and she burst into an agony of tears.

"And here's a letter," she presently found voice enough to say, "here's a letter from Mr. Mortimer, to say that his brother's coming to look at the house. Perhaps Mr. John Mortimer will come with him. Oh, what shall I do if they hear of this?"

Laura was very much impressed. If scorn, or anger, or incredulity had confronted her, she would have held to her intentions; but this alarm and grief at least had the merit of allowing all importance to the affair, and consequently to her.

Her imagination conjured up visions of her sister-in-law's future years. She saw her always wringing her hands, and she was touched for her. "And then so happy as we meant to be, having a foreign tour, and seeing Paris, and so as we had talked it over together. And such friends as we always are."

This was perfectly true; Mrs. Melcombe and Laura were not of the nagging order of women, they never said sarcastic or ill-natured things to one another, the foibles of the one suited the other; and if they had a few uncomfortable words now and then between themselves, they had enough *esprit de corps* to hide this from all outsiders.

An affecting scene took place, Laura rose and threw herself into Amelia's arms weeping passionately.

"You'll give it up, Laura dear, for my sake, and for our poor dear Peter's sake, who's gone."

No; Laura could not go quite so far in heroic self-sacrifice as that; but she did promise solemnly, that however many times Joseph might say he was dying for her, she would—what? She would promise to decide nothing till she had been to Paris.

She was very happy that morning; Amelia had not made game of her, and there had been such a scene! Laura enjoyed a scene; and Amelia had pleaded so hard and so long with her for that promise. At last she had given it. If she had not been such a remarkably foolish woman, she would have known she was glad on the whole that the promise had been extorted from her. As it was she thought she was sorry, but after a little more urging and pleading she gave up the precious valentine, and saw it devoured by the flames. It had a Birmingham postmark, and Mrs. Melcombe heard with pleasure that Joseph would be away at least a fortnight.

Laura had wanted a little excitement, just the least amusement; and if not that, just the least recognition of her place in nature as a woman, and a young one. At present, her imagination had not been long at work on this unpromising payer of the tribute. If some one, whose household ways and daily English were like her own, had come forward she would soon have forgotten Joseph; for he himself, as an individual, was almost nothing to her, it was only in his having paid the tribute that his power lay.

Late in the afternoon Mr. Augustus Mortimer arrived. He was received by Mrs. Melcombe almost, as it seemed, with the devotion of a daughter.

The room was strewed with account-books and cards. It had been intended that he should make some remark about them, and then she was to say, with careless ease, "Only the accounts of the parish charities." But he courteously feigning to see none of the litter, she was put out.

He presently went to inspect the repairs and restorations, to look over the garden and the stables; and it was not till the next morning that she found occasion to ask some advice of him.

The cottages on the land were let with the farms, so that the farmers put their labourers into them, charged, it is true, very little rent, but allowed them to get very much out of repair. It was the farmers' duty to keep them in repair; but there was no agent, no one to make them do it. Moreover, they would have it that no repairs worth mentioning were wanted. Did Mr. Mortimer think if she spent the money she had devoted to charity in repairing these cottages, she could fairly consider that she had spent it in charity?

It was a nice point, certainly, for it would be improving her son's property, and avoiding disputes with valuable and somewhat unmanageable tenants; and, on the other hand, it would be escaping the bad precedent of paying for repairs out of the estate; so she went on laying this casuistry before the old man while he pulled down his shaggy white brows, and looked very stern over the whole affair. "Some of the poor old women do suffer so sadly from rheumatism," she continued, "and our parish doctor says it comes from the damp places they live in, and then there is so much fever in the lower part of the hamlet."

"You had better let me see the farmers and the cottagers," said old Augustus. "I will go into the whole affair, and tell you what I think of it."

Accordingly he went his way among the people, and if he had any sorrowful reason for being glad of what rendered it his duty to pick up all the information he could, this did not make him less energetic in fighting the farmers.

Very little, however, could be done with them; an obvious hole in a roof they would repair, a rotting door they would replace, but that was all, and he felt strongly the impolicy of taking money out of the estate to do all the whitewashing, plastering, carpenters' work, and painting that were desirable; besides which, he was sure the water was not pure that the people drank, and that they ought to have another well.

When Mrs. Melcombe heard his report of it all, and when he acknowledged that he could do hardly anything with the farmers, she wished she had not asked his advice, particularly as he chose to bring certain religious remarks into it. He was indeed a most inconveniently religious man; his religion was of a very expensive kind, and was all mixed up with his philanthropy, as if one could not be religious at all without loving those whom God loved and as if one could not love them without serving them to the best of one's power.

She listened with dismay. If it was useless to expect much of the farmers, and impolitic to take much out of the estate, what was the use of talking? But Mr. Augustus Mortimer did talk for several minutes; first he remarked on the expressed wish of his mother that all needful repairs should be attended to, then he said his brother began to feel the infirmities of age, and also was a poor man; then he made Mrs. Melcombe wince by observing that the condition of the tenements was perfectly disgraceful, and next he went on to say that, being old himself, he did not wish to waste any time, for he should have but little, and therefore as he was rich he was content to do what was wanted himself.

"This house," he continued, "is a great deal too large for the small income your son will have. Very large sums have been spent, as the will directed, in putting it into perfect repair. I am not surprised, therefore, that you have felt perplexed, but now, if you have no objection, I will have estimates made at once."

Excessively surprised, a little humiliated, but yet, on the whole, conscious that such an offer relieved her of a great responsibility, Mrs. Peter Melcombe hesitated a moment, then said in a low voice—

"Thank you, Mr. Mortimer, but you will give me a little time to think of this."

"Certainly," he answered, with all composure, "till to-morrow morning;" then he went on as if that matter was quite settled, and enough had been said about it. "There is one person whom I should much like to point out to you as an object for your charity—the old shepherd's wife who is bedridden. If you were inclined to provide some one to look after her—— "

"Oh, Becky Maddison," interrupted Mrs. Melcombe; "the dear grandmother did not approve of that woman. She used to annoy her by telling an absurd ghost story."

"Indeed!"

"But still, as you think I ought to do something for her, I certainly will."

"I shall go and see her myself this afternoon," answered Mr. Augustus Mortimer hastily. "I will not fail to report to you how I find her."

"Her talk was naturally painful to the dear grandmother," continued Mrs. Melcombe.

Mr. Mortimer looked keenly attentive, but he did not ask any question, and as she said no more, he almost immediately withdrew, and walked straight across the fields to the cottage of this old woman.

Nothing more was said that evening concerning the repairs, or concerning this visit; but the next morning Mr. Mortimer renewed his proposition, and after a little modest hesitation, she accepted it; then, remembering his request concerning old Becky, she told him she had that morning sent her a blanket and some soup. "And, by-the-bye, Mr. Mortimer, did she tell you the story that used to annoy the dear grandmother?" she inquired.

Mr. Mortimer was so long in answering, that she looked up at him, and when he caught her eye he answered "Yes."

"He doesn't like it any more than his mother did," she thought, so she said no more, and he almost immediately went away to give orders about the proposed estimates.

Mrs. Melcombe and Laura made Mr. Mortimer very comfortable, and when he went away he left them highly pleased, for, having been told of their intended journey to Paris, he had proposed to them to come and spend a few days at his house, considering it the first stage of their tour.

So he departed, and no more dirt was thrown at him. The tide began to turn in favour of the Mortimers, people had seen the mild face and venerable gentleness of the Mortimer who was poor, they had now handled the gold of the one that was rich.

"Old Madam was a saint," they observed, "but she couldn't come and look arter us *hersen*, poor dear. Farmers are *allers* hard on poor folk. So he was bent on having another well atop o' the hill 'stead o' the bottom. Why let him, then, if he liked! Anyhow, there was this good in it—the full buckets would be to carry down hill 'stead of up. As to the water o' the ould well being foul and breeding fevers, it might be, and then again it might not be; if folks were to be for ever considering whether water was foul, they'd never drink in peace!"

The moment he was gone, Mrs. Melcombe turned her thoughts to Laura's swain, and excited such hopes of pleasure from the visit to Paris in the mind of her sister-in-law, that Joseph's devotion began to be less fascinating to her, besides which there was something inexpressibly sweet to her imaginative mind in the notion of being thwarted and watched. She pictured to herself the fine young man haunting the lonely glen, hoping to catch a sight of her, and smiting his brow as men do in novels, sighing and groaning over his lowly birth and his slender means. She wished Joseph would write that her sister-in-law might rob her of the letter; but Joseph didn't write, he knew better. At the end of the fortnight he appeared; coming to church, and sitting in full view of the ladies, looking not half so well in his shining Sunday clothes of Birmingham make, as he had done in his ordinary working suit.

Laura was a good deal out of countenance, but Mrs. Melcombe perceived, not without surprise, that while she felt nothing but a feminine exultation in being admired, the young man's homage was both deep and real. Nothing was either fancied or feigned.

So by Monday morning Mrs. Melcombe had got ready a delightful plan to lay before Laura—she actually offered to take her to London, and fired her imagination with accounts of the concerts, the theatres, and all that they were to do and see.

No mortal plumber could hold his own against such a sister-in-law. Laura let herself be carried off without having any interview with Joseph, who began to think " it was a bad job," and did not know how his supposed faithless lady wept during the railway journey. But then he did not know how completely when she went to her first oratorio she was delighted and consoled.

The longer they stayed in London the more delighted they were; so was Peter; the Polytechnic alone was worth all the joys of the country put together; but when they came back again at the end of April, and all the land was full of singing-birds, and the trees were in blossom, and the sweet smiling landscape looked so full of light, and all was so fresh and still, then the now absent Joseph got hold of Laura's imagination again; she went and gazed at the window that he had been glazing, when, as she passed, he lifted up his fine eyes and looked at her in such a particular manner.

What really had taken place was this. Joseph, with a lump of putty in his palm, was just about to dig a bit out of it with a knife that he held in his other hand. Laura passed, and when the young man looked up, she affected to feel confused, and turned away her face with a sort of ridiculous self-consciousness. Joseph was surprised, and the knife held suspended in his hand, he was staring at her when she glanced again, and naturally he was a little put out of countenance.

So Laura now walked about the place, recalled the romantic past, and if Joseph had appeared (which he did not, because he had no means of knowing that she had returned), it is highly doubtful whether Laura would ever have seen Paris.

As it was, with sighs and smiles, with regrets over a dead nosegay that the young man had given her, and with eager longings to see Paris, and perhaps Geneva, Laura spent the next fortnight, and then, taking leave of Melcombe again, was received in due time by Mr. Augustus Mortimer on the steps of his house, his son being with him.

It was nearly dinner-time, she and her sister-in-law were delighted to meet this gentleman, and find that he was going to dine that day with his father. Peter, too, was as happy as a king, for he hoped Mr. John Mortimer would and could give him information concerning all the well-remembered puppies, kittens, magpies, and white mice that he had made acquaintance with during his happy visit to the little Mortimers.

Mr. Augustus Mortimer's house was just outside the small town of Wigfield; it appeared to be quite in the country, because it was on the slope of a hill, and was so well backed up with trees that not a chimney could be seen from any of its windows. It was built with its back to the town, and commanded a pretty view over field, wood, and orchard, and also over its own beautiful lawn and slightly-sloping garden, which was divided from some rich meadows by the same little river that ran nearly two miles further on, past the bottom of John Mortimer's garden. "And there," said John Mortimer, after dinner, pointing out a chimney which could be seen against the sky, just over the tops of some trees—"there lives my uncle Daniel, in a house which belongs to his stepson, Giles Brandon; his house is just two miles from this, and mine is two miles from each of them, so that we form a triangle."

Mr. Mortimer's daughter came the next day to call on the relatives from Melcombe; she brought his step-daughters with her; and these young ladies when they returned home gave their step-brothers a succinct account of the impressions they had received.

"Provincial, both of them. The married one looks like a faded piece of wax-work. Laura Melcombe is rather pretty, but unless she is a goose, her manners, voice, and whole appearance do her the greatest injustice possible."

Mrs. Melcombe and Laura also gave judgment in the same manner when these visitors were gone.

"Mrs. Henfrey looks quite elderly. She must be several years past fifty; but I liked her kind, slow way of talking; and what a handsome gown she had on, Laura, real lace on it, and a real Maltese lace shawl!"

"She has a good jointure," said Laura; "she can afford to dress well. The girls, the Miss Grants, have graceful, easy manners, just the kind of manners I should like to have; but I can't say I thought much of their dress. I am sure those muslins must have been washed several times. In fact, they were decidedly shabby. I think it odd and old-fashioned of them always to call Mrs. Henfrey 'Sister.'"

"I do not see that; she is older than their mother was; they could not well address her by her Christian name. They do not seem to be a marrying family, and that is odd, as their mother married three times. The Grants are the children of the second marriage, are they not?"

"Yes; but three times! Did she marry three times? Ah, I remember—how shocking!"

"Shocking," exclaimed Mrs. Melcombe, "O, Laura, I consider it quite irreligious of you to say that."

Laura laughed. "But only think," she observed, "what a number of names one must remember in consequence of her three marriages. First, there is Uncle Daniel's own daughter, Mrs. Henfrey; I do not mind her; but then there is Mr. Brandon, the son of Aunt Mortimer's first husband; then these Grants, the children of her second husband; and then Valentine, uncle's son and hers by this third marriage. It's a fatigue only to think of them all!"

CHAPTER VIII.

THEY MEET AN AUTHOR.

"People may be taken in *once*, who imagine that an author is greater in private life than other men. Uncommon parts require uncommon opportunities for their exertion."

DR. JOHNSON.

MRS. HENFREY in taking leave of Amelia had expressed her pleasure at the prospect of shortly seeing her again. They were all coming by invitation to lunch, the next day, at her Uncle Augustus Mortimer's house, because in the afternoon there was to be a horticultural show in the town. They always went to these shows, she continued, and this one would have a particular interest for them, as John Mortimer's gardener, who had once been their gardener, was to carry off the first prize. "And if you ask him what the prize is for," said one of the girls, "he will tell you it is for 'airly 'tates.'"

Accordingly the next day there was a gathering of Mortimers and their families. Augustus Mortimer was not present, he generally took his luncheon at the bank; but his son John, to Peter's delight, appeared with the twins, and constituting himself master of the ceremonies, took the head of the table, and desired his cousin Valentine to take the other end, and make himself useful.

Peter asked after his little love, Anastasia.

"Oh, she is very happy," said Gladys Mortimer; "she and Janie have got a WASH."

"Got what?" asked Mrs. Henfrey.

"A wash, sister," said Valentine. "I passed through the garden, and saw them with lots of tiny dolls' clothes that they had been washing in the stream spread out to bleach on the grass."

"It's odd," observed Brandon, "that so wise as children are, they should be fond of imitating us who are such fools."

"Janie has been drawing from the round, in imitation of her sisters," observed John Mortimer. "She brought me this morning a portrait of a flat tin cock, lately bought for a penny, and said, 'I drew him from the round, father.'"

By this time the dishes were uncovered and the servants had withdrawn. Laura was very happy at first. She had been taken in to luncheon by the so-called St. George, he was treating her with a sort of deference that she found quite to her mind, and she looked about her on these newly-known relatives and connections with much complacency. There was John Mortimer, with Amelia at his right hand, in the place of honour; then there were the two Miss Grants (in fresh muslin dresses), with a certain Captain Walker between them, whose twin brother, as Laura understood, had married their elder sister. This military person was insignificant in appearance and small of stature, but he was very attentive to both the young ladies. Then there was Valentine, looking very handsome, between Mrs. Henfrey and Miss Christie Grant, and being rebuked by one and advised by the other as to his carving, for he could not manage the joint before him, and was letting it slip about in the dish and splash the white sauce.

"You must give your mind to it more," said Mrs. Henfrey, "and try to hit the joints."

"It's full of bones," exclaimed Valentine in a deeply-injured voice.

"Well, laddie," said Miss Christie, "and if I'm not mistaken, ye'll find when you get more used to carving, that a breast of veal always is full of bones."

"Nobody must take any notice of him till he has finished," said Brandon. "Put up a placard on the table, 'You are requested not to speak to the man at the veal.' Now, Aunt Christie, you should say, 'aweel, aweel,' you often do so when there seems no need to correct me."

"Isn't it wonderful," observed Valentine, "that he can keep up his spirits as he does, when only last week he was weighed in the columns of the *Wigfield Advertiser and True Blue*, and expressly informed that he was found wanting."

"If you would only let politics alone," observed Mrs. Henfrey, "the *True Blue* would never interfere with you. I always did hate politics," she continued, with peaceable and slow deliberation.

"They are talking of some Penny Readings that St. George has been giving," said John Mortimer, for he observed a look of surprise on Laura's face.

"'Our poet,' though, has let him alone lately," remarked Valentine. "Oh I wish somebody would command Barbara to repeat his last effusion. I am sure by the look in her eyes that she knows it by heart."

"We all do," said John Mortimer's eldest daughter.

"Ah! it's a fine thing to be a public character," observed her father; "but even I aspire to some notice from the *True Blue* next week in consequence of having old Nicholas for my gardener."

"I am very fond of poetry," said Laura simpering. "I should like to hear the poem you spoke of."

Thereupon the little girl immediately repeated the following verses:—

"If, dear friends, you've got a penny
(If you haven't steal one straight),
Go and buy the best of any
Penn'orth that you've bought of late.

"At the schoolroom as before
(Up May Lane), or else next door
(As last Monday) at the Boar,
Hear the Wigfield lion roar.

"What a treat it was, good lack!
Though my bench had ne'er a back,
With a mild respectful glee
There to hear, and that to see.

"Sweetly slept the men and boys,
And the girls, they sighed meanwhile
'O my goodness, what a voice!
O my gracious, what a smile!'"

The man with no ear for music feels his sense of justice outraged when people shudder while his daughter sings. Why won't they listen to her songs as to one another's? There is no difference.

With a like feeling those who have hardly any sense of humour are half-offended when others laugh, while they seem to be shut out for not perceiving any cause. Occasionally knowing themselves to be sensible people, they think it evident that their not seeing the joke must be because it is against them.

Laura and Mrs. Melcombe experienced a certain discomfort here. Neither would have been so rude as to laugh; in fact, what was there to laugh at? They were shut out not only from the laugh, but from that state of feeling which made these cousins, including the victim, enjoy it, against one of themselves.

As for Mrs. Henfrey, who also was without any perception of the humorous side of things, she looked on with a beaming countenance; pleased with them all for being in such good spirits, whatever might be the reason, for, as she always expressed it, she did so love to see young people happy.

"It's capital," said John, but not so good as the prose reviewing they give you; and all this most excellent fun we should lose, you know, Giles, if you might have your way, and all sorts of criticism and reviewing had to be signed with the writer's name."

"But it would make the thing much more fair and moderate," said Brandon "(not that I intended to include such little squibs as this); besides, it would secure a man against being reviewed by his own rivals—or his enemies."

"Yes," said Valentine; "but that sort of thing would tell both ways."

As he spoke with great gravity Mrs. Melcombe, mainly in the kind hope of helping dear Laura's mistake into the background, asked with an air of interest what he meant.

"Well," said Valentine, with calm audacity, "to give an example. Suppose a man writes something, call it anything you please—call it a lecture if you like—say that it is partly political, and that it is published by request; and suppose further that somebody, name unknown, writes an interesting account of its scope and general merits, and it is put into some periodical—you can call it anything you please—say a county paper, for instance. The author is set in the best light, and the reviewer brings forward also some of his own views, which is quite fair—"

As he seemed to be appealing to Laura, Laura said, "Yes; perfectly fair."

"His own views—on—on the currency or anything else you like to mention." Here John Mortimer asked Mrs. Melcombe if she would take some more wine, Valentine proceeding gravely: "Now do you or do you not think that if that review had been signed by the lecturer's father, brother, or friend almost as intimate as a brother, it would have carried more weight or less in consequence?"

As several of them smiled, Mrs. Melcombe immediately felt uncomfortable again.

"If what he said was true," she said, "I cannot exactly see——" and here she paused.

"Well," said John Mortimer, observing that the attention of his keen-witted little daughter was excited, and being desirous, it seemed, to give a plainer example of what it all meant, "let us say now, for once, that I am a poet. I send out a new book, and sit quaking. The first three reviews appear. Given in little they read thus:—

"One. 'He copied from Snooks, whose immortal

work, "The Loves of the Linendraper," is a comfort and a joy to our generation."

"Two. 'He has none of the culture, the spontaneity, the suavity, the reticence, the *abandon*, the heating power, the cooling power, the light, the shade, or any of the other ingredients referred to by the great Small in his noble work on poesy.'

"Three. 'This man doesn't know how to write his own language.'

"As I am a poet, fancy my state of mind! I am horribly cast down; don't like to go out to dinner; am sure my butler, having read these reviews, despises me as an impostor; but while I sit sulking, in comes a dear friend and brother-poet. 'How do you know,' says he, 'that Snooks didn't write number one himself? Or perhaps one of his clique did, for whom he is to do the same thing.' I immediately shake hands with him. This is evidently his candid opinion, and I love candour in a friend; besides, we both hate Snooks. 'And it is a well-known fact,' he continues with friendly warmth, 'that Small's great work won't sell; how do you know that number two was not written by a brother or friend of the publisher's, by way of an advertisement for it?' By this time I am almost consoled. Something strikes me with irresistible force. I remember that that fellow Smith, who contested with me the election for the borough of Wigfield in eighteen hundred and fifty or sixty, has taken to literature. He was at the head of the poll on that occasion, but my committee proving that he bribed, he lost his seat. I came in. It was said that I bribed too; but to discuss that now would be out of place. I feel sure that Smith must have written number three. In fact he said those very words concerning me on the hustings."

"Gladys," said Brandon, observing the child's deep attention, "it is right you should know that the brother-poet had written a tragedy on tin-tacks. Your father reviewed it, and said no family ought to be without it."

"But you didn't bribe father, and you didn't copy from Snooks, I am sure," said Gladys, determined to defend her father, even in his assumed character.

"What was the name of your *thing*, papa?" asked Barbara.

"I don't know, my dear, I have not considered that matter."

"It was called 'The Burglar's Betrothal,'" said Valentine.

"And do you think that Snooks really wrote that review?" she continued, contemplating her father through her eyeglass, for she was shortsighted.

"If you ask my sincere opinion, my dear, I must say that I think he did not; but if some other man had signed it, I should have been sure. Which now I never shall be."

Here the door was slowly opened, and the portly butler appeared, bearing in his own hands a fine dish of potatoes; from the same plot, he remarked to John, with those that had obtained the prize. The butler looked proud.

"I feel as much elated," said John, "as if I had raised them myself. Is Nicholas here?"

"Yes, sir, and he has been saying that if the soil of your garden could only be kept dry, they would be finer still."

"Dry!" exclaimed Valentine, "you can't keep anything dry in such a climate as this—not even your jokes."

"Hear, hear," said John Mortimer; "if the old man was not a teetotaler, and I myself were not so nearly concerned in this public recognition of *our* merits, I should certainly propose his health."

"Don't let such considerations sway you," exclaimed Valentine rising. "Jones, will you tell him that you left me on my legs, proposing his health in ginger-pop—'Mr. Nicholas Swan.'"

Mr. Nicholas Swan. Not one word of the ridiculous speech which followed the toast was heard by Laura, nor did she observe the respectful glee with which the butler retired, saying, "I think we've got a rise out of the *True Blue* now, sir. I'm told, sir, that the potatoes shown by the *other side*, compared with these, seemed no bigger than bullets."

Mr. Nicholas Swan. A sudden beating at the heart kept Mrs. Melcombe silent, and as for Laura, she had never blushed so deeply in her life. Joseph's name was Swan, and it flashed into her mind in an instant that he had told her his father was a gardener.

She sat lost in thought, and nervous, scarcely able to answer when some casual remark was made to her, and the meal was over before she had succeeded in persuading herself that this man could not be Joseph's father, because her coming straight to the place where he lived was *too* improbable.

"There goes Swanny across the lawn, father," said one of the twins, and thereupon they all went to the bow-window, and calling the old man, began to congratulate him, while he leaned his arms on the window-frame, which was at a convenient height from the ground, and gave them an account of his success.

They grouped themselves on the seats near. Mrs. Melcombe took the chair pushed up for her where, as John Mortimer said, she could see the view. Laura followed, having snatched up a book of photographs, with which she could appear to be occupied, for she did not want to attract the gardener's attention by sitting farther than others did from the window; and as she mechanically turned the leaves, she hearkened keenly to Swan's remarks, and tried to decide that he was not like Joseph.

"The markiss, sir? Yes, sir, his gardener, Mr. Fergus, took the best prize for strawberries and green peas. You'll understand that those airly tates were from seedlings of my own—that's where their great merit lies, and why they were first. They gave Blakis the cottagers' prize for lettuce; that I uphold was wrong. Said I, 'Those lettuce heads that poor Raby shows air the biggest ever I set my eyes on.' 'Swan,' says Mr. Tikey, 'we must encourage them that has good characters.' 'Well, now, if you come to think, sir,' says I, 'it's upwards of ten years since Raby stole that pair of boots,' and I say (though they was my boots) that should be forgot now, and he should have the cottagers' prize, but stealing never gets forgiven."

"Because it's such an inconvenient vice to those that have anything to lose," said Miss Christie.

"Yes, that's just it, ma'am. You see the vices and virtues have got overhauled again, and sorted differently to suit our convenience. Stealing's no worse *probly* in the eyes of our Maker than lying and slandering; not so bad, mayhap, as a deep *sweer.* But folks air so tenacious like, they must have every stick and stone respected that they reckon theirs."

"We shouldn't hear ye talking in this *pheelosophical* way," said Miss Christie, "if yere new potatoes had been stolen last night, before ye got them to the show."

Laura took a glance at the gardener, as, with all the ease of intimacy, he leaned in at the window and gave his opinion on things in general. He was hale, and looked about sixty years of age. He was dressed in his Sunday suit, and wore an orange bandana handkerchief loosely tied round his neck. He had keen grey eyes. Joseph's eyes were dark and large, and Joseph was taller, and had a straighter nose.

"Swan's quite right," remarked Valentine; "we are a great deal too tenacious about our belongings. Now I've heard of a fellow who was waiting about, to horsewhip another fellow, and when this last came out he had a cane in his hand. His enemy snatched it from him, and laid it about his back as much as he liked, split it and broke it on him, and then carried off the bits. Now what would you have done, Swan, in such a case?"

"Well, sir, in which case? I can't consider anyhow as I could be in the case of him that was whipped."

"I mean what would you have done about the cane?—the property? A magistrate had to decide. The man that had been horsewhipped said the other had spoilt his cane, which was as good as new, and then had stolen it. The other said he did not carry off the cane till it had been so much used that it was good for nothing, and he didn't call that stealing."

"Well, sir," said Mr. Swan, observing a smile on the face of one and another, "I think I'll leave that there magistrate to do the best he can with that there case, and I'll abide by his decision."

"When ye come out in the character of Apollo," said Miss Christie to Valentine, "ye should compose yourself into a grander attitude, and not sit all of a heap while ye're drawing the long-bow. Don't ye agree with me, Mrs. Melcombe?"

Mrs. Melcombe looked up and smiled uneasily; but the gardener had no uncomfortable surmises respecting her, as she had respecting him, and when he caught her eye he straightened himself up, and said with pleasant civility, while putting on his hat on purpose to touch it and take it off again, "'Servant, ma'am; my son Joseph has had a fine spell of work, as I hear from him, at your place since I saw you last autumn, and a beautiful place it is, I'm told."

Mrs. Melcombe answered this civil speech, and John Mortimer said, "How is Joseph getting on, Swan?"

"Getting on first-rate, thank you kindly, sir," replied Swan, leaning down into his former easy attitude, and keeping his Sunday hat under his arm. "That boy, though I say it, allers was as steady as old Time. He's at Birmingham now. I rather expect he'll be wanting to *settle* shortly."

As he evidently wished to be asked a further question, Mrs. Henfrey did ask one.

"No, ma'am, no," was the reply; "he have not told me nor his mother the young woman's name; but he said if he got her he should be the luckiest fellow that ever was." Here, from intense confusion and shyness, Laura dropped the book, St. George picked it up for her, and nobody thought of connecting the fall with the story, the unconscious Nicholas continuing. "So thereby his mother judged that it would come to something, for that's what a young chap mostly says when he has made up his mind; but I shall allers say, sir," he went on, "that with the good education as I gave him, it's a pity he took to such a poor trade. He airly showed a bent for it; I reckon it was the putty that got the better of him."

"Ah," said John Mortimer, "and I only wonder, Swan, that it didn't get the better of me! I used to lay out a good deal of pocket-money in it at one time, and many a private smash have I perpetrated in the panes of out-houses, and at the back of the conservatory, that I might afterwards mend them with my own putty and tools. I can remember my father's look of pride and pleasure when he would pass and find me so quietly, and, as he thought, so meritoriously employed."

And now this ordeal was over. The gardener was suffered to depart, and the ladies went up-stairs to dress for the flower-show.

"Oh, Amelia!" exclaimed Laura, pressing her cold hands to her burning cheeks, "I feel as if I almost hated that man. What business had he to talk of Joseph in that way?"

Amelia, on the contrary, was very much pleased with Swan, because he had clearly shown that he was ignorant of this affair. "He seems a very respectable person," she replied. "His cottage, I know, is near the end of John Mortimer's garden. I've seen it; but I never thought of asking his name. It certainly would be mortifying for you to have to go and stay there with him and Joseph's mother. I suppose, though, that the Mortimers would have to call."

Amelia felt a certain delight in presenting this picture to Laura.

"I would never go near them!" exclaimed Laura, very angry with her sister-in-law.

"Why not?" persisted Amelia, determined to make Laura see things as they were. "You could not possibly wish to divide a man from his own family; they have never injured you."

"Oh that he and I were on a desert island together," said Laura. She had often said that before to Amelia. She now felt that if Joseph's father and mother were there also, and there was nobody else to see, she should not mind their presence; besides, it would be convenient, they would act almost as servants.

Amelia very seldom had intuitions; but one seemed to visit her then. "Do you know, Laura, it really seems to me *less shocking* that you should be attached to Joseph (if you are, which I don't believe), than that you should be so excessively ashamed of it, with no better cause."

This she said quite sincerely, having risen for the moment into a clearer atmosphere than that in which she commonly breathed. It was a great advance for her; but then, on the other hand, she had never felt so easy about the result as that old man's talk had now made her. Laura never could do it!

So off they set to the flower-show, which was held under a large tent in a field. Laura heard the hum and buzz about her; the jolly wives of the various gardeners and florists admiring their husbands' prizes; the band of the militia playing outside; Brandon's delightful voice—how she wished that Joseph's was like it!—all affected her imagination; together with the strong scent of flowers and strawberries and trodden grass, and the mellow light let down over them through the tent, and the moving flutter of dresses and ribbons as the various ladies passed and repassed, almost all being adorned with little pink and blue flowers, if only so much as a rose-bud or a forget-me-not—for a general election was near, and they were "showing their colours" (a custom once almost universal, and which was still kept up in that old-fashioned place).

Wigfield was a droll little town, and in all its ways was intensely English. There was hardly a woman in it or round it who really and intelligently concerned herself about politics; but they were all "blues" or "pinks," and you might hear them talk for a week together without finding out which was the Liberal and which was the Conservative colour; but the "pinks" all went to the pink shops, and the "blues" would have thought it WRONG not to give their custom to those tradesmen who voted "blue."

You might send to London for anything you thought you wanted; but the Marchioness herself, the only great lady in the neighbourhood, knew better than to order anything in Wigfield from a shop of the wrong colour.

The "pinks" that day were happy. "Markiss," in the person of his gardener, had three prizes; "Old Money-Bags" (Mr. Augustus Mortimer's name at election time) had two prizes, in the person of his son's gardener; in fact, the "pinks" triumphed almost at the rate of two to one, and yet, to their immortal honour, let it be recorded that the "blues" said it was all fair.

John Mortimer shortly went to fetch his father, and returned with him and all his own younger children. Mr. Mortimer had long been allowed to give three supplementary prizes, on his own account, to some of the exhibitors who were cottagers, and on this occasion his eyes, having been duly directed by his son, were observed to rest with great admiration on the big lettuces. Raby's wife could hardly believe it when she saw the bright sovereign laid on the broad top of one of them; while Mr. Swan, as one of the heroes of the day, and with Mrs. Swan leaning on his arm, looked on approvingly, the latter wearing a black silk gown and a shawl covered with fir-cones. She was a stout woman, and had been very pretty—she was supposed by her husband to be so still. On this occasion, pointing out the very biggest and brightest bunch of cut-flowers he saw, Mr. Swan remarked complacently—

"They remind me of you, Maria."

"And which on 'em came from our garden, dear," said Mrs. Swan, meaning which came from Mr. John Mortimer's garden.

Swan pointed out several. "Mr. Fergus came to me yesterday, and said he, 'We want a good lot of flowers to dress up the tent. You'll let us have some?' 'Certain,' said I; 'we allers do.' Then he marches up to my piccotees. 'Now these,' said he, 'would just suit us. We could do very well with pretty nigh all of 'em.' 'Softly,' said I; 'flowers you'll have; but leave the rest to me. If I'm to have one of my teeth drawn, it's fair I should say which.' Yes, William Raby air improved; but I shall allers say as nothing ever can raise that idle dog Phil. Raby. I don't hope for folks that take parish pay."

The said William Raby came in the evening and brought the big vegetables, wrapped in an old newspaper, for Mr. Mortimer's acceptance, and when the old man came out into his hall to speak to him, Raby said—

"It wer' not only the money. My wife, *her* feels, too—when a man's been down so long—as it does him a sight o' good to get a mouthful o' pride, and six penn'orth o' praise to make him hold his head up."

"St. George was dull yesterday," observed John Mortimer, when he and his father were alone the next morning in the bank parlour. "He was not like himself; he flashed out now and then, but I could see that it was an effort to him to appear in good spirits. I thought he had got over that attachment, for he seemed jolly enough some time ago."

"When does he sail for Canada?" asked the old man.

"At the end of this week, and I believe mainly for the sake of having something to do. It is very much to be lamented that my uncle did not manage to make him take up some profession. Here are his fine talents almost wasted; and, besides that, while he is running about on his philanthropic schemes, Valentine steals the heart of the girl he loves."

"But," said his father, "I think the young fellow is quite unconscious that St. George likes her."

"My dear father, then he has no business to be. He ought to know that such a thing is most probable. Here is St. George shipwrecked, floating on a raft, and half starved, when this impudent little yacht, that seems, by the way she flies about, to know the soundings of all harbours by special intuition—this impudent little yacht comes and looks round the corner of every wave, and actually overhauls the high seas till she finds him, and there the first time he opens his eyes is that sweet, quaint piece of innocence leaning over him. He is shut up with her for ten days or so; she is as graceful as a sylph, and has a tender sort of baby face that's enough to distract a man, and I don't see how he could possibly leave that vessel without being in love with her, unless some other woman had already got hold of his heart. No, even if St. George did not know himself that he cared for her, he ought to have been allowed time to find it out before any one else spoke. And there is Val in constant correspondence with her, and as secure as possible!"

Conversation then turned to the Melcombes. Old Augustus spoke uneasily of the boy, said he looked pale, and was not grown.

"He gets that pallor from his mother," said John. "I should not like to see any of my children such complete reproductions of either parent as that boy is of her. Family likeness is always strongest among the uncultivated, and among lethargic and stupid people. If you go down into the depths of the country, to villages, where the parents hardly think at all, and the children learn next to nothing, you'll find whole families of them almost exactly alike, excepting in size."

His father listened quietly, but with the full intention of bringing the conversation back to Peter as soon as he could.

"It is the same with nations," proceeded John, "those who have little energy and no keen desire for knowledge are ten times more alike in feature, complexion, and countenance than we are. No! family likeness is all very well in infancy, before the mind has begun to work on the face; but as a man's children grow, they ought to be less and less alike every year."

"That little fellow," said the father, "seems to me to be exactly like what he was a year ago."

"I observe no change."

"Do you think he is an average child, John?"

John laughed. "I think that little imp of mine, Hughie, could thrash him, if they chose to fight, and he is nearly three years the younger of the two. No, I do not think he is an average child; but I see nothing the matter with him."

Grand was not exempt from the common foibles of grandfathers, and he was specially infatuated in favour of the little Hugh, who was a most sweet-tempered and audacious child, and when his son went on, "Those two little scamps are getting so troublesome, that they will have to be sent to school very shortly," he said, almost in a grumbling tone, "They're always good enough when they're with *me*."

So, in course of time, Mrs. and Miss Melcombe set forth on their travels; it was their ambition to see exactly the same places and things that everybody else goes to see, and they made just such observations on them as everybody else makes.

In the meantime Brandon, not at all aware that several people besides John Mortimer had noticed that he was out of spirits—Brandon also prepared to set forth on his travels. He had persuaded several families to emigrate, and had also persuaded himself that he must go to their destination himself, that he might look out for situations for them, and settle them before the winter came on He was very busy for some days arranging his affairs; he meant to be away some time. Mr. Mortimer knew it—perhaps he knew more, for he said not a word by way of dissuasion, but only seemed rather depressed. The evening, however, before Brandon was to start, as, at about eight o'clock, he sat talking with his step-father, the old man lifted up his head and said to him—

"You find me quite as clear in my thoughts and quite as well able to express them as usual, don't you, St. George?"

"Yes," answered the step-son, feeling, however, a little dismayed, for the wistful earnestness with which this was said was peculiar.

"If you should ever be asked," continued Daniel Mortimer, "you would be able to say that you had seen no signs of mental decay in me these last few months?"

"Yes, I should."

"Don't disturb yourself, my dear fellow. I am as well as usual; better since my illness than I was for some time before. I quite hope to see you again; but in case I do not, I have a favour to ask of you."

The step-son assured him with all affection and fervour that he would attend to his wish, whatever it might be.

"I have never loved anything that breathed as I loved your mother," continued the old man, as if still appealing to him, "and you could hardly have been dearer to me if you had been my own."

"I know it," said Brandon.

"When you were in your own study this morning at the top of the house——"

"Yes, my liege?"

"I sent Valentine up to you with a desk. You were in that room, were you not?"

"Oh, yes."

"A small desk, that was once your mother's—it has a Bramah lock."

"I noticed that it had, and that it was locked."

"What have you done with it?"

"Valentine said you wished me to take particular care of it, so I locked it into my cabinet, where my will is, as you know, and where are most of my papers."

"Thank you; here is the key. You think you shall never forget where that desk is, Giles?"

"Never! such a thing is quite impossible."

"If I am gone when you return, you are to open that desk. You will find in it a letter which I wrote about three years ago; and if I have ever deserved well of you and yours, I charge you and I implore you to do your very best as regards what I have asked of you in that letter."

CHAPTER IX.

SIGNED "DANIEL MORTIMER."—CANADA.

"The logs burn red; she lifts her head
For sledge-bells tinkle and tinkle, O lightly swung.
'Youth was a pleasant morning, but ah! to think 'tis fled,
Sae lang, lang syne,' quo' her mother, 'I, too, was young.'

"No guides there are but the North star,
And the moaning forest tossing wild arms before,
The maiden murmurs, 'O sweet were yon bells afar,
And hark! hark! hark! for he cometh, he nears the door.'

"Swift north-lights show, and scatter and go.
How can I meet him, and smile not, on this cold shore?
Nay, I will call him, 'Come in from the night and the snow,
And love, love, love in the wild wood, wander no more.'"

AN hour after the conversation between Brandon and old Daniel Mortimer, they parted, and nothing could be more unlike than his travels were and those of the Melcombes. First, there was Newfoundland to be seen. It looked at a distance like a lump of perfectly black hill embedded in thick layers of cotton wool; then as the vessel approached, there was its harbour, which though the year was nearly half over, was crackling all over with brittle ice. Then there was Halifax Bay, blue as a great sapphire, full of light, and swarming with the spawn of fish. And there was the Bras d'Or, boats all along this yellow spit of sand, stranded, with their sails set and scarcely flapping in the warm still air; and then there was the port where he was to meet his emigrants, for they had not crossed in the same ship with him; and after that there were wild forests and unquiet waters far inland, where all night the noise of the "lumber" was heard as it leaped over the falls; while at dawn was added the screaming of white-breasted fowl jostling one another in their flight as they still thronged up towards the north.

We almost always think of Canada as a cold country. Its summer counts for little; nor meadow-grass waist deep, over which swarms of mosquitoes hover, tormenting man and horse; nor sunshine that blisters the face, nor natural strawberry-grounds as wide as Yorkshire, nor a sky clearer, purer, and more intensely blue than any that spans Italian plains. No; Canada means winter, snow, quivering northern lights, log-fires, and sledge-bells!

Brandon found Canada hot, but when he had finished his work there, he left it, and betook himself to the south, while it became the Canada of our thought.

He went through the very heart of the States, and pleased himself with wild rough living in lands where the rich earth is always moist and warm, and primeval forest still shelters large tracts of it.

Camping out at night, sometimes in swampy hollows, it was strange to wake when there was neither moon nor star, and see the great decaying trees that storm had felled or age had ruined, glow with a weird phosphorescent light, which followed the rents in them, and hovered about the seams in their bark, making them look like the ghosts of huge alligators prone in the places they had ravaged, and giving forth infernal gleams. Stranger yet it was to see in the dark, moving near the pine-wood fire, two feeble wandering lights, the eyes of some curious deer that had come to gaze and wonder, and show its whereabouts by those soft reflections.

And then, when he and his companions wanted venison, it was strange to go forth into the forest in the dark, two of them bearing a great iron pot slung upon a long rod, and heaped with blazing pine-cones.

Then several pairs of these luminous spots would be seen coming together, and perhaps a dangerous couple would glare down from a tree, and a wounded panther would come crashing into their midst.

After that, he went and spent Christmas in Florida. He had had frequent letters from home and from his step-father. He wished to keep away till a certain thing was settled one way or the other, but every letter showed that it was still unsettled; the sea-nymph that he had been wasting his heart upon had not yet decided to accept his brother's, but there was every likelihood that she would.

As time went on, however, he felt happy in the consciousness that absence was doing its work upon him, and that change had refreshed his mind. He was beginning to forget her. When the woman whom one loves is to marry one's brother, and that brother happens to be of all the family the one whom one prefers, what quality can be so admirable as inconstancy?

Still, for a man who was really forgetting, he argued the matter too much in his mind. Even when he got far south, among the Florida keys, and saw the legions of the heron and the ibis stalking with stately gait along the wet sand, and every now and then thrusting in their "javelin bills," spiking and bringing out long wriggling flashes of silver that went alive down their throats, he would still be thinking it over. Yes; he was forgetting her. He began to be in better spirits. He was in very good spirits one day in January when, quite unknown to him, the snow was shovelled away from the corner of a quiet churchyard in which his mother slept, and room was made beside her for the old man who had loved him as his own.

Old Daniel Mortimer had no such *following* as had attended the funeral of his mother, and no such peaceful sunshine sleeping on a landscape all blossom and growth. The wind raged, and the snow whirled all about his grave and in it. The coffin was white before the first clod of earth was thrown on it, and the mourners were driven out of the churchyard, when the solemn service was over, by such gusts of storm and whirling wind as they could hardly stand against.

His will was read. He had hardly anything to leave. His directions were very simple and few, and there was a little desk locked up in a cabinet that nobody thought about, and that the one person who could have opened it supposed to concern exclusively himself. So when he came, six months after, and looked about him with regretful affection; when he had put the old man's portrait up in a place of honour, and looked to the paying of all the debts, for everything, even to the furniture, was now his own; when he had read the will, and sealed up all such papers as he thought his half-brother Valentine might afterwards want to refer to—he betook himself to his own particular domain, his long room in the top of the house. There, locking himself in, he opened his cabinet, and taking out the little desk, sat down to look for and read this letter.

The desk was soon opened. He lifted one half, saw several old miniatures which had belonged to his own father's family, a lock of his father's hair which he remembered to have seen in his mother's possession, and one or two trinkets. No letter.

It was not without some slight trepidation that he opened the other side, and there, nothing else being with it, a large letter sealed with black and directed to himself in his step-father's well-known hand, it was lying.

As he took the letter up, a sensation so faint, so ethereal that it is hard to describe or characterize it, but which most of us have felt at least once, came over him, or rather came about him, as if something from without suggested a presence.

He was free from any sensation of fear, but he chose to speak; lifting up his face as if the old man had been standing before him, he said aloud, "Yes, I promised." The feeling was gone as he spoke, and he broke the seal.

A long letter. His eyes, as it was folded, fell first on these surprising words, "I forbade my mother to leave her property to me," and then, "I have never judged her," the aged writer continued, "for in her case I know not what I could have done."

Brandon laid the letter down, and took a moment for thought, before he could make up his mind to read it through. Some crime, some deep disgrace, he perceived was about to be confided to him. With a hurried sense of dislike and shrinking from acquaintance with it, he wondered whether his own late mother had known anything of it, then whether he was there called upon to divulge it now, and to act. If not, he argued with himself, why was it to be confided to him?

Then he addressed himself to his task, and read the letter through, coming to its last word only to be still more surprised, as he perceived plainly that beyond what he could gather from those two short sentences already quoted, nothing was confided or confessed, nothing at all—only a request was made to him, and that very urgently and solemnly, but it concerned not himself, but his young brother Valentine, for not content with repudiating the family property for himself, the old father was desirous, it was evident, through his step-son, to stand in the way and bar his own son's very remote chance of inheriting it either.

A thing that is very unexpected and moderately strange, we meet with wide-opened eyes, with a start and perhaps exclamations; but a thing more than strange, utterly unaccounted for, quite unreasonable, and the last thing one could have supposed possible as coming from the person who demanded it, is met in far quieter fashion.

Brandon leaned back in his chair and slowly looked about him. He was conscious that he was drawing deeper breath than usual, and that his heart beat quickly, but he was so much surprised that for the moment his thoughts appeared to scatter themselves about, and he knew not how to marshal them and make them help him as to what this might mean.

Mystery in romance and in tales is such a common vulgar thing, in tragedy and even in comedy it is so completely what we demand and expect, that we seldom consider what an astonishing and very uncommon thing it is when it appears in life. And here in a commonplace, well-conducted, happy, and united family was a mystery pointing to something that one of its best-loved members had never had a hint of. Whatever it was, it concerned a place little more than fifty miles off, and a man in whose presence he had lived from his early childhood; the utmost caution of secrecy was demanded, and the matter spoken of entirely changed the notions he had always held concerning his step-father, whom he had thought he knew better than any man living. When one had believed that one absolutely understood another, how it startles the mind to discover that this is a mistake! A beautiful old man this had been—pious, not very worldly-wise, but having a sweetness of nature, a sunny smile, and a native ease about him that would not have been possible without a quiet conscience. This he had possessed, but "I forbade my mother to leave her property to me." His step-son turned back the page, and looked at those words again. Then his eyes fell lower. "In her case I know not what I could have done." "When did he forbid this—was it ten years ago, twenty years, fifty years? He was really very well off when he married my mother. Now where did he get the property that he lost by his speculations? Not by the law; his profession never brought him in more than two hundred a year. Oh! he had it from the old cousin that he and Grand often talk of, old John Mortimer. And that's where the old silver plate came from. Of course, and where John got his name.

"We always knew, I think, that there was an aged mother; now why did I take for granted that she must be in her second childhood? I wonder whether John put that into my head. I think I did remark to him once when I was a boy and he was living at home, that it was odd there was no portrait of her in either of the houses. (But no more there is of Grand now I come to think of it; John never could make him sit.) Before the dear old man got so infirm he used generally to go out about once a year and come back in low spirits, not liking to be questioned. He may have gone then to see his mother, but I know sister used to think he went to see the relations of that wretched woman, his first wife. Who shall say now?"

And then he sat down and thought and thought, but nothing came of his thinking. Peter Melcombe, so far as he knew, was perfectly well; that was a comfort. Valentine was very docile; that was also a comfort; and considering that what his father had wished for him nearly four years ago was actually coming to pass, and everything was in train for his going to one of the very best and healthiest of our colonies, there seemed little danger that even if Melcombe fell to him he should find the putting it from him a great act of self-denial.

And what a strange thing it was, Brandon thought, that through the force of circumstances he himself should have been made to bring about such an unlikely thing! That so young a man should want to marry was strange enough. It was more strange that he should have fixed on the only woman in the world that his brother wanted. This said brother had thought it the very climax of all that was strange that it should have devolved on him who had command of money and who knew the colonies, to make this early marriage possible. But surely the climax of strangeness was rather here, that he had all this time been working as if on purpose to bring about the longing desire of his old step-father, which till then he had never heard of, depriving Valentine as much as was possible of his freedom, shutting him up to the course his father wanted him to follow, and preparing to send him as far as in this world he could be sent from the dreaded precincts of Melcombe.

Brandon had devoted out of his moderate patrimony a thousand pounds each to his step-brother and his step-sisters. In the case of Valentine he had done more; he had in a recent visit to New Zealand bought some land with a dwelling-house on it, and to this place it was arranged that immediately on his marriage Valentine should sail.

Brandon felt a strong desire to go and look at Melcombe, for his step-father's conduct with regard to it kept coming back to his mind with ever-fresh surprise; but though he searched his memory it could yield him nothing, not a hint, not a look, from any one which threw the least light on this letter.

"But that there's crime at the core of it, or some deep disgrace," he soliloquized, "appears to me most evident, and I take his assurance in its fullest meaning that he had nothing to do with it."

The next morning, having slept over the contents of the letter, he went to his upper room, locked himself in, and read it again. Then after pausing a while to reconsider it, he went up to the wall to look at a likeness of Dorothea Graham. Valentine had a photographing machine, and had filled the house with portraits of himself and his beloved. This was supposed to be one of the best. "Lucky enough that I had the sense to leave this behind me," thought Brandon. "Yes, you sweet thing, I am by no means breaking my heart now about you and your love for that boy. You are sure to marry him; you have a faithful heart, so the best thing for him will be to let you marry as soon as possible. I'll tell him so as we walk to John Mortimer's to-day. I'll tell him he may do it as soon as he likes."

Accordingly as about six o'clock he and Valentine walked through a wood, across a common, and then over some fields, Brandon began to make some remarks concerning the frequent letters that passed between these youthful lovers. "It is not to be supposed," he observed, "that any lady would correspond with you thus for years if she had not fully made up her mind to accept you in the end."

"No," answered Valentine with perfect confidence; "but she knows that I promised my father to wait a few months more before I decidedly engaged myself, but for that promise I was to have had an answer from her half a year ago."

Brandon fully believed that Dorothea Graham loved his brother, and that her happiness was in his own hands. He had found it easy to put the possibility of an early marriage in Valentine's way, but nothing could well go forward without his sanction, and since his return he had hitherto felt that the words which would give it were too difficult for him to say. Now, however, that remarkable letter, cutting in across the usual current of his thoughts, had thrown them back for awhile. So that Dorothea seemed less real, less dear, less present to him.

The difficult words were about to be said.

"If she knows why you do not speak, and waits, there certainly is an understanding between you, which amounts almost to the same thing."

"Yes," said Valentine, "and in August, *as she knows*, I shall ask her again."

"Then," said Brandon, almost taking Valentine's breath away with sudden delight, "I think, old fellow, that when she has once said 'yes,' you had better make short work with the engagement; you will never be more ready to marry than you are now; you are a few months older than John was when he went and did it; and here you are, with your house in New Zealand ready built, your garden planted, a flock of sheep bought, and all there is to do is to turn out the people now taking care of the place, as soon as you are ready to come in."

Brandon was standing on a little plank which bridged a stream about two feet wide; he had turned to say this, for Valentine was behind him.

Valentine received the communication first with silence, then with a shout of triumph, after which he ran completely round his brother several times, jumping over the stream and flourishing a great stick that he held, with boyish ecstasy, not at all dignified, but very sincere. When he had made at least three complete circles, and jumped the stream six times, Giles gravely walked on, and Valentine presently followed, wiping his forehead.

"Nobody could have expressed my own sentiments in more charming English," he exclaimed; "I never heard such grammar in my life; what a brick you are, St. George!"

Giles had great faith in his theory that absence always cured love, also in his belief that his was cured and half forgotten. At that moment he experienced a sharp pang, however, that was not very like forgetfulness, but which Valentine converted almost into self-scorn when he said—

"You know, Giles, she always did show the most undisguised liking for me from our first meeting; and then look how constant she has been, and what beautiful letters she writes, always trying, too, to improve me. Of course I cannot even pretend to think she would not have engaged herself to me months ago if I might have asked her."

"All true, perfectly true," he thought to himself; "he loves her and she loves him, and I believe if she had never met with Valentine, she would still never have married me. What a fool I am!"

"Why wouldn't you take this view of things yesterday, when I tried to make you?" asked Valentine.

"I was not ready for it," answered Giles, "or it was not ready for me."

Thereupon they passed through a wicket-gate into a kind of glen or wilderness, at the end of John Mortimer's garden, and beyond the stream where his little girls acted Nausicaa and his little boys had preserves of minute fishes, ingeniously fenced in with sticks and fine netting.

"There's Grand," exclaimed Valentine, "they've brought him out to look at their water-snails. What a venerable old boy he is! he looks quite holy, doesn't he?"

"Hold your tongue," said Brandon, "they'll hear you. He's come to see their newts; they had a lot yesterday at the bottom of the punt. Little Hugh had one in his hand, a beast with an orange breast, and it was squinting up at him."

It would be hard to say of any man that he is *never* right. If he is always thinking that he has forgotten a certain lady, surely he is right sometimes.

They went in to dinner, a party of four, for John Mortimer since his wife's death did not entertain ladies, and Miss Christie Grant always presided at an early dinner, when the governess and the children dined.

As the dinner advanced St. George and Valentine both got into high spirits, the former because a stronger conviction than usual assured him that he was forgetting Dorothea Graham; the latter, because instead of being pulled back, he had at last got a shove in the other direction. In short, Valentine was so happy in his jokes and so full of fun, that the servants had no sooner withdrawn than John Mortimer taxed him with having good reason for being so, mentioned the probable cause, and asked to see Miss Graham's portrait, "which, no doubt," he said, "you have got in your pocket."

"Why I have had that for years," said Valentine scornfully.

"And dozens of them," said Brandon; "they took them themselves."

"When is it to be?" asked old Grand with great interest.

"I don't exactly know, uncle; *even Giles* doesn't know that! If he had known, I'm sure he would have told you, and asked your advice, for I always brought him up to be very respectful to his elders."

"Come, sir, come," said the old man laughing, "if you don't *exactly* know, I suppose you have a tolerably distinct notion."

"I know when I should like it to be, and when I think D. would like it. Not too late for a wedding tour, say October, now, or," seeing his brother look grave, "or November; suppose we say November."

"I'm afraid there is no wedding tour in the programme," observed Brandon. "The voyage must be the tour."

"Then I'll go without my cart. We must have a tour; it will be the only fun I shall ever be able to give her."

Valentine had inherited only about two hundred pounds from his father, he having been left residuary legatee, and he was much more inclined to spend this on luxuries than on necessaries.

"You've bought me land, and actually paid for it yourself, and you've bought me a flock, and made me a barn, and yet you deny me the very necessaries of life, though I can pay for them myself! I must have a tour, and D. must have a basket-carriage."

"Well, my dear fellow," said Grand, "though that matter is not yet settled, it is evident things are so far advanced that we may begin to think of the wedding presents. Now, what would you like to have from me, I wonder? I mean how would you prefer to have it? John and I have already considered the amount, and he quite agrees with me as to what I ought to give to my only brother's only son."

"*Only brother's!*" The word struck Brandon both as showing that the old man had almost forgotten other dead brothers, and also as evidently being the preface to a larger gift than he had anticipated.

"Thank you, uncle," said Valentine, almost accomplishing a blush of pride and pleasure. "As you are so kind as to let me choose, I should like your present in money, in my pocket, you know, because there is the tour, and it would go towards that."

"In your pocket!" exclaimed John Mortimer, with a laugh of such amusement and raillery as almost put Valentine out of countenance. "Why, do you think my father wants to give you a school-boy's tip?"

"I think a good deal depends on the lady," said Grand, who also seemed amused; "if she has no fortune, it might be wise to settle it on her; if she has, you might wish to lay it out in more land, or to invest it here; you and Giles must consider this. I mean to give you two thousand pounds." Then, when he saw that Valentine was silent from astonishment, he went on, "And if your dear father had been here he would not have been at all surprised. Many circumstances, with which you are not acquainted, assure me of this, and I consider that I owe everything to him." There was a certain sternness about these words; he would have, it was evident, no discussion.

John Mortimer heard his father say this with surprise. "He must mean that he owes his religious views to my uncle," was his thought; but to Brandon, who did not trouble himself about those last words, the others were full of meaning; the amount of the gift, together with the hint at circumstances with which Valentine was not acquainted, made him feel almost certain that the strange words, "I forbade my mother to leave her property to me," alluded to something which was known to the next brother.

Valentine, at first, was too much surprised to be joyous, but he thanked his uncle with something of the cordial ingenuousness and grace which had distinguished his father.

"I can have a tour *now*, can't I, old fellow," he said after a time to his brother; "take my wife"—here a joyous laugh—"my WIFE on the Continent; we shall go dashing about from place to place, you know, staying at hotels, *and all that!*"

"To be sure," said Brandon, "staying at hotels, of course, and ordering wonderful things for breakfast. I think I see you now—

'Happy married lovers,
Phillis trifling with a plover's
Egg, while Corydon uncovers
With a grace the Sally Lun.'"

"That's the way this fellow is always making game of me," exclaimed Valentine; "why I'm older than you were, John, when you married."

"And wild horses shall never drag the words out of me that I was too young," said John Mortimer, "whatever I may think," he continued.

"John was a great deal graver than you are," said Brandon; "besides, he knew the multiplication table."

"So do I, of course," exclaimed Valentine.

"Well," answered Brandon, "I never said you did not."

CHAPTER X.

CAUSES AND CONSEQUENCES.

"Now I am at a loss to know whether it be my hare's foot that is my preservation; for I never had a fit of the collique since I wore it; or whether it be my taking of a pill of turpentine every morning."

Diary of Mr. Samuel Pepys.

"JOHN, the Melcombes have stayed on the Continent so much longer than I expected that I hardly remember whether I told you I had invited them to come round this way, and remain here a few days on their return." Old Augustus Mortimer said this to his son, who was dining with him a few days after the conversation concerning the wedding present. "I supposed," he added, "that you would not invite that child or his mother again?"

John Mortimer replied, in clear and vigorous English, that he never should—never!

The manner in which he was looked after by the ladies had become quite a joke in the family, though one of his chief tormentors had lately been moved out of his way, Louisa Grant was married. Captain Walker had at first, after Mr. Mortimer's death, agreed to wait for her till Brandon's return; but his regiment being ordered abroad, he had induced her to hasten the wedding, which took place about three months before Brandon reached England. And as Louisa did not, out of respect to her step-father, like to be married from his house so soon after his death, old Grand had received and entertained all the wedding guests, and John Mortimer had given away the bride.

On that occasion it was confidently asserted by the remaining Miss Grant and Valentine, that there were four ladies present who would at any time with pleasure undertake to act the loving mother to dear John's seven children.

John was becoming rather sensitive; he remembered how sweetly Mrs. Melcombe had smiled on him, and he remembered the ghost story too.

"I rather want to see how that boy is getting on," continued Augustus.

"By-the-bye," said the son, "I heard to my surprise the other day from Swan, whose son, it seems, was doing some work at Melcombe this spring (making a greenhouse, I think), that Mrs. Melcombe wintered at Mentone, partly on her boy's account, for he had a feverish or aguish illness at Venice, and she was advised not to bring him to England."

"I never heard of it," said Grand, with anxiety.

"Nor I, my dear father; but I meant to have told you before; for I see you take an interest in the child."

"What imprudence!" continued Grand; "those people really have no sense. I begged them particularly not to go to Venice in the autumn."

"Yes," said John, "it was foolish; but Swan went on to say that he heard the boy was all right again."

"I hope so," replied Grand, almost fervently; "and his mother wants to consult us now about his going to school."

John could not forbear to smile when his father said "us."

"So you have written to say you shall be glad to see them?" he inquired.

"Yes; it is very little I ever see of my relations."

John thought that perhaps his father's mind was turning with affection towards his family, from whom he did not now doubt that he had been estranged owing to some cause which had terminated with the old mother's death. So he said cordially—

"Would you like, when Mrs. Melcombe goes home, to invite Laura to remain with you for a few weeks? I have no doubt, if you would, that Lizzy Grant would be charmed to come at the same time, and taste the sweetness of freedom. The two girls could have the carriage, you know, and the canoes, and the riding-horses. They might enjoy themselves very much, and give croquet parties and picnics to their hearts' content. I would get old Christie to come to you whenever a chaperone was wanted. She is a most valuable possession, my dear father, but I would lend her."

"You are very kind, my dear," answered the father, who often addressed his son in this fashion when they were alone. "I think it would be a pleasure to me to have the girls. You can't think, John, how cheerful the house used to be before your sisters were married; you can hardly remember it, you were so young."

"Why did I never think of proposing such a visit to him before?" thought John, almost with compunction.

"I seem to know them pretty well," he answered, "from their letters and from hearing you talk of them; but what I really remember, I believe, is four grand young ladies who used to carry me a pick-a-back, and give me sugared almonds."

Of the four Miss Mortimers, the eldest had married a clergyman, and died soon after; the second and third had married "shepherd kings," and were living with the said kings in Australia; and the fourth was in India with her husband and a grown-up family. Their father had given to each of them an ample fortune, and parted with her before his only son was five years old, for John Mortimer was fifteen years younger than his youngest sister, and had been, though the daughters were much beloved, a greater joy and comfort to his father than all four of them put together.

He was glad that his father showed this willingness to have Lizzy Grant to stay in his house, for he was fond of all the Grants; there was a kind of plain-spoken intimacy between him and them that he enjoyed. The two elder had always been his very good friends, and during his wife's lifetime had generally called him "John dear," and looked to him and his wife to take them about whenever their brother was away. Liz, who was rather a plain girl, he regarded more in the light of a niece than of a step-cousin.

A day or two after this, therefore, while sitting alone writing his letters (Grand being gone out for his constitutional), when he was told that Miss Grant wanted to speak to him, he desired that she might be shown in.

She was sitting at the back door in a little pony carriage, and giving the reins to her boy, she passed through it, to the wonder of all beholders.

Very few young ladies were shown in there.

"What is it?" exclaimed John, for Liz looked almost sulky.

"Oh John," she answered, with a sort of whimsical pathos, "isn't it sad, so few delightful things as there are, that two of them should come together, so that I can't have both!"

"What are the delightful things—offers?"

"Don't be so tiresome. No, of course not. You know very well that nothing of that kind ever happens to me."

"Indeed, if that is the case, it can only be because your frocks are almost always crumpled, and—what's that long bit of blue ribbon that I see?"

"It's all right—that's how it's meant to go. I can't think why you fancy that I'm not tidy. St. George is always saying so too."

"That's very hard. Well, child?"

"I thought perhaps you knew that Grand had invited me to stay six weeks at his house—Laura Melcombe to be there also, and we two to do just as we liked. The whole of August, John, and part of September, and that's the very time when I can't come, because we are going to be at the seaside. Dorothea is to join us, you know, and if I do not see her then I never shall, for they are to sail at Christmas."

"There is a world of misery to be got out of conflicting pleasures," said John philosophically. "You can't come, that's evident; and I had just given orders that the new canoe should be painted and the old one caulked. Two quiet ponies for you to drive (you are a very tolerable whip, I know). As to the grapes, a house is being kept back on purpose to be ripe just at that time; and the croquet balls are all sent to be painted. Melancholy facts! but such is life."

"No but, John——"

"I'm extremely busy to-day."

"Not so busy that you have not time to laugh at me. This would have been almost the greatest pleasure I ever had."

"And I've been reminding my father," proceeded John, "that when Emily came to stay with him she always sat at the head of the table. She asked him if she might, and so should you have done, because, though Laura is a relation, he has known you all your life."

"No but, John," repeated Lizzie, "can't you do something for me? Tell me whether Laura Melcombe has been already invited?"

"She has not, Miss Grant."

"I have no doubt, if you asked Grand to let the visit be put off till the middle of September, he would."

"I shouldn't wonder."

"Then you'll do it, won't you? because you know you and I have always been such friends."

"Now you mention it, I think we have; at any rate,

I don't dislike you half so much as I do some of my other friends. Yes, child, your confidence is not misplaced."

"Then I may leave the matter in your hands?" exclaimed Liz joyfully.

"You really may," replied John Mortimer, and he took her back to the pony carriage in a high state of bliss and gratitude.

This change, however, which was easily effected, made a difference to several people whom Miss Grant had no wish to disoblige. First, Mrs. Melcombe, finding that Laura was invited to pay a long visit, and that the invitation was not extended to her, resolved not to come home by Wigfield at all; but when Laura wrote an acceptation, excused herself from coming also, on the ground of her desire to get home.

Grand, therefore, did not see Peter, and this troubled him more than he liked to avow. Brandon was also disappointed, for he particularly wanted to see the boy and his mother again. The strangeness of his step-father's letter grew upon him, and it rather fretted him to think that he could not find any plausible reason for going over to Melcombe to look about him. He was therefore secretly vexed with his sister when he found that, in consequence of her request to John, the plans of all the Melcombes had been changed. So Liz with a cheerful heart went to the sea-side with Mrs. Henfrey and Valentine, and very soon wrote home to Miss Christie Grant that Dorothea had joined them, that the long-talked-of offer had been made and (of course) accepted, and that Giles was come. She did not add that Giles had utterly lost his heart again to his brother's bride elect, but that she would not have done if she had known it.

Miss Christie was wroth on the occasion.

"It's just shameful," she remarked. "Everybody knew Miss Graham would accept him, but why can't she say how it was and when it was? She's worse than her mother. 'Dear Aunt,' her mother wrote to me, 'I'm going to marry Mr. Mortimer on Saturday week, and I hope you'll come to the wedding, but you're not to wear your blue gown. Your affectionate niece, EMILY GRANT.' That was every word she said, and I'd never heard there was anything between her and Mr. Mortimer before."

"And why were you not to wear your blue gown?" inquired John Mortimer.

"Well," replied Miss Christie, "I don't deny that if she hadn't been beforehand with me I might just slyly have said that my blue gown would do, for I'd *only* had it five years. I was aye thrifty; she knew it was as good as ever—a very excellent lutestring, and made for her wedding when she married Mr. Grant—so she was determined to take my joke against her out of my mouth."

If Miss Christie had not found plenty to do during the next six weeks, she would have grumbled yet more than she did over her wrongs. As it was, Master Augustus John Mortimer came home from school for his long holidays, and he and his friends excited more noise, bustle, and commotion in the house than all the other children put together.

John Mortimer's eldest son, always called Johnnie, to distinguish him from his father, was ridiculously big for his age, portentously clever and keen-witted, awkward, blunt, rude, full of fun, extremely fond of his father, and exceedingly unlike him in person. His hair was nearly black, his forehead was square and high, his hands and feet almost rivalled those of his parent in size, and his height was five feet three.

In any other eyes than those of a fond parent he must have appeared as an awkward, noisy, plain, and intolerably active boy; but his father (who almost from his infancy had pleased himself with a mental picture of the manner of man he would probably grow into) saw nothing of all this, but merely added in his mind two inches to the height of the future companion he was to find in him, and wished that the boy could get over a lisp which still disfigured some of his words.

He brought such a surprising account of his merits with him—how he could learn anything he pleased, how he never forgot anything, how, in fact, his master, as regarded his lessons, had not a fault to find with him, that when his twin sisters had seen it, there seemed to them something strange in his being as fond of tarts and lollipops as ever.

. As for John, nothing surprised him. Miss Christie saw great diversities in his children, but in regard to them all he showed an aggravating degree of contentment with what Providence had sent him. Miss Christie wore through Johnnie's sojourn at home as well as she could, and was very happy when she saw him off to school again; happier still when walking towards home across the fields with John Mortimer and the four younger children, they saw Brandon and Valentine at a distance coming to meet them.

"So they are at home again," she exclaimed; "and now we'll hear all about the wedding that is to be. I've been just wearying for the *parteeculars*, and there never were such bad letter-writers as those girls. Anyhow there'll be a handsome bridegroom."

"Ah!" said John Mortimer, "all the ladies admire Val. He's quite a woman's man."

"Well, and St. George is a man's man, then," retorted Miss Christie; "ye all admire him, I am sure."

"And what are you, papa, dearest?" asked Janie, who had hold of his hand.

"I'm my own man, my little queen-regnant," answered her father with a somewhat exultant laugh.

"Ay, Mr. Mortimer, I'm just surprised at ye," quoth Miss Christie, shaking her head over these vainglorious words.

"I think father's the most beautifullest man of all," said little Janie, with a sort of jealous feeling as if somehow he had been disparaged, though she did not exactly know how. "And the goodest, too," she presently added, as if not satisfied with her first tribute to him.

Valentine, who was seldom out of countenance on any occasion, received the congratulations of all the party with a certain rather becoming pride and complacency. He seemed, however, to be taking things very easily; but he presently became rather silent, and John, who felt keenly that Brandon was not so indifferent to the bride-elect as he wished to be, turned the conversation as soon as he could to other matters. There was some talk about Valentine's land which had been bought for him in New Zealand, after which Brandon said suddenly,—

"John, when this fellow is gone, or perhaps before, I mean to have something to do—some regular work—and I think of taking to literature in good earnest."

"All right," answered John, "and as you evidently intend me to question you, I will ask first whether you, Giles Brandon, mean to write on some subject that you understand, or on one that you know nothing about?"

Brandon laughed. "There is more to be said in favour of that last than you think," he answered.

"It may be that there is everything to be said; but if you practise it, don't put your name to your work, that's all."

"I shall not do so in any case. How do I know whether the only use people may make of it (and that a metaphorical one) may not be to throw it at me ever after."

"I don't like that," said Miss Christie. "I could wish that every man should own his own."

"No," remarked John Mortimer; "if a man in youth writes a foolish book and gives his name to it, he has, so far as his name is concerned, used his one chance; and if, in maturer life, he writes something high and good, then if he wants his wise child to live, he must consent to die himself with the foolish one. It is much the same with one who has become notorious through the doing of some base or foolish action. If he repent, rise to better things, and write a noble book, he must not claim it as if it could elevate him. It must go forth on its own merits, or it will not be recognised for what it is, only for what he is or was. No, if a man wants to bring in new thoughts or work elevating changes, he must not clog them with a name that has been despised."

"I think Dorothea and I may as well write a book together," said Valentine. "She did begin one, but somehow it stuck fast."

"You had better write it about yourselves, then," said John, "that being nearly all you study just now, I should think. Many a novel contains the author and little else. He explains himself in trying to describe human nature."

"Human nature!" exclaimed Valentine; "we must have something grander than that to write of, I can tell you. We have read so many books that turn it 'the seamy side outward,' and point out the joins as if it was a glove, that we cannot condescend to it."

"No," said John, setting off on the subject again as if he was most seriously considering it, Valentine meanwhile smiling significantly on the others. "It is a mistake to describe too much from within. The external life as we see it should rather be given, and about as much of the motives and springs of action as an intelligent man with good opportunity could discover. We don't want to be told all. We do not know all about those we live with, and always have lived with. If ever I took to writing fiction I should not pretend to know all about my characters. The author's world appears small if he makes it manifest that he reigns there. I don't understand myself thoroughly. How can I understand so many other people? I cannot fathom them. My own children often surprise me. If I believed thoroughly in the children of my pen, they would write themselves down sometimes in a fashion that I had not intended."

"John talks like a book," observed Valentine. "You propose a subject, and he lays forth his views as if he had considered it for a week. 'Drive on, Samivel.'"

"But I don't agree with him," said Miss Christie. "When I read a book I aye dislike to be left in any doubt what the man means or what the story means."

"I always think it a great proof of power in a writer," said Brandon, "when he consciously or unconsciously makes his reader feel that he knows a vast deal more about his characters than he has chosen to tell. And what a keen sense some have of the reality of their invented men and women! So much so that you may occasionally see evident tokens that they are jealous of them. They cannot bear to put all the witty and clever speeches into the mouths of these 'fetches' of their own imagination. Some must be saved up to edge in as a sly aside, a sage reflection of the author's own. There never should be any author's asides."

"I don't know about that," John answered, "but I often feel offended with authors who lack imagination to see that a group of their own creations would not look in one another's eyes just what they look in his own. The author's pretty woman is too often pretty to all; his wit is acknowledged as a wit by all. The difference of opinion comes from the readers. They differ certainly."

"Even I," observed Valentine, "if I were an author's wit, might be voted a bore, and how sad that would be, for in real life it is only right to testify that I find little or no difference of opinion."

He spoke in a melancholy tone, and heaved up a sigh.

"Is cousin Val a wit?" asked little Hugh.

"I am afraid I am," said Valentine; "they're

always saying so, and it's very unkind of them to talk about it, because I couldn't help it, could I?"

Here the little Anastasia, touched with pity by the heartfelt pathos of his tone, put her dimpled hand in his and said tenderly, "Never mind, dear, it'll be better soon, p'raps, and you didn't do it on purpose."

"Does it hurt?" asked Hugh, also full of ruth.

"Be ashamed of yourself," whispered Miss Christie, "to work on the dear children's feelings so. No, my sweet mannie, it doesn't hurt a bit."

"I'm very much to be pitied," proceeded Valentine. "That isn't all"—he sighed again—"I was born with a bad French accent, and without a single tooth in my head, or, out of it, while such was my weakness, that it took two strong men, both masters of arts, to drag me through the rudiments of the Latin grammar."

Anastasia's eyes filled with tears. It seemed so sad; and the tender little heart had not gone yet into the question of *seeming*.

"They *teached* you the Latin grammar did they?" said Bertram, who had also been listening, and was relieved to hear of something in this list of miseries that he could understand; "that's what Miss Crampton teaches me. I don't like it, and you didn't either, then. I'm six and three quarters; how old were you?"

Before Valentine had answered, John and Brandon, finding themselves before the party, had stopped and turned. Brandon was surprised to see how earnestly the two elder children, while he talked, had been looking at him, and then at their father and Valentine. At last, when this pause occurred, and the two groups met, Janie said—

"I am sure papa is a great deal prettier than Mr. Brandon, and Cousin Val looks quite ugly beside him."

"Yes, Janie," said Bertram, with an air of high satisfaction, "papa's much more beautiful than either of the others. I shall ask Miss Crampton when I go in if she doesn't think so. You would like to know what she thinks, wouldn't you, father?"

John had opened his mouth to say no, when his better sense coming to his aid, he forbore to speak. For this lady taught his children to perfection, but his friends always would insist that she wanted to teach him too—something that he wouldn't learn.

Aunt Christie, his constant friend and champion, presently spoke for him.

"No, children," she said, as soon as she had composed her voice to a due gravity, "it's natural ye should admire your father, good children generally do, but, now, if I were you, I would never tell anybody at all, not even Miss Crampton—do ye hear me, all of you? I would never tell anybody your opinion of him. If ye do, they will certainly think ye highly conceited, for ye know quite well that people say you four little ones are just as exactly like him as ye can be."

The children were evidently impressed.

"In fact," said Valentine, "now I take a good look at him, I should say that you are even more like him than he is himself—but—I may be mistaken."

"I won't say it then," said Bertram, now quite convinced.

"And I won't, and I won't," added others, as they ran forward to open a gate.

"Cheer up, John," said St. George, "let us not see so much beauty and virtue cast down. There's Miss Crampton looking out of the school-room window."

But though he laughed he did not deceive John Mortimer, who knew as well as possible that the loss of Dorothea Graham pressed heavily on his heart.

"You two are going to dine with me, of course," he said, when all the party had passed into the wilderness beyond his garden.

"On the contrary, with your leave," answered

Valentine, "we are going to take a lesson of Swan in the art of budding roses. We cannot manage it to our minds. We dined early."

"And I suppose you will agree with Val," observed Brandon, "that a rose-garden is one of the necessaries of life."

"Dorothea must have one, must she, out in New Zealand? Well, Swan will be proud to teach you anything he knows or doesn't know, and he will give you an opinion if you ask it on any subject whatever."

Accordingly John went into the house to dine, and perhaps it was in consequence of this assertion that the two young men asked their old friend's opinion on various points not at all in his line. Valentine even told him that his brother intended to write a book, and asked him what he thought it had better be about; whereupon Swan, while deftly shaping his *bud*, shook his head gravely, and said that wanted a deal of thinking over.

"But if I was you, sir," he continued, speaking to Brandon, "I should get Mr. Mortimer—Mr. John—to help you, specially if there's going to be any foreign talk in it. My word, I don't believe there's any language going that Mr. Mortimer can't lay his tongue to!"

CHAPTER XI.

WANTED A DESERT ISLAND.

> We, too, have autumns, when our leaves
> Drop loosely through the dampened air;
> When all our good seems bound in sheaves,
> And we stand reaped and bare."
>
> LOWELL.

LAURA and Mrs. Melcombe went home, and Laura saw the window again that Joseph had so skilfully glazed. Joseph was not there, and Laura would not have occupied herself with constant thoughts about him if there had been anything, or rather anybody else to think of. She soon began to feel low-spirited and restless, while, like a potato-plant in a dark cellar, she put forth long runners towards the light, and no light was to be found. This homely simile ought to be forgiven, because it is such a good one.

Peter was getting too old for her teaching. He had a tutor, but the tutor was a married man, and had taken lodgings for himself and his wife in one of the farm-houses.

Laura had no career before her, and no worthy occupation. All that came to pass in her day was a short saunter, or a drive, or a visit to the market-town, where she sat looking on while her sister-in-law did some shopping.

Melcombe was six or seven miles from any *visitable* families, excepting two or three clergymen and their wives; it was shut up in a three-cornered nook of land, and could not be approached excepting through turn-pikes, and up and down some specially steep hills. These things make havoc with country sociability.

As long as there had been plenty to do and see, Laura had enjoyed her life on the Continent, and had fed herself with hope. So many people as passed before her, it would be strange, she thought, if not one of them had been made for her, not one was to give her the love she wanted, the devotion she knew she could return.

It was certainly strange, and yet it came to pass, though the travelled fool returned, improved in style, dress, and even in appearance, while her conversation was naturally more amusing than before, for she had seen most places and things that people like to talk of.

Not one man had asked her to spend her life with him, and she came back more given to flights of fancy than ever, but far better acquainted with herself and more humble, for she had spent so much of her time (in imagination) with Joseph that she had become accustomed to his slightly provincial accent, and had ceased to care about it. Joseph, however, did not speak like his good father, and he had been endowed with as much learning as he would consent to acquire, Swan having felt a great ambition to make him a certified schoolmaster, but Joseph having been at an early age rather an idle young dog, had tormented his father into letting him take to a mere handicraft, and had left school writing a hand almost like copperplate, and being a very fair accountant, but without thirst for knowledge, and without any worthy ambition.

Laura had always known that nothing but a desert island was wanted, and she could be his contented wife; but a desert island was not to be had, such things are getting rare in the world, and she now thought that any remote locality, where nobody knew her, would do.

But where was Joseph?

She had certainly gone away without giving him any interview, she had persistently kept away, yet though she was doing what she could, by fits and starts, to forget him, that perverse imagination of hers always pictured *him* as waiting, constant, ready. There was a particular tree in the glen behind which she had so frequently represented him to herself as standing patiently while she approached with furtive steps, that when she came home and went to look at it, there was a feeling almost akin to surprise in her mind at seeing the place drenched in sparkling dew, and all overgrown with moss. Footsteps that are feigned never tread anything down; they leave no print, excepting in the heart that feigns them.

When Laura saw this place in the glen, she perceived plainly that there was no one with whom she might be humbly happy and poor—not even a plumber!

This form of human sorrow—certainly one of the worst—is not half enough pitied by the happy.

Of course Laura was a fool—nobody claims for her that she was not; but fools are not rare, either male or female; as they arrange the world and its ways in great measure, it is odd that they do not understand one another better, and whether Laura showed her folly most or least in thinking that she could have been obscurely happy as the wife of a man who belonged to a different class of life from her own (she herself having small intellectual endowments, and but little culture), is a subject too vast, too overwhelming, for decision here; it ought to have a treatise in twelve volumes all to itself.

Mrs. Melcombe had come home also somewhat improved, but a good deal disappointed. She had fully hoped and intended to marry again, because her son, who was to live to be old, would wish to marry early, and her future daughter-in-law would be mistress of the house. It was desirable, therefore, that Peter's mother should not be dependent on him for a home. She had twice been invited, while on the Continent, to change her name; but in each case it would have been, in a worldly point of view, very much to her disadvantage, and that was a species of second marriage that she by no means contemplated. She did not want her second husband to take her that she might nurse him in his old age, fast approaching, and that he might live upon her income.

So she came home *Mrs. Melcombe*, and she continued to be kind to Laura, though she did not sympathize with her; and that was no fault of hers: sympathy is much more an intellectual than a moral endowment. However kind, dull, and stupid people may be, they can rarely sympathize with any trouble unless they have gone through one just like it themselves.

You may hear it said, "Ah, I can sympathize with him, poor fellow, for I have a wooden leg myself," or, "Yes, being a widow, I know what a widow's feelings are," and so on.

No one has a right to blame these people; they are as kind as any; it is not their fault that some are living among them to whom no experience at all is necessary, and who not only could sympathize, but do in thought, with the very angel that never fell, when they consider what it must be to him if the mortal child he has to watch goes wrong; with the poor weak drunkard who wishes he could keep sober, but feels, when he would fain pass by it, that the gin-shop, like a devil-fish, sends forth long tentacles and ruthlessly sucks him in; with the mother-whale, when her wilful young one insists on swimming up the fiord, and she who has risked her life to warn him must hear the thud of the harpoon in his side; with the old tired horse, when they fetch him in from his sober reverie in the fields, and put his blinkers on; with anything else?—yes, with the bluebells, whose life above ground is so short, when wasteful children tread them down;—these all feel something that one would fain save them from. So perhaps does the rose-tree also, when some careless boy goes by whooping in the joy of his heart, and whips off her buds with his cane.

Fruitful sympathy must doubtless have some likeness of nature, and also a certain kindliness to found itself on; but it comes more from a penetrative keenness of observation, from the patient investigations of thought, from those vivid intuitions that wait on imagination, from a good memory, which can live over again in circumstances that are changed, and from that intelligent possession of the whole of one's foregone life, which makes it impossible to ignore the power of any great emotion or passion merely because it is past. Where these qualities are there should be, for there can be, sympathy.

Mrs. Melcombe was fond of her one child; but she had forgotten what her own nature, thoughts, fears, and wishes, as well as joys, had been in childhood. In like manner, as she was, on the whole, contented herself, she not only thought that her own example ought to make Laura contented, but she frequently pointed this out to her.

The child is to the father and mother, who imparted life to him, and who see his youth, the most excellent consolation that nature can afford them for the loss of their own youth, and for the shortness of life in themselves; but if a mother is therefore convinced that her child is a consoler to those who have none, he is sure, at some time or other, to be considered an unmitigated bore.

Mrs. Melcombe often thought, "Laura has my child with her constantly to amuse her, and has none of the responsibility about him that I have. Laura goes to the shops with me, sees me give the orders, and I frequently even consult her; she goes with me into the garden, and sees the interest I take in the wall-fruit and the new asparagus-bed, and yet she never takes example by me. She will eat just as many of these things as I shall, though she often follows me about the place looking as if she scarcely cared for them at all."

Laura was pleased, however, to go to Wigfield and stay with Grand, and have for a companion a careless, childish girl, who undertook with enthusiasm to teach her to drive, and if old Grand wanted his horses, would borrow any rats of ponies that she could get.

Laura spent many happy hours with Liz and the Mortimer children, now huddled into an old tub of a punt, eating cakes and curd for lunch, now having a picnic in the wood, and boiling the kettle out of doors, and at other times welcomed into the long loft called "Parliament;" but she seldom saw John Mortimer himself, for Lizzie was always anxious to be back in good time for dinner. She valued her place at the head of the table, and the indulgent old Grand perceived this plainly. He liked Laura well enough; but Liz was the kind of creature whom he could be fond of. They were both foolish girls. Liz took no manner of pains to improve herself any more than Laura did; but Laura was full of uneasy little affectations, capricious changes of manner, and shyness, and Liz was absolutely simple, and as confiding as a child.

The only useful thing the girls did while they stayed with Grand was to go into the town twice a week and devote a couple of hours to a coal and clothing club, setting down the savings of the poor, and keeping the books. This bi-weekly visit had consequences as regarded one of them, but it was the one who did not care what happened; and they parted at the end of their visit, having become a good deal attached to each other, and intending to correspond as fully and frequently as is the manner of girls.

The intelligent mind, it may be taken for granted, is able to grasp the thought that one may be a very fair, and even copious, letter-writer, and yet show nothing like diffusiveness in writing to an ancient aunt.

The leaves were all dropping when Laura came home, and was received into the spirit of the autumn, breathing in that sense of silence that comes from absence of the birds, while in still mornings, unstirred of any wind, the leaves let themselves go, and the flowers give it up and drop and close. She was rather sad; but she found amusement in writing to Liz, and as the days got to their shortest, with nothing to relieve their monotony, there was pleasure to be got out of the long answers, which set forth how Valentine was really going to be married soon after Christmas, and what Liz was going to wear, how Dorothea was coming down to be married from Wigfield House, to please "sister," and how it would all be such fun—"Only three weeks, Laura dear, to the delightful day!" Finally, how Dorothea had arrived—and oh, such a lovely *trousseau!* and she had never looked half so sweet and pretty before, "and in four days, dear, the wedding is to be; eighty people to breakfast—only think! and you shall be told all about it."

Laura felt herself slightly injured when, a week after this, she had not been told anything. She felt even surprised when another week passed, and yet there was silence; but at the end of it, she came rushing one morning into Amelia's room, quite flushed from excitement, and with an open letter in her hand.

"They're not married at all," she exclaimed, "Valentine and Miss Graham! There has been no wedding, and there is none coming off. Valentine has jilted her."

"Nonsense," cried Mrs. Melcombe. "You must be dreaming—things had gone so far," and she sat down, feeling suddenly weak from amazement.

"But it is so," repeated Laura, "here is the whole account, I tell you. When the time came he never appeared."

"What a disgraceful shame!" exclaimed Amelia, and Laura proceeded to read to her this long-expected letter:—

"DEAREST LAURA,—I don't know how to begin, and I hardly know what to tell you, because I am so ashamed of it all; and I promised to give you an account of the wedding, but I can't. What will you think when I tell you that there was none? Valentine never came. I told you that Dorothea was in the house, but that he had gone away to take leave of various friends, because, after the wedding, they were to sail almost immediately, and so,—I must make short work with this, because I hate it to that degree. There was the great snowstorm, as you know, and when he did not come home we thought he must be blocked up somewhere, and then we were afraid he was very ill. At last when still it snowed, and still he did not come, Giles went in search of him, and it was not till the very day before the wedding that he got back, having found out the whole detestable thing.

"Poor Val! and we used to think him such a dear fellow. Of course I cannot help being fond of him still, but, Laura, he has disgracefully attached himself to another girl; he could not bear to come home and be married, and he knew St. George would be in such a rage that he did not dare to tell."

"Young scamp!" exclaimed Amelia; "such a tall, handsome fellow to, who would have believed it of him?"

"Well, Laura dear, when I saw St. George come in, I was so frightened that I fainted. Dorothea was quite calm—quite still—she had been so all the time. It makes me cry to think what she must have felt, dear sweet thing; but such a day as that one was, Laura, I cannot describe, and you cannot imagine. The whole country was completely snowed up. St. George had telegraphed to John Mortimer, from London, to be at our house, if possible, by four o'clock, for something had gone wrong, and his horses, because of the deep drift, overturned the phaeton into a ditch. John rolled out, but managed to wade on to us; he was half covered with snow when I came down just as light was failing, and saw him in the hall stamping about and shaking the snow out of his pockets and from his hair. I heard him sighing and saying how sad it was, for we thought Val must be ill, till Giles came up to him, and in two minutes told him what had happened. Oh I never saw anybody in such a fury as he put himself into! I was quite surprised. He almost stuttered with rage. What was the use either of his storming at Giles, as if he could help it, or indeed any of us? And then sister was very much hurt, for she came hurrying into the hall, and began to cry; she does so like, poor thing, that people should take things quietly. And presently, grinding and crunching through the snow, with four horses, came dear old Grand, done up in comforters, in the close carriage. He had driven round the other way; he knew something was wrong, and he came into the hall with such trembling hands, thinking Val was dying or perhaps dead. And then what a passion he got into, too, when John told him, it's no use at all my trying to explain to you; he actually cried, and when he had dried his eyes, he shook his fists, and said he was ashamed of his name.

"It was very disagreeable for us, as you may suppose. It was dusk before sister and St. George could get them to think of what we had to do. To send and stop the bells from ringing early the next morning; to stop several people who were coming by rail to dinner that day, and expecting to sleep in the house on account of the unusual weather; to let Dick A'Court know, and the other clergyman, who were to have married them; and to prevent as many people as possible from coming to the breakfast, or to the church; to stop the men who were making a path to it through the drift—Oh you can't think what a confusion there presently was, and we had four or five hired flys in the stable, ready to fetch our friends, and take them to church, too; and there was such a smell all over, of roasting things and baking things. Well, Laura, off we all set into the kitchen, and sent off the hired men with the flys, and every servant we had in the house, male or female—and Grand's men too—excepting sister's little maid to attend to Dorothea. They went with messages and letters and telegrams right and left, to prevent the disgrace of any more people coming to look at us. And then, when they were all gone, we being in the kitchen, John soon recollected how the cook had begged us to be very particular, and put water every now and then into the boiler, for the pipe that supplied it was frozen, and if we didn't mind it would burst. So off he and Giles had to go into the dark yard and get in some water, and then they had to fetch in coals for the fires, and when John found that all the water in the back kitchen was frozen, and there was none but what was boiling to wash his hands in, he broke out again and denounced Val, and that minute up came the carrier's cart to the back door, having rescued the four smallest Mortimers and Aunt Christie and the nurse, who had been found stuck fast in the sociable in a drift, and in the children burst, full of ecstasy and congratulations, and thinking it the greatest fun in the world that we should all be in the kitchen. And while Grand sat in low spirits at one side of the fire, and they began to amuse themselves by pulling in all the fish-baskets, and parcels, and boxes, and wedding presents, that the carriers had left outside in the snow (because John wouldn't let them come in and see us), St. George sat at the end of the dresser with his arms folded, smoked a cigar, and held his peace. He must have been very much tired, as well as disgusted, poor fellow, for he had been rushing about the country for three days and nights; so he left all the others to do just what they liked, and say what they liked. And very soon the whole confusion got to its height, by the elder children coming in and being told, and flying at John to condole and cry over him, and entreat him not to mind. John, indeed! just as if we didn't care at all! It was intended that all the children should sleep in our house, for it is so near the church, and nothing could prevent the younger ones from thinking it all the most glorious fun. What with having been stuck fast, and then coming on in the cart and finding us in the kitchen, and having supper there, they were so delighted that they could not conceal their ecstasy.

"As for little Anastasia, when the weights of the great kitchen clock ran down, and it stopped with an awful sort of gasping click, I believe she thought *that was the wedding*, for she ran up to St. George, who still sat on the dresser, and said—

"'Shan't we have another one to-morrow?'

"'No, you *stoopid* little thing!' Bertie said. 'You know Cousin Val won't come to do the marrying.'

"'But somebody must,' she went on, 'else we can't have our new *nopera* cloaks and our satin frocks. Can't papa?'

"'No, papa doesn't wish,' said Bertie; 'I asked him.'

"'Then,' she said, looking up at St. George, and speaking in a very pathetic tone, 'you will, *dear*, won't you? because you know you're so kind.'

"I just happened to glance at St. George then, and you can't think, Laura, how astonished I was.

He turned away his face, and sister, who was stand ing close by, lifted up the child and let her kiss him. Then he got down from the dresser and went away; but, Laura, if he had wished more than anything in the world to marry Dorothea, he might have looked just so.

"Don't tell any one what I have said about this. Perhaps I was mistaken. I will write again soon.

"Ever affectionately yours,

"ELIZABETH GRANT."

"Well," said Mrs. Melcombe, "it's the most disgraceful thing I ever heard of."

"And here is a postscript," remarked Laura; "nothing particular, though:—'P.S.—Dorothea was ill at first; but she is better. I must tell you that dear old Grand, the next morning, apologized to sister for having so lost his temper; he said it was the old Adam that was strong in him still.'"

CHAPTER XII.

VALENTINE.

"If he had known where he was going to fall, he could have put down straw."—*Russian Proverb.*

LAURA wrote with difficulty an answer to Lizzy Grant's letter. It is easier for the sister to say, "My brother is a dishonourable young fellow, and has behaved shamefully," than for the friend to answer without offence, "I quite agree with you."

But the next letter made matters in some degree easier, for it at least showed the direction that his family gave to the excuses they now offered for the behaviour of the young scapegrace. First, he had been very unwell in London—almost seriously unwell; and next, Lizzy said she had been quite right as to St. George's love for Dorothea, for he had made her an offer before she left the house.

"In fact," continued Liz, "we have all decided, so far as we can, to overlook what Val has done, for he is deeply attached to the girl who, without any fault of her own, has supplanted Dorothea. He is already engaged to her, and if he is allowed to marry her early in the spring, and sail for New Zealand, he is not likely ever to return; at any rate, he will not for very many years. In that case, you know, Laura, we shall only be with him about six weeks longer; so I hope our friends will forgive us for forgiving him."

"They are fond of him, that is the fact," observed Mrs. Melcombe; "and to be sure the other brother, wanting to marry Miss Graham, does seem to make some difference, some excuse; but as to his illness, I don't think much of that. I remember when his old father came here to the funeral, I remarked that Valentine looked overgrown, and not strong, and Mr. Mortimer said he had been very delicate himself all his youth, and often had a cough (far more delicate, in fact, than his son was); but he had outgrown 't, and enjoyed very fair health for many years."

Then Laura went on reading:—

"Besides, we think that, though Dorothea refused St. George point blank when he made her an offer, yet she would hardly write to him every week as she does, if she did not like him, and he would hardly be so very silent and reserved about her, and yet evidently in such good spirits, if he did not think that something in the end would come of it."

"No," said Mrs. Melcombe, laughing in a cynical spirit, "the ridiculous scrape they are in does not end with Valentine. If he was really ill, there could be no thought of his marriage with this other girl; and, besides, Miss Graham (if this is true) will have far the best of the two brothers. *St. George*, as they are so fond of calling him (I suppose because Giles is such an ugly name), is far better off than Valentine, and has ten times more sense."

"Dorothea is gone to the Isle of Wight," continued Laura, finishing the letter, "to live with some old friends. She has no relatives, poor girl, excepting a father, who is somewhere at the other end of the world, and he seems to take very little notice of her. There is, indeed, an old uncle, but he lives at sea; he is almost always at sea in his yacht, and her only brother sails with him; but nobody knows in the least where they are now. It is very sad for her, and she told St. George, and sister too, that she had only loved Val out of gratitude, because he seemed so much attached to her, and because she wanted somebody to devote herself to."

In her next letter Liz told Laura that she herself was to be married shortly to Dick A'Court, "who says he fell in love with me when we two used to add up the coal-and-clothing cards." In these words, and in no more, the information was imparted, and the rest of the letter was so stiff and formal that Laura's pleasure in the correspondence ended with it. The realities of life were beginning to make her child-friend feel sober and reticent.

Laura wrote a long effusive letter in reply, full of tender congratulations on the high lot that awaited Liz as the helpmeet of a devoted clergyman, also on the joys of happy lovers; but this composition did not touch the feelings of Liz in the right place. "Just as if I had not told her," she thought, "that Emily was come home from India, and that I had consented to accept Dick partly to please her, because she was sure I should be sorry for it afterwards if I didn't. So I dare say I should have been," she continued thoughtfully. "In fact, I am almost sure of it. But I know very well, whatever Emily may say, that Dick will make me do just as he likes. I am sure I shall have to practise those quire boys of his, and they will bawl in my ears and call me teacher."

So thinking, Liz allowed herself to drift towards matrimony without enthusiasm, but with a general notion that, as most people were married sooner or later, no doubt matrimony was the proper thing and the best thing on the whole. "And I shall certainly go through with it, now I have promised," she further reflected, "for it would never do for another of us to behave badly just at the last."

It was the last week in March, and Laura was loitering through the garden one morning before breakfast, when Mrs. Melcombe came out to her in some excitement with a note in her hand, which had been sent on from the inn, and which set forth that Mr. Brandon, having business in that immediate neighbourhood, would, if agreeable to her, do himself the pleasure of calling some time that morning. He added that he had brought a book for Miss Melcombe from his sister.

"I have sent to the inn," said Mrs. Melcombe, "to beg that he will come on here to breakfast."

Laura had been gathering a bunch of violets, and she rushed up-stairs and put them into her hair. Then in a great hurry she changed her toilette, and, after ascertaining that the guest had arrived, she came languidly into the breakfast-room, a straw-hat hanging by its strings from her arm, and filled with primroses and other flowers. She felt as she approached that all this looked quite romantic, but it did not look so real and so unpremeditated as might have been wished.

Mrs. Melcombe had also changed her array. Little Peter, like most other children, was always the picture of cleanly neatness when first he left his nurse's hand in the morning, and his mother was much pleased at the evident interest with which their guest regarded him, asking him various questions about his lessons, his sports, and his pony. She had been deeply gratified at the kind way in which all the Mortimers and their connections had received her boy; none of them seemed at all jealous. Even Valentine had never hinted or even looked at her as if he felt that the property ought not to have gone to the younger branch.

Peter, now ten years old, and but a small boy for his age, had an average degree of intelligence; and as he sat winking and blinking in the morning sunshine, he constantly shook back a lock of hair that fell over his forehead, till Brandon, quietly putting his hand to it, moved it away, and while the boy related some childish adventure that he had encouraged him to talk of, looked at him with scrutinizing and, as it seemed to his mother, with almost anxious attention.

"Peter has been very poorly several times this winter," she remarked. "I mean shortly to take him out for change of air."

"His forehead looks pale," said Brandon, withdrawing his hand, and for a minute or two he seemed lost in thought, till Mrs. Melcombe, expressing a hope that he would stay at her house as long as his affairs detained him in that neighbourhood, he accepted her invitation with great readiness. He would spend that day and the next with her, and, if she would permit it, he would walk with young hopeful to his tutor's house, and come back again in time for luncheon.

"I declare, he scarcely spoke to me all breakfast-time," thought Laura. "I consider him decidedly a proud man, and any one might think he had come to see Peter rather than to see us."

Brandon evidently did wish to walk with the boy, and accordingly rose as soon as he had finished his breakfast, Mrs. Melcombe giving him some directions, and a key to let himself in with by a side gate.

All the intelligence Brandon possessed, and all his keenness of observation, he exercised during his walk with the little heir. He could generally attract children, and Peter was already well inclined toward him, for he had shown himself to be knowing about a country boy's pleasures; also he knew all about the little Mortimers and their doings.

Brandon wished to see Melcombe, even to examine some parts of the house and grounds, and he wanted if possible to hear something more about the ghost story; but it did not suit him to betray any special interest. So he left it to work its way to the surface if it would. It was not the business he had come about, but he had undertaken to transact that, on purpose because it gave him a chance of looking at the place.

This was the deep glen, then, that he had heard Valentine speak of?

"Yes; and mother says the old uncle Mortimer (that one who lived at Wigfield) improved it so much; he had so many trees thinned out, and a pond dug where there used to be a swamp. We've got some carp in that pond. Do you think, if I fed them, they would get tame?"

Brandon told some anecdote of certain carp that he had seen abroad, and then asked—

"Do you like the glen, my boy—is it a favourite place of yours?"

"Pretty well," answered Peter. "There are not so many nests, though, as there used to be. It used to be quite dark with trees."

"Did you like it then?"

"Yes, it was jolly; but——"

"But what?" asked Brandon carelessly.

"Grandmother didn't like it," said the boy.

Brandon longed to ask why.

"She was very old, my grandmother."

"Yes. And so she didn't like the glen?"

"No; but the old uncle has had a walk, a sort of path, made through it; and mamma says I may like it as much as I please, so does aunt Laura. "You know," continued the child, in an argumentative tone, "there's no place in the world where somebody hasn't died."

"Now, what does this mean?" thought Brandon. "I would fain raise the ghost if I could. Is he coming up now, or is he not?"

Presently, however, Peter made some allusion to the family misfortune—the death of the eldest son, by which Brandon perceived that it had taken place in the glen. He then dropped the subject, nothing more that was said till a few minutes before they reached the tutor's lodgings being of the least interest. Then, as they turned the edge of a wood, Peter looked back.

"You won't forget the turn of the lane you are to take, will you, Mr. Brandon? and you've got the key?"

"Yes," said Brandon.

"It's a green sort of door, in the park-paling. A new one has been made, because that one was so shabby. It's the one my uncles went through when they ran away, you know."

"What uncles?" asked Brandon, not at all suspecting the truth, and not much interested.

"Why, that one who belonged to you," said Peter, "and the other one who belongs to Bertie and Hugh. Didn't you know?" he exclaimed, having observed the momentary flash of surprise that Brandon made haste to conceal. "They ran away," he repeated, as Brandon walked beside him making no answer, "a very long time before my mamma was born, and they never came back any more. till I was nearly six years old."

"So that's your tutor's house, is it?" said Brandon, and thereupon he took leave of him.

"Amazing!" he said to himself as he walked away. "What next, I wonder?"

As he returned he revolved this information in his mind with increasing surprise. John Mortimer had a proud and confident way of talking about his father that did not sound as if he knew that he had begun life by running away from home. Valentine, he was well aware, knew nothing about it.

Coming on, he turned aside to talk to some men who were digging a well. He knew how to talk to working people, and, what is more to the purpose, he knew how to make them talk; but though they proffered a good deal of information about the neighbourhood, nothing was said that gave him any of the knowledge he wanted. And shortly he went on, and let himself in at the little gate with his key. It was not yet eleven o'clock, and as he did not want to see the ladies of the family so soon, he determined to go down into the steep glen and look about him.

He had no doubt now that to this place the superstitious story belonged.

First, he skirted it all about. From above it was nearly as round as a cup, and as deep in proportion to its size. The large old trees had been left, and appeared almost to fill it up, their softly rounded heads coming to within three feet of the level where he stood. All the mother birds — rooks, jays, thrushes, and pigeons—were plainly in view under him, as they sat brooding on their nests among the topmost twigs, and there was a great cawing and crowing of the cock-birds while they flew about and fed their mates. The leaves were not out; their buds only looked like green eggs spotting the trees, excepting that here and there a horse-chestnut, forwarder than its brethren, was pushing its crumpled foliage out of the pale-pink sheath. Everywhere saplings had been cut down, and numbers of them strewed the damp mossy ground; but light penetrated, and water trinkled, there was a pleasant scent of herbs and flowers, and the whole place was cheerful with growth and spring.

A set of winding steps cut in the soft, red rock led into the glen just where the side was steepest, and Brandon, intent on discovery, sprang lightly down them. He wandered almost everywhere about the place. It seemed to hold within itself a different climate from the world above, where keen spring air was stirring; here hardly a breath moved, and in the soft sheltered warmth the leaves appeared visibly to be expanding. He forgot his object, also another object that he had in view (the business, in fact, which had brought him), leaned against the trunk of a horse-chestnut, listened to the missel-thrushes, looked at a pine-tree a little way off, that was letting down a mist of golden dust, and presently lost himself in a reverie, finding, as is the way with a lover, that the scene present, whatever it may happen to be, was helping to master his every-day self, was indeed just the scene to send him plunging yet further down into the depths of his passionate dream.

He had stood leaning against the tree, with his hat at his feet and his arms folded, for perhaps half an hour. He had inherited a world (with an ideal companion), had become absorbed into a lifetime of hope; and his love appeared to grow without let or hindrance in the growing freshness and glorious expansion of the spring.

Half an hour of hope and joy consoles for much foregone trouble, and further satisfies the heart by making it an easier thing to believe in more yet to come.

A sudden exclamation and a little crash roused him.

Laura! She had come to visit her favourite tree, and lo! a man there at last, leaning against it lost in thought, and so absolutely still that she had not noticed him.

She knew in an instant that this was not Joseph, and yet as the sight of him flashed on her sense before recognition, the nothingness she always found gave way to a feeling as of something real, that almost might have been the right thing. As for him, though he saw her flitting figure, she did not for the twinkling of an eye pass for the ghost he had come to look for. He roused himself up in an instant. "Whew!" was his inward thought, "she is alone; what could be so lucky! I'll do the business at once, and get it over."

Picking up his hat, and sinking at every step into the soft cushions of moss, he accordingly approached her and said, but perhaps just a little coldly, "I did not expect to see you here, Miss Melcombe."

Laura perceived this slight tinge of coldness as plainly as he did the improvement in her appearance since he had first seen her in the morning, for surprise at detecting him had overpowered her affectation. She had coloured from having been startled, and while she, from habit, moved on mechanically to the tree, she answered quite simply and naturally that she walked that way almost every day.

Brandon turned and walked with her. Opposite to the said tree, and very near it, was another, under which stood a bench. Laura sat down, and while pointing out the spot where certain herons had built their platform-like nests, began to recover herself, or rather to put on the damaging affectation which in a moment of forgetfulness she had thrown off.

Brandon did not sit beside her, but while she arranged her dress to her mind, threw her plaid shawl into becoming folds, and laying her hand on her bracelet, furtively drew the ornament upon it to the upper side, he looked at her and thought what a goose she was.

She wore a straw hat with so wide a brim that as he stood before her he did not see her face, and he was not sorry for this; it was not his business to reprove her, but what he had to say would, he supposed, put her a good deal out of countenance.

He was just about to speak, and Laura was in the full enjoyment of feeling how romantic it was to be there alone with a young man, was just wishing that some of her friends could be looking down from above to see this interesting picture, and draw certain conclusions, when a decidedly sharp voice called out from behind, "Laura! what can you be doing here? You know I don't like you to be for ever coming to that tree.—Laura!"

"Yes, I'm here," said Laura, and Mrs. Melcombe, arrayed in blue poplin, stepped into view, and made Brandon feel very foolish and Laura very cross.

"Oh! you've brought Mr. Brandon here to see the carp," said Amelia graciously, but she hardly knew what to think, and they all presently went to the pond, and watched the creatures flashing up their golden sides, each wondering all the time what the two others were thinking of. Then as it was nearly lunch time, Amelia and Laura proceeded to leave the dell, Brandon attending them and helping them up the steps. He was rather vexed that he had not been able to say his say and give Laura a certain packet that he had in his possession; and as the afternoon presently clouded over and it began to pour with rain, he hardly knew what to do with himself till the bright idea occurred to him that he would ask Mrs. Melcombe to show him the old house.

Up and down stairs and into a good many rooms they all three proceeded together. Hardly any pictures to found a question or a theory on; no old china with a story belonging to it; no brown books that had been loved by dead Melcombes. This could not have been a studious race. Not a single anecdote was told of the dead all the time they went over the place, till at last Mrs. Melcombe unlocked the door of a dark, old-fashioned sitting-room upstairs, and going to the shutters opened one of them, saying, "This is the room in which the dear old grandmother spent the later years of her life."

This really was an interesting old room. Laura and Amelia folded back the shutters with a genuine air of reverence and feeling. It was most evident that they had loved this woman whose son had forbidden her to leave her property to him.

Two or three dark old pictures hung on the walls, and there was a cabinet on which Laura laying her hand, said—

"The dear grandmother kept all her letters here."

"Indeed," Brandon answered; "it must have been very interesting to you to look them over. (And yet," he thought "you don't look as if you had found in them anything of much interest.")

"We have never opened it," said Mrs. Melcombe. "Mr. Mortimer, when he was here, proposed to look over and sort all the letters for me, but I declined his offer."

("And no doubt made him miserable by so doing") was Brandon's next thought.

"I shall keep the key for my dear boy," she continued, "and give it to him when he comes of age."

("To find out something that he will wish he didn't know,") thought Brandon again. ("That cabinet, as likely as not, contains the evidence of *it*, whatever *it* is.")

"And in this gallery outside," she proceeded, "the dear grandmother used to walk every day."

Brandon perceived that he had got to the core and heart of the place at last. His interest was so intense that he failed to conceal it. He walked to the window and noticed the pouring rain that was streaming between the rustic pillars of the balustrades into the garden below. He examined the pictures; only two of them were portraits, but in the background of one was an undoubted representation of the house itself; the other was a portrait of a beautiful boy in a blue jacket and a shirt with a wide frill laid back and open at the neck. Under his arm appeared the head of a greyish dog.

"That creature," Brandon thought, "is almost exactly like my old dog Smokey. I am very much mistaken if this is not the portrait of one of his ancestors."

He turned to ask some question about it, and observed to his surprise that Mrs. Melcombe had left the room, and he was alone with Laura, who had seated herself on a sofa and taken a long piece of crochet-work from her pocket, which she was doing almost with the air of one who waits patiently till somebody else has finished his investigations.

"I thought you would be interested in that picture," she said; "you recognise it, I suppose?"

"No!" he exclaimed.

"It used not to be here," said Laura; "the dear grandmother, as long as she lived, always had it in her bedroom. It's Mr. Mortimer, your step-father, when he was a boy, and that was his dog, a great favourite; when he ran away the dog disappeared—it was always supposed that it ran after him. I suppose," continued Laura, impelled to say this to some one who was sure to be impressed by it—"I suppose nobody ever did mourn as my grandmother did over the loss of those two sons. Yet she never used to blame them."

They did run away then, and they did keep away, and yet she did not blame them. How deeply pathetic these things seemed. Whatever it might be that had made his step-father write that letter, it appeared now to be thrown back to the time when he had divided himself thus from his family and taken his boy brother with him.

"And that other portrait," said Laura, "we found up in one of the garrets, and hung here when the house was restored. It is the portrait of my grandmother's only brother, who was sixteen or eighteen years younger than she was. His name was Melcombe, which was her maiden name, but ours, you know, was really Mortimer. It is very much darkened by time and neglect, and never was of any particular value."

"What has he got under his arm?" said Brandon.

"I think it is a cocked hat or some kind of hat. I think they wore cocked hats then in the navy; he was a lieutenant in the navy. You see some sort of gold lace on it, and on the hilt of his sword."

"Did he die at sea?" asked Brandon.

"Yes. My great-grandfather left this place to his son, and as he died unmarried it was to come to our eldest uncle, and then to grandmother, as it did, you know."

"'Its name was Melcombe, and it came from the sea,'" Brandon repeated inwardly, adding, "Well, the *ghost* can have had nothing to do with this mystery. I shall trouble myself no more about him."

"He was only about a year older than my oldest

uncle," proceeded Laura, "for grandmother married at seventeen."

Brandon looked again. Something in the two pictures reminded him of the portraits of the Flambourgh family. They had evidently been done by the same artist. Each youth had something under his left arm, each was turning his face slightly, and they both looked the same way. Young Daniel Mortimer was so placed that his quiet eyes seemed to be always regarding the hearth, now empty of warmth. The other, hung on the same wall, seemed to look out into the garden, and Laura said in a sentimental way that, considering the evident love she had borne her grandmother, was not at all out of place.

"There is a bed of lilies that dear grandmother used to love to watch, and Amelia and I thought it interesting when we had had this picture put up to observe that its eyes seemed to fall on the same place. They were not friends, my grandmother and her brother, and no doubt after his death my grandmother laid their frequent quarrels to heart, for she could never bear to mention him, though she had a beautiful monument put up to his memory. You must go and see it, Mr. Brandon. We have lately had it cleaned, and dear grandmother's name added under his."

"I will," said Brandon.

CHAPTER XIII.

VENERABLE ANCIENTRY.

"Even as the sparrow findeth an house, and the swallow a nest for herself where she may lay her young, so I seek thine altars, O Lord of Hosts, my King and my God."—PSALM lxxxiv., Marginal Translation.

RISING early the next morning, Brandon found that he had an hour to spare before breakfast, and sallied forth for an early walk. A delicate hoar-frost still made white the shade, and sparkled all over the sombre leaves of some fine yew-trees that grew outside the garden wall.

Walking up a little rise, he saw the weathercock and one turret of a church tower peering over the edge of a small steep hill, close at hand, and turning toward it he went briskly on, under the lee of a short fir plantation, all the grass being pure and fresh with hoar-frost, which melted in every hollow and shadow as fast as the sun came round to it.

The house was too large and pretentious for the grounds it stood in, these being hardly extensive enough to be called a park; they consisted of finely varied wood and dell, and were laid out in grass and fed off by sheep.

He passed through a gate into the churchyard, which had a very little valley all to itself, the land rising on every side so as to make a deep nest for it. Such a venerable, low, long church! taking old age so quietly, covering itself with ivy and ferns, and having a general air of mossiness, and subsidence into the bosom of the earth again, from whence its brown old stones had been quarried. For, as is often the case with an old burial-place, the soil had greatly risen, so that one who walked between the graves could see the whole interior of the place through the windows. The tiled roof, sparkling and white with the morning frost, was beginning to drip, and dew shone on the melting rime, while all around the enclosure orchards were planted, and the trees leaned over their boughs.

A woman, stepping from a cottage on the rise, held up a great key to him, and he advanced, took it, and told her he would return it.

A large heavy thing it was, that looked as if it might be hundreds of years old; he turned the lock with it and stepped in, walking down the small brick aisle, observing the ancient oaken seats, the quaint pulpit, and strange brasses; till, white, staring, obtrusive, and all out of taste, he saw in the chancel what he had come to look for, a great white marble monument, on the south side; four fluttering cherubs with short wings that appeared to hold up a marble slab, while two weeping figures knelt below. First was recorded on the slab the death of Augustus Cuthbert Melcombe, only son of Cuthbert Melcombe, gent., of this place. Then followed the date of his birth, and there was no date of death, merely the information that he was a lieutenant in the Royal Navy. Brandon copied this inscription into his note-book.

Below was the name of the young man's only sister, aged ninety-seven, "universally beloved and respected;" then the solemn words used before death by the aged patriarch, "I have waited for Thy Salvation, O Lord." All about the chancel were various small tablets in memory of the successive vicars of the place and their families, but no others with the name of Melcombe on them. The whole building was so overflowing with the records of human creatures, inside and out, it appeared as if so saturated with man's thoughts, so used to man's prayers and tears, so about presently to decline and subside into the earth as he does, that there was almost an effort in beliving that it was empty of the beings it seemed to be a part of—empty of those whom we call the living.

It was easy to move reverently and feel awed in the face of this venerable ancientry. This was the place, then, where that poor woman had worshipped whose son "had never judged her."

"If I settled," he thought, "in a new country, this is the sort of scene that, from time to time, would recur to my thoughts and get hold of me, with almost intolerable power to make life one craving for home.

"How hard to take root in a soil my fathers never ploughed! Let me abide where my story grew, where my dead are laid, in a country full of days, full of the echoes of old Englishmen's talk, and whose sunsets are stained as if with the blood shed for their liberties."

He left the church, noticing, as he went down the aisle, numbers of dogs'-eared books in the different pews, and the narrow window at the east end now letting in long shafts of sunshine; but there was nothing to inform him of any fact that threw light on his step-father's letter, and he returned the key to the sexton's wife, and went back to breakfast, telling Mrs. Melcombe where he had been, and remarking that there was no date of death on Augustus Melcombe's tomb.

"I think they did not know the date," she replied. "It was during the long French war that he died, and they were some time uncertain of the fact, but at length the eldest son going to London, wrote his mother an account of how he had met with the captain of his young uncle's ship, and had been told of his death at sea, somewhere near the West Indies. The dear grandmother showed me that letter," observed Mrs. Melcombe, "when first I married."

Brandon listened attentively, and when he was alone set that down also in his note-book, then considering that neither the ghost nor the young lieutenant need trouble him further, he felt that all his suspicions were cast loose into a fathomless sea, from which he could fish nothing up; but the little heir was well and happy, and he devoutly hoped that he would remain so, and save to himself the anxiety of showing, and to Valentine the pain and doubt that would come of reading the letter.

Mrs. Melcombe, narrow as were her thoughts, was, notwithstanding, a schemer in a small way. She had felt that Brandon must have had something to say to Laura when she herself coming up had interrupted him. Laura had few reserves from her, so when she had ascertained that nothing had occurred when she had left them together in the grandmother's sitting-room but such talk as naturally arose out of the visit to it, she resolved to give him another opportunity, and after breakfast was about to propose a walk, when he helped her by asking her to show him that room again.

"I should like so much to have a photograph of Mr. Mortimer's picture," he said; "may I see it again?"

Nothing more easy. They all went up to the room; a fire had been lighted to air it, because its atmosphere had felt chilly the day before. Laura seated herself again on the sofa. Brandon, with pen and ink, began trying to make a sketch of the portrait, and very soon found himself alone with Laura, as he had fully expected would be the case. Whereupon, sitting with his back to her, and working away at his etching, he presently said—

"I mentioned yesterday to Mrs. Melcombe that I had come on business."

"Yes," Laura answered.

"So as it concerns only you, I will, if you please, explain it now."

As he leaned slightly round towards her Laura looked up, but she was mute through surprise. There was something in this voice at once penetrative and sweet; but now she was again conscious of what sounded like a delicately-hinted reproof.

"A young man," he proceeded, "whom I have known almost all my life—in fact, I may call him a friend of mine—told me of an event that had taken place—he called it a misfortune that had befallen him. It had greatly unsettled him, he said, for a long time; and now that he was getting over it, and wanted to forget it, he wished for a change, would like to go abroad, and asked if I could help him. I have many foreign acquaintances. It so chanced that I had just been applied to by one of them to send him out an Englishman, a clerk, to help him with his English correspondence. So I proposed to this young fellow to go, and he gladly consented."

Laura said nothing. Brandon's words did not lead her to think of Joseph. So she thought of him, wishing she had been so led. She noticed, however, a slight emphasis in the words which informed her that the young man, whoever he was, "was getting over his misfortune, and wanted to forget it."

"It was very kind of you," she said at last, after a long pause.

Brandon turned. Her words were ambiguous, and he wished to be understood. "You observe, no doubt, Miss Melcombe," he said, "that I am speaking of Joseph Swan?"

"Joseph Swan!" Laura repeated, "then he is going away?"

"Yes; but when I had secured this situation for him, he said he felt that he must tell me what had occurred. He told me of an attachment that he had formed, and whatever I may think as to the prudence displayed in the affair, you know best whether *he* was at all to blame. He had received certain promises, so he assured me, and for a long time he had buoyed himself up with hope, but after that, feeling himself very much injured, and knowing that he had been deceived, he had determined to go away."

Laura had never expected to have her conduct brought home to her, and she had actually been almost unaware that she was to blame.

"It was Amelia's doing," she murmured.

Brandon was anxious to speak guardedly, and would not mention Joseph's name again lest Mrs. Melcombe should enter suddenly and hear it, so he answered, "Yes; and the young man told me he knew you were very much afraid of your sister-in-law. It appears, however, that you had written to him."

"I did, two or three times," said Laura.

"So in case you should in after years feel anxious as to what had become of those letters, or should feel some compunction for groundless hopes excited and for causeless caprice, I undertook to tell you as a message from this young man, that, considering you to be completely under the dominion of your sister-in-law, he does not at all blame you, he does not admit that you are in fault; in one sense, now that he can look back on his attachment as over, he declares that he is the better for it, because it induced him to work hard at improving himself. He is to go out to Santo Domingo, where, in a new climate, and hearing a new language, he can begin life afresh; but he wishes you to be assured that he shall never trouble or annoy you, and he returns you your letters. I promised to say all this to you as a message from this young man—a young man who, whatever the world may call him, deserves, I think, by you (and me) to be from henceforth always regarded as a gentleman. Will you allow me to give you this packet?"

He had risen as he spoke, and while approaching

her produced a small packet carefully done up; but Laura did not stir. She had dropped her hands on her knees, and he, stooping, laid it upon them, when meeting her eyes for a moment, he observed with amazement and discomfiture that she was silent not from shame and compunction for what had seemed very unfeminine and heartless conduct, but from a rapture that seemed too deep for words.

"Miss Melcombe!" he exclaimed.

"Yes," she answered, in a low voice. "It is an island that he is going to then. I always thought I should not mind marrying him if he would go to a desert island. And so he loved me, really and truly?"

"It appears that he did, *some time ago*," said Brandon, rather pointedly.

"Does any one else know," Laura asked, "but you?"

"Yes; John Mortimer does."

Laura blushed deeply.

"Joseph told him first about this affair, but did not divulge the lady's name. After all was settled, he acknowledged to us both that you were the lady. John was very glad that I was willing personally to give the letters into your own hands again."

"I suppose he thought I had been very imprudent?"

Brandon recalled the scene. John had in fact expressed himself to that effect in no measured terms; but he had been pleasant and even cordial to Joseph, partly because the young man declared the thing to be quite over, partly because he did him the justice to remember that such an acquaintance must always have been begun by the woman. It could not possibly be Joe's doing that he had corresponded with Laura Melcombe.

Laura repeated her words.

"I suppose he thought I had been very imprudent?"

"Perhaps he did."

"Perhaps he thought I had been heartless too?"

"Not to bring the thing to a decided and honourable termination?—yes, probably. He remarked that it certainly was most unnecessary to have behaved as you have done."

"How so, Mr. Brandon?"

"I believe, indeed I am sure, that you are of age?"

"Yes, I am. He meant that no one can really prevent my doing as I please; but Amelia wanted me to ignore the whole thing because she was so ashamed of him and his people."

"He told John so."

"And what did he answer?"

"Among other things, he said he was glad it was all over."

"Yes," said Laura, not in the least impressed by this hint, "but what else?"

"He said, 'Joe, you ought to have been above wanting to marry any woman who was ashamed of you. *I* wouldn't do such a thing on any account.'"

"He said that?" cried Laura, rather startled.

"Yes, and I quite agreed with him—I told Joe that I did."

"Did he say anything more?"

Brandon hesitated, and at length, finding that she would wait till he spoke, he said—

"He told Joe he ought to be thankful to have the thing over, and said that he had come out of it well, and the lady had not."

"Amelia is not half so unkind as you are," said Laura, when she had made him say this, and a quiet tear stole down her cheek and dropped on her hand.

"Pardon me! I think that for myself I have expressed no opinion but this one, that Joe Swan deserves your respect for the manly care he has taken to shield you from blame, spare you anxiety, and terminate the matter properly."

"Terminate!" repeated Laura; "yes, that is where you are so unkind."

"Am I expected to help her to bring it on again?" thought Brandon. "No; I have a great respect for fools, and they must marry like other people; but oh, Joey, Joey Swan, if you are one, which I thought you the other day (and the soul of honour too!), I think if you still cared about it, you could soon get yourself mated with a greater one still! Laura Melcombe would be at least a fair match for you in that particular. But no, Joey, I decline to interfere any further."

CHAPTER XIV.

EMILY.

"Not warp'd by passion, awed by rumour,
Not grave through pride, nor gay through folly,
An equal mixture of good humour,
And sensible, soft melancholy.

"'Has she no faults then,' Envy says, 'Sir?'
'Yes, she has one, I must aver;
When all the world conspires to praise her
The woman's deaf, and does not hear.'"

JOHN MORTIMER was sitting at breakfast the very morning after this conversation had taken place at Melcombe. No less than four of his children were waiting on him; Gladys was drying his limp newspaper at a bright fire, Barbara spreading butter on his toast, little Hugh kneeling on a chair, with his elbows on the table, was reading him a choice anecdote from a child's book of natural history, and Anastasia, while he poured out his coffee with one hand, had got hold of the other, which she was folding up industriously in her pinafore and frock, because she said it was cold. It was a windy, chilly, and exasperatingly bright spring morning; the sunshine appeared to prick the traveller all over rather than to warm him. Not at all the morning for an early walk, but John, lifting up his eyes, saw a lady in the garden, and in another instant Mrs. Frederic Walker was shown in.

"What, Emily!" exclaimed John, starting up.

"Yes, John; but my soldier and my valuable infant are both quite well. Now, if you don't go on with your breakfast, I shall depart. Let me sit by the fire and warm my feet."

"You have breakfasted?"

"Of course. How patriarchal you look, John, sitting in state to be adored!"

Thereupon, turning away from the fire, she began to smile upon the little Anastasia, and without any more direct invitation, the small coquette allowed herself to be decoyed from her father to sit on the visitor's knee. Emily had already thrown off her fur wraps, and the child, making herself very much at home in her arms, began presently to look at her brooch and other ornaments, the touch of her small fingers appearing to give pleasure to Emily, who took up one of the fat little pink hands, and kissed it fondly.

"What is that lady's name, Nancy?" said John.

"Mrs. Nemily," answered the child.

"You have still a little nursery English left about you, John," said Emily. "How sweet it is! My boy has that yet to come; he can hardly say half-a-dozen words."

Then Gladys entering the room with a cup and saucer, she rose and came to the table.

"That milk looks so nice—give me some of it. How pleasant it is to feel cold and hungry, as one does in England! No, John, not ham; I will have some bread and marmalade. Do the children always wait on you, John, at breakfast?"

There was something peculiarly sweet and penetrative in the voices of Brandon and his sister; but this second quality sometimes appeared to give more significance to their words than they had intended.

"Always. Does it appear an odd arrangement in your eyes?"

"Father," said Barbara, "here is your paper. I have cut the leaves."

"Thank you, my dear; put it down. You should consider, Emily, my great age and exaltation in the eyes of these youngsters. Don't you perceive that I am a middle-aged man, madam?"

"Middle-aged, indeed! You are not thirty-six till the end of September, you know—the 28th of September. And oh, John, you cannot think how young you look! just as if you had stolen all these children, and they were not really yours. You have so many of them, too, while I have only one, and he such a little one—he is only two years old."

While she spoke a bell began to ring, and the two elder children, wishing her good-bye, left the room.

"Do you think those girls are growing like their mother?" asked John.

"I think they are a little. Perhaps that pretty way they have of taking up their eye-glasses when they come forward to look at anything, makes them seem more like than they are."

John scarcely ever mentioned his wife, but before Emily most people spoke without much reserve.

"Only one of the whole tribe is like her in mind and disposition," he continued.

"And that's a good thing," thought Emily, but she did not betray her thought.

While this talk went on the two younger children had got possession of Mrs. Nemily's watch (which hung from her neck by a long Trichinopoly chain), and were listening to a chime that it played. Emily took the boy on her knee, and it did not appear that he considered himself too big to be nursed, but began to examine the watch, putting it to his ear, while he composedly rested his head on her shoulder.

"Poor little folk," thought John, "how naturally they take to the caresses of a young mother!"

Another bell then rang.

"What order is kept in your house!" said Emily, as both the children departed, one with a kiss on her dimpled cheek and the other on his little scratched fist, which already told of much climbing.

"That is the school-room bell," John answered; and then Mrs. Frederic Walker laughed, and said, with a look half whimsical, half wistful—

"Oh, John, you're going to be so cross?"

"Are you going to make me cross? You had better tell me at once, then, what you are come for. Has Giles returned?"

"He came in late last night. I know what he went for, John. He thought it best to tell me. He is now gone on to the station about some affairs of his own. It seems that you both took Joey Swan's part, and were displeased with that Laura."

"Of course. She made the poor fellow very miserable for a long time. Besides, I am ashamed of the whole derogatory affair. Did Giles see that she burnt those letters—foolish, cold-hearted creature?"

"'Foolish,' I dare say; but 'cold-hearted,' I don't know. St. George declared to me that he thought she was as much in love now as that goose Joseph ever was."

"Amazing!" exclaimed John, very much discomfited.

"And she tried hard to make him promise that he would keep the whole thing a profound secret, especially from you; and so of course he declined, for he felt that you must be the proper person to tell it to, though we do not know why. He reasoned with her, but he could make nothing of her."

"Perhaps she wants to bring it on again," said John. "What a pity he returned the letters before Joe had sailed!"

"No, it was the right thing to do. And, John, if love is really the sacred, strong, immortal passion made out by all the poets and novelists, I cannot see, somehow, that putty ought to stand in its light. It ought to have a soul above putty."

"With all my heart," said John; "but you see in this case it hadn't."

"It would be an *astonishingly* disadvantageous thing for our family if she ran away and married him just now, when Valentine has been making himself so ridiculous. But there is no doubt we could bring it on again, and have it done if we chose," said Emily.

John looked at her with surprise.

"But then," she continued, "I should say that the man ought to be thought of as well as herself, and she might prove a thoroughly unsuitable, foolish wife, who would soon tire of him. SHE might be very miserable also. She would not have half the chance of happiness that an ordinary marriage gives. And, again, Santo Domingo is notoriously unhealthy. She might die, and if we had caused the marriage, we should feel that."

"Are you addressing this remarkable speech to yourself or to *the chair?*" said John, laughing.

"To the chair. But, if I am the meeting, don't propose as a resolution that this meeting is *tête montée*. John, you used to say of me before I married that I was troubled with intuitions."

"I remember that I did."

"You meant that I sometimes saw consequences very clearly, and felt that the only way to be at peace was to do the right thing, having taken some real trouble to find out what it was."

"I was not aware that I meant that. But proceed."

"When Laura was here in the autumn she often talked to Liz about little Peter Melcombe's health, and said she believed that his illness at Venice had very much shaken his constitution. His mother, she said, never would allow that there had been much the matter with him, though she had felt frightened at the time. It was the heat, Laura thought, that had been too much for him. Now, you know if that poor little fellow were to die, Valentine, who has nothing to live on, and nothing to do, is his heir. What a fine thing it would be for him!"

"I don't see yet what you mean."

"Mrs. Melcombe found out before Giles left Melcombe all about these letters. She came into the room, and Laura, who seems to have been filled with a ridiculous sort of elation to think that somebody had really loved her, betrayed it in her manner, and between her and Giles it was confessed. Mrs. Melcombe was very wroth."

"Laura has a right to do as she pleases," said John; "no one can prevent it."

"She has the right, but not the power. WE can do as we please, or we can let Mrs. Melcombe do as SHE pleases."

"You mean that we can tell my gardener's son that my cousin (whom he no longer cares for) is in love with him, and, by our assistance and persuasion, we can, if we choose, bring on as foolish a marriage as ever was contemplated, and one as disadvantageous to ourselves. Now for the alternative. What can it be?"

"Mrs. Melcombe can take Laura on the Continent again, and she proposed to do it forthwith."

"And leave her boy at school? A very good thing for him."

"No, she means to take him also, and not come back till Joseph is at the other end of the world."

"Two months will see him there."

"Well, John, now you have stated the case, it does seem a strange fancy of mine to wish to interfere, and if to interfere could possibly be to our advantage——"

"You would not have thought of it! No, I am sure of that. Now my advice is, that we let them alone all round. I don't believe, in the first place, that Joe Swan, now he has change, freedom, and a rise in life before him, would willingly marry Laura if he might. I am not at all sure that, if it came to the point, she would willingly marry him at such short notice, and leave every friend she has in the world. I think she would shrink back, for she can know nothing worth mentioning of him. As to the boy, how do you know that a tour may not be a very fine thing for him? It must be better than moping at Melcombe under petticoat government; and even if Joe married Laura to-morrow, we could not prevent Mrs. Melcombe from taking him on the Continent whenever she chose."

Emily was silent.

"And what made you talk of a runaway match?" continued John.

"Because she told Giles that the last time she saw Joseph he proposed to her to sneak away, get married before a magistrate, and go off without saying a word to anybody."

"Fools," exclaimed John, "both of them! No, we cannot afford to have any runaway matches—and of such a sort too! I should certainly interfere if I thought there was any danger of that."

"I hope you would. He wanted her to propose some scheme. I think scorn of all scheming. If she had really meant to marry him, his part should have been to see that she did it in a way that would not make it worse for her afterwards. He should have told Mrs. Melcombe fairly that she could not prevent it, and he should have taken her to church and married her like a man before plenty of witnesses in the place where she is known. If he had not shown such a craven spirit, I almost think I would have taken his part. Now, John, I know what you think; but I should have felt just the same if Valentine had not made himself ridiculous, and if I was quite sure that this would not end in a runaway match after all, and the *True Blue* be full of it."

"I believe you," said John; "and I always had a great respect for you, 'Mrs. Nemily.'"

"What are you laughing at, then?"

"Perhaps at the matronly dignity with which you have been laying down the law."

"Is that all? Oh, I always do that now I am married, John."

"You don't say so! Well, Joe Swan has worked hard at improving himself; but though good has come out of it in the end for him, it is certainly a very queer affair. Why, in the name of common sense, couldn't Laura be contented with somebody in her own sphere?"

"I should like to know why Laura was so anxious the matter should be concealed from you," said Emily.

"Most likely she remembers that Swan is in my employment, or she may also be 'troubled with intuitions,' and know by intuition what I think of her."

"And how is Aunt Christie?" asked Emily, after little more talk concerning Joseph's affairs.

"Well and happy; I do not believe it falls to the lot of any old woman to be happier in this *oblate spheroid.* The manner in which she acts dragon over Miss C. is a joy to me, the only observer. She always manages that we shall never meet excepting in her presence; when I go into the schoolroom to read prayers, I invariably find her there before me. She insists, also, on presiding at all the schoolroom meals. How she found out the state of things here I cannot tell, but I thankfully let her alone. I never go out to smoke a cigar in the evening, and notice a stately female form stepping forth also, but Aunt Christie is sure to come briskly stumping in her wake, ready to join either her or me."

"You don't mean to imply anything?"

"Of course not! but you yourself, before you married, were often known to take my arm at flower-shows, &c., in order to escape from certain poor fellows who sighed in vain."

"Yes, you were good about that; and you remind me of it, no doubt, in order to claim the like friendli-

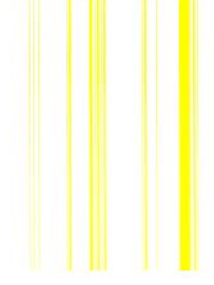

ness from me now the tables are turned. John, the next time I take your arm in public it will be to extend my matronly countenance to those modest efforts of yours at escaping attention, for you know yourself to be quite unworthy of notice!"

"Just so; you express my precise feeling."

"It is a pity you and Grand are so rich!"

"Why? You do not insinuate, I hope, that I and my seven are merely eligible on that account! Now, what are you looking at me for, with that little twist in your lips that always means mischief?"

"Because I like you, and I am afraid you are being spoilt, John. I do so wish you had a nice wife. I should; at least, if you wished it yourself."

"A saving clause! Have you and Fred discussed me, madam?"

"No, I declare that we have not."

"I hope you have nobody to recommend, because I won't have her! I always particularly disliked red hair."

"Now what makes you suppose I was thinking of any one who has red hair?"

"You best know yourself whether you were *not*."

"Well," said Emily, after a pause for reflection, "now you mention it (I never did), I do not see that you could do better."

"I often think so myself, and that is partly why I am so set against it! No, Emily, it would be a shame to joke about an excellent and pleasant woman. The fact is, I have not the remotest intention of ever marrying again at all."

"Very well," said Emily, "it is not my affair; it was your own notion entirely that I wanted to help you to a wife."

And she sat a moment cogitating, and thinking that the lady of the golden head had probably lost her chance by showing too openly that she was ready.

"What are you looking at?" said John. "At the

paths worn in my carpets? That's because all the rooms are thoroughfares. Only fancy any woman marrying a poor fellow whose carpets get into that state every three or four years."

"Oh," said Emily, "if that was likely to stand in your light, I could soon show you how to provide a remedy."

"But my father hates the thoughts of bricks and mortar," said John, amused at her seriousness, "and I inherit that feeling."

"John, the north front of your house is very ugly. You have five French windows on a line—one in each of these rooms, one in the hall; you would only have to run a narrow passage-like conservatory in front of them, enter it by the hall window, and each room by its own window, put a few plants in the conservatory, and the thing is done in a fortnight. Every room has its back window; you would get into the back garden as you do now; you need not touch the back of the house, that is all smothered in vines and creepers, as you are smothered in children!"

"The matter shall have my gravest consideration," said John, "provided you never mention matrimony to me again as long as you live."

"Very well," said Emily, "I promise; but there is St. George coming. I must not forget to tell you that I saw Joseph this morning at a distance; he was standing in the lea of the pigstye, and cogitating in the real moony style."

"It was about his outfit," exclaimed John; "depend upon it it was not about Laura."

And so the colloquy ended, and John walked down his own garden, opened the wicket that led to his gardener's cottage, and saw Joseph idly picking out a weed here and there, while he watched the bees, some of whom, deluded by the sunshine, had come forth, and were feebly hanging about the opening of the hive.

"Joe," said John, with perfect decision and directness, "I have a favour to ask of you."

Joseph was startled at first; but as no more was said, he presently answered, "Well, sir, you and yours have done me so many, that I didn't ought to hesitate about saying I'll grant it, whatever it is."

"If you should think of marrying before you go——"

"Which I don't, sir," interrupted the young man rather hastily.

"Very good; then if you change your mind, I want your promise that you will immediately let me know."

"Yes, sir," said Joseph, as if the promise cost him nothing, and suggested nothing to his mind, "I will."

"There," thought John, as he turned away, "he does not know what he is about; but if she brings the thing on again, I believe he will keep faith with me, and a clandestine marriage I am determined shall not be."

He then went into the town and found, to his surprise, that Brandon had already seen his father, and had told him that Dorothea Graham had engaged herself to him. John was very much pleased, but his father treated the matter with a degree of apathy which rather startled and disturbed him.

Old Augustus was in general deeply interested in a marriage; he had helped several people to marry, and whether he approved or disapproved of any one in particular, he was almost sure, when he had been lately told of it, to make some remarks on the sacredness of the institution, and on the advantages of an early marriage for young men.

He, however, said nothing, though Brandon was one of his chief favourites; but having just related the fact, took up the *Times*, and John opened his letters, one of them being from his son Johnny, written in a fully-formed and beautiful hand, which made its abrupt style and boyish vehemence the more observable.

"MY DEAREST FATHER,—It's all right. Mr. —— took me to Harrow, and Dr. B. examined me, and he said—oh, he said a good deal about my Latin verses, and the books I'm *in*, but I can't tell you it, because it seems so muffish. And, papa, I wish I might bring Crayshaw home for the Easter holidays; you very nearly promised I should; but I wanted to tell you what fun I and the other fellows had at the boat-race. You can hardly think how jolly it was. I suppose when I get into the great school I shall never see it. We ran down shouting and yelling after the boats. I thought I should never be happy again if Cambridge didn't win. It was such a disgustingly sleety, blowy, snowy, windy, raspy, muddy day, as you never saw. And such crowds of fellows cheering and screeching out to the crews. Such a rout!

'The Lord Mayor lent the City P'lice,
The cads ran down by scores and scores
With shouting roughs, and scented muffs,
While blue were flounces, frills, and gores.
On swampy meads, in sleeted hush,
The swarms of London made a rush,
And all the world was in the slush.'

Etcetera. That's part of Crayshaw's last; it's a parody of one of those American fogies. Dear father, you will let me come home, won't you; because I do assure you I shall get in with the greatest ease, even if I'm not coached for a day more. A great many fellows here haven't a tutor at all.—I remain, your affectionate son,

"A. J. MORTIMER.

"P.S.—Will you tell Gladys that my three puppies, which she says are growing nicely, are not, on any account, to be given away; and will you say that Swan is not to drown them, or do anything with them, till I've chosen one, and then he may sell the

N

others. And I hope my nails and screws and my tools have not been meddled with. The children are not to take my things. It often makes me miserable to think that they get my nails and my paddle when I'm gone."

John Mortimer smiled, and felt rather inclined to let the boy come home, when, looking up, he observed that his father was dozing over the newspaper, and that he shivered.

Master Augustus John did not get an answer so soon as he had hoped for it, and when it came it was dated from a little, quiet place at the seaside, and let him know that his grandfather was very poorly, very much out of sorts, and that his father had felt uneasy about him. Johnny was informed that he must try to be happy, spending the Easter holidays at his tutor's. His grandfather sent him a very handsome "tip," and a letter written in such a shaky hand, that the boy was a good deal impressed, and locked it up in his desk, lest he should never have another.

CHAPTER XV.

THE AMERICAN GUEST.

"Shall we rouse the night-owl with a catch that will draw three souls out of one weaver?"

IN less than a week from the receipt of his son's letter, John Mortimer wrote again, and gave the boy leave to come home, but on no account to bring young Crayshaw with him, if a journey was likely to do him harm.

Johnny accordingly set off instantly (the holidays having just begun), and, travelling all night, reached the paternal homestead by eight o'clock in the morning.

His father was away, but he was received with rapture by his brothers and sisters. His little brothers admired him with the humble reverence of small boys for big ones, and the girls delighted in his school-boy slang, and thought themselves honoured by his companionship.

Crayshaw was an American by birth, but his elder brother (under whose guardianship he was) had left him in England as his best chance of living to manhood, for he had very bad health, and the climate of his native place did not suit him.

Young Gifford Crayshaw had a general invitation to spend the holidays at Brandon's house, for his brother and Brandon were intimate friends; but boys being dull alone, Johnny Mortimer and he contrived at these times to meet rather often, sometimes to play, sometimes to fight—even the latter is far better than being without companionship, more natural, and on the whole more cheerful.

"And I'm sure," said Aunt Christie, when she heard he was coming, "I should never care about the mischief he leads the little ones into when he's well, if he could breathe like other people when he's ill; you may hear him half over the house when he has his asthma."

Crayshaw came by the express train in the afternoon, and was met by the young Mortimers in the close carriage. He was nearly fifteen, and a strange contrast to Johnny, whose perfect health, ardent joyousness, and lumbering proportions never were so observable as beside the clear-cut face of the other, the slow gait, an expression of countenance at once audacious, keen, and sweet, together with that peculiar shadow under the eyelids which some people consider to betoken an early death.

Crayshaw was happily quite well that afternoon, and accordingly very noisy doings went on; Miss Crampton was away for her short Easter holiday, and Aunt Christie did not interfere if she could help it when Johnny was at home.

That night Master Augustus John Mortimer, his friend, and all the family were early asleep; not so the next. It was some time past one o'clock A.M. when John Mortimer and Brandon, who had been dining together at a neighbour's house, one having left his father rather better, and the other having come home from the Isle of Wight, walked up towards the house deep in conversation, till John, lifting up his eyes, saw lights in the schoolroom windows. This deluded father calmly remarked that the children had forgotten to put the lamp out when they went to bed. Brandon thought he heard a sound uncommonly like infant revelry, but he said nothing, and the two proceeded into the closed house, and went softly up-stairs.

"Roast pork," said Brandon, "if ever I smelt that article in my life!"

They opened the schoolroom door, and John beheld, to his extreme surprise, a table spread, his eldest son at the head of it, his twin daughters, those paragons of good behaviour, peeling potatoes, and the other children, all more or less dishevelled, sitting round, blushing and discomfited.

"My dears!" exclaimed John Mortimer, "this I never could have believed of you! One o'clock in the morning!"

Perfect silence. Brandon thought John would find it beneath his dignity to make a joke of this breach of discipline. He was rather vexed that he should have helped to discover it, and feeling a little *de trop*, he advanced to the top of the table. "John," he said with a resigned air and with a melancholy cadence in his voice that greatly impressed the children.

"Come," thought John as he paused, "they deserve a 'wigging,' but I don't want to make a 'Star-chamber matter' of this. I wish he would not be so supernaturally serious."

"John," repeated Brandon, "on occasion of this unexpected hospitality, I feel called upon to make a speech."

John sat down, wondering what would come next.

"John, ladies and gentlemen," said Brandon, "when I look around me on these varied attractions, when I behold those raspberry turnovers of a flakiness and a puffiness so ethereal, that one might think the very eyes of the observer should drop lightly on them, lest that too appreciative glance should flatten them down—I say, ladies and gentlemen, when I smell that crackling, when I cast my eyes on those cinders in the gravy, I am irresistibly reminded of occasions when I myself, arrayed in a holland pinafore, have presided over like entertainments; and of one in particular when, being of tender age—of one occasion, I say, that is never to be forgotten, when, during the small hours of the night, I was hauled out of bed to assist in mixing hardbake, by one very dear to us all—who shall be nameless."

What more he would have added will never be known, for with ringing laughter that spoke for the excellence of their lungs, the whole tableful of young Mortimers, with the exception of Johnnie, rose, and, as if by one impulse, fell upon their father.

"Hold hard," he was heard to shout, "don't smother me." But he received a kissing and hugging of great severity; the elder ones who had understood Brandon's speech, closing him in; the little ones, who only perceived to their delight that the occasion had become festive again, hovering round, and getting at him where they could. So that when they parted, and he was visible again, sitting radiant in the midst of them, his agreeable face was very red, and he was breathing fast and audibly. "I'll pay you for this!" he exclaimed, when he observed, to his amusement, that Brandon's serious look was now really genuine, as if he was afraid the experiment might be repeated on himself. "Johnnie, my boy, shake hands, I forgive you this once. And you may pass the bottle." Johnnie, who knew himself to be the real offender, made haste to obey. "It's not blacking, of course," continued John, looking at the thick liquor with distrust.

"The betht black currant," exclaimed his heir, "at thirteen-penth a bottle."

"And where's Cray?" exclaimed John, suddenly observing the absence of his young guest.

"He's down in the kitchen, dishing up the pudding," said Barbara blushing, and she darted out of the room, and presently returned, other footsteps following hers.

"Cray," exclaimed John, as the boy seemed inclined to linger outside, "don't stand there in the draught.

And so it is not by your virtuous inclinations that you have hitherto been excluded from this festive scene?"

"No, sir," said Crayshaw with farcical meekness of voice and air, "quite the contrary. It was that I've met with a serious accident. I've been run over."

John looked aghast. "You surely have not been into the loose-box," he said anxiously.

"Oh no, father, nothing of the sort," said Barbara. "It was only that he was down in the kitchen on his knees, and two blackbeetles ran over his legs. You should never believe a word he says, father."

"But that was the reason the pudding came to grief," continued Crayshaw; "they were very large and fierce, and in my terror I let it fall, and it was squashed. When I saw their friends coming on to fall upon it, I was just about to cry, 'Take it all, but spare my life!' when Barbara came and rescued me. I hope," he went on, yet more meekly, "I hope it was not an unholy self-love that prompted me to prefer my life to the pudding!"

The children laughed, as they generally did when Crayshaw spoke, but it was more at his manner than at his words. And now, peace being restored, everybody helped everybody else to the delicacies, John discreetly refraining from any inquiry as to whether this was the first midnight feast over which his son had presided, but he could not forbear to say, "I suppose your grandfather's 'tip' is to blame for this?"

"If everybody was like the Grand," remarked Crayshaw, "Tennyson never need have said—

'Vex not thou the schoolboy's soul
With thy shabby *tip*.'"

"Now, Cray," said Brandon, "don't you emulate Valentine's abominable trick of quoting."

"And I have often begged you two not to parody the Immortals," said John. "The small fry you may make fun of, if you please, but let the great alone."

"But he ithn't dead," reasoned Master Augustus John; "I don't call any of thoth fellowth immortal till they're dead."

"It's a very bad habit," continued his father.

"And he's made me almost as bad as himself," observed Crayshaw in the softest and mildest of tones. "Miss Christie said this very morning that there was no bearing me, and I never did it till I knew him. I used to be so good, everybody loved me."

John laughed, but was determined to say his say. "You never can take real pleasure again in any poetry that you have mauled in that manner. Miss Crampton was seriously annoyed when she found that you had altered the girl's songs, and made them ridiculous."

The last time, in fact, that Johnnie and Crayshaw had been together, they had deprived themselves of their natural rest in order to carry out these changes; and the first time Miss Crampton gave a music lesson after their departure, she opened the book at one of their improved versions, which ran as follows:—

> "Wink to me only with thy nose,
> And I will sing through mine."

Miss Crampton hated boyish vulgarity; she turned the page, but matters were no better. The two youths had next been at work on a song in which a muff of a man, who offers nothing particular in return, requests 'Nancy' to gang wi' him, leaving her home, her dinner, her brooches, her best gowns, &c., behind, to walk through snow-drifts, blasts, and other perils by his side, and afterwards strew flowers on his clay. Desirous as it seemed to show that the young person was not so misguided as her silence has hitherto left the world to think, they had added a verse, which ran as follows:—

> "'Ah, wilt thou thus, for his loved sake,
> All manner of hardships dare to know?'
> The fair one smiled whenas he spake,
> And promptly answered, 'No, sir; no.'"

"Cray," said John Mortimer, observing the boy's wan appearance, "how could you think of sitting up so late?"

"Why, the thupper wath on purpoth for him," exclaimed Johnnie. "We gave it in hith honour, ath a mark of thympathy."

"Because he was burnt out," said Gladys. "Papa, did you know? his tutor's house was burnt down, and the boys had to escape in the night."

"But it wath a great lark," observed Johnnie, "and he knowth he thought tho."

"Yes," said Crayshaw, folding his hands with farcical mock meekness, "but I saved hardly anything — nothing whatever, in fact, but my Yankee accent, and that only by taking it between my teeth."

"There was not enough of it to be worth saving, my dear boy," said Brandon.

Crayshaw's face for once assumed a genuine expression, one of alarm. He was distinguished at school for the splendid Yankee dialect he could put on, as Johnnie was for his mastery of a powerful Devonshire lingo; but if scarcely a hint of his birthplace remained in his daily speech, and he had not noticed any change, there was surely danger lest this interesting accomplishment should be declining also.

"I am always imitating the talk I hear in the cottages," he remarked; "I may have lost it so."

"Perhaps, as Cray goes to so many places, it may get scattered about," said little Bertram; but he was speedily checked by Johnnie, who observed with severity that they didn't want any "thrimp thauth."

"He mutht thimmer," said Johnnie, "thath what he mutht do. He mutht be thrown into an iron pot, with a gallon of therry cobbler, and a pumpkin pie, and thome baked beanth, and a copy of the Biglow Paperth, and a handful of thalt, and they mutht all thimmer together till he geth properly flavoured again."

"Wouldn't it be safer if he was only dipped in?" asked the same "shrimp" who had spoken before.

As this was the second time he had taken this awful liberty, he would probably have been dismissed the assembly but for the presence of his father. As it was, Johnnie and Crayshaw both looked at him, not fiercely but steadily, whereupon the little fellow with deep blushes slid gently from his chair under the table.

A few days after this midnight repast, Emily, knowing that John Mortimer was away a good deal, and having a perfectly gratuitous notion that his children must be dull in consequence, got Valentine to drive her over one morning to invite them to spend a day at Brandon's house.

A great noise of shouting, drumming on battledores, and blowing through discordant horns, let them know, as they came up the lane, that the community was in a state of high activity; and when they reached the garden gate they were just in time to see the whole family vanish round a corner, running at full speed after a donkey on which Johnnie was riding.

The visitors drove inside the gate, and waited five minutes, when the donkey, having made the circuit of the premises, came galloping up, the whole tribe of young Mortimers after him. They received Emily with loving cordiality, and accounted for the violent exercise they had been taking by the declaration that this donkey never would go at all, unless he heard a great noise and clatter at his heels.

"So that if Johnnie wanted to go far, as far as to London," observed one of the panting family, "it would be awkward, wouldn't it?"

"And he's only a second-hand donkey, either," exclaimed little Janie in deep disparagement of the beast; "father bought him of the blacksmith."

"But isn't it good fun to see him go so fast?" cried another. "Would you like to see our donkey do it again?"

"And see him 'witch the world with noble ass-manship," said Valentine.

Whereupon a voice above said rather faintly, "Hear, hear!" and Crayshaw appeared leaning out of a first-floor window, the pathetic shadow more than commonly evident in his eyes, in spite of a mischievous smile. He had but lately recovered from a rheumatic fever, and was further held down by frequent attacks of asthma. Yet the moment one of these went off, the elastic spirits of boyhood enabled him to fling it into the background of his thoughts, and having rested awhile, as he was then doing, he became, according to the account Gladys gave of him at that moment, "just like other boys, only ten times more so!"

Emily now alighted, and as they closed about her and hemmed her in, donkey and all, she felt inclined to move her elbows gently, as she had sometimes seen John do, in order to clear a little space about him. "Why does not Cray come down, too?" she asked.

"I think he has had enough of the beast," said Barbara, "for yesterday he was trying to make him jump; but the donkey and Cray could not agree about it. He would not jump, and at last he pitched Cray over his head."

"Odd," said Valentine; "that seems a double contradiction to the proverb that 'great wits jump.'" Valentine loved to move off the scene, leaving a joke with his company. He now drove away, and Johnnie informed Emily that he had already been hard at work that morning.

"I've a right to enjoy mythelf after it," he added, looking round in a patronising manner, "and I have. I've not had a better lark, in fact, since Grand was a little boy."

By these kind, though preposterous words, the assembly was stimulated to action. The frightful clatter, drumming, and blowing of horns began again, and the donkey set off with all his might, the Mortimers after him. When he returned, little Bertram was seated on his back. "Johnnie and Cray have something very particular to do," she was informed with gravity.

"For their holiday task?"

"Oh no, for that lovely electrifying machine of cousin Val's. Cray is always writing verses; he is going to be a poet. Johnnie was saying last week that it was not at all hard to turn poetry into Latin, and Val said he should have the machine if he could translate some that Cray wrote the other day. Do you think the Romans had any buttons and buttonholes?"

"I don't know. Why?"

"Because there are buttons in one of the poems. Cray says it is a tribute—a tribute to this donkey that father has just given us. He was inspired to write it when he saw him hanging his head over the yard gate."

Thereupon the verses, copied in a large childish hand, were produced and read aloud:—

A TRIBUTE.

The jackass brayed;
And all his passionate dream was in that sound
Which, to the stables round
And other tenements, told of packs that weighed
On his brown haunches; also that, alas!
His true heart sighed for Jenny, that fair ass
Who backward still and forward paced
With panniers and the curate's children graced.
Then, when she took no heed, but turned aside
Her head, he shook his ears
As much as to say "Great are—as these—my fears."
And while I wept to think how love that preyed
On the deep heart not worth a button seemed
To her for whom he dreamed;
And while the red sun stained the welkin wide,
And summer lightnings on the horizon played,
Again the jackass brayed.

"And here's the other," said Gladys. "Johnnie

says, it would be much the easier to do, only he is doubtful about the 'choker.'"

THE SCHOOLBOY TO HIS DRESS SUIT.

Nice is broiled salmon, whitebait's also nice
  With bread and butter served, no shaving thinner.
Entrées are good; but what is even ice—
  Cream ice—to him that's made to dress for dinner?
Oh my dress boots, my studs, and my white tie
  Termed choker (emblem of this heart's pure aim),
Why are good things to eat your meed? Oh why
  Must swallow-tails be donned for tasting game?
The deep heart questions vainly,—not for ease
  Or joy were such invented;—but this know,
I'd rather dine off hunks of bread and cheese
  Than feast in state rigged out in my dress clo'.

G. C.

Emily, after duly admiring these verses, gave her invitation, and it was accepted with delight. Nothing, they said, could be more convenient. Father had told them how Mr. Brandon was having the long wing of the house pulled down, the part where cousin Val's room used to be; so he had been obliged to turn out his nests, and his magic lantern, and many other things that he had when he was a little boy.

"And he says we shall inherit them."

"And when father saw him sitting on a heap of bricks among his things, he says it put him in mind of Marius on the ruins of Carthage."

"So now we can fetch them all away."

Emily then departed, after stipulating that the two little ones, her favourites, should come also. "Darlings!" she exclaimed, when she saw their stout little legs so actively running to ask Miss Christie's leave. "Will my boy ever look at me with such clear earnest eyes? Shall I ever see such a lovely flush on his face, or hear such joyous laughter from him?"

Time was to answer this question for her, and a very momentous month for the whole family began its course. Laura, writing from Paris to Liz, made it evident to those who knew anything of the matter, that Mrs. Melcombe, as she thought, had carried her out of harm's way; and it is a good thing Laura did not know with what perfect composure and ambitious hope Joseph made his preparations for the voyage. The sudden change of circumstances and occupation, and the new language he had to learn, woke him thoroughly from his dream, and though it had been for some long time both deep and strong, yet it was to him now as other dreams "when one awaketh;" and Laura herself, now that she had been brought face to face, not with her lover, but with facts, was much more reasonable than before. Brandon had said to her pointedly, in the presence of her sister-in-law, "If you and this young man had decided to marry, no law, human or divine, could have forbidden it." But at the same time Amelia had said, "Laura, you know very well that though you love to make romances about him, you would not give up one of the comforts of life for his sake."

Laura, in fact, had scarcely believed in the young man's love till she had been informed that it was over. She longed to be sought more than she cared to be won; it soothed and comforted what had been a painful sense of disadvantage to know that one man at least had sighed for her in vain. He would not have been a desirable husband, but as a former lover she could feign him what she pleased, and while, under new and advantageous circumstances, he became more and more like what she feigned, it was not surprising that in the end she forgot her feigning, and found her feet entangled for good and all in the toils she herself had spread for them.

In the meantime Johnnie and Crayshaw, together with the younger Mortimers, did much as they liked, till Harrow school reopened, when the two boys returned, departing a few hours earlier than was necessary that they might avoid Miss Crampton, a functionary whom Johnny held in great abhorrence.

At the same period Grand suddenly rallied, and, becoming as well as ever, his son, who had made many journeys backwards and forwards to see him, brought him home, buying at the railway station, as he stepped into his father's carriage, the *Times* and the *Wigfield Advertiser*, and *True Blue*, in each of which he saw a piece of news that concerned himself, though it was told with a difference.

In the *Times* was the marriage of Giles Brandon, Esq., &c., to Dorothea, elder daughter of Edward Graham, Esq.; and in the local paper, with an introduction in the true fustian style of mock concealment, came the same announcement, followed by a sufficiently droll and malicious account of the terrible inconvenience another member of this family had suffered a short time since by being snowed up, in which state he still continued, as snow in that part of the world had forgotten how to melt.

A good deal that was likely to mortify Valentine followed this, but it was no more than he deserved.

John laughed. "Well, Giles is a dear fellow," he said, throwing down the paper. "I am pleased at his marriage, and they must submit to be laughed at like other people."

CHAPTER XVI.

WEARING THE WILLOW.

> "My Lord Sebastian,
> The truth you speak doth lack some gentleness
> And time to speak it in; you rub the sore
> When you should bring the plaster."
> *The Tempest.*

WHEN John Mortimer reached the banking-house next morning, he found Valentine waiting for him in his private sitting-room.

"I thought my uncle would hardly be coming so early, John," he said, "and that perhaps you would spare me a few minutes to talk things over."

"To be sure," said John, and looking more directly at Valentine, he noticed an air of depression and gloom which seemed rather too deep to be laid to the account of the *True Blue.*

He was stooping as he sat, and slightly swinging his hat by the brim between his knees. He had reddened at first, with a sullen and half-defiant expression, but this soon faded, and, biting his lips, he brought himself with evident effort to say—

"Well, John, I've done for myself, you see; Giles has married her. Serves me right, quite right. I've nothing to say against it."

"No, I devoutly hope you have not," exclaimed John, to whom the unlucky situation became evident in an instant.

"Grand always has done me the justice to take my part as regards my conduct about this hateful second engagement. He always knew that I would have married poor Lucy if they would have let me—married her and made the best of my frightful, shameful mistake. But as you know, Mrs. Nelson, Lucy's mother, made me return her letters a month ago, and said it must be broken off, unless I would let it go dragging on and on for two years at least, and that was impossible, you know, John, because—because, I so soon found out what I'd done."

"Wait a minute, my dear fellow," John interrupted hastily, "you have said nothing yet but what expresses very natural feelings. I remark, in reply, that your regret at what you have long seen to be unworthy conduct need no longer disturb you on the lady's account, she having now married somebody else."

"Yes," said Valentine, sighing restlessly.

"And," John went on, looking intently at him, "on your own account I think you need not at all regret that you had no chance of going and humbly offering yourself to her again, for I feel certain that she would have considered it insulting her to suppose she could possibly overlook such a slight. Let me speak plainly, and say that she could have regarded such a thing in no other light."

Then, giving him time to think over these words, which evidently impressed him, John presently went on, "It would be ridiculous, however, now, for Dorothea to resent your former conduct, or St. George either. Of course they will be quite friendly towards you, and you may depend upon it that all this will very soon appear as natural as possible; you'll soon forget your former relation towards your brother's wife; in fact you must."

Valentine was silent awhile, but when he did speak he said, "You feel sure, then, that she would have thought such a thing an insult?" He meant, you feel sure, then, that I should have had no chance even if my brother had not come forward.

"Perfectly sure," answered John with confidence. "That was a step which, from the hour you made it, you never could have retraced."

Here there was another silence; then—

"Well, John, if you think so," said the poor fellow —"this was rather a sudden blow to me, though."

John pitied him; he had made a great fool of himself, and he was smarting for it keenly. His handsome young face was very pale, but John was helping him to recollect his better self, and he knew it. "I shall not allude to this any more," he continued.

"I'm very glad to hear you say so," said John.

"I came partly to say — to tell you that now I am better, quite well, in fact, I cannot live at home any longer. At home! Well, I meant in St. George's house, any longer."

The additional knowledge John had that minute acquired of the state of Valentine's feeling, or what he supposed himself to feel, gave more than usual confidence and cordiality to his answer.

"Of course not. You will be considering now what you mean to do, and my father and I must help you. In the first place there is that two thousand pounds; you have never had a shilling of it yet. My father was speaking of that yesterday."

"Oh," answered Valentine, with evident relief, and with rather a bitter smile, "I thought he proposed to give me that as a wedding present, and if so, goodness knows I never expect to touch a farthing of it."

"That's as hereafter may be," said John, leading him away from the dangerous subject. Valentine began every sentence with a restless sigh.

"I never chose to mention it," he remarked. "I had no right to consider it as anything else, nor did I."

"He does not regard it in any such light," said John. "He had left it to you in his will, but decided afterwards to give it now. You know he talks of his death, dear old man, as composedly as of to-morrow morning. He was reminding me of this money the other day when he was unwell, and saying that, married or unmarried, you should have it made over to you."

"I'm very deeply, deeply obliged to him," said Valentine, with a fervour that was almost emotion. "It seems, John, as if that would help me,—might get me out of the scrape, for I really did not know where to turn. I've got nothing to do, and had nothing to live on, and I'm two and twenty."

"Yes."

"I do feel as if I was altogether in such an ignominious position."

As John quite agreed with him in this view of his position, he remained silent.

Valentine went on, "First, my going to Cambridge came to nothing on account of my health. Then a month ago, as I didn't want to go and live out in New Zealand by myself, couldn't in fact, the New Zealand place was transferred to Liz, and she and Dick are to go to it, Giles saying that he would give me a thousand pounds instead of it. I shall not take that, of course."

"Because he will want his income for himself," John interrupted.

Valentine proceeding, "And now since I left off learning to farm,—for that's no use here,—I've got nothing on earth to do."

"Have you thought of anything yet?"

"Yes."

"Well, out with it."

"John," remarked Valentine, as the shadow of a smile flitted across John's face, "you always seem to me to know what a fellow is thinking of! Perhaps you would not like such a thing,—wouldn't have it?"

John observed that he was getting a little less gloomy as he proceeded.

"But whether or not, that two thousand pounds

will help me to some career, certainly, and entirely save me from what I could not bear to think of, *her* knowing that I was dependent on Giles, and despising me for it."

"Pooh," exclaimed John, a little chafed at his talking in this way, "what is St. George's wife likely to know, or to care, as to how her brother-in-law derives his income? But I quite agree with you that you have no business to be dependent on Giles; he has done a great deal for his sisters he should now have his income for himself."

"Yes," said Valentine.

"You have always been a wonderfully united family," observed John pointedly; "there is every reason why that state of things should continue."

"Yes," repeated Valentine, receiving the covert lecture resignedly.

"And there is no earthly end, good or bad, to be served," continued John, "by the showing of irritation or gloom on your part, because your brother has chosen to take for himself what you had previously and with all deliberation thrown away."

"I suppose not, John," said Valentine quite humbly.

"Then what can you be thinking of?"

"I don't know."

"You have not talked to any one as you have done to me this morning?"

"No, certainly not."

"Well, then, decide while the game is in your own hand that you never will."

So far from being irritated or sulky at the wigging that John was bestowing on him, Valentine was decidedly the better for it. The colour returned to his face, he sat upright in his chair, and then he got up and stood on the rug, as if John's energy had roused him, and opened his eyes also, to his true position.

"You don't want to cover yourself with ridicule, do you?" continued John, seeing his advantage.

"Why, even if you cared to take neither reason, nor duty, nor honour into the question, surely the only way to save your own dignity from utter extinction is to be, or at least seem to be, quite indifferent as to what the lady may have chosen to do, but very glad that your brother should have taken a step which makes it only fair to you that he and his wife should forget your former conduct."

"John," said Valentine, "I acknowledge that you are right."

John had spoken quite as much, indeed more, in Brandon's interest than in Valentine's. The manner in which the elder had suffered the younger to make himself agreeable and engage himself to Dorothea Graham, and how, when he believed she loved him, he had made it possible for them to marry, were partly known to him and partly surmised. And now it seemed in mockery of everything that was decent, becoming, and fair that the one who had forsaken her should represent himself as having waked, after a short delusion, and discovered that he loved her still, letting his brother know this, and perhaps all the world. Such would be a painful and humiliating position also for the bride. It might even affect the happiness of the newly-married pair; but John did not wish to hint at these graver views of the subject; he was afraid to give them too much importance, and he confidently reckoned on Valentine's volatile disposition to stand his friend, and soon enable him to get over his attachment. All that seemed wanting was some degree of present discretion.

"John, I acknowledge that you are right," repeated Valentine, after an interval of thought.

"You acknowledge—now we have probed this subject and got to the bottom of it—that it demands of you absolute silence, and at first some discretion?"

"Yes; that is settled."

"You mean to take my view?"

"Yes, I do."

As he stood some time lost in thought, John let him alone and began to write, till, thinking he had pondered enough, he looked up and alluded to the business Valentine had come about.

"You may as well tell it me, unless you want to take my father into your council also: he will be here soon."

"No; I thought it would be more right if I spoke to you first, John, before my uncle heard of it," said Valentine.

"Because it is likely to concern me longer?" asked John.

"Yes; you see what I mean; I should like, if uncle and you would let me, to go into the bank; I mean as a clerk—nothing more, of course."

"I should want some time to consider that matter," said John. "I was half afraid you would propose this, Val. It's so like you to take the easiest thing that offers."

"Is it on my account or on your own that you shall take time?"

"On both. So far as you are concerned, it is no career to be a banker's clerk."

"No; but, John, though I hardly ever think of it, I cannot always forget that there is only one life between me and Melcombe."

"Very true," said John coolly; "but if it is ill waiting for a dead man's shoes, what must it be waiting for a dead child's shoes?"

"I do not even wish or care to be ever more than a clerk," said Valentine; "but that, I think, would fill up my time pleasantly."

"Between this and what?"

"Between this and the time when I shall have finally decided what I will do. I think eventually I shall go abroad."

John knew by this time that he would very gladly not have Valentine with him, or rather under him;

but an almost unfailing instinct, where his father was concerned, assured him that the old man *would* like it.

"Shall I speak to my father about it for you?" he said.

"No, John, by no means, if you do not like it. I would not be so unfair as let him have a hint of it till you have taken the time you said you wanted."

"All right," said John; "but where, in case you became a clerk here, do you propose to live?"

"Dick A'Court lived in lodgings for years," said Valentine, "so does John A'Court now, over the pastrycook's in the High Street."

"And you think you could live over the shoemaker's?"

"Why not?"

"I have often met Dick meekly carrying home small parcels of grocery for himself. I should like to catch you doing anything of the sort!"

"I believe I can do anything now. I have learned to leave off quoting. I used to be always doing it, and to please Dorothea I have quite given it up."

"Well," said John, "let that pass."

He knew as well as possible what would be his father's wish, and he meant to let him gratify it. He was a good son, and, as he had everything completely in his own power, he may be said to have been very indulgent to his father, but the old man did not know it any more than he did.

Mr. Augustus Mortimer had a fine house, handsomely appointed and furnished. From time to time, as his son's family had increased, he had added accommodation. There was an obvious nursery; there was an evident school-room, perfectly ready for the son, and only waiting, he often thought, till it should be said to his father, "Come up higher."

It was one of John's theories that there should be a certain homely simplicity in the dress, food, and general surroundings of youthful humanity; that it should not have to walk habitually on carpets so rich that little dusty feet must needs do damage, and appear intruders; nor be made to feel all day that somebody was disturbed if somebody else was making himself happy according to his lights, and in his own fashion.

But of late Mr. Augustus Mortimer had begun to show a degree of infirmity which sometimes made his son uncomfortable that he should have to live alone. To bring those joyous urchins and little, laughing, dancing, playful girls into his house was not to be thought of. What was wanted was some young relative to live with him, who would drive him into the town and home again, dine with him, live in his presence, and make his house cheerful. In short, as John thought the matter over, he perceived that it would be a very good thing for his father to have Valentine as an inmate, and that it would be everything to Valentine to be with his father.

People always seemed to manage comfortable homes for Valentine, and make good arrangements for him, as fast as he brought previous ones to nought.

Very few sons like to bring other people into their fathers' houses, specially in the old age of the latter; but John Mortimer was not only confident of his own supreme influence, but he was more than commonly attached to his father, and had long been made to feel that on his own insight and forethought depended almost all that gave the old man pleasure.

His father seldom disturbed any existing arrangements, though he often found comfort from their being altered for him; so John decided to propose to him to have his brother's son to live with him. In a few days, therefore, he wrote to Valentine that he had made up his mind, and would speak to his father for him, which he did, and saw that the nephew's wish gave decided pleasure; but when he made his other proposal he was quite surprised (well as he knew his father) at the gladness it excited, at those thanks to himself for having thought of such a thing, and at certain little half-expressed hints which seemed intended to meet and answer any future thoughts his son might entertain as to Valentine's obtaining more influence than he would approve. But John was seldom surprised by an after-thought; he was almost always happy enough to have done his thinking beforehand.

He was in the act of writing a letter to Valentine the next morning at his own house, and was there laying the whole plan before him, when he saw him driving rapidly up to the door in the little pony chaïse, now the only carriage kept at Brandon's house. He sprang out as if in urgent haste, and burst into the room in a great hurry.

"John," he exclaimed, "can you lend me your phaeton, or give me a mount as far as the junction? Fred Walker has had one of his attacks, and Emily is in a terrible fright. She wants another opinion: she wishes Dr. Limpsey to be fetched, and she wants Grand to come to her."

This last desire, mentioned as the two hurried together to the stable, showed John that Emily apprehended danger.

Emily's joyous and impassioned nature, though she lived safely, as it were, in the middle of her own sweet world—saw the best of it, made the best of it, and coloured it all, earth and sky, with her tender hopefulness—was often conscious of something yet to come, ready and expectant of *the rest of it.* The rest of life, she meant; the rest of sorrow, love, and feeling.

She had a soul full of unused treasures of emotion, and pure, clear depths of passion that as yet slumbered unstirred. If her heart was a lute, its highest and lowest chords had never been sounded hitherto. This also she was aware of, and she knew what their music would be like when it came.

She had been in her girlhood the chief idol of

many hearts; but joyous, straightforward, and full of childlike sweetness, she had looked on all her adorers in such an impartially careless fashion, that not one of them could complain. Then, having confided to John Mortimer's wife that she could get up no enthusiasm for any of them, and thought there could be none of that commodity in her nature, she had at last consented, on great persuasion, to take the man who had loved her all her life, "because he wouldn't go away, and she didn't know what else to do with him; he was such a devoted little fellow, too, and she liked him so much better than either of his brothers!"

So they were married; Captain Walker was excessively proud and happy in his wife, and Mrs. Walker was as joyous and sweet as ever. She had satisfied the kindly pity which for a long while had made her very uncomfortable on his account; and, O happy circumstance! she became in course of time the mother of the most attractive, wonderful, and interesting child ever born. In the eyes, however, of the invidious world, he was uncommonly like his plain sickly father, and not, with that exception, at all distinguished from other children.

John made haste to send Valentine off to the junction, undertook himself to drive his father over to see Emily, and gathered from the short account Valentine gave whilst the horse was put too, that Fred Walker had been taken ill during the night with a fainting fit. He had come from India for his year's leave in a very poor state of health, and with apprehended heart disease. Only ten days previously Emily had persuaded him that it would be well to go to London for advice. But a fainting fit had taken place, and the medical man called in had forbidden this journey for the present. He had appeared to recover, so that there seemed to be no more ground for uneasiness than usual; but this second faintness had lasted long enough to terrify all those about him.

Grand was very fond of his late brother's step-daughter; she had always been his favourite, partly on account of her confiding ease and liking for him, partly because of the fervent religiousness that she had shown from a child.

The most joyous and gladsome natures are often most keenly alive to impressions of reverence, and wonder, and awe. Emily's mind longed and craved to annex itself to all things fervent, deep, and real. As she walked on the common grass, she thought the better of it because the feet of Christ had trodden it also. There were things which she—as the angels—"desired to look into;" but she wanted also to do the right thing, and to love the doing of it.

With all this half Methodistic fervour, and longing to lie close at the very heart of Christianity, she had by nature a strange fearlessness; her religion, which was full of impassioned loyalty, and her faith, which seemed to fold her in, had elements in them of curiosity and awed expectation, which made death itself appear something grand and happy, quite irrespective of a simply religious reason. It would show her "the rest of it." She could not do long without it; and often in her most joyous hours she felt that the crown of life was death's most grand hereafter.

CHAPTER XVII.

AN EASY DISMISSAL.

"Admired Miranda!
Indeed the top of admiration! worth
What's dearest to the world."
The Tempest.

"WELL, father, it's too true!"

"You don't say so?"

"Yes; he died, Dr. Mainby's housekeeper says, at five o'clock this morning. The doctor was there all night, and he's now come home, and gone to bed."

"One of the most unfortunate occurrences I ever heard of. Well, that that is, is—and can't be helped. I'd have given something (over and above the ten-and-sixpence) to have had it otherwise; but I 'spose, Jemmy, I 'spose we understand the claims of decency and humanity." It was the editor of the *True Blue* who said this.

"I 'spose we do," answered the son sturdily, though sulkily; "but that's the very best skit that Blank Blank ever did for us."

"Blank Blank" was the signature under which various satirical verses appeared in the *True Blue.*

"Paid for, too—ten-and-six. Well, here goes, Jemmy." He took a paper from his desk, read it over with a half smile. "One or two of the jokes in it will keep," he observed; then, when his son nodded assent, he folded it up and threw it in the fire. This was a righteous action. He never got any thanks for doing it; also a certain severity that he was inclined to feel against the deceased for dying just then, he quickly turned (from a sense of justice) towards the living members of his family, and from them to their party, the " pinks " in general. Then he began to moralise. " Captain Walker—and so he's dead—died at five o'clock this morning. It's very sudden. Why Mrs. Walker was driving him through the town three days ago."

" Yes," answered the son; " but when a man has heart complaint, you never know where you are with him."

A good many people in Wigfield and round it discussed that death during the day; but few, on the whole, in a kindlier spirit than had been displayed by the editor of the opposition paper. Mrs. A' Court, wife of the vicar, and mother of Dick A' Court, remarked that she was the last person to say anything unkind, but she did value consistency.

" Everybody knows that my Dick is a high churchman; they sent for him to administer the holy communion, and he found old Mr. Mortimer there, a layman, who is almost, I consider, a Methodist, he's so low church; and poor Captain Walker was getting him to pray extempore by his bed. Even afterward he wouldn't let him out of his sight. And Dick never remonstrated. Now, that is not what I could have hoped of my son; but when I told him so, he was very much hurt, said the old man was a saint, and he wouldn't interfere. 'Well, my dear,' I said, 'you must do as you please; but remember that your mother values consistency.' "

When Mrs. Melcombe, who, with her son and Laura, was still at Paris, heard of it, she also made a characteristic remark. " Dear me, how sad!" she exclaimed; " and there will be that pretty bride, Mrs. Brandon, in mourning for months, till all her wedding dresses, in fact, are out of fashion."

Mrs. Melcombe had left Melcombe while it was at its loveliest, all the hawthorns in flower, the peonies and lilies of the valley. She chose first to go to Paris, and then when Peter did not seem to grow, was thin and pale, she decided—since he never seemed so well as when he had no lessons to do—that she would let him accompany them on their tour.

Melcombe was therefore shut up again; and the pictures of Daniel Mortimer and the young lieutenant, his uncle, remained all the summer in the dark. But Wigfield House was no sooner opened after Captain Walker's funeral than back came the painters, cleaners, and upholsterers, to every part of it; and the whole place, including the garden, was set in order for the bride.

Emily was not able to have any of the rest and seclusion she so much needed; but almost immediately took her one child and went to stay with her late husband's father till she could decide where to live.

Love that has been received affects the heart which has lost it quite differently from a loss where the love has been bestowed. The remembrance of it warms the heart towards the dear lost donor; but if the recollection of life spent together is without remorse, if, as in Emily's case, the dead man has been wedded as a tribute to his acknowledged love, and if he has not only been allowed to bestow his love in peace without seeing any fault or failing that could give him one twinge of jealousy—if he has been considered, and liked thoroughly, and, in easy affectionate companionship, his wife has walked beside him, delighting him, and pleased to do so—then, when he is gone, comes, as the troubled heart calms itself after the alarms of death and parting, that one, only kind of sorrow which can ever be called with truth "the luxury of grief."

In her mourning weeds, when she reached Fred's father's house, Emily loved to sit with her boy on her lap, and indulge in passionate tears, thinking over how fond poor Fred had been, and how proud of her. There was no sting in her grief, no compunction, for she knew perfectly well how happy she had made him; and there was not the anguish of personal loss, and want, and bereavement.

She looked pale when she reached Mr. Walker's house, but not worn. She liked to tell him the details of his son's short illness; and the affectionate, irascible old man not only liked to hear them, but derived pleasure from seeing this fine young woman, this interesting widow, sitting mourning for his son. So he made much of her, and pushed her sister Louisa at once into the background for her sake.

The sisters having married twin brothers, Mr. Walker's elder sons, neither had looked on himself as heir to the exclusion of the other; but Emily's pale morsel of a child was at once made more important than his father had ever been. Louisa, staying also with her husband in the house, was only the expectant mother of a grandson for him; and the rich old man now began almost immediately to talk of how he should bring up Emily's boy, and what he should do for him—taking for granted, from the first, that his favourite daughter-in-law was to live with him and keep his house.

Louisa took this change in Mr. Walker very wisely and sweetly—did not even resent it, when, in the presence of his living son, he would aggravate himself into lamentations over the dead one, as if in him he had lost his all.

Sometimes he wondered a little himself at this quiescence—at the slight impression he seemed to make on his son, whom he had fully intended to rouse to remonstrance about it—at the tender way in which the young wife ministered to her sister, and at the great change for the worse that he soon began to observe in Emily's appearance.

Nobody liked to tell him the cause, and he would not see it; even when it became an acknowledged fact, which every one else talked of, that the little one was ill, he resolutely refused to see it; said the weather was against a child born in India—blamed the east wind. Even when the family doctor tried to let him know that the child was not likely to be long for this world, he was angry, with all the unreasonable volubility of a man who thinks others are deceiving him, rather than grieved for the peril of the little life and the anguish of the mother's heart.

Now came indeed "the rest of it." What a rending away of heart and life it seemed to let go the object of this absorbing, satisfying love! Now she was to lose, where the love had been bestowed; and she felt as if death itself was in the bitter cup.

It was not till the child was actually passing away, after little more than a fortnight's illness, that his grandfather could be brought to believe in his danger. He had been heaping promises of what he would do for him on the mother, as if to raise her courage. With kindly wrong-headed obstinacy he had collected and detailed to her accounts of how ill other children had been and had recovered, had been getting fresh medical opinions, and proposing to try new remedies; but no sooner was all over, and the afflicted mother was led from her dead child by his son, than he tormented himself and the doctors by demanding why he had been kept in the dark so long, why he had not been allowed to try change of air, why, if the symptoms showed mortal disease from the first, he had been allowed to set his heart on the child as he had done. No one now had anything to say to Emily. She had only been a widow a month, and the first loss had had no bitterness in it, though she had sorrowed with the tender affection of a loyal heart. The death of her child was almost the loss of all.

Valentine in the meantime had taken his sister Liz to a little quiet place; there, as her marriage could not be put off, and the ship was decided on in which they were to sail for New Zealand, he acted the part of father, and gave her away at the quietest wedding possible, seeing her off afterwards, and returning to take up his abode in his uncle's house, about three weeks after the death of Emily's little child. Not one of the late inhabitants had been left in his old home excepting Mrs. Henfrey, who remained to receive the bride, and was still there, though the newly-married pair had been home a week. Valentine had found ample time to consider how he should behave to Dorothea, Mrs. Brandon. He had also become accustomed to the thought of her being out of his reach, and the little excitement of wonder as to how they should meet was not altogether displeasing to him. "Giles will be inclined, no doubt, to be rather jealous of me," was his thought; "I shall be a bad fellow if I don't take care to show him that there is no need for it. D. must do the same. Of course she will. Sweet D.! Well, it can't be helped now."

It was natural enough that he should cogitate over the best way of managing his first meeting with them; but he had not been an hour in his uncle's house before he found that Grand was shortly going to give a great dinner party for the bride mainly consisting of relatives and very old friends. This, it was evident, would be the most natural time for him to present himself.

Valentine loved comfort and luxury, and finding himself established quite as if he had been a younger son in the house—a horse kept for him to ride, and a small sitting-room set aside in which he could see his friends—he experienced a glow of pleasure at first, and he soon perceived that his presence was a real pleasure to his old uncle; so, settling himself with characteristic ease in his place, he felt hourly more and more content with his new home.

It was not till he came down into the drawing-room before dinner on the day of the party that he began to feel excited and agitated. A good many of the guests were already present, he went up to one and to another, and then advanced to speak to Miss Christie, who was arrayed in a wonderful green gown, bought new for the occasion.

"Mr. and Mrs. Brandon," sounded clearly all down the long room, and he turned slowly and saw them. For one instant they appeared to be standing quite still, and so he often saw them side by side in his thoughts ever after. The bride looked serenely sweet, a delicate blush tinging her face, which was almost of infantine fairness and innocence; then old Grand's white head came in the way as he advanced to meet her and take her hand, bowing low with old-fashioned formality and courtesy. Several other people followed and claimed her acquaintance, so that they were closed in for the moment. Then he felt that now was the time for him to come forward, which he did, and as the others parted again to let Grand take her to a seat, they met face to face.

"Ah, Valentine," she said, so quietly, with such an unexcited air; she gave him her hand for a moment, and it was over. Then he shook hands with his brother, their eyes met, and though both tried hard to be grave, neither could forbear to smile furtively; but Giles was much the more embarrassed of the two.

During dinner, though Valentine talked and laughed, he could not help stealing a minute now and then to gaze at the bride, till John, darting a sudden look at him, brought him to his senses; but he cogitated about her, though he did not repeat the offence. "Is it lilac, or grey, or what, that she has on? That pale stuff must be satin, for it shines. Oh, meant for mourning perhaps. How wonderfully silent Giles is! How quiet they both are!"

This observation he made to himself several times during the evening, catching the words of one and the other whatever part of the room he was in, almost as distinctly as they did themselves; but he only looked once at Dorothea, when something made him feel or think that she had drawn her glove off. His eyes wandered then to her hand. Yes, it was so—there was the wedding ring.

With what difficulty, with what disgrace he had contrived to escape from marrying this young woman! His eyes wandered round the room. Just so she would have looked, and every one else would have looked, if this wedding dinner had been made for *his* bride, but he would not have been sitting up in the corner with three girls about him, laughing and making laugh. No, and he would not have stood rather remote from her, as Giles did. He thought he would have been proudly at her side. Oh, how could he have been such a fool? how could he? how could he?

"She would have loved me just as well, just so she would have lifted up her face, as she does now, and turned towards me."—No! The bride and her husband looked at one another for an instant, and in one beat of the heart he knew not only that no such look had ever been in her eyes for him, but he felt before he had time to reason his conviction down, that in all likelihood there never would have been. Then, when he found that Dorothea seemed scarcely aware of his presence, he determined to return the compliment, got excited, and was the life and soul of the younger part of the company. So that when the guests dispersed, many were the remarks they made about it.

"Well, young Mortimer need not have been quite so determined to show his brother how delighted he was not to be standing in his shoes." "Do you think Brandon married her out of pity?" "She is a sweet young creature. I never saw newly-married people take so little notice of one another. It must have been a trial to her to meet young Mortimer again, for no doubt she was attached to him."

A quarter of an hour after the bride had taken her

leave, and when all the other guests were gone, Valentine went into the hall, feeling very angry with himself for having forgotten that, as he was now a member of her host's family, he might with propriety have seen Dorothea into the carriage. "This," he thought, "shall not occur again."

The hall doors were open, servants stood about as if waiting still. He saw a man's figure. Some one, beyond the stream of lamplight which came from the house, stood on the gravel, where through a window he could command a view of the staircase.

It was little past eleven, the moon was up, and as the longest day was at hand, twilight was hardly over, and only one star here and there hung out of the heavens.

"Why, that is Giles," thought Valentine. "Strange! he cannot have sent Dorothea home alone, surely."

Giles approached the steps, and Valentine, following the direction of his eyes, saw a slender figure descending the stairs.

Dorothea! She was divested now of the shimmering satin and all her bridal splendour. How sweet and girlish she looked in this more simple array! Evidently they were going to walk home through the woods and lanes, see glow-worms and smell the hedge roses. For an instant Valentine was on the point of proposing to accompany them part of the way, but recollected himself just in time to withdraw into the shadow made by a stand of greenhouse plants, and from thence see Giles come up the steps, take the delicate ungloved hand and lay it on his arm, while the hall doors were closed behind them.

Adam and Eve were returning to Paradise on foot. The world was quite a new world. They wanted to see what it was like by moonlight, now they were married.

Valentine walked disconsolately up the stairs, and there at the head of them, through a wide-open door, he saw a maid. The pale splendours of Dorothea's gown were lying over her arm, and she was putting gold and pearls into a case. He darted past as quickly as he could, so glad to get out of sight, lest she should recognise him, for he shrewdly suspected that this was the same person who had been sent with Dorothea to Wigfield, when she first went there—one Mrs. Brand. So, in fact, it was; her husband was dead, she no longer sailed in old Captain Rollin's yacht, and Brandon had invited her to come and stay in the house a while, and see her young lady again.

How glad he was to get away and shelter himself in his own room!—an uncomfortable sensation this for a fine young man. "What should I have done but for Grand and John?" was his thought. Grand and John were very considerate the next day. In the first place, Grand scarcely mentioned the bride during breakfast; in fact, so far as appeared, he had forgotten the party altogether. John was also considerate, gave Valentine plenty to do, and in a way that made him feel the yoke, took him in hand and saw that he did it.

It is often a great comfort to be well governed. John had a talent for government, and under his dominion Valentine had the pleasure of feeling, for the first time in his life, that he had certain things to do which must and should be done, after which he had a full right to occupy himself as he pleased.

CHAPTER XVIII.

A MORNING CALL.

> "Learn now for all
> That I, which know my heart, do here pronounce
> By the very truth of it, I care not for you."—*Cymbeline.*

"JOHN," said Valentine, ten days after this dinner party, "you have not called on D. yet, nor have I."

"No," John answered, observing his wish, "and it might not be a bad plan for us to go together."

"Thank you, and if you would add the twins to —to make the thing easier and less formal."

"Nonsense," said John; "but yes, I'll take some of the children, for of course you feel awkward." He did not add, "You should not have made such a fool of yourself," lest Valentine should answer, "I devoutly wish I had not;" but he went on, "And why don't you say Dorothea, instead of using a nick-name?"

"I always used to call her D.," said Valentine.

"All the more reason why you should not now," answered John.

And Valentine murmured to himself—

"'These strong Egyptian fetters I must break, or lose myself in dotage' (*Antony and Cleopatra*)." This he added from old habit. "I'll quote everything I can think of to D., just to make her think I have forgotten her wish that I should leave off quoting; and if that is not doing my duty by St. George, I should like to know what is. Only that might put it into his head to quote too, and perhaps he might have the best of it. I fancy I hear him saying, 'Art thou learned?' I, as William, answer, 'No, sir.' 'Then learn this of me,' he makes reply, 'to have is to have; for all your writers do consent that *ipse* is he. Now you are not *ipse*, for I am he. He, sir, that hath married this woman. Therefore, you clown, abandon, which is—,' &c., &c. What a fool I am!"

John, adding the twins and little Bertram to the party, drove over on a Saturday afternoon, finding no one at home but Mrs. Henfrey.

"St. George," she said, "has taken to regular work, and sits at his desk all the morning, and for an hour or two in the afternoon, excepting on Saturday, when he gives himself a half-holiday, as if he was a schoolboy."

"And where was he now?" John asked.

"Somewhere about the place with Dorothea; he had been grubbing up the roots of the trees in a corner of the little wood at all leisure times; he thought of turning it into a vegetable garden."

"Why, we always had more vegetables than we could use," exclaimed Valentine, "and we were three times as large a family."

"Very true, my dear, but they are full of schemes—going to grow some vegetables, I think, and flowers, for one of the county hospitals. It would not be like him, you know, to go on as other people do."

"No," Valentine answered. "And he always loved a little hard work out of doors; he is wise to take it now, or he would soon get tired of stopping peaceably at home, playing Benedict in this dull place."

The children were then sent out to find where the young wife was, and come and report to their father, telling her that he would pay his call out of doors.

"And so you are still here, sister," observed Valentine, willing to change the subject, for he had been rather disconcerted by a quiet smile with which she had heard his last speech.

"Yes, my dear, the fact is, they won't let me go."

"Ah, indeed?"

"Of course I never thought they would want me. And the morning after they came home I mentioned that I had been looking out for a house—that small house that I consulted John about, and, in fact, took."

Mrs. Henfrey was hardly ever known to launch into narration. She almost always broke up her remarks by appeals to one and another of her listeners, and she now did not go on till John had made the admission that she had consulted him. She then proceeded with all deliberation—

"But you should have seen how vexed St. George looked. He had no idea, he said, that I should ever think of leaving him; and, indeed, I may mention to you in confidence, both of you, that he always drew for me what money I said was wanted for the bills, and he no more thought of looking at my housekeeping books than my father did."

"Really," said Valentine.

He was quite aware of this, to him, insignificant fact, but to have said more would only have put her out, and he wanted her to talk just then.

"And so," she continued slowly, "I said to him, I said, 'My dear Giles, I have had a pleasant home in this house, many, many years, indeed, ever since you were a child; but it is my opinion (and you will find it is the general opinion) that every young wife should have her house to herself.' I did not doubt at all that this was her opinion too; only I considered that as he had spoken so plainly, she might not like to say so."

"No, very likely not," said John, when she stopped, as if stranded, till somebody helped her on with a remark.

"You are quite right, John, any one might have thought so; but in a minute or two. 'Well,' said

St. George, 'this is rather a blow;' and what does that pretty creature do but come and sit by me, and begin to coax me. 'She wanted me so much, and it would be so kind if I would but stop and do as I always had done, and she would be so careful to please me, and she had always thought the house was so beautifully managed, and everything in such order, and so regular.'"

"So it is," Valentine put in. "She is quite right there."

"'And she didn't know how to order the dinner,' she said; and so she went on, till I said, 'Well, my dears, I don't wish that there should be any mistake about this for want of a little plain speaking.'"

"Well?" said John, when she came to a dead stop.

"And she said, 'You love St. George, don't you, just as much as if he was related to you?' 'How can any one help loving him?' 'And I know if you leave us he won't be half so comfortable. And nobody should ever interfere with you.' So I said I would keep their house for them, and you may suppose how glad I was to say it, for I'm like a cat, exactly like a cat—I don't like to leave a place that I am used to, and it would have been difficult for her to manage."

"Yes, very."

"I had often been thinking, when I supposed I had to go, that she would never remember to see that the table-linen was all used in its proper turn, and to have the winter curtains changed for white ones before the sun faded them."

"You're such a comfortable, dear thing to live with," observed Valentine, now the narrative was over. "Everybody likes you, you know."

Mrs. Henfrey smiled complacently, accepting the compliment. She was, to all strangers, an absolutely uninteresting woman; but her family knew her merits, and Giles and Valentine were both particularly alive to them.

"And so here I am," continued 'sister,' "but it is a pity for poor Emily, for she wanted me to live in that house, you know, John, with her."

"But I thought old Walker was devoted to her," said John.

"So he was, my dear, so long as her boy was with her; but now she is nobody, and I am told he shows a willingness to let her go, which is almost like dismissing her."

"I hope she will not get my old woman away to live with her," thought John, with a sudden start. "I don't know what I may be driven to, if she does. I shall have to turn out of my own house, or take the Golden Head into it by way of protection. No, not that! I'll play the man. But," he thought, continuing his cogitations, "Emily is too young and attractive to live alone, and what so natural as that she should ask her old aunt to come to her?"

John was still deeply cogitating on this knotty point when the children came back, and conducted him and Valentine to the place where Brandon was at work, and Dorothea sitting near him on a tree-stump knitting.

None of the party ever forgot that afternoon, but each remembered it as an appeal to his own particular circumstances. Brandon was deep in the contentment of a great wish fulfilled. The newly-perfected life was fresh and sweet, and something of reserve in the character and manners of his wife seemed to restrain him from using up the charm of it too fast. His restless and passionate nature was at once satisfied and kept in check by the freshness and moderation of hers. She received his devotion very quietly, made no demonstrations, but grew to him, laid up his confidences in her heart, and let him discover—though she never said it—that all the rest of the world was becoming as nothing for his sake. Accordingly it did not occur to him, excepting on Valentine's own account, to consider how he might feel during this interview. He noticed that he was a little sulky and perhaps rather out of countenance; he did not wonder at these things; but being absolutely secure of his wife's love, he never even said to himself how impossible it was that her affection should revert to Valentine; but this was for the simple reason that he had never thought about that matter at all. He talked to Valentine on indifferent subjects, and felt that he should be glad when he had got over the awkwardness he was then evidently enduring, for they had been accustomed, far more than most brothers, to live together on terms of familiar intimacy, and only one of them at present was aware that this could never be again.

Valentine also never forgot, but often saw that picture again with the fresh fulness of the leaves for a background to the girlish figure; and the fair face so innocent and candid and so obviously content. She was seated opposite to him, with Brandon on the grass close to her. In general they addressed each other merely by the Christian name, but just before John rose to take leave, Dorothea dropped her ball. It rolled a little way, and pointing it out to Brandon with her long wooden knitting-pin, she said, in a soft quiet tone, "Love, will you pick it up?" and Valentine, who had overheard the little speech, was inexpressibly hurt, almost indignant. He could not possibly have told why, but he hoped she did not say that often, and when Brandon gave it into her hand again, and said something to her that Valentine could not hear, he felt almost as if he had been unkindly used, as if his feelings had been insulted, and he vowed that it should be a long time before he came to see them again.

"It won't do," he thought to himself. "I see this means a great deal more than I ever thought it did. I thought Giles would be jealous, and I should have to set things in a light that would satisfy him; but it is I who am jealous, and he does not care what I feel at all. She is all I could wish; but I don't know whether looking at her is most bitter or most sweet."

As for John, he had walked down to the wood as usual, in full possession of his present self, and as he supposed of his future intentions, and yet, sitting opposite to these married lovers for a quarter of an hour, wrought a certain change in him that nothing ever effaced. It was an alien feeling to him to be overcome by a yearning discontent. Something never yet fed and satisfied made its presence known to him. It was not that sense which comes to all, sooner or later, that human life cannot give us what we expected of it, but rather a passionate waking to the certainty that he never even for one day had possessed what it might have given. He had never been endowed for one day with any deep love, with its keen perceptions and high companionship.

"Well, I suppose I didn't deserve it," he thought, half angrily, while he tried to trample the feeling down and stifle it. But his keener instincts soon rose up in him and let him know that he did deserve it. It was very extraordinary that he had not won it—there were few men, indeed, who deserved it half so well.

"But it's too late now," he chose to say to himself, as he drove home. "It's not in my line either to go philandering after any woman. Besides, I hate red hair. The next *Dissolution* I'll stand for the borough of Wigfield. Seven children to bring up, and one of them almost as big as myself—what a fool I am! What can I have been thinking of?"

"What are you laughing at, papa?" said Barbara, who was sitting beside him.

"Not at you, my darling," he replied; "for you are something real."

For the next few weeks neither he nor Valentine saw much of Dorothea: excepting at three or four dinners, they scarcely met at all. After this came the Harrow holidays. Johnny came home, and with him the inevitable Crayshaw. The latter was only to stay a week, and that week should have been spent with Brandon, but the boys had begged hard to be together, having developed a peculiar friendship for one another which seemed to have been founded on many fights, in consequence of which they had been strictly forbidden to meet.

This had taken place more than a year before, when Crayshaw, having been invited by John to spend the holidays with his boy, the two had quarrelled, and even fought, to such a degree that John at last in despair had taken Johnnie over to his grandfather's house, with the declaration that if he so much as spoke to Crayshaw again, or crossed the wide brook that ran between the two houses, he would fine him half-a-crown every time he did it.

"Ith all that hateful map," said young hopeful sulkily, when he was borne off to his banishment.

"You ought to be ashamed of yourself," quoth his father. "I don't care what it's about. You have no notion of hospitality. I won't have you fight with your guest."

Crayshaw was in very weak health, but full of mischief and fun. For a few days he seemed happy enough, then he flagged, and on the fifth morning he laid half-a-crown beside John's plate at breakfast.

"What's this for?" asked John.

"Because it is not fair that he should be fined, and not I."

"Put it in the missionary box," said John, who knew very well that the boys had been constructing a dam together all the previous day.

"It was about their possessions that they quarrelled," said Gladys in giving an account of the matter afterwards. "They made a plan that they would go into partnership, and conquer all the rest of the world; but when they looked at the great map up in Parliament, and Johnnie found how much the most he had got, he said Cray must annex Japan, or he would not join. Cray said it was against his principles. So they quarrelled, and fought once or twice; but perhaps it was just as well, for you know the rest of the world would rather not be conquered. Then, when they were fined for playing together, they did every day. They made a splendid dam over the brook, which was very low; but one night came a storm, father's meadows were flooded, they could not get the dam undone, and some sheep were drowned. So they went to Grand, and begged him to tell father, and get them off. They said it was a strange thing they were never to be together, and neither of them had got a penny left. So Grand got them forgiven, and we went all over the meadows for two or three days in canoes and punts."

And now these two desirable inmates were to be together for a week. A great deal can be done in a week, particularly by those who give their minds to it because they know their time is short. That process called turning the house out of windows took place when John was away. Aunt Christie, who did not like boys, kept her distance, but Miss Crampton being very much scandalized by the unusual noise, declared, on the second morning of these holidays, that she should go up into Parliament, and see what they were all about. Miss Crampton was not supposed ever to go up into Parliament; it was a privileged place.

"Will the old girl really come, do you think?" exclaimed Crayshaw.

"She says she shall, as soon as she has done giving Janie her music lesson," replied Barbara, who had rushed up the steep stairs to give this message.

"Mon peruke!" exclaimed Johnnie looking round, "you'd better look out, then, or vous l'attrapperais."

The walls were hung with pictures, maps, and caricatures; these last were what had attracted Johnnie's eyes, and the girls began hastily to cover them.

"It's very unkind of her," exclaimed Barbara. "Father never exactly said that we were to have our own playroom to ourselves, but we know, and she knows, that he meant it."

Then, after a good deal of whispering, giggling, and consulting among the elder ones, the little boys were dismissed; and in the meantime Mr. Nicholas Swan, who, standing on a ladder outside, was nailing the vines (quite aware that the governess was going to have a reception which might be called a warning never to come there any more), may or may not have intended to make his work last as long as possible. At any rate, he could with difficulty forbear from an occasional grin, while, with his nails neatly arranged between his lips, he leisurely trained and pruned; and when he was asked by the young people to bring them up some shavings and a piece of wood, he went down to help in the mischief, whatever it might be, with an alacrity ill suited to his years and gravity.

"Now, I'll tell you what, young gentlemen," he remarked, when, ascending, he showed his honest face again, thrust in a log of wood, and exhibited an armful of shavings, "I'm agreeable to anything but gunpowder, or that there spark as comes cantering out o' your engine with a crack. No, Miss Gladys, ex-cuse me, I don't give up these here shavings till I know it's all right."

"Well, well, it *ith* all right," exclaimed Johnnie, "we're not going to do any harm! O Cray, he'th brought up a log ath big ath a fiddle. Quelle alouette!"

"How lucky it is that she has never seen Cray!" exclaimed Barbara. "Johnnie, do be calm; how are we to do it, if you laugh so? Now then, you are to be attending to the electrifying machine."

"Swanny," asked Crayshaw, "have you got a pipe in your pocket? I want one to lie on my desk."

"Well, now, to think o' your asking me such a question, just as if I was ever *known* to take so much as a whiff in working hours—no, not in the tool-house, nor nowhere."

"But just feel. Come, you might."

"Well, now, this here is remarkable," exclaimed Swan, with a start as if of great surprise, when, after feeling in several pockets, a pipe appeared from the last one.

"Don't knock the ashes out."

"She's coming," said Swan, furtively glancing down, and then pretending to nail with great diligence. "And, my word, if here isn't Miss Christie with her!"

A great scuffle now ensued to get things ready. Barbara darted down-stairs, and what she may have said to Aunt Christie while Swan received some final instructions above, is of less consequence than what Miss Crampton may have felt when she found herself at the top of the stairs in the long room, with its brown high-pitched roof—a room full of the strangest furniture, warm with the sun of August, and sweet with the scent of the creepers.

Gladys and Johnnie were busy at the electrifying machine, and with a rustling and crackling noise the "spunky little flashes," as Swan called them, kept leaping from one leaden knob to another.

Miss Crampton saw a youth sitting on a low chair, with his legs on rather a higher one; the floor under him was strewed with shavings, which looked, Swan thought, "as natural as life," meaning that they looked just as if he had made them by his own proper whittling.

The youth in question was using a large pruning knife on a log that he held rather awkwardly on his knee. He had a soft hat, which had been disposed over one eye. Miss Crampton gave the sparks as wide a berth as she could, and as she advanced, "Well, sir," Swan was saying in obedience to his instructions, "if you've been brought up a republican, I spose you can't help it. But whatever *your* notions may be, Old Master is staunch. He's all for Church and Queen and he hates republican institootions like poison. Which is likewise my own feelings to a T."

No one had taken any notice of Miss Crampton, and she stopped amazed.

"Wall," answered the youth, diligently whittling, "I think small potatoes of ye-our lo-cation myself—but ye-our monarchical government, I guess, hez not yet corrupted the he-eart of the Grand. He handed onto me and onto his hair a tip which"—here he put his hand in his waistcoat pocket, and fondly regarded two or three coins; then feigning to become aware of Miss Crampton's presence, "Augustus John, my yound friend," he continued, "ef yeow feel like it, I guess yeou'd better set a chair for the school marm—for it is the school marm, I calculate?"

Here Miss Christie, radiant with joy and malice, could not conceal her delight, but patted him on the shoulder, and then hastily retreated into the background, lest she should spoil the sport; while as Johnnie, having small command of countenance, did not dare to turn from the window out of which he was pretending to look, Crayshaw rose himself, shook hands with Miss Crampton, and setting a chair for her, began to whittle again.

"Wall," he then said, "and heow do yeou git along with ye-our teaching, marm? Squire thinks a heap of ye-our teaching, as I he-ear, specially ye-our teaching of the eye-talian tongue."

"Did I understand you to be arguing with the gardener when I came in, respecting the principles and opinions of this family?" inquired Miss Crampton, who had now somewhat recovered from her surprise, and was equal to the resenting of indignities.

"Wall, mebby I was, but it's a matter of science that we're mainly concerned with, I guess, this morning—science, electricity. We're gitting on first-rate—those rods on the stairs——"

"Yes?" exclaimed Miss Crampton.

"We air of a scientific turn, we air—Augustus

John and I—fixing wires to every one of them. They air steep, those steps," he continued pensively.

Here Miss Crampton's colour increased visibly.

"And when the machine is che-arged, we shall electrify them. So that when yeou dew but touch one rod, it'll make yeou jump as high as the next step, without any voluntary effort. Yeou'll find that an improvement."

Here Swan ducked down, and laughed below at his ease.

"We air very scientific in my country."

"Indeed!"

"Ever been to Amurica?"

"Certainly not," answered Miss Crampton with vigour, "nor have I the slightest intention of ever doing so. Pray, are you allowed, in consideration of your nationality, to whittle in Harrow School?"

This was said by way of a reproof for the state of the floor.

"Wall," began Crayshaw, to cover the almost audible titters of the girls; but, distracted by this from the matter in hand, he coughed, went on whittling, and held his peace.

"I have often told Johnnie," said Miss Crampton with great dignity, at the same time darting a severe glance at Johnnie's back, "that the delight he takes in talking the Devonshire dialect is likely to be very injurious to his English, and he will have it that this country accent is not permanently catching. It may be hoped," she continued, looking round, "that other accents are not catching either."

Crayshaw, choosing to take this hint as a compliment, smiled sweetly. "I guess I'm speaking better than usual," he observed, "for my brother and his folks air newly come from the Ste-ates, and I've been with them. But," he continued, a sudden gleam of joy lighting up his eyes as something occurred to him that he thought suitable to "top up" with, "all the Mortimers talk with such a peowerful English ac-*cent*, that when I come de-own to this *lo*-cation, my own seems to melt off my tongue. Neow, yeou'll skasely believe it," he continued, "but it's tre-u, that ef yeou were tew hea-ar me talk at the end of a week, yeou'd he-ardly realise that I was an Amurican at all."

"Cray, how can ye?" exclaimed Aunt Christie, "and so wan as ye look this morning too."

"Seen my brother?" inquired Crayshaw meekly.

"No, I have not," said Miss Crampton bridling.

"He's merried. We settle airly in my country; it's one of our institootions." Another gleam of joy and impudence shot across the pallid face. "I'm thinking of settling shortly myself."

Then, as Aunt Christie was observed to be struggling with a laugh that, however long repressed, was sure to break forth at last, Barbara led her to the top of the stairs, and loudly entreated her to mind she didn't stumble, and to mind she did not touch the stair-rods, for the machine, she observed, was just ready.

"The jarth are all charged now, Cray," said Johnnie, coming forward at last. "Mith Crampton, would you like to have the firtht turn of going down with them?"

"No, thank you," said Miss Crampton almost suavely, and rising with something very like alacrity. Then, remembering that she had not even mentioned what she came for, "I wish to observe," she said, "that I much disapprove of the noise I hear up in Parliament. I desire that it may not occur again. If it does, I shall detain the girls in the schoolroom. I am very much disturbed by it."

"You don't say so!" exclaimed Crayshaw with an air of indolent surprise; and Miss Crampton thereupon retreated down-stairs, taking great care not to touch any metallic substance.

CHAPTER XIX.

MR. MORTIMER GOES THROUGH THE TURNPIKE.

"I hear thee speak of the happy land."

SWAN looked down as Miss Crampton and Miss Christie emerged into the garden.

"Most impertinent of Swan," he heard the former say, to be arguing thus about political affairs in the presence of the children. And what Mr. Mortimer can be thinking of, inviting young Crayshaw to stay so much with them, I cannot imagine. We shall be having them turn republican next."

"Turn republican!" repeated Miss Christie with infinite scorn; "there's about as much chance of that as of his ever seeing his native country again, poor laddie; which is just no chance at all."

Crayshaw at this moment inquired of Swan, who had mounted his ladder step by step as Miss Crampton went on, "Is the old girl gone in? And what was she talking of?"

"Well, sir, something about republican institootions."

"Ah! and so you hate them like poison?"

"Yes, in a manner of speaking I do. But I've been a-thinking," continued Swan, taking the nails out of his lips and leaning in at the window, "I've been a-thinking as it ain't noways fair, if all men is ekal—which you're allers upholding—that you should say Swan, and I should say Mister Crayshaw."

"No, it isn't," exclaimed Crayshaw, laughing;

"let's have it the other way. You shall say Crayshaw to me, and I'll say Mr. Swan to you, sir."

"Well, now, you allers contrive to get the better of me, you and Mr. Johnnie, you're so sharp! But, anyhow, I could earn my own living before I was your age, and neither of you can. Then, there's hardly a year as I don't gain a prize."

"I'm like a good clock," said Crayshaw, "I neither gain nor lose. I can strike, too. But how did you find out, sir, that I never gained any prizes?"

"Don't you, sir?"

"Never, sir—I never gained one in my life, sir. But I say, I wish you'd take these shavings down again."

"No, I won't," answered Swan, "if I'm to be 'sirred' any more, and the young ladies made to laugh at me."

"Let Swanny alone, Cray," said Gladys. "Be as conservative as you like, Swan. Why shouldn't you? It's the only right thing."

"Nothing can be very far wrong as Old Master thinks," answered Swan. "He never interfered with my ways of doing my work either, no more than Mr. John does, and that's a thing I vally; and he never but once wanted me to do what I grudged doing."

"When was that?" asked Mr. Augustus John.

"Why, when he made me give up that there burial club," answered Swan. "He said it was noways a moral institootion; and so I shouldn't have even a decent burying to look forward to for me and my wife (my poor daughters being widows, and a great expense to me), if he hadn't said he'd bury us himself if I'd give it up, and bury us respectably too, it stands to reason. Mr. John heard him."

"Then, thath the thame thing ath if he'd thaid it himthelf," observed Johnnie, answering the old man's thought about a much older man.

"Did I say it wasn't, sir? No, if ever there was

a gentleman—it's not a bit of use argufying that all men are ekal. I'm not ekal to either of them two."

"In what respect?" asked Crayshaw.

"In what respect? Well, sir, this is how it is. I wouldn't do anything mean nor dishonest; but as for them two, they couldn't. I never had the education neither to be a gentleman, nor wished to. Not that I talk as these here folks do down here—I'd scorn it. I'm a Sunbury man myself, and come from the valley of the Thames, and talk plain English. But one of my boys, Joey," continued Swan, "talking of wishes, he wished he'd had better teaching. He's been very uppish for some time (all his own fault he hadn't been more edicated); told his mother and me, afore he sailed for the West Indies, as he'd been trying hard for some time to turn gentleman. 'I shall give myself all the airs that ever I can,' he says, 'when once I get out there.' 'Why, you young ass!' says I, 'for it's agen my religion to call you a fool (let alone your mother wouldn't like it), arn't you awear that giving himself airs is exactly what no real gentleman ever does?' 'A good lot of things,' says he, 'father, goes to the making of a gentleman.' 'Ay, Joey,' says I, 'but ain't a gentleman a man with good manners? Now a good-manner'd man is allers saying by his ways and looks to them that air beneath him, "You're as good as I am!" and a bad-manner'd man is allers saying by his ways and looks to them that air above him, "I'm as good as you air!" There's a good many folks,' I says (not knowing I should repeat it to you this day, Mr. Crayshaw), 'as will have it, that because we shall all ekally have to be judged in the next world, we must be all ekal in this. In some things I uphold we air, and in others I say we're not. Now your real gentleman thinks most of them things that make men ekal, and t'other chap thinks most of what makes them unekal.'"

"Hear, hear!" said Johnnie. "And what did Joey thay to that, Thwan?"

"He didn't say much," answered Swan in his most pragmatical manner. "He knows well enough that when I'm argufying with my own children (as I've had the expense of bringing up), I expect to have the last word, and I have it. It's dinner-time, Mr. Johnnie; will you pass me out my pipe? I don't say but what I may take a whiff while the dinner's dishing up."

"It was very useful, Swan," said Gladys. "No doubt it made Miss Crampton think that Cray smokes."

"My word!" exclaimed Swan, "it was as good as a play to see him give himself those meek airs, and look so respectful."

He went down, and the two little boys came up. They had been turned out of Parliament, and had spent the time of their exile in running to the town, and laying out some of their money in the purchase of a present for Crayshaw; they were subject to humble fits of enthusiasm for Crayshaw and Johnnie. They came in, and handed him a "Robinson Crusoe" with pictures in it.

Crayshaw accepted it graciously.

"You must write my name in it," he observed, with exceeding mildness, "and mind you write it with a soft G."

"Yes, of course," said little Hugh, taking in, but hesitating how to obey.

"A hard G is quite wrong, and very indigestible too," he continued, yet more mildly; "though people will persist that it's a capital letter."

The young people then began to congratulate themselves on their success as regarded Miss Crampton.

"She scarcely stayed five minutes, and she was so afraid of the machine, and so shocked at the whittling and the talk, and Cray's whole appearance, that she will not come near us while he is here. After that, the stair-rods will protect us."

"No," said Crayshaw, "but it's no stimulus to my genius to have to talk Yankee to such ignorant people. I might mix up North, South, and West as

I liked, and you would be none the wiser. However, if she chances to hear me speak a week hence, she'll believe that my accent has entirely peeled off. I thought I'd better provide against that probability. It was an invention worthy of a poet, which I am."

"Que les poètes thoient pendus," said Augustus John, with vigour and sincerity. "Ekthepting Homer and Tennython," he added, as if willing to be just to all men.

"What for? they've done nothing to you."

"Haven't they! But for them I need not watht my life in making Latin verthéth. The fighting, though, in Homer and Tennython I like."

In the meantime the four younger children were whispering together over a large paper parcel, that crackled a good deal.

"Which do you think is the grandest word?" said Bertram.

"I like *fallacious*, Janie."

"But you said you would put *umbrageous*," observed Hugh, in a discontented tone.

"No, those words don't mean *it*," answered Janie. "I like *ambrosial* best. Put 'For our dear ambrosial Johnnie.'"

The parcel contained as many squibs and crackers as the seller thereof would trust with his young customers; also one rocket.

Johnnie's little brothers and sisters having written these words, rose from the floor on which they had been seated, and with blushes and modest pride presented the parcel.

"For a birthday present," they said, "and, Johnnie, you're to let off every one of them your own self; and lots more are coming from the shop."

"My wig!" exclaimed Johnnie, feigning intense surprise, though he had heard every word of the conference. "Let them all off mythelf, did you thay? Well, I do call that a motht egregiouth and tender lark."

These epithets appeared to give rarity and splendour to his thanks. Janie pondered over them a little, but when Crayshaw added, "Quite parenthetical," she gave it up. That was a word she could not hope to understand. When a difficulty is once confessed to be unconquerable, the mind can repose before it as before difficulties overcome, so says Whately. "If it had only been as hard a word as *chemical*," thought Janie, "I would have looked it out in the spelling-book; but this word is so very hard that perhaps nobody knows it but Cray."

For the remainder of the week, though many revolutionary speeches were made in Parliament against the constituted schoolroom authorities, there was, on the whole, better behaviour and less noise.

After that, John took his three elder children on the Continent, keeping the boy with him till Harrow School opened again, and remaining behind with the girls till the first week in November. During this time he by no means troubled himself about the domestic happiness that he felt he had missed, though he looked forward with fresh interest to the time when his intelligent little daughters would be companions for him, and began, half unconsciously, to idealise the character of his late wife, as if her death had cost him a true companion—as if, in fact, it had not made him much nobler and far happier.

He was not sorry, when he returned home, to find Valentine eager to get away for a little while, for it had been agreed that the old man should not be left by both of them. Valentine was improved; his comfortable and independent position in his uncle's house, where his presence was so evidently regarded as an advantage, had made him more satisfied with himself; and absence from Dorothea had enabled him to take an interest in other women.

He went away in high spirits and capital health, and John subsided into his usual habits, his children continuing to grow about him. He was still a head taller than his eldest son, but this did not promise to be long the case. And his eldest girls were so clever, and so forward with their education, that he was increasingly anxious to propitiate Miss Crampton. It was very difficult to hold the balance even; he scarcely knew how to keep her at a distance, and yet to mark his sense of her value.

"I am going to see the Brandons to-morrow," he remarked to Miss Christie one day, just before the Christmas holidays.

"Then I wish ye would take little Nancy with ye," observed the good lady, "for Dorothea was here yesterday. Emily is come to stay with them, and she drove her over. Emily wished to see the child, and when she found her gone out for her walk she was disappointed."

"What did she want with her?" asked John.

"Well, I should have thought it might occur to ye that the sweet lamb had perhaps some sacred reason for feeling attracted towards the smallest creatures she could conveniently get at."

"Let the nestling bird be dressed up, then," said John. "I will drive her over with me to lunch this morning. Poor Emily! she will feel seeing the child."

"Not at all. She has been here twice to see the two little ones. At first she would only watch them over the blinds, and drop a few tears; but soon she felt the comfort of them, and when she had got a kiss or two, she went away more contented."

Accordingly John drove his smallest daughter over to Wigfield House, setting her down rosy and smiling from her wraps, and sending her to the ladies, while he went up to Brandon's peculiar domain to talk over some business with him.

They went down into the morning-room together, and Emily rose to meet John. It was the first time he had seen her in her mourning-dress and with the cap that did not seem at all to belong to her.

Emily was a graceful young woman. Her face, of a fine oval shape, was devoid of ruddy hues; yet it was more white than pale; the clear dark grey eyes shining with health, and the mouth being red and beautiful. The hair was dark, abundant, and devoid of gloss, and she had the advantage of a graceful and cordial manner, and a very charming smile.

There were tears on her eyelashes when she spoke to John, and he knew that his little cherub of a child must have caused them. She presently went back to her place, taking little Anastasia on her knee; while Dorothea, sitting on the sofa close to them, and facing the child, occupied and pleased herself with the little creature, and encouraged her to talk.

Of English children this was a lovely specimen, and surely there are none lovelier in the world. Dorothea listened to her pretty tongue, and mused over her with a silent rapture. Her hair fell about her face like flakes of floss-silk, loose, and yellow as Indian corn; and her rosy cheeks were deeply dimpled. She was the only one of the Mortimers who was small for her years. She liked being nursed and petted, and while Dorothea smoothed out the fingers of her tiny gloves, the little fat hands, so soft and warm, occupied themselves with the contents of her work-box.

She was relating how Grand had invited them all to spend the day. "Papa brought the message, and they all wanted to go; and so—" she was saying, when John caught the sound of her little voice—"and so papa said, 'What! not one of you going to stay with your poor old father?'"—these words, evidently authentic, she repeated with the deepest pathos—"and so," she went on, "I said, 'I will.'" Then, after a pause for reflection, "That was kind of me, wasn't it?"

A few caresses followed.

Then catching sight of Emily's brooch, in which was a portrait of her child, little Nancy put the wide tulle cap-strings aside, and looked at it earnestly.

"I know who that is," she said, after bestowing a kiss on the baby's face.

"Do you, my sweet? who is it, then?"

"It's Freddy; he's gone to the happy land. It's full of little boys and girls. Grand's going soon," she added, with great cheerfulness. "Did you know? Grand says he hopes he shall go soon."

"How did Emily look?" asked Miss Christie, when John came home.

"Better than usual, I think," said John carelessly. "There's no bitterness in her sorrow, poor thing! She laughed several times at Nancy's childish talk."

"She looks a great deal too young and attractive to live alone," said Miss Christie pointedly.

"Well," answered John, "she need not do that long. There are several fellows about here, who, unless they are greater fools than I take them for, will find her, as a well-endowed young widow, quite as attractive as they did when she was an almost portionless girl."

"But in the meantime?" said Miss Christie.

"If you are going to say anything that I shall hate to hear," answered John, half-laughing, "don't keep me lingering long. If you mean to leave me, say so at once, and put me out of my misery."

"Well, well," said Miss Christie, looking at him with some pleasure, and more admiration, "I've been torn in pieces for several weeks past, thinking it over. Never shall I have my own way again in any man's house, or woman's either, as I have had it here. And the use of the carriage and the top of the pew," she continued, speaking to herself as much as to him; "and the keys; and I always *knew* I was welcome, which is more than being told so. And I thank ye, John Mortimer, for it all, I do indeed; but if my niece's daughter is wanting me, what can I do but go to her?"

"It was very base of Emily not to say a word about it," said John, smiling with as much grimness as utter want of practice, together with the natural cast of his countenance, would admit of.

Miss Christie looked up, and saw with secret joy the face she admired above all others coloured with a sudden flush of most unfeigned vexation. John gave the footstool before him a little shove of impatience, and it rolled over quite unknown to him, and lighted on Miss Christie's corns.

She scarcely felt the pain. It was sweet to be of so much importance. Two people contending for one lonely, homely old woman.

"Say the word," she presently said, "and I won't leave ye."

"No," answered John, "you ought to go to Emily. I had better say instead that I am very sensible of the kindness you have done me in staying so long."

"But ye won't be driven to do anything rash?" she answered, observing that he was still a little chafed, and willing to pass the matter off lightly.

"Such as taking to myself the lady up-stairs!" exclaimed John. "No, but I must part with her; if one of you goes, the other must."

This was absolutely the first time the matter had even been hinted at between them, and yet Miss Christie's whole conduct was arranged with reference to it, and John always fully counted on her protective presence.

"Ay, but if I might give myself the liberty of a very old friend," she answered, straightway taking the ell because he had given her an inch, "there is something I would like to say to ye."

"What would you like to say?"

"Well, I would like to say that if a man is so more than commonly a fine man, that it's just a pleasure to set one's eyes on him, and if he's well endowed with this world's gear, it's a strange thing if there is no excellent, desirable, and altogether sweet young woman ready, and even sighing, for him."

"Humph!" said John.

"I don't say there is," proceeded Miss Christie; "far be it from me."

"I hate red hair," answered the attractive widower.

"It's just like a golden oriole. It isn't red at all," replied Miss Christie dogmatically.

"*I* call it red," said John Mortimer.

"The painters consider it the finest colour possible," continued the absent lady's champion.

"Then let them paint her," said John; "but—I shall not marry her; besides," he chose to say, "I know if I asked her she would not have me: therefore, as I don't mean to ask her, I shall not be such an unmannerly dog as to discuss her, further than to say that I do not wish to marry a woman who takes such a deep and sincere interest in herself."

"Why, don't we all do that? I am sure *I* do."

"You naturally feel that you are the most important and interesting of all God's creatures *to yourself*. You do not therefore think that you must be so to *me*. Our little lives, my dear lady, should not turn round upon themselves, and as it were make a centre of their own axis. The better lives revolve round some external centre; everything depends on that centre, and how much or how many we carry round with us besides ourselves. Now, my father's centre is and always has been Almighty God—our Father and his. His soul is as it were drawn to God and lost, as a centre to itself in that great central soul. He looks at everything—I speak it reverently—from God's high point of view."

"Ay, but she's a good woman," said Miss Christie, trying to adopt his religious tone, and as usual not knowing how. "Always going about among the poor. I don't suppose," she continued with enthusiasm—"I don't suppose there's a single thing they can do in their houses that she doesn't interfere with."

Then observing his amusement, "Ye don't know what's good for ye," she added, half laughing, but a little afraid she was going too far.

"If ever I am so driven wild by the governesses that I put my neck, as a heart-broken father, under the yoke, in order to get somebody into the house who can govern as you have done," said John, "it will be entirely your doing, your fault for leaving me."

"Well, well," said Miss Christie, laughing, "I must abide ye're present reproaches, but I feel that I need dread no future ones, for if ye should go and do it, ye'll be too much a gentleman to say anything to me afterwards."

"You are quite mistaken," exclaimed John, laughing, "that one consolation I propose to reserve to myself, or if I should not think it right to speak, mark my words, the more cheerful I look the more sure you may be that I am a miserable man."

Some days after this the stately Miss Crampton departed for her Christmas holidays, a letter following her, containing a dismissal (worded with studied politeness) and a cheque for such an amount of money as went far to console her.

"Mr. Mortimer was about to send the little boys to school, and meant also to make other changes in his household. Mr. Mortimer need hardly add, that should Miss Crampton think of taking another situation, he should do himself the pleasure to speak as highly of her qualifications as she could desire."

Aunt Christie gone, Miss Crampton gone also! What a happy state of things for the young Mortimers! If Crayshaw had been with them, there is no saying what they might have done; but Johnnie, by his father's orders, had brought a youth of seventeen to spend three weeks with him, and the young fellow turned out to be such a dandy, and so much better pleased to be with the girls than with Johnnie scouring the country and skating, that John for the first time began to perceive the coming on of a fresh source of trouble in his house. Gladys and Barbara were nearly fourteen years old, but looked older; they were tall, slender girls, black-haired and grey-eyed, as their mother had been, very simple, full of energy, and in mind and disposition their father's own daughters. Johnnie groaned over his unpromising companion, Edward Conyngham by name; but he was the son of an old friend, and John did what he could to make the boys companionable, while the girls, though they laughed at young Conyngham, were on the whole more amused with his compliments than their father liked. But it was not till one day, going up into Parliament, and finding some verses pinned on a curtain, that he began to feel what it was to have no lady to superintend his daughters.

"What are they?" Gladys said. "Why, papa, Cray sent them; they are supposed to have been written by Conyngham."

"What does he know about Conyngham?"

"Oh, I told him when I last wrote."

"When you last wrote," repeated John, in a cogitative tone.

"Yes; I write about once a fortnight, of course, when Barbara writes to Johnnie."

"Did Miss Crampton superintend the letters?" was John's next inquiry.

"Oh no, father, we always wrote them up here."

"I wonder whether Janie would have allowed this," thought John. "I suppose as they are so young it cannot signify."

"Cray sent them because we told him how Conyngham walked after Gladys wherever she went. That boy is such a goose, father; you never heard such stuff as he talks when you are away."

John was silent.

"Johnnie and Cray are disgusted with his rubbish," continued Barbara, "pretending to make love and all that."

"Yes," said John; "it is very ridiculous. Boys like Conyngham and Crayshaw ought to know better." Nothing, he felt, could be so likely to make the schoolroom distasteful to his daughters as this early admiration. Still he was consoled by the view they took of it.

"Cray does know better, of course," said Gladys carelessly.

"Still, he was extremely angry with Conyngham, for being so fond of Gladys," remarked Barbara; "because you know she is *his* friend. He would never hear about his puppy, that old Patience Smith takes care of for sixpence a week, or his rabbits that we have here, or his hawk that lives at Wigfield, unless Gladys wrote; Mr. Brandon never writes to him."

"Now shall I put a stop to this, or shall I let it be?" thought John; and he proceeded to read Crayshaw's effusion.

TO G. M. IN HER BRONZE BOOTS

As in the novel skippers say,
"Shiver my timbers!" and "Belay!"
While a few dukes so handy there
Respectfully make love or swear;

As in the poem some great ass
For ever pipes to his dear lass;
And as in life tea crowns the cup
And muffins sop much butter up;

So, naturally, while I walk
With you, I feel a swell—and stalk—
Consecutively muttering "Oh,
I'm quite a man, I feel I grow."

But loudliest thumps this heart to-day,
While in the mud you pick your way,
(You fawn, you flower, you star, you gem,)
In your new boots with heels to them.

YOUR ELDEST SLAVE.

"I don't consider these verses a bit more *consecutive* than Conyngham's talk," said John, laughing.

"Well, father, then he shouldn't say such things! He said Mr. Brandon walked with an infallible stride, and that you were the most consecutive of any one he had ever met with."

"But, my dear little girl, Crayshaw would not have

known that unless you had told him; do you think that was the right thing to do by a guest?"

Gladys blushed. "But, father," said Barbara, "I suppose Cray may come now; Conyngham goes to-morrow. Cray never feels so well as when he is here."

"I had no intention of inviting him this Christmas," answered John.

"Well," said Gladys, "it doesn't make much difference; he and Johnnie can be together just the same nearly all day, because his brother and Mrs. Crayshaw are going to stay with the Brandons, and Cray is to come too."

John felt as if the fates were against him.

"And his brother was so horribly vexed when he found that he hardly got on at school at all."

"That's enough to vex any man. Cray should spend less time in writing these verses of his."

"Yes, he wrote us word that his brother said so, and was extremely cross and unpleasant, when he replied that this was genius, and must not be repressed."

John, after this, rode into the town, and as he stopped his horse to pay the turnpike, he was observed by the turnpike-keeper's wife to be looking gloomy and abstracted; indeed, the gate was no sooner shut behind him than he sighed, and said with a certain bitterness, "I shouldn't wonder if, in two or three years time, I am driven to put my neck under the yoke after all."

"No, we can't come," said little Hugh, when a few days after this Emily and Dorothea drove over and invited the children to spend the day, "we couldn't come on any account, because something very grand is going to happen."

"Did you know," asked Anastasia, "that Johnnie had got into the *shell?*"

"No, my sweet," said Emily, consoling her empty arms for their loss, and appeasing her heart with a kiss.

"And father always said that some day he should come home to early dinner," continued Hugh, "and show the great magic lantern up in Parliament. Then Swan's grandchildren and the coachman's little girls are coming; and every one is to have a present. It will be such fun."

"The shell," observed Bertram, "means a sort of a class between the other classes. Father's so glad Johnnie has got into the shell."

"She is glad too," said Anastasia. "You're glad, Mrs. Nemily."

"Yes, I am glad," answered Emily, a tear that had gathered under her dark eyelashes falling, and making her eyes look brighter, and her smile more sweet.

Emily was not of a temperament that is ever depressed. She had her times of sorrow and tears; but she could often smile, and still oftener laugh.

CHAPTER XX.

THE RIVER.

"Now there was a great calm at that time in the river; wherefore Mr. Standfast, when he was about half way in, he stood awhile, and talked to his companions that had waited upon him thither; and he said, . . . 'I have formerly lived by hearsay and faith; but now I go where I shall live by sight, and shall be with Him in whose company I delight myself. I have loved to hear my Lord spoken of; and wherever I have seen the print of his shoe in the earth, there have I coveted to set my foot too.'"—*Pilgrim's Progress.*

AND now the Christmas holidays being more than half over, Mr. Augustus Mortimer desired that his grandson might come and spend a few days with him, for Valentine had told him how enchanted John was with the boy's progress, but that he was mortified almost past bearing by his lisp. Grand therefore resolved that something should be done; and Crayshaw having now arrived, and spending the greater part of every day with his allies the young Mortimers, was easily included in the invitation. If anybody wants a school-boy, he is generally most welcome to him. Grand sent a flattering message to the effect that he should be much disappointed if Cray did not appear that day at his dinner table. Cray accordingly did appear, and after dinner the old man began to put before his grandson the advantage it would be to him if he could cure himself of his lisp.

"I never lithp, Grand," answered the boy, "when I talk thlowly, and—— No, I mean when I talk s-lowly and take pains."

"Then why don't you always talk slowly and take

pains, to please your father, to please me, and to improve yourself?"

Johnnie groaned.

"This is very little more than an idle childish habit," continued Grand.

"We used to think it would do him good to have his tongue slit," said Crayshaw, "but there's no need. When I torment him and chaff him, he never does it."

"I hope there *is* no need," said Grand, a little uncertain whether this remedy was proposed in joke or earnest. "Valentine has been reminding me that he used to lisp horribly when a child, but he entirely cured himself before he was your age."

Johnnie, in school-boy fashion, made a face at Valentine when the old man was not looking. It expressed good-humoured defiance and derision, but the only effect it produced was on himself, for it disturbed for the moment the great likeness to his grandfather that grew on him every day. John had clear features, thick light hair, and deep blue eyes. His son was dark, with bushy eyebrows, large stern features, and a high narrow head, like old Grand.

It was quite dark, and the depth of winter, but the thermometer was many degrees above freezing-point, and a warm south wind was blowing. Grand rose and rang the bell. "Are the stable lanterns lighted?" he asked.

"Yes, sir."

"Then you two boys come with me."

The boys, wondering and nothing loth, followed to the stable, and the brown eyes of two large ponies looked mildly into theirs.

"Trot them out," said Grand to the groom, "and let the young gentlemen have a good look at them."

Not a word did either of the boys say. An event of huge importance appeared to loom in the horizon of each: he cogitated over its probable conditions.

"I got a saddle for each of them," said Grand. "Valentine chose them, Johnnie. There now, we had better come in again." And when they were seated in the dining-room as before, and there was still silence, he went on, "You two, as I understand, are both in the same house at Harrow?"

"Yes, sir."

"And it is agreed that Johnnie could cure himself of his lisp if he chose, and if you would continually remind him of it?"

"Oh yes, certainly it is."

"Very well, if the thing is managed by next Easter, I'll give each of you one of those ponies; and," continued Grand cunningly, "you may have the use of them during the remainder of these holidays, provided you both promise, upon your honour, to begin the cure directly. If Johnnie has not left off lisping at Easter, I shall have the ponies sold."

"I'll lead him such a life that he shall wish he'd never been born; I will indeed," exclaimed Crayshaw fervently.

"Well," said Johnnie, "never wath a better time. *Allez le*, or, in other wordth, go it."

"And every two or three days you shall bring him to me," continued Grand, "that I may hear him read and speak."

The next morning, before John went into the town, he was greeted by the two boys on their ponies, and came out to admire and hear the conditions.

"We mayn't have them at school," said Johnnie, bringing out the last word with laudable distinctness, "but Grand will let them live in hith—in his—stables."

John was very well contented to let the experiment alone; and a few days after this, his younger children, going over with a message to Johnnie, reported progress to him in the evening as he sat at dinner.

"Johnnie and Cray were gone into the town on their grand new ponies, almost as big as horses; they came galloping home while we were there," said Janie.

"And, father, they are going to show up their exercises, or something that they've done, to Grand tomorrow; you'll hear them," observed Hugh.

"But poor Cray was so ill on Saturday," said the little girl, "that he couldn't do nothing but lie in bed and write his poetry."

"But they got on very well," observed Bertram philosophically. "They had up the stable-boy with a great squirt; he had to keep staring at Cray while Johnnie read aloud, and every time Cray winked he was to squirt Johnnie. Cray didn't have any dinner or any tea, and his face was so red."

"Poor fellow!"

"Yes," said the youngest boy, "and he wrote some verses about Johnnie, and said they were for him to read aloud to grandfather. But what do you think? Johnnie said he wouldn't! That doesn't sound very kind, does it?"

Johnnie's resolution, however, was not particularly remarkable; the verses, compounded during an attack of asthma, running as follows:—

AUGUSTUS JOHN CONFESSES TO LOSS OF APPETITE.

I cannot eat rice pudding now,
Jam roll, boiled beef, and such;
From Stilton cheese this heart I vow
Turns coldly as from Dutch.

For crab, a shell-fish erst loved well,
I do not care at all,
Though I myself am in the shell
And fellow-feelings call.

I mourn not over tasks unsaid—
This child is not a flat—
My purse is empty as my head,
But no—it isn't that;

I cannot eat. And why? To shrink
From truth is like a sinner,
I'll speak or burst; it is, I think,
That I've just had my dinner.

Crayshaw was very zealous in the discharge of his promise; the ponies took a great deal of exercise; and old Grand, before the boys were dismissed to school, saw very decided and satisfactory progress on the part of his grandson, while the ponies were committed to his charge with a fervour that was almost pathetic. It was hard to part from them; but men are tyrannical; they will not permit boys to have horses at a public school; the boys therefore returned to their work, and the ponies were relieved from theirs, and entered on a course of life which is commonly called eating their heads off.

John in the meanwhile tried in vain to supply the loss of the stately and erudite Miss Crampton. He wanted two ladies, and wished that neither should be young. One must be able to teach his children and keep them in order; the other must superintend the expenditure and see to the comforts of his whole household, order his children's dress, and look after their health.

Either he was not fortunate in his applicants, or he was difficult to please, for he had not suited himself with either lady when a new source of occupation and anxiety sprung up, and everything else was set aside on account of it; for all on a sudden it was perceived one afternoon that Mr. Augustus Mortimer was not at all well.

It was after bank hours, but he was dozing in his private sitting-room at the bank, and his young nephew, Mr. Mortimer, was watching him.

Valentine had caused his card to be printed "Mr. Mortimer:" he did not intend because he was landless, and but for his uncle's bounty almost penniless, to forego the little portion of dignity which belonged to him.

The carriage stood at the door, and the horses now and then stamped in the lightly-falling snow, and were sometimes driven a little way down the street and back again to warm them.

At his usual time John had gone home, and then his father, while waiting for the carriage, had dropped asleep.

Though Valentine had wakened him more than

once, and told him the men and horses were waiting, he had not shown any willingness to move.

"There's plenty of time; I must have this sleep out first," he said.

Then, when for the third time Valentine woke him, he roused himself. "I think I can say it now," he observed. "I could not go home, you know, Val, till it was said."

"Till what was said, uncle?"

"I forget," was the answer. "You must help me."

Valentine suggested various things which had been discussed that day; but they did not help him, and he sank into thought.

"I hope I was not going to make any mistake," he shortly said, and Valentine began to suppose he really had something particular to say. "I think my dear brother and I decided for ever to hold our peace," he next murmured, after a long pause.

Valentine was silent. The allusion to his father made him remember how completely all the more active and eventful part of their lives had gone by for these two old men before he came into the world.

"What were you and John talking of just before he left?" said the old man, after a puzzled pause.

"Nothing of the least consequence," answered Valentine, feeling that he had forgotten what he might have meant to say. "John would be uneasy if he knew you were here still. Shall we go home?"

"Not yet. If I mentioned this, you would never tell it to my John. There is no need that my John should ever have a hint of it. You will promise not to tell him?"

"No, my dear uncle, indeed I could not think of such a thing," said Valentine, now a little uneasy. If his uncle really had something important to say, this was a strange request, and if he had not, his thoughts must be wandering.

"Well," said Grand, in a dull, quiet voice, as of

one satisfied and persuaded, "perhaps it is no duty of mine, then, to mention it. But what was it that you and John were talking of just before he went away?"

"You and John were going to send your cards, to inquire after Mrs. A'Court, because she is ill. I asked if mine might go too, and as it was handed across you took notice of what was on it, and said it pleased you; do you remember? But John laughed about it."

"Yes; and what did you answer, Val?"

I said that if everybody had his rights, that ought not to have been my name at all. You ought to have been Mr. Mortimer now, and I Mr. Melcombe.

"I thought it was that," answered Grand, cogitating. "Yes, it was never intended that you should touch a shilling of that property."

"I know that, uncle," said Valentine. "My father always told me he had no expectations from his mother. It was unlucky for me, that's all. I don't mean to say," he continued, "that it has been any particular disappointment, because I was always brought up to suppose I should have nothing; but as I grow older I often think it seems rather a shame I should be cut out; and as my father was, I am sure, one of the most amiable of men, it is very odd that he never contrived to make it up with the old lady."

"He never had any quarrel with her," answered old Augustus. "He was always her favourite son."

Valentine looked at him with surprise. He appeared to be oppressed with the lassitude of sleep, and yet to be struggling to keep his eyes open and to say something. But he only managed to repeat his last words. "I've told John all that I wish him to know," he next said, and then succumbed and was asleep again.

"The favourite son, and natural heir!" thought Valentine. "No quarrel, and yet not inherit a shilling! That is queer, to say the least of it. I'll go up to

London and have another look at that will. And he has told John something or other. Unless his thoughts are all abroad then, he must have been alluding to two perfectly different things."

"Valentine now went to the carriage and fetched in the footman, hoping that at sight of him his uncle might be persuaded to come home; but this was done with so much difficulty that, when at last it was accomplished, Valentine sent the carriage on to fetch John, and sat anxiously watching till he came, and a medical man with him.

Sleep and weakness, but no pain, and no disquietude. It was so at the end of a week; it was so at the end of a fortnight, and then it became evident that his sight was failing; he was not always aware whether or not he was alone; he often prayed aloud also, but sometimes supposed himself to be recovering.

"Where is Valentine?" he said one afternoon, when John, having left him to get some rest, Valentine had taken his place. "Are we alone?" he asked, when Valentine had spoken to him. "What time is it?"

"About four o'clock, uncle; getting dusk, and snow falls."

"Yes, I heard you mention snow when the nurse went down to her tea. I am often aware of John's presence when I cannot show it. Tell him so."

"Yes, I will."

"He is a dear good son to me."

"Yes."

"He ought not to make a sorrow of my removal. It disturbs me sometimes to perceive that he does. He knows where my will is, and all my papers. I have never concealed anything from him; I had never any cause."

"No, indeed, uncle."

"Till now," proceeded old Augustus. Valentine looked attentively in the failing light at the majestic wreck of the tall, fine old man. He made out that the eyes were closed, and that the face had its usual immobile, untroubled expression, and the last words startled him. "I have thought it best," he continued, "not to leave you anything in my will."

"No," said Valentine, "because you gave me that two thousand pounds during your lifetime."

"Yes, my dear; my memory does not fail me. John will not be cursed with one guinea of ill-gotten wealth. Valentine!"

"Yes, uncle, yes; I am here; I am not going away."

"You have the key of my cabinet, in the library. Go and fetch me a parcel that is in the drawer inside."

"Let me ring, then, first for some one to come; for you must not be left alone."

"Leave me, I say, and do as I tell you."

Valentine, vexed, but not able to decline, ran down in breathless haste, found the packet of that peculiar sort and size usually called a banker's parcel, locked the cabinet, and returned to the old man's bed.

"Are we alone?" he asked, when Valentine had made his presence known to him. "Let me feel that parcel. Ah, your father was very dear to me. I owe everything to him—everything."

Valentine, who was not easy as to what would come next, replied like an honourable man, "So you said, uncle, when you generously gave me that two thousand pounds."

"Ill-gotten wealth," old Augustus murmured, "never prospers; it is a curse to its possessor. My son, my John, will have none of it. Valentine!"

"Yes."

"What do you think was the worst-earned money that human fingers ever handled?"

The question so put suggested but one answer.

"*That* thirty pieces of silver," said Valentine.

"Ah!" replied Augustus with a sigh. "Well, thank God, none of us can match that crime. But murders have been done, and murderers have profited by the spoil! When those pieces of silver were lying on the floor of the temple, after the murderer was dead, to whom do you think they belonged?"

Valentine was excessively startled; the voice seemed higher and thinner than usual, but the conversation had begun so sensibly, and the wrinkled hand kept such firm hold still of the parcel, that it surprised him to feel, as he now did, that his dear old uncle was wandering, and he answered nothing.

"Not to the priests," continued Augustus, and as a pause followed, Valentine felt impelled to reply.

"No," he said, "they belonged to his family, no doubt, if they had chosen to pick them up."

"Ah, that is what I suppose. If his father, poor wretch, or perhaps his miserable mother, had gone into the temple that day, it would have been a strange sight, surely, to see her gather them up."

"Yes," said Valentine faintly. The shadow of something too remote to make its substance visible appeared to fall over him then, causing him a vague wonder and awe, and revulsion of feeling. He knew not whether this old man was taking leave of sober daylight reason, or whether some fresh sense of the worthlessness of earthly wealth, more especially ill-gotten wealth, had come to him from a sudden remembrance of this silver—or——

He tried gently to lead his thoughts away from what seemed to be troubling him, for his head turned restlessly on the pillow.

"You have no need to think of that," he said kindly and quietly, "for as you have just been saying, John will inherit nothing but well-earned property."

"John does not know of this," said Augustus. "I have drawn it out for years by degrees, as he supposed, for household expenses. It is all in Bank of England notes. Every month that I lived it would have become more and more."

Uncommonly circumstantial this!

"It contains seventeen hundred pounds; take it in your hand, and hear me."

"Yes, uncle."

"You cannot live on a very small income. You have evidently very little notion of the value of money. You and John may not agree. It may not suit him to have you with him; on the other hand—on the other hand—what was I saying?"

"That it might not suit John to have me with him."

"Yes, yes; but, on the other hand (where is it gone), on the other hand, it might excite his curiosity, his surprise, if I left you more in my will. Now what am I doing this for? What is it? Daniel's son? Yes."

"Dear uncle, try to collect your thoughts; there is something you want me to do with this money, try to tell me what it is."

"Have you got it in your hand?"

"Yes, I have."

"Keep it then, and use it for your own purposes."

"Thank you. Are you sure that is what you meant? Is that all?"

"Is that all? No. I said you were not to tell John."

"Will you tell him yourself then?" asked Valentine. "I do not think he would mind my having it."

By way of answer to this, the old man actually laughed. Valentine had thought he was long past that, but it was a joyful laugh, and almost exultant.

"Mind," he said, "my John! No; you attend to my desire, and to all I have said. Also it is agreed between me and my son that if ever you two part company, he is to give you a thousand pounds. I tell you this that you may not suppose it has anything to do with the money in that parcel. Your father was everything to me," he continued, his voice getting fainter, and his speech more confused, as he went on, "and—and I never expected to see him again in this world.. And so you have come over to see me, Daniel? Give me your hand. Come over to see me, and there are no lights! God has been very good to me, brother, and I begin to think He will call me into his presence soon."

Valentine started up, and it was really more in order to carry out the old man's desires, so solemnly expressed, than from any joy of possession, that he put the parcel into his pocket before he rang for the nurse and went to fetch John.

He had borne a part in the last-sustained conversation the old man ever held, and that day month, in just such a snow-storm as had fallen about his much-loved brother, his stately white head was laid in the grave.

CHAPTER XXI.

THE DEAD FATHER ENTREATS.

"*Prospero.* I have done nothing but in care of thee,
Of thee, my dear one."

The Tempest.

VALENTINE rose early the morning after the funeral; John Mortimer had left him alone in the house, and gone home to his children.

John had regarded the impending death of his father more as a loss and a misfortune than is common. He and the old man, besides being constant companions, had been very intimate friends, and the rending of the tie between them was very keenly felt by the son.

Nothing, perhaps, differs more than the amount of affection felt by different people; there is no gauge for it—language cannot convey it. Yet instinctive perception shows us where it is great. Some feel little, and show all that little becomingly; others feel much, and reveal scarcely anything; but, on the whole, men are not deceived, each gets the degree of help and sympathy that was due to him.

Valentine had been very thoughtful for John; the invitations and orders connected with a large funeral had been mainly arranged by him.

Afterwards, he had been present at the reading of the will, and had been made to feel that the seventeen hundred pounds in that parcel which he had not yet opened could signify nothing to a son who was to enter on such a rich inheritance as it set forth and specified.

Still he wished his uncle had not kept the giving of it a secret, and, while he was dressing, the details of that last conversation, the falling snow, the failing light, and the high, thin voice, changed, and yet so much more impressive for the change, recurred to his thoughts more freshly than ever, perhaps because before he went down he meant to open the parcel, which accordingly he did.

Bank of England notes were in it, and not a line of writing on the white paper that enfolded them. He turned it over, and then mechanically began to count and add up the amount. Seventeen hundred pounds, neither more nor less, and most assuredly his own. With the two thousand pounds he already possessed, this sum would, independently of any exertions of his own, bring him in nearly two hundred a-year. In case of failing health this would be enough to live on modestly, either in England or on the Continent.

He leaned his chin on his hand, and, with a dull contentment looked at these thin, crisp papers. He had cared for his old uncle very much, and been exceedingly comfortable with him, and now that he was forbidden to mention his last gift, he began to feel (though this had fretted him at first) that it would make him more independent of John.

But why should the old father have disliked to excite his son's surprise and curiosity? Why, indeed, when he had laughed at the notion of John's being capable of minding his doing as he pleased.

Valentine pondered over this as he locked up his property. It was not yet eight o'clock, and as he put out the candle he had lighted to count his notes by (for the March morning was dark), he heard wheels, and, on going down, met John in the hall. He had come in before the breakfast-hour, as had often been his custom when he meant to breakfast with his father.

John's countenance showed a certain agitation.

Valentine observing it, gave him a quiet, matter-of-fact greeting, and talked of the weather. A thaw had come on, and the snow was melting rapidly. For the moment John seemed unable to answer, but when they got into the dining-room, he said—

"I overtook St. George's groom. He had been to my house, he said, thinking you were there. Your brother sent a message, rather an urgent one, and this note to you. He wants you, it seems."

"Wants me, wants ME!" exclaimed Valentine. What for?"

John shrugged his shoulders.

"Is he ill?" continued Valentine.

"The man did not say so."

Valentine read the note. It merely repeated that his brother wanted him. What an extraordinary piece of thoughtlessness this seemed! Brandon might have perceived that Valentine would be much needed by John that day.

"You told me yesterday," said Valentine, "that there were various things you should like me to do for you in the house to-day, and over at the town too. So I shall send him word that I cannot go"

"I think you had better go," said John.

Valentine was sure that John would have been glad of his company. It would be easier for a man with his peculiarly keen feelings not to have to face all his clerks alone the first time after his father's death.

"You must go," he repeated, however. "St. George would never have thought of sending for you unless for some urgent reason. If you take my dog-cart you will be in time for the breakfast there, which is at nine. The horse is not taken out."

Valentine still hesitating, John added—

"But, I may as well say now that my father's removal need make no difference in our being together. As far as I am concerned, I am very well pleased with our present arrangement. I find in you an aptitude for business affairs that I could by no means have anticipated. So if St. George wants to consult you about some new plan for you (which I hardly think can be the case), you had better hear what I have to say before you turn yourself out."

Valentine thanked him cordially. Emily had pointedly said to him, during his uncle's last illness, that in the event of any change, she should be pleased if he would come and live with her. He had made no answer, because he had not thought John would wish the connection between them to continue. But now everything was easy. His dear old uncle had left him a riding-horse, and some books. He had only to move these to Emily's house, and so without trouble enter another home.

It was not yet nine o'clock when Valentine entered the dining-room in his brother's house.

The gloom was over, the sun had burst forth, lumps of snow, shining in the dazzle of early sunlight, were falling with a dull thud from the trees, while every smaller particle dislodged by a waft of air, dropped with a flash as of a diamond.

First Mrs. Henfrey came in and looked surprised to see Valentine; wondered he had left John; had never seen a man so overcome at his father's funeral. Then Giles came in with some purple and some orange crocuses, which he laid upon his wife's plate. He said nothing about his note, but went and fetched Dorothea, who was also evidently surprised to see Valentine.

How lovely and interesting she looked in his eyes that morning, so serene herself, and an object of such watchful solicitude both to her husband and his old step-sister!

"Any man may feel interested in her now," thought Valentine, excusing himself to himself for the glow of admiring tenderness that filled his heart. "Sweet thing! Oh! what a fool I have been!"

There was little conversation; the ladies were in mourning, and merely asked a few questions as to the arrangements of the late relative's affairs.

Brandon sat at the head of the table, and his wife at his right hand. There was something very cordial in his manner, but such an evident turning away from any mention of having sent for him, that Valentine, perceiving the matter to be private, followed his lead, and when breakfast was over went with him up-stairs to his long room, at the top of the house, his library and workshop.

"Now, then," he exclaimed, when at last the door was shut and they were alone, "I suppose I may speak? What can it be, old fellow, that induced you to send for me at a time so peculiarly inconvenient to John?"

"It was partly something that I read in a newspaper," answered Giles, "and also—also a letter. A letter that was left in my care by your father."

"Oh! then you were to give it to me after my uncle's death, were you?"

For all answer Giles said, "There it is," and Valentine, following his eyes, saw a sealed parcel, not unlike in shape and size to the one he had already opened that morning. It was lying on a small, opened desk. "Take your time, my dear fellow," said Giles, "and read it carefully. I shall come up again soon, and tell you how it came into my possession."

Thereupon he left the room, and Valentine, very much surprised, advanced to the table.

The packet was not directed to any person, but outside it was written in Brandon's clear hand, "Read by me on the 3rd of July, 18—, and sealed up the following morning. G. B."

Valentine sat down before it, broke his brother's seal, and took out a large letter, the seal of which (his father's) had already been broken. It was addressed, in his father's handwriting, "Giles Brandon, Esq., Wigfield House."

We are never so well inclined to believe in a stroke of good fortune as when one has just been dealt to us. Valentine was almost sure he was going to read of something that would prove to be to his advantage. His uncle had behaved so strangely in providing him with his last bounty, that it was difficult for him not to connect this letter with that gift. Something might have been made over to his father on his behalf, and, with this thought in his mind, he unfolded the sheet of foolscap and read as follows:—

"My much-loved Son,—You will see by the date of this letter that my dearest boy Valentine is between seventeen and eighteen years of age when I write it. I perceive a possible peril for him, and my brother being old, there is no one to whom I can so naturally appeal on his behalf as to you.

"I have had great anxiety about you lately, but now you are happily restored to me from the sea, and I know that I may fully trust both to your love and your discretion.

"Some men, my dear Giles, are happy enough to have nothing to hide. I am not of that number; but I bless God that I can say, if I conceal aught, it is not a work of my own doing, nor is it kept secret for my own sake.

"It is now seven weeks since I laid in the grave the body of my aged mother. She left her great-grandson, Peter Melcombe, the only son of my nephew Peter Melcombe, whose father was my fourth brother, her sole heir.

"I do not think it wise to conceal from you that I, being her eldest surviving son, desired of her, that she would not—I mean, that I forbad my mother to leave her property to me.

"It is not for me to judge her. I have never done so; for in her case I know not what I could have done, but I write this in the full confidence that both of you will respect my wishes; and that you, Giles, will never divulge my secret, even to Valentine, unless what I fear should come to pass, and render this necessary.

"If Peter Melcombe, now a child, should live to

marry, and an heir should be born to him, then throw this letter into the fire, and let it be to you as if it had never been written. If he even lives to come of age, at which time he can make a will and leave his property where he pleases, you may destroy it.

"I do not feel afraid that the child will die, it is scarcely to be supposed that he will. I pray God that it may not be so; but in case he should—in case this child should be taken away during his minority, I being already gone—then my grandfather's will is so worded that my son Valentine, my only son, will be his heir.

"Let Valentine know in such a case that I, his dead father, who delighted in him, would rather have seen him die in his cradle, than live by that land and inherit that gold. I have been poor, but I have never turned to anything at Melcombe with one thought that it could mend my case; and as I have renounced it for myself, I would fain renounce it for my heirs for ever. Nothing is so unlikely as that this property should ever fall to my son, but if it should, I trust to his love and duty to let it be, and I trust to you, Giles, to make this easy for him, either to get him away while he is yet young, to lead a fresh and manly life in some one of our colonies, or to find some career at home for him which shall provide him with a competence, that if such a temptation should come in his way, he may not find it too hard to stand against.

"And may the blessing of God light upon you for this (for I know you will do it), more than for all the other acts of dutiful affection you have ever shown me.

"When I desire you to keep this a secret (as I hope always), I make no exception in favour of any person whatever.

"This letter is written with much thought and full deliberation, and signed by him who ever feels as a loving father towards you.

"DANIEL MORTIMER."

Valentine had opened the letter with a preconceived notion as to its contents, and this, together with excessive surprise, made him fail for the moment to perceive one main point that it might have told him.

When Brandon just as he finished reading came back, he found Valentine seated before the letter amazed and pale.

"What does it mean?" he exclaimed, when the two had looked searchingly at one another. "What on earth can it mean?"

"I have no idea," said Giles.

"But you have had it for years," continued Valentine, very much agitated. "Surely you have tried to find out what it means. Have you made no inquiries?"

"Yes. I have been to Melcombe. I could discover nothing at all. No," in answer to another look, "neither then, or at any other time."

"But you are older than I am, so much older, had you never any suspicion of anything at all? Did nothing ever occur before I was old enough to notice things which roused in you any suspicions?"

"Suspicions of what?"

"Of disgrace, I suppose. Of crime perhaps I mean; but I don't know what I mean. Do you think John knows of this?"

"No. I am sure he does not. But don't agitate yourself," he went on, observing that Valentine's hand trembled. "Remember, that whatever this secret was that your father kept buried in his breast, it has never been found out, that is evident, and therefore it is most unlikely now that it ever should be. In my opinion, and it is the only one I have fully formed about the matter, this crime or this disgrace—I quote your own words—must have taken place between sixty and seventy years ago, and your father expressly declares that he had nothing to do with it."

"But if the old woman had," began Valentine vehemently, and paused.

"How can that be?" answered Giles. "He says, 'I know not in her case what I could have done,' and that he has never judged her."

Valentine heaved up a mighty sigh, excitement made his pulses beat and his hands tremble.

"What made you think," he said, "that it was so long ago? I am so surprised that I cannot think coherently."

"To tell you why I think so, is to tell you something more that I believe you don't know."

"Well," said the poor fellow, sighing restlessly, "out with it, Giles."

"Your father began life by running away from home."

"Oh, I know that."

"You do?"

"Yes, my dear father told it to me some weeks before he died, but I did not like it, I wished to dismiss it from my thoughts."

"Indeed! but will you try to remember now, how he told it to you and what he said."

"It was very simple. Though now I come to think of it, with this new light thrown upon it—— Yes; he did put it very oddly, very strangely, so that I did not like the affair, or to think of it. He said that as there was now some intercourse between us and Melcombe, a place that he had not gone near for so very many years, it was almost certain, that, sooner or later, I should hear something concerning himself that would surprise me. It was singular that I had not heard it already. I did not like to hear him talk in his usual pious way of such an occurrence; for though of course we know that all things *are* overruled for good to those who love God——"

"Well?" said Brandon, when he paused to ponder.

"Well," repeated Valentine, "for all that, and though he referred to that very text, I did not like to hear him say that he blessed God he had been led to do it; and that, if ever I heard of it, I was to remember that he thought of it with gratitude."

Saying this, he turned over the pages again. "But there is nothing of that here," he said, "how did you discover it?"

"I was told of it at Melcombe," said Brandon, hesitating.

"By whom?"

"It seemed to be familiarly known there." He glanced at the *Times* which was laid on the table just beyond the desk at which Valentine sat. "It was little Peter Melcombe," he said gravely, "who mentioned it to me."

"What! the poor little heir!" exclaimed Valentine, rather contemptuously. "I would not be in his shoes for a good deal! But Giles—but Giles—you have shown me the letter!"

He started up.

"Yes, there IT is," said Giles, glancing again at the *Times*, for he perceived instantly that Valentine for the first time had remembered on what contingency he was to be told of this matter.

There it was indeed! The crisis of his fate in a few sorrowful words had come before him.

"At Corfu, on the 28th of February, to the inexpressible grief of his mother, Peter, only child of the late Peter Melcombe, Esq., and great-grandson and heir of the late Mrs. Melcombe, of Melcombe. In the twelfth year of his age."

"Good heavens!" exclaimed Valentine, in an awestruck whisper. "Then it has come to this, after all?"

He sat silent so long, that his brother had full time once more to consider this subject in all its bearings, to perceive that Valentine was trying to discover some reasonable cause for what his father had done, and then to see his countenance gradually clear and his now flashing eyes lose their troubled expression.

"I know you have respected my poor father's confidence," he said at last.

"Yes, I have."

"And you never heard anything from him by word of mouth that seemed afterwards to connect itself with this affair?"

"Yes, I did," Brandon answered, "he said to me just before my last voyage, that he had written an important letter, told me where it was, and desired me to observe that his faculties were quite unimpaired long after the writing of it."

"I do not think they could have been," Valentine put in, and he continued his questions. "You think that you have never, never heard him say anything, at any time which at all puzzled or startled you, and which you remembered after this?"

"No, I never did. He never surprised me, or excited any suspicion at any time about anything, till I had broken the seal of that letter."

"And after all," Valentine said, turning the pages, "how little there is in it, how little it tells me!"

"Hardly anything, but there is a great deal, there is everything in his having been impelled to write it."

"Well, poor man" (Giles was rather struck by this epithet), "if secrecy was his object, he has made that at least impossible. I must soon know all, whatever it is. And more than that, if I act as he wishes, in fact, as he commands, all the world will set itself to investigate the reason."

"Yes, I am afraid so," Brandon answered, "I have often thought of that."

Valentine went on. "I always knew, felt rather, that he must have had a tremendous quarrel with his elder brother. He never would mention him if he could help it, and showed an ill-disguised unforgiving sort of—almost dread, I was going to say, of him, as if he had been fearfully bullied by him in his boyhood and could not forget it; but," he continued, still pondering, "it surely is carrying both anger and superstition a little too far, to think that when he is in his grave it will do his son any harm to inherit the land of the brother he quarrelled with."

"Yes," said Giles, "when one considers how most of the land of this country was first acquired, how many crimes lie heavy on its various conquerors, and how many more have been perpetrated in its transmission from one possessor to another;" then he paused, and Valentine took up his words.

"It seems incredible that he should have thought an old quarrel (however bitter) between two boys ought, more than half a century afterwards, to deprive the son of one of them from taking his lawful inheritance."

"Yes," Brandon said. "He was no fool; he could not have thought so, and therefore it could not have been that, or anything like it. Nor could he have felt that he was in any sense answerable for the poor man's death, for I have ascertained that there had been no communication between the two branches of the family for several years before he laid violent hands on himself."

Valentine sighed restlessly. "The whole thing is perfectly unreasonable," he said; "in fact, it would be impossible to do as he desires, even if I were ever so willing."

"Impossible?" exclaimed Brandon.

"Yes, the estate is already mine; how is it possible for me not to take it? I must prove the will, the old will, the law would see to that, for there will be legacy duty to pay. Even if I chose to fling the income into the pond, I must save out enough to satisfy the tax-gatherers. You seem to take for granted that I will and can calmly and secretly let the estate be. But have you thought out the details at all? Have you formed any theory as to how this is to be done?"

He spoke with some impatience and irritation, it vexed him to perceive that his brother had fully counted on the dead father's letter being obeyed. Brandon had nothing to say.

"Besides," continued Valentine, "where is this

sort of thing to stop? If I die to-morrow, John is my heir. Is he to let it alone? Could he?"

"I don't know," answered Brandon. "He has not the same temptation to take it that you have."

"Temptation!" repeated Valentine.

Brandon did not retract or explain the word.

"And does he know any reason, I wonder, why he should renounce it?" continued Valentine, but as he spoke his hand, which he had put out to take the *Times*, paused on its way, and his eyes involuntarily opened a little wider. Something, it seemed, had struck him, and he was recalling it and puzzling it out. Two or three lilies thrown under a lilac tree by John's father had come back to report themselves, nothing more recent or more startling than that, for he was still thinking of the elder brother. "And he must have hated him to the full as much as my poor father did," was his thought. "That garden had been shut up for his sake many, many years. Wait a minute, if that man got the estate wrongfully, I'll have nothing to do with it after all. Nonsense! Why do I slander the dead in my thoughts? as if I had not read that will many times—he inherited after the old woman's sickly brother, who died at sea." After this his thoughts wandered into all sorts of vague and intricate paths that led to no certain goal; he was not even certain at last that there was anything real to puzzle about. His father might have been under some delusion after all.

At last his wandering eyes met Brandon's.

"Well!" he exclaimed, as if suddenly waking up.

"How composedly he takes it, and yet how amazed he is!" thought Brandon. "Well," he replied, by way of answer.

"I shall ask you, Giles, as you have kept this matter absolutely secret so long, to keep it secret still; at any rate for awhile, from every person whatever."

"I think you have a right to expect that of me. I will."

"Poor little fellow! died at Corfu then. The news is all over Wigfield by this time, no doubt. John knows it of course, now." Again he paused, and this time it was his uncle's last conversation that recurred to his memory. It was most unwelcome. Brandon could see that he looked more than disturbed; he was also angry; and yet after awhile, both these feelings melted away, he was like a man who had walked up to a cobweb, that stretched itself before his face, but when he had put up his hand and cleared it off, where was it?

He remembered how the vague talk of a dying old man had startled him.

The manner of the gift and the odd feeling he had suffered at the time, as if it might be somehow connected with the words said, appeared to rise up to be looked at. But one can hardly look straight at a thing of that sort without making it change its aspect. Sensations and impressions are subject to us; they may be reasoned down. His reason was stronger than his fear had been, and made it look foolish. He brought back the words, they were disjointed, they accused no one, they could not be put together. So he covered that recollection over, and threw it aside. He did not consciously hide it from himself, but he did know in his own mind that he should not relate it to his brother.

"Well, you have done your part," he said at length; "and now I must see about doing mine."

"No one could feel more keenly than I do, how hard this is upon you," said Brandon; but Valentine detected a tone of relief in his voice, as if he took the words to mean a submission to the father's wish, and as if he was glad. "My poor father might have placed some confidence in me, instead of treating me like a child," he said bitterly; "why on earth could he not tell me all."

"Why, my dear fellow," exclaimed Brandon; "surely if you were to renounce the property, it would have been hard upon you and John to be shamed or tortured by any knowledge of the crime and disgrace that it came with."

"That it came with!" repeated Valentine; "you take that for granted, then? You have got further than I have."

"I think, of course, that the crime was committed, or the disgrace incurred, for the sake of the property."

"Well," said Valentine, "I am much more uncertain about the whole thing than you seem to be. I shall make it my duty to investigate the matter. I must find out everything; perhaps it will be only too easy; according to what I find I shall act. One generation has no right so to dominate over another as to keep it always in childlike bondage to a command for which no reason is given. If, when I know, I consider that my dear father was right, I shall of my own free-will sell the land, and divest myself of the proceeds. If that he was wrong, I shall go and live fearlessly and freely in that house, and on that land which, in the course of providence, has come to me."

"Reasonable and cool," thought Brandon. "Have I any right to say more? He will do just what he says. No one was ever more free from superstition; and he is of age, as he reminds me."

"Very well," he then said aloud; "you have a right to do as you please. Still, I must remind you of your father's distinct assertion, that in this case he has set you an example. He would not have the land."

"Does he mean," said Valentine, confused between his surprise at the letter, his own recollections, and his secret wishes—"Does he, can he mean, that his old mother positively asked him to be her heir, and he refused?"

"I cannot tell; how is the will worded?"

"My great-grandfather left his estate to his only son, and if *he* died childless, to his eldest grandson; both these were mere boys at the time, and if neither lived to marry, then the old man left his estate to his only daughter. That was my grandmother, you know, and she had it for many years."

"And she had power to will it away, as is evident."

"Yes, she might leave it to any one of her sons, or his representative; but she was not to divide it into shares. And in case of the branch she favoured dying out, the estate was to revert to his heir-at-law—the old man's heir-at-law, you know, his nearest of kin. That would have been my father, if he had lived a year or two longer, he was the second son. It is a most complicated and voluminous will."

Brandon asked one more question. "But its provisions come to an end with you, is it not so? It is not entailed, and you can do with it exactly as you please."

Valentine's countenance fell a little when his brother said this; he perceived that he chanced to be more free than most heirs, he had more freedom than he cared for.

"Yes," he replied, "that is so."

CHAPTER XXII.

SOPHISTRY.

"'As he has not trusted me, he will never know how I should scorn to be a thief,' quoth the school boy yesterday, when his master's orchard gate was locked; but, 'It's all his own fault,' quoth the same boy to-day while he was stealing his master's plums, 'why did he leave the gate ajar?'"

"VAL," said Brandon, "I do hope you will give yourself time to consider this thing in all its bearings before you decide. I am afraid if you make a mistake, it will prove a momentous one."

He spoke with a certain feeling of restraint, his advice had not been asked; and the two brothers began to perceive by this time that it was hard to keep up an air of easy familiarity when neither felt really at ease. Each was thinking of the lovely young wife down-stairs. One felt that he could hardly preach to the man whose folly had been his own opportunity, the other felt that nothing would be more sweet than to let her see that, after all, she had married a man not half so rich nor in so good a position as her first love, for so he chose to consider himself. How utter, how thorough an escape this would be also from the least fear of further dependence on Giles! And, as to his having made a fool of himself, and having been well laughed at for his pains, he was perfectly aware that as Melcombe of Melcombe, and with those personal advantages that he by no means undervalued, nobody would choose to remember that story against him, and he might marry almost wherever he pleased.

As he turned in his chair to think, he caught a glimpse of his old uncle's house, just a corner through some trees, of his own bedroom window there, the place where that parcel was.

He knew that, think as long as he would, Giles would not interrupt. "Yes, that parcel! Well, I'm independent, anyhow," he considered exultingly; and the further thought came into his mind, "I am well enough off. What if I were to give this up and stay with John? I know he is surprised and pleased to find me so useful. I shall be more so; the work suits me, and brings out all I have in me; I like it. Then I always liked being with Emily, and I should soon be master in that house. Bother the estate! I felt at first that I could not possibly fling it by, but really—really I believe that in a few years, when John goes into Parliament, he'll make me his partner. It's very perplexing; yes, I'll think it well over, as Giles says. I'll do as I please; and I've a great mind to let that doomed old den alone after all."

Though he expressed his mind in these undignified words, it was not without manly earnestness that he turned back to his brother, and said seriously, "Giles, I do assure you that I will decide nothing till I have given the whole thing my very best attention. In the meantime, of course, whatever you hear, you will say nothing. I shall certainly not go to Melcombe for a few days, I've got so attached to John, somehow, that I cannot think of leaving him in the lurch just now when he is out of spirits, and likes to have me with him."

Thereupon the brothers parted, Valentine going downstairs, and Brandon sitting still in his room, a smile dawning on his face, and a laugh following.

"Leaving John in the lurch!" he repeated. "What would my lord John think if he could hear that; but I have noticed for some time that they like one another. What a notion Val has suddenly formed of his own importance! There was really something like dignity in his leave-taking. He does not intend that I should interfere, as is evident. And I am not certain that if he asked for my advice I should know what to say. I was very clear in my own mind that when he consulted me I should say, 'Follow your father's desire.' I am still clear that I would do so myself in such a case; but I am not asked for my opinion. I think he will renounce the inheritance, on reflection; if he does, I shall be truly glad that it was not at all by my advice, or to please me. But if he does not? Well, I shall not wish to make the thing out any worse than it is. I always thought that letter weak as a command, but strong as a warning. It would be, to say the least of it, a dutiful and filial action to respect that warning. A warning not to perpetuate some wrong, for instance; but what wrong? I saw a miniature of Daniel Mortimer the elder, smiling, handsome, and fair-haired. It not only reminded me strongly of my step-father, but of the whole race, John, Valentine, John's children, and all. Therefore, I am sure there need be 'no scandal about Queen Elizabeth' Mortimer, and its discovery on the part of her son."

Meanwhile, Valentine, instead of driving straight back to Wigfield, stopped short at his sister Emily's new house, intending to tell her simply of the death of little Peter Melcombe, and notice how she took it. O that the letter had been left to him instead of to Giles! How difficult it was, moreover, to believe that Giles had possessed it so long, and yet that its contents were dead to every one else that breathed! If Giles had not shown him by his manner what he ought to do, he thought he might have felt better inclined to do it. Certain it is that being now alone, he thought of his father's desire with more respect.

Emily had been settled about a month in her new house, and Miss Christie Grant was with her. There was a pretty drawing-room, with bow windows at the back of it. Emily had put there her Indian cabinets, and many other beautiful things brought from the east, besides decorating it with delicate ferns, and bulbs in flower. She was slightly inclined to be lavish so far as she could afford it; but her Scotch blood kept her just on the right side of prudence, and so gave more grace to her undoubted generosity.

This house, which had been chosen by Mrs. Henfrey, was less than a quarter of a mile from John Mortimer's, and was approached by the same sandy lane. In front, on the opposite side of this lane, the house was sheltered by a great cliff, crowned with fir trees, and enriched with wild plants and swallows' caves; and behind, at the end of her garden ran the same wide brook which made a boundary for John Mortimer's ground.

This circumstance was a great advantage to the little Mortimers, who with familiar friendship made themselves at once at home all over Mrs. Nemily's premises, and forthwith set little boats and ships afloat on the brook in the happy certainty that sooner or later they would come down to their rightful owners.

Valentine entered the drawing-room, and a glance as he stooped to kiss his sister served to assure him that she knew nothing of the great news.

She put her two hands upon his shoulders, and her sweet eyes looked into his. A slightly shamefaced expression struck her. "Does the dear boy think he is in love again?" she thought; "who is it, I wonder?" The look became almost sheepish; and she, rather surprised, said to him, "Well, Val, you see the house is ready."

"Yes," he answered, looking round him with a sigh.

Emily felt that he might well look grave and sad; it was no common friend that he had lost. "How is John?" she asked.

"Why, he was very dull; very dull indeed, when I

left him this morning; and natural enough he should be."

"Yes, most natural."

Then he said, after a little more conversation on their recent loss, "Emily, I came to tell you something very important—to me at least," here the shamefaced look came back. "Oh, no," he exclaimed, as a flash of amazement leaped out of her eyes; "nothing of that sort."

"I am glad to hear it," she answered, not able to forbear smiling; "but sit down then, you great, long-legged fellow, you put me out of conceit with this room; you make the ceiling look too low."

"Oh, do I?" said Valentine, and he sat down in a comfortable chair, and thought he could have been very happy with Emily, and did not know how to begin to tell her.

"I must say I admire your taste, Emily," he then said, looking about him, and shirking the great subject.

Emily was a little surprised at his holding off in this way, so she in her turn took the opportunity to say something fresh; something that she thought he might as well hear.

"And so John's dull, is he? Poor John! Do you know, Val, the last time I saw him he was very cross."

"Indeed! why was he cross?"

"It was about a month ago. He laughed, but I know he was cross. St. George and I went over at his breakfast-time to get the key of this house, which had been left with him; and, while I ran up-stairs to see the children, he told St. George how, drawing up his blind to shave that morning, he had seen you chasing Barbara and Miss Green (that little temporary governess of theirs) about the garden. Barbara threw some snowballs at you, but you caught her and kissed her."

"She is a kind of cousin," Valentine murmured; "besides, she is a mere child."

"But she is a very tall child," said Emily. "She is within two inches as tall as I am. Miss Green is certainly no child."

Valentine did not wish to enter on that side of the question. "I'm sure I don't know how one can find out when to leave off kissing one's cousins," he observed.

"Oh! I can give you an easy rule for that," said Emily; "leave off the moment you begin to care to do it: they will probably help you by beginning, just about the same time, to think they have bestowed kisses enough."

"It all arose out of my kindness," said Valentine. "John had already begun to be anxious about the dear old man, so I went over that morning before breakfast, and sent him up a message. His father was decidedly better; and as he had to take a journey that day, I thought he should know it as soon as possible. But Emily——"

"Yes, dear boy?"

"I really did come to say something important." And instantly as he spoke he felt what a tragical circumstance this was for some one else, and that such would be Emily's first thought and view of it.

"What is it?" she exclaimed, now a little startled.

Valentine had turned rather pale. He tasted the bitter ingredients in this cup of prosperity more plainly now; and he wished that letter was at the bottom of the sea. "Why—why it is something you will be very sorry for, too," he said, his voice faltering. "It's poor little Peter Melcombe."

"Oh!" exclaimed Emily, with an awestruck shudder. "There! I said so."

"WHAT did you say?" cried Valentine, so much struck by her words that he recovered his self-possession instantly.

"Poor, poor woman," she went on, the ready tears falling on her cheeks; "and he was her only child!"

"But what do you mean, Emily?" continued

Valentine, startled and suspicious. "*What* did you say?"

"Oh!" she answered, "nothing that I had any particular reason for saying. I felt that it might be a great risk to take that delicate boy to Italy again, where he had been ill before, and I told John I wished we could prevent it. I could not forget that his death would be a fine thing for my brother, and I felt a sort of fear that this would be the end of it."

Valentine was relieved. She evidently knew nothing, and he could listen calmly while she went on.

"My mere sense of the danger made it a necessity for me to act. I suppose you will be surprised when I tell you"—here two more tears fell—"that I wrote to Mrs. Melcombe. I knew she was determined to go on the Continent, and I said if she liked to leave her boy behind, I would take charge of him. It was the day before dear Fred was taken ill."

"And she declined!" said Valentine. "Well, it was very kind of you, very good of you, and just like you. Let us hope poor Mrs. Melcombe does not remember it now."

"Yes, she declined; said her boy had an excellent constitution. Where did the poor little fellow die?"

"At Corfu."

Emily wept for sympathy with the mother, and Valentine sat still opposite to her, and was glad of the silence; it pleased him to think of this that Emily had done, till all on a sudden some familiar words out of the Bible flashed into his mind, strange, quaint words, and it seemed much more as if somebody kept repeating them in his presence than as if he had turned them over himself to the surface, from among the mass of scraps that were lying littered about in the chambers of his memory. "The words of Jonadab the son of Rechab, that he commanded his sons."

"May I see the letter?" asked Emily.

"There was no letter; we saw it in the *Times*,"

said Valentine; and again the mental repetition began. "The son of Rechab, that he commanded HIS sons, are performed; for unto this day——"

Emily had dried her eyes now. "Well, Val dear," she said, and hesitated.

"Oh, I wish she would give me time to get once straight through to the end, and have done with it," thought Valentine. "'The words of Jonadab the son of Rechab, that he commanded *his* sons, are——' (yes, only the point of it is that they're not—not yet, at any rate) the words of Jonadab."

Here Emily spoke again. "Well, Val, nobody ever came into an estate more naturally and rightly than you do, for, however well you may have behaved about it, and nobody could have behaved better, you must have felt that as the old lady chose to leave all to one son, that should not have been the youngest. I hope you will be happy; and I know you will make a kind, good landlord. It seems quite providential that you should have spent so much time in learning all about land and farming. I have always felt that all which was best and nicest in you would come out, if you could have prosperity, and we now see that it was intended for you."

Cordial, delightful words to Valentine; they almost made him forget this letter that she had never heard of.

"Oh, if you please, ma'am," exclaimed a female servant, bursting into the room, "Mr. Brandon's love to you. He has sent the pony-carriage, and he wants you to come back in it directly."

Something in the instant attention paid to this message, and the alacrity with which Emily ran up-stairs, as if perfectly ready, and expectant of it, showed Valentine that it did not concern his inheritance, but also what and whom it probably did concern, and he sauntered into the little hall to wait for Emily, put her into the carriage and fold the rug round her, while he observed without much surprise that she had for the moment quite forgotten his special affairs, and was anxious and rather urgent to be off.

Then he drove into Wigfield, considering in his own mind that if John did not know anything concerning the command in this strange letter, he and he only was the person who ought to be told and consulted about it.

It rained now, and when he entered the bank and paused to take off his wet coat, he saw on every face as it was lifted up that his news was known, and his heart beat so fast as he knocked at John's door that he had hardly strength to obey the hearty "Come in."

Two minutes would decide what John knew, and whether he also had a message to give him from the dead. John was standing with his back to the fire, grave and lost in thought. Valentine came in, and sat down on one side of the grate, putting his feet on the fender to warm them. When he had done this, he longed to change his attitude, for John neither moved nor spoke, and he could not see his face. His own agitation made him feel that he was watched, and that he could not seem ill at ease, and must not be the first to move; but at last when the silence and immobility of John became intolerable to him, he suddenly pushed back his chair, and looked up. John then turned his head slightly, and their eyes met.

"You know it," said Valentine.

"Yes," John answered gravely, "of course."

"Oh! what next, what next?" thought Valentine, and he spent two or three minutes in such a tumult of keen expectation and eager excitement, that he could hear every beat of his heart quite plainly, and then—

"It is a very great upset of all my plans," John said, still with more gravity than usual. "I had fully intended—indeed, I had hoped, old fellow, that you and I would be partners some day."

"Oh, John," exclaimed Valentine, a sudden revulsion of feeling almost overcoming him now he found that his fears as to what John might be thinking of were groundless. "Oh, John, I wish we could! It might be a great deal better for me. And so you really did mean it? You are more like a brother than anything else. I hate the thought of that ill-starred house; I think I'll stop here with you."

"Nonsense," said John, just as composedly and as gravely as ever; "what do you mean, you foolish lad?" But he appreciated the affection Valentine had expressed for him, and kindly put his hand on his young relative's shoulder.

Valentine had never found it so hard to understand himself as at that moment. His course was free, Giles could not speak, and John knew nothing; yet either the firm clasp of a man's hand on his shoulder roused him to the fact that he cared for this man so much that he could be happier under his orders than free and his own master, or else his father's words gathered force by mere withdrawal of opposition.

For a moment he almost wished John did know; he wanted to be fortified in his desire to remain with him; and yet—— No! he could not tell him; that would be taking his fate out of his own hands for ever.

"You think then I must—take it up; in short, go and live in it?" he said at length.

"Think!" exclaimed John, with energy and vehemence; "why, who could possibly think otherwise?"

"I've always been accustomed to go in and out amongst a posse of my own relations."

"Your own relations must come to you then," answered John pleasantly, "I, for one. Why, Melcombe's only fifty or sixty miles off, man!"

"It seems to me now that I'm very sorry for that poor little fellow's death," Valentine went on.

"Nobody could have behaved better during his lifetime than you have done," John said. "Why,

Val," he exclaimed, looking down, "you astonish me!"

Valentine was vainly struggling with tears. John went and bolted the door; then got some wine, and brought him a glass.

"As calm as possible during my father's death and funeral," he thought, "and now half choking himself, forsooth, because his fortune's made, and he must leave his relations. I trust and hope, with all my heart, that Dorothea is not at the bottom of this! I supposed his nerves to be strong enough for anything."

Valentine was deadly pale. He put up a shaking hand for the glass, and as he drank the wine, and felt the blood creeping warmly about his limbs again, he thought "John knows nothing whatever. No wonder he is astonished, he little thinks what a leap in the dark it is."

And so the die was cast.

A few days after this Gladys and Barbara received letters; the first ran as follows:—

"MY DEAR YOUNG FRIENDS,—Owe you three-and-sixpence for Blob's biscuits, do I? Don't you know that it is not polite to remind people of their debts? When you would have been paid that money I cannot think, if it were not for a circumstance detailed below. I have just been reading that the finest minds always possess a keen sense of humour, so if you find nothing to laugh at in this, it will prove that there is nothing particular in you. Did I ever think there was? Well, why *will* you ask such awkward questions?—Off!

THE NOBLE TUCK-MAN.

Americus as he did wend
  With A. J. Mortimer, his chum,
The two were greeted by a friend,
  "And how are you, boys, Hi, Ho, **Hum**?"

He spread a note so crisp, so neat
  (Ho and Hi, and tender Hum),

"If you of this a fifth can eat
I'll give you the remainder. Come!"

To the tuck-shop three repair
(Ho and Hum, and pensive Hi),
One looks on to see all's fair
Two call out for hot mince pie.

Thirteen tarts, a few Bath buns
(Hi and Hum, and gorgeous Ho),
Lobster cakes (the butter'd ones),
All at once they cry "No go."

Then doth tuck-man smile. "Them there
(Ho and Hi, and futile Hum)
Jellies three and sixpence air,
Use of spoons an equal sum."

Three are rich. Sweet task 'tis o'er,
"Tuckman, you're a brick," they cry,
Wildly then shake hands all four
(Hum and Ho, the end is Hi).

"N.B.—He spoke as good English as we did, and we did not shake hands with him. Such is poetic license. I may have exaggerated a little, as to the number of things we ate. I repeat, I *may* have done. You will never be able to appreciate me till you have learned to make allowance for such little eccentricities of genius.

"Yours, with sentiments that would do anybody credit,

"GIFFORD CRAYSHAW."

The second letter, which was also addressed to both sisters, was from Johnnie, and ran as follows:—

"Now look here, you two fellows are not to expect me to spend all my spare time in writing to you. Where do you think I am now? Why, at Brighton.

"Val's a brick. Yesterday was our *Exeat*, and he came down to Harrow, called for me and Cray, and brought us here to the Old Ship Hotel. We two chose the dinner, and in twenty minutes that dinner was gone like a dream. Val and Cray made the unlucky waiter laugh till he dropped the butter-boat. The waiter was a proud man—I never saw a prouder. He had made up his mind that nothing should make him laugh, but at last we had him. Beware of pride, my friends.

"Then we went to the Aquarium. My wig! I never saw anything so extraordinary. It ought to be called the Aquaria, for there are dozens of them. They are like large rooms full of water, and you go and look in at the fish through the windows. No, they're more like caves than rooms, they have rocks for walls. Talk of the ancient Greeks! I'll never wish to be one of those fogies again! I've seen turtles now under water, sitting opposite to one another, bowing and looking each in his fellow's face, just like two cats on a rug. Why the world's full of things that *they* knew nothing about.

"But I had no notion that fish were such fools, some of them, at least. There were some conger eels seven feet long, and when we stared at them they went and stuck their little heads into crevices in the rocks. I should like to have reasoned with them, for they evidently thought they were hidden, while, in fact, they were wriggling upside down, full in view. Well, so then we went to see the octopus. One was just like a pink satin bag, covered with large ivory buttons, but that was only because it was inside out. While I was watching it I rather started, for I saw in a corner of the den close to me an enormous sort of bloated sea toadstool (as I thought), but it had eyes, it was covered with warts, it seemed very faint, and it heaved and panted. By that time a conglomeration like a mass of writhing serpents was letting itself down the side of the den, and when it got to the bottom it shot out a head, made itself into the exact shape of an owl without wings, and began to fly about the place. That made three.

"An old woman who was looking at them too, called out then, 'Oh, you brute, I hate you,' and Val said to her, 'My good lady, allow me to suggest that it is not hatred you feel, but envy. Envy is a very bad passion, and it is our duty to try and restrain it.' 'Sir,' said the old lady, rather fiercely. 'No, we must not give way to envy,' Val persisted, 'though, indeed, what are we in comparison with creatures who can turn themselves inside out as soon as look at you, fly without wings, and walk up a precipice by means of one pearl button?' 'If the police were after you, it might be handy to turn yourself inside out, I'll allow,' she answered, in a very loud, angry voice, 'so as they should not know you; but I wouldn't, if I could, I'll assure you, young man, no, that I wouldn't, not for all the pearl buttons in the world.'

"Well, I never wrote such a long letter in my life, it must count for three, mind. We had a great deal more fun after that, but Val and I got away, because a little crowd collected. Cray stayed behind, pretending he did not belong to us, and he heard a man say, 'Perhaps the gentleman's a parson; that sort always think they ought to be *moralising* about something or other.' And he found out by their talk that the old lady was a clearstarcher, so when she was alone again we went back. Val said he should be some time at Brighton, and he gave her his address and offered her his washing. She asked for his name, too, and he replied—you know how grave Val is—'Well, ma'am, I'm sorry to say I cannot oblige you with my name, because I don't know it. All I am sure about is, that it begins with an M; but I've written up to London, and I shall know for a certainty the week after next.' So she winked at me, and tapped herself on the forehead. Val is very much vexed because he came up to London about the will, and the lawyers say he cannot —or somebody else, I don't know which—cannot administer it unless he takes the name of Melcombe. So what he said was quite true, and afterwards we heard the old lady telling her friends that he was demented, but he seemed very harmless and good.

"It's an extraordinary thing, isn't it, that Val has

turned out to be rich. Please thank father for writing and telling me about it all. Val doesn't seem to care, and he hates changing his name. He was quite crusty when we congratulated him.

"Give my love to the kids, and tell them if they don't weed my garden they will catch it when I come home.

"I remain, your deservedly revered brother,

"A. J. M."

A postscript followed, from Crayshaw :—

"What this fellow says is quite right, our letters are worth three of yours. You never once mentioned my guinea-pigs in your last, and we don't care whether there is a baby at Wigfield or not. Pretty, is he? I know better, they are all ugly. Fanny Crayshaw has just got another. I detest babies; but George thinks (indeed many parents do) that the youngest infant is just as much a human being as he is himself, even when it is squalling, in fact more so."

CHAPTER XXIII.

DANTE AND OTHERS.

"He climbed the wall of heaven, and saw his love
Safe at her singing; and he left his foes
In vales of shadow weltering, unassoiled,
Immortal sufferers henceforth, in both worlds."

IT was the middle of April. Valentine was gone, and the Mortimer children were running wild, for their nurse had suddenly departed on account of the airs of the new lady-housekeeper, who, moreover, had quarrelled with the new governess.

John was now without doubt Mr. Mortimer, the head of his family and all alone of his name, for Valentine had been obliged to take the name of Melcombe, and, rather to the surprise of his family, had no sooner got things a little settled than he had started across the Continent to meet Mrs. Peter Melcombe, and bring her home to England.

Mr. Mortimer still felt his father's death, and he regretted Valentine's absence more than he cared to confess. He lost his temper rather often, at that particular season, for he did not know where to turn. The housekeeper and the governess insisted frequently on appealing to him against each other, about all sorts of matters that he knew nothing of, and the children took advantage of their feuds to do precisely as they pleased. John's house, though it showed evidently enough that it was a rich man's abode, had a comfortable homeliness about it, but it had always been a costly house to keep, and now that it was less than ever needful to him to save money, he did not want to hear recriminations concerning such petty matters as the too frequent tuning of the school-room piano, and the unprofitable fabrics which had been bought for the children's dresses.

In less than two years Parliament would dissolve. It was now frequently said that Mr. Mortimer was to stand for the borough of Wigfield; but how this was compatible with the present state of his household he did not know.

"I suppose," he said to himself one morning, with a mighty sigh, "I suppose there is only one way out of it all. I really must take a liking to red hair. Well! not just yet."

It was about ten o'clock in the morning when he said this, and he was setting out to walk across the fields, and call for the first time on Mrs. Frederic Walker. He was taking his three younger children with him to make an apology to her.

Now that Mrs. Walker was a widow, she and Mr. Mortimer had half unconsciously changed their manner slightly towards each other; they were just as friendly as before, but not so familiar; the children, however, were very intimate with her.

"She didn't want that bit of garden," argued little Hugh, as one who felt aggrieved; "and when she saw that we had taken it she only laughed."

The fact was, that finding a small piece of waste ground at the back of Mrs. Walker's shrubbery, the children had dug it over, divided it with oyster-shells into four portions, planted it with bulbs and roots, and in their own opinion it was now theirs. They came rather frequently to dig in it. Sometimes on these occasions they went in-doors to see "Mrs. Nemily," and perhaps partake of bread and jam. Once they came in to complain of her gardener, who had been weeding in *their* gardens. They wished her to forbid this. Emily laughed, and said she would.

Their course of honest industry was, however, discovered at last by the twins; and now they were to give up the gardens, which seemed a sad pity, just when they had been intending to put in spring crops.

Some people never really *have* anything. It is not only that they can get no good out of things (that is common even among those who are able both to have and to hold), but that they don't know how to reign over their possessions and appropriate them.

Their chattels appear to know this, and despise them; their dogs run after other men; the best branches of their rose-trees climb over the garden-wall, and people who smell at the flowers there appear to supply a reason for any roses being planted inside. Such people always know their weak point, and spend their own money as if they had stolen it.

The little Mortimers were not related to them. Here was a piece of ground which nobody cultivated; it manifestly wanted owners; they took it, weeded it, and flung out all the weeds into Mrs. Walker's garden.

The morning was warm; a south wind was fluttering the half-unfolded leaf-buds, and spreading abroad the soft odour of violets and primroses which covered the sunny slopes.

John's children, when they came in at Mrs. Walker's drawing-room window, brought some of this delicate fragrance of the spring upon their hair and clothes. Grown-up people are not in the habit of rolling about, or tumbling down over beds of flowers. They must take the consequences, and leave the ambrosial scents of the wood behind them.

John himself, who had not been prepared to see them run off from him at the last moment, beheld their active little legs disappearing as they got over the low ledge of the open window. He, however, did not follow their example, but walked round to the front of the house, and was shown into the drawing-room, after ringing the bell, Emily lifting up her head at his entrance with evident surprise. He was surprised too, even startled, for on a sofa opposite to her sat a lady whom he had been thinking of a good deal during the previous month—her of the golden head, Miss Justina Fairbairn. It was evident that the children had not announced his intended call.

Miss Justina Fairbairn was the daughter of an old K.C.B. deceased. She and her mother were poor, but they were much respected as sensible, dignified women; and they had that kind of good opinion of themselves which those who hold in sincerity (having no doubt or misgiving) can generally spread among their friends.

Miss Fairbairn was a fine, tall woman, with something composed and even motherly in her appearance; her fair and rather wide face had a satisfied, calm expression, excepting when she chanced to meet John, and then a flash would come from those cold blue eyes, a certain hope, doubt, or feeling of suspense would assert itself in spite of her. It never rose to actual expectation, for she was most reasonable; and John had never shown her any attention; but she had a sincere conviction that a marriage with her would be the best and most suitable that was possible for him. It was almost inconceivable, she thought, that he could escape the knowledge of this fact long. She was so every way suitable. She was about thirty-two years of age, and she felt sure he ought not to marry a younger woman.

Many people thought as she did, that Mr. Mortimer could not do better than marry Miss Fairbairn; and it is highly probable that this opinion had originated with herself, though it must be well understood that she had not expressed it. Thoughts are certainly able to spread themselves without the aid of looks or language. Invisible seed that floats from the parent plant can root itself wherever it settles and thoughts must have some medium through which they sail till they reach minds that can take them in, and there they strike root, and whole crops of the same sort come up, just as if they were indigenous, and naturally belonging to their entertainers. This is even more true in great matters than in small.

Miss Fairbairn, as usual when she saw John, became gracious. John was thought to be a very intellectual man; she was intellectual, and meant to be more so. John was specially fond of his children; her talk concerning children should be both wise and kind.

Real love of children and childhood is, however, a quality that no one can successfully feign. John had occasionally been seen, by observant matrons and maids, to attempt with a certain uncouth tenderness to do his children womanly service. He could tie their bonnet-strings and sashes when these came undone. They had been known to apply to him during a walk to take stones out of their boots, and also to lace these up again.

Why should we write of children as if they were just like grown-up people? They are not in the least like, any more than they are like one another; but here they are, and if we can neither love nor understand them, woe betide us!

"No more crying, my dear," John had said that morning to his youngest daughter.

He had just administered a reproof to her as he sat at breakfast, for some infantile delinquency; and she, sniffing and sobbing piteously, testified a desire to kiss him in token of penitence.

"I'm good now," she remarked.

"Where's your pocket-handkerchief?" said her father, with magisterial dignity.

The infant replied that she had lost it, and straightway asked to borrow his.

John lent the article, and having made use of it,

she pushed it back with all good faith into his breast-pocket, and repeating, "I'm good now," received the coveted kiss, and presently after a donation of buttered toast, upon which she became as happy as ever.

In ordinary life it devolves on the mother to lend a handkerchief; but if children have none, there are fathers who can rise to such occasions, and not feel afterwards as if heroic sacrifices had been demanded of them.

John Mortimer felt that Miss Fairbairn had never before greeted him with so much *empressement*. They sat down, and she immediately began to talk to him. A flattering hope that he had known of her presence, and had come at once to see her, gave her just the degree of excitement that she wanted to enable her to produce her thoughts at their best; while he, accustomed by experience to caution, and not ready yet to commit himself, longed to remark that he had been surprised as well as pleased to see her. But he found no opportunity at first to do it; and in the meantime Emily sat and looked on, and listened to their conversation with an air of easy *insouciance* very natural and becoming to her. Emily was seven-and-twenty, and had always been accustomed to defer to Miss Fairbairn as much older as well as wiser than herself; and this deference did not seem out of place, for the large, fair spinster made the young matron look slender and girlish.

John Mortimer remembered how Emily had said a year ago that he could not do better than marry Justina. He thought she had invited her there to that end; and as he talked he took care to express to her by looks his good-humoured defiance; whereupon she defended herself with her eyes, and punished him by saying—

"I thought you would come to-day perhaps and see my little house. Do you like it, John? I have been in it less than three months, and I am already quite attached to it. Miss Fairbairn only came last night, and she is delighted with it."

"Yes," said Justina, "I only came last night;" and an air of irrepressible satisfaction spread itself over her face - that Mr Mortimer should have walked over to see her this very first morning was beyond her utmost hopes. She had caused Emily to invite her at that particular time that she might often see John; and here he was.

"Emily thinks it a pointed thing, my coming at once," he cogitated. "She reminds me, too, that friendship for her did not bring me. Well, I was too much out of spirits to come a month ago."

Emily's eyes flashed and softened when she saw him out of countenance, and a little twist came in her lips where a smile would like to have broken through. She was still in crape, and wore the delicate gossamer of her widow's cap, with long, wing-like streamers falling away at her back; and while she sat at work on a cumbersome knitted shawl she listened with an air of docility to Justina's conversation, without noticing that a touch of dismay was beginning to show itself in John's face; for Miss Fairbairn had begun to speak of Italian literature, a subject she had been getting up lately for certain good reasons of her own. She dared to talk about Dante, and John was almost at once keenly aware that all this learning was sham—it was the outcome of no real taste; and he felt like a fool while one of the ladies did the wooing and the other, as he thought, amused herself with watching it. He was accustomed to be wooed, and to be watched, but he had been trying for some time to bring his mind to like the present wooer. While away from her he fancied that he had begun to succeed, and now he knew well that this sort of talk would drive him wild in a week. It represented nothing real. No; the thing would not do. She was a good-woman; she would have ruled his house well; she would have been just to his children; and if he had established her in all comfort and elegance over his family, he might have left her, and attended to those prospective Parliamentary duties as long as he liked, without annoying her. She was a lady too, and her mother, old Lady Fairbairn, was a pleasant and unexceptionable woman. But she was making herself ridiculous now. No; it would not do.

Giving her up then and there, he suddenly started from his seat as if he felt relieved, and drawing himself to his full height, looked down on the two ladies, one of whom, lifting her golden head, continued the wooing with her eyes, while the other said carelessly and with a dispassionate air—

"Well, I cannot think how you or John or any one can like that bitter-hearted, odious, cruel Dante."

"Emily," exclaimed Miss Fairbairn, "how can you be so absurd, dear?"

"I wonder they did not tear him into little bits," continued Emily audaciously, "instead of merely banishing him, which was all they did—wasn't it, John?"

"I cannot imagine what you mean," exclaimed Miss Fairbairn, while John laughed, and felt that at least here was something real and natural.

"You cannot? That's because you don't consider, then, what we should feel if somebody now were to write a grand poem about our fathers, mothers, aunts, uncles, and dear friends deceased, setting forth how he had seen them all in the nether regions; how he had received their confidences, and how penitent most of them were. Persecuted, indeed! and misunderstood! I consider that his was the deadliest revenge any man ever took upon his enemies."

Miss Fairbairn's brow, on hearing this, contracted with pain; for John laughed again, and turning slightly towards Emily as he stood leaning against the window-frame, took the opportunity to get away from the subject of Italian literature, and ask her some question about her knitting.

"It must be something to give away, I am sure. You are always giving."

"But you know, John," she answered, as if excusing herself, "we are not at all sure that we shall have any possessions, anything of our own, in the future life—anything, consequently, to give away. Perhaps it will all belong to all. So let us have enough of giving while we can, and enjoy the best part of possession."

"Dear Emily," said Miss Fairbairn kindly, "you should not indulge in these unauthorised fancies."

"But it so chances that this is not for a poor person," observed Emily, "but for dear Aunt Christie."

"Ah, she was always very well while she lived with me," said John; "but I hear a very different account of her now."

"Yes; she has rheumatism in her foot; so that she is obliged to sit up-stairs. John, you should go and see her."

"I will take Mr. Mortimer to her," said Justina, rising serenely. This she thought would break off the conversation, in which she had no part.

So John went up to Miss Christie's little sitting-room, and there she was, bolt upright, with her lame foot on a cushion. By this visit he gave unmixed pleasure to the old lady, and afforded opportunity to the younger one for some pleasant, reasonable speeches, and for a little effective waiting on the invalid, as well as for some covert compliments.

"Ay, John Mortimer," quoth Miss Christie, with an audacious twinkle in her eyes, "I'm no that clear that I don't deserve all the pain I've got for my sins against ye."

"Against me!" exclaimed John, amazed.

"Some very bad advice I gave ye, John," she continued, while Miss Fairbairn, a little surprised, looked on.

"Make your mind easy," John answered with

mock gravity, for he knew well enough what she meant. "I never follow bad advice. I promise not to follow yours."

"What was your advice, dear?" asked Miss Fairbairn sweetly, her golden head within a yard of John's as she stooped forward. "I wonder you should have ventured to give advice to such a man as Mr. Mortimer. People always seem to think that in any matter of consequence they are lucky if they can get advice from him."

John drew a long breath, and experienced a strong sense of compunction; but Miss Christie was merely relieved, and she began to talk with deep interest about the new governess and the new housekeeper.

Miss Fairbairn brought John down again as soon as she could, and took the opportunity to engage his attention on the stairs, by asking him a question on some political subject that really interested him; and he, like a straightforward man, falling into the trap, began to give her his views respecting it.

But as he opened the drawing-room door for her, his three children, who all this time had been in the garden, came running in at the window, and before he and Miss Fairbairn were seated, his two little boys, treading on Mrs. Walker's crape, were thrusting some large handfuls of flowers almost into her face, while Anastasia emptied a lapful on to her knees. Emily accepted them graciously.

"And so," little Hugh exclaimed, "as father said we were not to have the gardens, we thought we had better gather all the flowers, because *they* are our own, you know," he proceeded; "for we bought most of the bulbs with our own money; and they're all for you."

Hyacinths, narcissus, wallflowers, polyanthus, they continued to be held up for her inspection.

"And you'll let us put them in water ourselves, won't you?" said Bertram.

"Yes, she will, Bertie," cried Hugh.

"Don't tread on Mrs. Walker's dress," John began, and the sprites, as if in ready obedience, were off in an instant; but in reality they were gone to find vases for the flowers, Emily looking up with all composure, though a good deal of scrambling and arguing were heard through the open door.

"We found these in the pantry," exclaimed the two little boys, returning, each with a dish in his hand. "Nancy wanted to get some water, but we wouldn't let her."

"Come here," exclaimed John with gravity; "come here, and shut the door. Emily, I brought these imps on purpose to apologize for their high misdemeanours."

Thereupon the two little boys blushed and hung their heads. It was nothing to have taken the garden, but it daunted them to have to acknowledge the fault. Before they had said a word, however, a shrill little voice cried out behind them—

"But I can't do my *apologize* yet, father, because I've got a pin in my cape, and it pricks, and somebody must take it out."

"I cannot get the least pretence of penitence out of any one of them," exclaimed John, unable to forbear laughing. "I must make the apology myself, Emily. I am very much afraid that these gardens were taken without leave; they were not given at all."

"I have heard you say more than once," answered Emily, with an easy smile, "that it is the privilege of the giver to forget. I never had a very good memory."

"But they confessed themselves that they *took* them."

"Well, John, then if you said they were to apologize," answered Emily, giving them just the shadow of a smile, "of course they must;" and so they did, the little boys with hot blushes and flashing eyes, the little girl with innocent unconsciousness of shame. Then "Mrs. Nemily" rather spoilt the dignity of the occasion by taking her up and kissing her; upon which the child inquired in a loud whisper—

"But now we've done our *apologize*, we may keep our gardens, mayn't we?"

At this neither she nor John could help laughing.

"You may, if papa has no objection," said Emily, suddenly aware of a certain set look about Miss Fairbairn's lips, and a glance of reproof, almost of anguish, from her stern blue eye.

Miss Fairbairn had that morning tasted the sweetness of hope, and she now experienced a sharp pang of jealousy when she saw the children hanging about Emily with familiar friendliness, treading on her tucks, whispering confidences in her ears, and putting their flowers on the clean chintz of her ottomans. These things Justina would have found intolerable if done to herself, unless in their father's presence. Even then she would have only welcomed them for the sake of diverting them from Emily.

She felt sure that at first all had been as she hoped, and as it ought to be; and she could not refrain from darting a glance of reproof at Emily. She even felt as if it was wrong of John to be thus beguiled into turning away when he ought to have been cultivating his acquaintance with her mind and character. It was still more wrong of Emily to be attracting his notice and drawing him away from his true place, his interest, and now almost his duty.

Emily, with instant docility, put the little Anastasia down and took up her knitting, while Miss Fairbairn, suddenly feigning a great interest in horticulture, asked after John's old gardener, who she heard had just taken another prize.

"The old man is very well," said John, "and if you and Mrs. Walker would come over some morning, I am sure he would be proud to show you the flowers."

Miss Fairbairn instantly accepted the proposal.

"I always took an interest in that old man," she observed; "he is so original."

"Yes, he is," said John.

"But at what time of day are you generally at home," she continued, not observing, or perhaps not intending to observe that the flowers could have been shown during their owner's absence. "At luncheon time, or at what time?"

John, thus appealed to, paused an instant; he had never thought of coming home to entertain the ladies, but he could not be inhospitable, and he concluded that the mistake was real. "At luncheon time," he presently said, and named a day when he would be at home, being very careful to address the invitation to Mrs. Walker.

He then retired with his children, who were now in very good spirits; they gave their hands to Justina, who would have liked to kiss them, but the sprites skipped away in their father's wake, and while he walked home, lost in thought on grave and serious things, they broke in every now and then with their childish speculations on life and manners.

"Swanny must put on his Sunday coat when they come, and his orange handkerchief that Janie hemmed for him because Mrs. Swan's fingers are all crumpled up," said the little girl.

"Father, what's a Methodist?" asked Hugh.

Before John could answer little Bertram informed his brother, "It is a thing about not going to church. It has nothing to do with her fingers being crumpled up, that's rheumatism."

CHAPTER XXIV.

SELF-WONDER AND SELF-SCORN.

"Something there is moves me to love, and I
Do know I love, but know not how, nor why."
A. BROME.

AS John and his children withdrew together through the garden, Justina Fairbairn sat with her work on her knees, watching them.

"Mr. Mortimer is six-and-thirty, is he not?" she asked.

"Yes," answered Emily.

"How much he improves in appearance!" she observed; "he used not to be thought handsome when he was very young—he is both handsome and stately now."

"It is the way with the Mortimers, I think," said Emily. "I should not wonder if in ten years' time Val is just as majestic as the old men used to be, though he has no dignity at all about him now."

"Yes, majesty is the right word," said Justina serenely. "Mr. Mortimer has a finer presence, a finer carriage than formerly; it may be partly because he is not so very thin as he used to be."

"Perhaps so," said Emily.

"And this was his first call," continued Justina, obliged to make openings for herself through which to push what she had to say. "I suppose, dear, you could hardly fail to notice how matters were going. This calling at once, and his bringing the children too; and his wish to find out my opinions, and tell me his own on various subjects."

Silence on the part of the hostess.

"I could almost have wished, dear Emily, that you had not——"

She paused. "Had not what?" asked Emily.

Miss Fairbairn remembered that she was Mrs. Walker's guest, and that it behoved her not to offend her hostess, because she wanted to stay in that house as long as possible. She would like to have finished her speech thus: "that you had not engrossed the children so completely;" but she said instead, with a little smile meant to look conscious, "I believe I meant, dear, that I should have been very glad to talk to the children myself."

She felt that this reply fell rather flat, but she knew that Emily must immediately be made aware of what she now hoped was really the state of the case, and must also be made to help her.

No surprise was expressed, but Mrs. Walker did not make any reply whatever, so she continued,—

"You look surprised, dear, but surely what I have hinted at cannot be a new thought to you," and as it did not suit her to drop the subject yet, she proceeded. "No, I see by your smile that it is not. I confess I should have liked to talk to them, for," she added, with a sigh of contentment, "the task, I see very plainly before me, is always a difficult one to undertake."

Still Emily was silent; she seemed lost in thought; indeed, she was considering among other things that it was little more than a year since she and John had discussed Justina together; was there, could there really be, anything between them now?

Justina watched her, and wished she could know what effect these hints had taken. Emily had always behaved in such a high-minded, noble way to her lovers, and been so generous to other women, that Justina depended on her now. The lower nature paid homage to the higher, even to the point of believing in a sense of honour quite alien to its own experience. There was not the least reason to suppose that Emily cared about John Mortimer, but she wanted her to stand aside lest he should take it into his head to begin to care for her. So many men had been infatuated about Emily, but Emily had never wished to rob another woman for the mere vanity of spoliation, and Justina's opinion of her actually was that if she could be made to believe that she, Justina, had any rights in John Mortimer, she would not stand in her light, even though she might have begun to think highly of his house, and his position, as advantageous for herself. Love she did not take into her consideration, she neither felt that nor imputed it to others.

She was thoroughly mean herself, but if Emily had done anything mean, it would positively have shaken her faith and trust in Goodness itself. It would actually have been bad for her, and there is no saying how much lower she might have declined, if one of the few persons she believed in had made a descent.

Though she thought thus of Emily, she had notwithstanding felt towards her a kind of serene superiority, as might be felt towards one who could only look straight before her, by one who could see round a corner; but that morning, for the first time, she had begun to fear her, to acknowledge a certain charm in her careless, but by no means ungracious indifference; in her sweet, natural ways with John's children, and in those dark lashes which clouded her soft grey eyes.

The contradictions in her face were dangerous; there was a wistful yearning in her smile; joyous as her laugh sounded, she often put a stop to its sudden sweetness with a sigh.

Justina felt Emily's silence very oppressive, and while it lasted she fully expected that it would be broken at last by some important words.

Emily might tell her that she must be deceiving herself, and might be able to give such decisive proof of the fact as would oblige her to give up this new hope. That was what Justina feared. On the other hand, she might show her ignorance and lighten Justina's heart by merely asking her whether she thought she could love and bear with another woman's children. She might even ask whether John Mortimer had made his intentions plain.

But no, when Emily did speak, she appeared completely to ignore these hints, though her face retained its air of wonder and cogitation.

"By-the-bye, Justina," she said, "you put me a little out of countenance just now. John Mortimer never meant to ask us to luncheon; I know he seldom or ever comes home in the middle of the day."

"Are you sure of that?" said Justina.

"Quite sure; you invited yourself."

"Did I make a mistake? Well, if he did not at first intend it, he certainly caught at the notion afterwards."

"Do you think so? I thought, on the contrary, that he spent some moments in considering what day he could spare to come and receive us."

"Perhaps it is just as well," answered Justina; "I should have felt very awkward going about his house and garden in his absence."

"Justina," said Emily, driven at last to front the question, "how much do you wish me to understand?"

"Nothing at all, dear, but what you see," she replied, without lifting her head from her work; then she added, "Do those children come here often?"

"Two or three times a week, I think," answered Emily, with a degree of carelessness that attracted Miss Fairbairn's attention. She had appeared more than commonly indifferent that morning, she had hardly responded to the loving caresses of John's children, but this had seemed to signify nothing, they came and hung about her just the same.

"They had taken those gardens some time before I found it out," she continued. "They run through the copses and through those three or four fields that belong to John, and get into my garden over the stepping-stones in the brook."

"They must feel very sure of their welcome," said Justina, rather pointedly.

"Yes," answered Emily, also rather pointedly; "but I have never invited them to come, never once; there is, as you see, no occasion."

Holding her graceful head a little higher than usual, she folded up her now finished shawl, ran up-stairs with it to Miss Christie's room, and was conscious almost at once (or she fancied so) that her old aunt looked at her with a certain air of scrutiny, not unmixed with amusement. She was relieved when she had put on her gift to hear Miss Christie say, "Well, ye'll be glad to know that I feel more at my ease now than I've done for some time."

There had been such an air of triumph in Miss Christie's glance that Emily was pleased to find she was only exultant on account of her health. She expressed her gladness, and assured the old lady she would soon be as active as ever.

"It's no my foot I'm thinking of," answered Miss Christie, "but some bad advice that weighed on my mind—bad advice that I've given to John Mortimer." Thereupon she related the conversation in which she had recommended Miss Fairbairn to him.

Emily sat very still—so still, that she hardly seemed to breathe, then, looking up, she said, perhaps rather more calmly and quietly than was her wont—

"Several people have thought it would be a good thing for John to marry Justina Fairbairn."

"And I was one of them," quoth Miss Christie, her eyes sparkling with joy and malice, "but I've thought lately that I was just mistaken," and she presently related what had passed between her and John that morning.

Emily's fair cheek took a slight blush-rose tint. If she felt relieved, this did not appear; perhaps she thought, "Under like circumstances John would speak just so of me." The old lady had been silent some moments before Emily answered, and when she did speak she said—

"What! you and John actually joked about poor Justina in her presence, auntie?"

"Did I see him in her absence?" inquired Miss Christie, excusing herself. "I tell ye, child, I've changed my mind. John Mortimer's a world too good for her. Aye, but he looked grand this morning."

"Yes," answered Emily, "but it is a pity he thinks all the women are in love with him!" Then, feeling that she had been unjust, she corrected herself, "No, I mean that he is so keenly aware how many women there are in the neighbourhood who would gladly marry him."

"Aware!" quoth Miss Christie, instantly taking his part. "Aware, indeed! Can he ever go out, or stop at home, that somebody doesn't try to make him aware! Small blame to them," she added with a laugh, "few men can hold their heads higher, either moreally or pheesically, and he has his pockets full of money besides."

Emily got away from Miss Christie as soon as she could, put on her bonnet, and went into the garden.

The air was soft, and almost oppressively mild, for the bracing east wind was gone, and a tender wooing zephyr was fluttering among the crumbled leaves, and helping them to their expansion. Before she knew what instinct had taken her there, she found herself standing by the four little gardens, listening to the cheerful dance of the water among the stepping-stones, and looking at the small footsteps of the children, which were printed all over their property.

Yes, there was no mistake about that, her empty heart had taken them in with no thought and no fear of anything that might follow.

Only the other day and her thoughts had been as free as air, there was a sorrowful shadow lying behind her; when she chose, she looked back into it, recalled the confiding trust, and marital pride, and instinctive courage of her late husband, and was sufficiently mistress of her past to muse no more on his unopened mind, and petty ambitions, and small range of thought. He was gone to heaven, he could see farther now, and as for these matters, she had hidden them; they were shut down into night and oblivion, with the dust of what had once been a faithful heart.

Fred Walker had been as one short-sighted, who only sees things close at hand, but sees them clearly.

Emily was very long-sighted, but in a vast range of vision are comprehended many things that the keenest eyes cannot wholly define, and some that are confused with their own shadows.

Things near she saw as plainly as he had done, but the wondrous wide distance drew her now and again away from these. The life of to-day would sometimes spend itself in gazing over the life in her whole day. Her life, as she felt it, yearning and passioning, would appear to overflow the little cup of its separation, or take reflections from other lives, till it was hardly all itself, so much as a small part of the great whole, God's immortal child, the wonderful race of mankind, held in the hand of its fashioner, and conscious of some yearning, the ancient yearning towards its source.

Emily moved slowly home again, and felt rather sensitive about the proposed luncheon at John Mortimer's house. She wished she had managed to spare him from being obliged to give the invitation. She even considered whether Justina could be induced to go alone. But there was no engagement that could be pleaded as a reason for absenting herself. What must be done was before they went, to try, without giving needless pain, to place the matter in a truer light. This would only be fair to poor Justina.

Emily scarcely confessed to her own heart that she was glad of what Miss Christie had said. She was not, from any thought that it could make the least difference to herself, but, upon reflection, she felt ashamed of how John Mortimer had been wooed, and of how he had betrayed by his smile that he knew it.

That day was a Tuesday, the luncheon was to take place on Saturday, but on Friday afternoon Emily had not found courage or occasion to speak to her friend. The more she thought about it, the more difficult and ungracious the matter seemed.

Such was the state of things. Miss Christie was still up-stairs, Justina was seated at work in the drawing-room, and Emily, arrayed in a lilac print apron, was planting some fresh ferns in her *jardinière* when the door was opened, and the servant announced Mr. Mortimer. Emily was finishing her horticulture, and was not at all the kind of person to be put out of countenance on being discovered at any occupation that it suited her fancy to be engaged in. She, however, blushed beautifully, just as any other woman might have done, on being discovered in her drawing-room so arrayed, and her hands acquainted with peat.

She presently left the room. John knew she was gone to wash her hands, and hoped she would not stay away long. "For it won't do, my lady," he thought, "however long you leave me. I will not make an offer to the present candidate, that I am determined!"

In the meantime Justina, wishing to say something of Emily that would sound amiable, and yet help her own cause, remarked pleasantly—

"Emily is a dear, careless creature—just like what

she was as a girl" (careless creatures, by-the-bye, are not at all suited to be stepmothers).

"Yes," answered John, in an abstracted tone, and as if he was not considering Mrs. Walker's mental characteristics, which was the case, for he was merely occupied in wishing she would return.

"But she wishes to look well, notwithstanding," continued Justina, as if excusing her, "so no wonder she goes to divest herself of her housemaid's apron."

"Ah," said John, who was no great observer of apparel, "I thought she was not dressed as usual;" but he added, "she is so graceful, that in any array she cannot fail to look well."

Justina looked up feeling hurt, and also a little surprised. Here she was, alone with John Mortimer for the first time in her life, and he was entertaining her with the praise of another woman; but she had a great deal of self-command, and she began almost at once to ask him some questions about his children. She had a most excellent governess to recommend, and was it not true that they wanted a nurse also? Yes, Mr. Mortimer did want both, and, as Justina had been writing to every friend she had about these functionaries, and had heard of several, she mentioned in each case the one she thought most suitable, and John, much pleased at the happy chance which brought such treasures before him, was deep in conversation about them when Emily reappeared, and then, to Justina's great annoyance, he took down two addresses, and broke off the conversation with her instantly to say—

"Emily, I am come to make the humblest apologies possible. I find that I am absolutely obliged to go to London to-morrow on a matter that cannot be postponed."

Justina was greatly mortified, but she answered instantly, and not Emily—

"Ah, then of course you are come to put us off, Mr. Mortimer?"

There was no undue stress on the words "put us off," but they suggested an idea to John that was new to him, and he would have felt called upon to act upon them, and renew the invitation, if Emily had not answered just as if she had heard not a syllable.

"We shall be sorry to miss you, John, when we come, but no doubt the children will be at home, and the girls."

"Yes," said John, slipping into this arrangement so easily, that how little he cared about her visit ought to have been at once made plain to Justina. "Oh yes, and they will be so proud to entertain you. I hope you will honour them, as was intended, by coming to lunch."

"Yes, to be sure," Emily answered with readiness. "I hope the auriculas will not have begun to fade, they are Miss Fairbairn's favourite flower."

Then, to the intense mortification of Justina, John changed the subject, as if it had been one of no moment to him. "I have been over to Wigfield-house this afternoon to pay my respects to Mrs. Brandon and her boy."

"You found them well, I know, for we were there this morning."

"Perfectly well," said John, and he laughed. "Giles was marching about in the garden with that astonishing infant lying flat on his arm, and with its long robes dangling down. Dorothea (come out, I was told, for the first time) was walking beside him, and looking like a girl of sixteen. I believe when I approached they were discussing to what calling in life they would bring up the youngster. I was desired to remark his uncommon likeness to his father; told that he was considered a very fine child, and I should have had the privilege of looking at his little downy black head, but his mother decided not to accord it, lest he should take cold."

"And so you laugh at her maternal folly," said

Justina smiling, but not displeased at what sounded like disparagement of an attractive young woman.

"I laugh at it?—yes! but as a man who feels that it is the one lovely folly of the world. Who could bear to think of all that childhood demands of womanhood, if he did not bear in mind the sweet delusive glamour that washes every woman's eyes ere she catches sight of the small mortal sent to be her charge."

Then Justina, who had found a few moments for recovering herself and deciding how to act, took the conversation again into her own hands, and very soon, in spite of Emily, who did not dare to interfere again, John Mortimer was brought quite naturally and inevitably to add to the desire that they would the next day visit his children, an invitation to luncheon after he should have returned.

Justina accepted.

"But it must not be this day week," she observed with quiet complacency, "for that is to be the baby's christening day, and I am asked to be his god-mother."

Emily could not forbear to look up; John's face was quite a study. He had just been asked to stand for the child, had consented, and whom he might have for companions he had not thought of asking.

"It will be the first anniversary of their wedding," said Emily by way of saying something, for John's silence began to be awkward.

Mrs. Brandon, having been charmed with the sensible serenity of Miss Fairbairn's conversation, and with the candour and straightforwardness that distinguished her, had cultivated her acquaintance with assiduity, and was at that moment thinking how fortunate she was in her baby's sponsors.

When Justina found that John Mortimer was to be present at this christening, and in such a capacity too, she accomplished the best blush her cheek had worn for years. It was almost like an utterance, so completely did it make her feelings known. As for John, he had very seldom in his life looked as foolish as he did then.

Why had he been asked together with Miss Fairbairn? Whatever he might have thought concerning her, his thought was his own; he had never made it manifest by paying her the least attention. He did not like her now so well as he might have done, if he had not tried and failed to make himself like her more. She was almost the only woman now concerning whom he felt strongly that she would not do for him. Surely people did not think he had any intentions towards her. He sat silent and discomfited till Emily, again quite aware of his feelings, and sure he wanted to go, made the opportunity for him, helped him to take advantage of it, and received a somewhat significant smile of thanks as he departed.

"Emily," exclaimed Justina, as soon as the door was shut, "what can you be thinking of? You almost dismissed Mr. Mortimer! Surely, surely you cannot wish to prevent his coming here to see me."

Justina spoke with a displeasure that she hardly cared to moderate. Emily stood listening till she was sure John Mortimer had left her house, then she said something that was meant to serve for an answer, got away as soon as she could, ran up-stairs, hurried to her own room, and locked the door.

"Not alone!" was her first startled thought, but it was so instantaneously corrected that it had scarcely time to shape itself into words. The large cheval glass had been moved by her own orders, and as she stood just within the door, it sent back her image to her, reflected from head to foot.

She advanced gazing at herself, at the rich folds of her black silk gown made heavy with crape, and at the frail gossamer she carried on her head, and which, as she came on, let its long appendages float out like pennons in her wake. Emily had such a high, almost fantastic notion of feminine dignity (fantastic because it left too much out of view that woman also is a human creature), that till this day it might almost have been said she had not taken even her own self into her confidence. She hardly believed it, and it seems a pity to tell.

Her eyes flashed with anger, while she advanced, as if they would defy the fair widow coming on in those seemly weeds.

"How dare you blush?" she cried out almost aloud. "Only a year and a fortnight ago kneeling by his coffin—how dare you blush? I scorn you!"

She put her hands to her throat, conscious of that nervous rising which some people call a ball in it; then she sat down full in view of herself, and felt as if she should choke. She was so new to the powerful fetters that had hold of her, were dragging her on, frightening her, subduing her.

Was she never to do or to be any more what she chose—never to know the rest and sweetness of forgetting even for a little while? Why must she be mastered by a voice that did not care at all whether its cadence and its fall were marked by her or not? Why must she tremble and falter even in her prayer, if a foot came up the aisle that she could not bear to miss, and yet that was treading down, and doomed, if this went on, to tread down all reviving joy, and every springtide flower that was budding in her heart?

"No more to be kept back than the rising of the tide"—these were her words—"but, oh, not foreseen as that is, and not to go down any more."

She almost raged against herself. How could she have come there—how could she, why had she never considered what might occur? Then she shed a few passionate tears. "Is it really true, Justina Fairbairn's would-be rival? And neither of us has the slightest chance in the world. Oh, oh, if anything—anything that ever was or could be, was able to work a cure, it would be what I have seen twice this week. It would be to watch another woman making a fool of herself to win his favour, and to see him smile and know it. Oh, this is too miserable, far too humiliating. The other day, when he came, I cared so little; to-day I could hardly look him in the face."

Then she considered a little longer, and turned impatiently from her image in the glass.

"Why, I have known him all my life, and never dreamed of such a thing! But for that rainy Sunday three weeks ago, I never might have done. Oh, this must be a mere fancy. While I talked to him I felt that it ought to be—that it was. Yes, it is."

Her eyes wandered over the lawn. She could see the edges of those little gardens. She had looked at them of late more often than was prudent. "Darlings!" she whispered with such a heartsick sigh, "how keenly I loved them for the sake of my little lost treasure, before ever I noticed their beautiful likeness to their father—no, that's a mistake. I say it is—I mean to break away from it. And even if it was none, after the lesson I have had to-day, it must and shall be a mistake for ever."

CHAPTER XXV.

THAT RAINY SUNDAY.

"He hath put the world in their hearts.'

THIS is how that had come about which was such a trouble and oppression to Emily.

Emily was walking to church on a Sunday morning, just three weeks before John Mortimer's first call upon her.

Her little nephew, Dorothea's child, was four days old. He had spent many of his new-found hours sleeping in her arms, while she cherished him with a keen and painful love, full of sweet anguish and unsatisfied memories.

The tending of this small life, which in some sort was to be a plenishing for her empty heart, had, however, made her more fully alive than usual to the loneliness of her lot, and as she walked on through a fir-wood, in the mild weather, everything seemed also to be more alive, waking, and going to change. The lights that slanted down were more significant. The little shaded hollows were more pathetic, but on the whole it seemed as if the best part of the year was coming on for the world. It made her heart ache to feel or fancy how glad the world was, and how the open sky laughed down upon it in helpful sympathy. The old question presents itself over and over again to be answered,—What is it that gives us so much joy in looking at earth and air and water?

We love a landscape, but not merely because remoteness makes blue the distant hills, as if the sky itself having come down, we could look through a portion of it, as through a veil. It is not the vague possibility of what may be shrouded in the blue that stirs our hearts. We know that if we saw it close it would be set full of villages, and farmhouses, lanes and orchards, and furrowed fields; no other, and not fairer than we have near.

Is it what we impart, or impute to nature from ourselves, that we chiefly lean upon? or does she truly impart of what is really in her to us?

What delight we find in her action, what sentiment in her rest! What passion we impute to her changes, what apathy of a satisfying calming sort to her decline!

If one of us could go to another world, and be all alone in it, perhaps that world would appear to be washed perfectly clean of all this kind of beauty, though it might in itself and for itself be far more beautiful than ours.

Who has not felt delight in the grand movements of a thunder-storm, when the heavens and earth come together, and have it out, and seem to feel the better for it afterwards, as if they had cleared off old scores? The sight of noble wrath, and vehement action, cannot only nerve the energetic; they can comfort those obliged to be still. There is so little these may do, but the elements are up and doing; and they are in some sort theirs.

And who does not like to watch the stately white cloud lying becalmed over the woods, and waiting in a rapture of rest for a wind to come and float it on? Yet we might not have cared to see the cloud take her rest, but for the sweetness of rest to ourselves. The plough turned over on one side under a hedge, while the ploughman rests at noon, might hint to us what is the key-note of that chord which makes us think the rest of the cloud so fair.

If the splendour of some intense passion had never suddenly glorified the spread-out ether of time in which our spirits float, should we feel such a strange yearning on looking at a sunset, with its tender preliminary flush, and then the rapid suffusions of scarlet and growth of gold? If it is not ourselves that we look at then, it is at one of the tokens and emblems which claim a likeness with us, a link to hold us up to the clear space that washes itself so suddenly in an elixir costly as the golden chances of youth, and the crimson rose of love. With what a sigh, even youth itself will mark that outpouring of coloured glory! It whelms the world and overcomes the sky, and then, while none withstand it, and all is its own, it will change as if wearied, and on a sudden be over; or with pathetic withdrawal faint slowly away.

Her apathy, too—her surrender, when she has had everything, and felt the toil in it, and found the hurry of living. The young seldom perceive the apathy of nature; eyes that are enlightened by age can often see her quiet in the autumn, folding up her best things, as they have done, and getting ready to put them away under the snow. They both expect the spring.

Emily was thinking some such thoughts as these while she walked on to the small country church alone. She went in. This was the first Sunday after the funeral of old Augustus Mortimer. A glance showed her that John was at church, sitting among his children.

The Mortimers were much beloved thereabout. This was not the place where the old man had worshipped, but a kindly feeling towards his son had induced the bringing out of such black drapery as the little church possessed. It was hung round the pulpit, and about the wall at the back of his pew; and as he sat upright, perfectly still, and with his face set into a grave, immobile expression, the dark background appeared to add purity to the fair clear tints of his hair and complexion, and make every line of his features more distinct.

And while she looked from time to time at this face, the same thing occurred to her, as does to us in looking at nature; either she perceived something she had never known of or looked for before, or she imparted to his manhood something from the tenderness of her womanhood, and mourned with him and for him.

For this was what she saw, that in spite of the children about him (all in deep mourning), his two tall young daughters and his sweet little girls and boys, there was a certain air of isolation about him, a sort of unconsciousness of them all as he towered above them, which gave him a somewhat desolate effect of being alone. The light striking down upon his head and the mourning drapery behind him, made every shadow of a change more evident. She knew how the withdrawal of this old father weighed on his heart, and his attitude was so unchanging, and his expression so guarded, that she saw he was keeping watch over his self-possession, and holding it well in hand.

All this appeared so evident to her that she was relieved, as the service went on, to find him still calm and able to command himself, and keep down any expression of trouble and pain. He began to breathe more freely too; but Emily felt that he would not meet any eyes that day, and she looked at him and his children many times.

In the middle of the sermon a dark cloud came over, and before the service was finished it poured with rain. Emily was not going back to her brother's house; she had only the short distance to traverse that led to her own, and she did not intend to speak to the Mortimers; so she withdrew into the porch, to wait there till they should have passed out by the little door they generally used. They scarcely ever had out a carriage on Sunday, for John preserved many of his father's habits, without, in all cases, holding the opinions which had led to them.

That day, however, the servants brought a carriage, and as the little girls were carried to it under umbrellas they caught sight of Emily, and to her annoyance, she presently saw John advancing to her. She had already begun to walk when he met her, and, sheltering her with his umbrella, proposed to take her home in the carriage; but she declined; she felt the oppression and sadness of his manner, and knew he did not want her company. "I would much rather walk," she declared.

"Would you?" he said, and waved to the men to take the carriage on. "Well, it is not far;" and he proceeded to conduct her. Indeed there was nothing else for him to do, for she could not hold up her umbrella. He gave her his arm, and for two or three minutes the wind and the rain together made her plenty of occupation; but when they got under the shelter of the cliff-like rock near her house she felt the silence oppressive, and thinking that nothing to the purpose, nothing touching on either his thoughts or her own, would be acceptable, she said, by way of saying something,—

"And so Valentine is gone! Has he written from Melcombe to you, John?"

"No," John answered, and added, after another short silence, "I feel the loss of his company; it leaves me the more alone."

Then, to her surprise, he began at once to speak of this much-loved old man, and related two or three little evidences of his kindness and charity that she liked to hear, and that it evidently was a relief to him to tell. She was just the kind of woman unconsciously to draw forth confidences, and to reward them. Something poignant in his feeling was rather set forth than concealed by his sober, self-restrained ways and quiet words; it suited Emily, and she allowed herself to speak with that tender reverence of the dead which came very well from her, since she had loved him living so well. She was rather eloquent when her feelings were touched, and then she had a sweet and penetrative voice. John liked to hear her; he recalled her words when he had parted with her at her own door, and felt that no one else had said anything of his father that was half so much to his mind. It was nearly four weeks after this that Emily fully confessed to herself what had occurred.

The dinner, after John Mortimer withdrew that day and Emily made to herself this confession, was happily relieved by the company of three or four neighbours, otherwise the hostess might have been made to feel very plainly that she had displeased her guest. But the next morning Justina, having had time to consider that Emily must on no account be annoyed, came down all serenity and kindliness. She was so attentive to the lame old aunt, and though the poor lady, being rather in pain, was decidedly snappish, she did not betray any feeling of disapproval.

"Ay," said Miss Christie to herself when the two ladies had set off on their short walk, "yon's not so straightforward and simple as I once thought her. Only give her a chance, and as sure as death she'll get hold of John, after all."

Emily and Justina went across the fields and came to John's garden, over the wooden bridge that spanned the brook.

The sunny sloping garden was full of spring flowers. Vines, not yet in leaf, were trained all over the back of the house, clematis and jasmine, climbing up them and over them, were pouring themselves down again in great twisted strands; windows peeped out of ivy, and the old red-tiled roof, warm and mossy, looked homely and comfortable. A certain air of old-fashioned, easy comfort pervaded the whole place; large bay windows, with little roofs of their own, came boldly forth, and commanded a good view of other windows—ivied windows that retired unaccountably. There were no right lines. Casements at one end of the house showed in three tiers, at the other there were but two. The only thing that was perfectly at ease about itself, and quite clear that it ought to be seen, was the roof. You could not possibly make a "stuck-up" house, or a smart villa, or a modern family house of one that had a roof like that. The late Mrs. Mortimer had wished it could be taken away. She would have liked the house to be higher and the roof lower. John, on the other hand, delighted in his roof, and also in his stables, the other remarkable feature of the place.

As the visitors advanced, children's voices greeted them; the little ones were running in and out; they presently met and seized Mrs. Walker, dancing round her, and leading her in triumph into the hall. Then Justina observed a good-sized doll, comfortably put to bed on one of the hall chairs, and tightly tucked up in some manifest pinafores; near it stood a child's wheel-barrow, half full of picture-books. "I shall not allow that sort of litter here when I come, as I hope and trust I soon shall do," thought Justina. "Children's toys are all very well in their proper places."

Then Justina, who had never been inside the house before, easily induced the children to take her from room to room, of those four which were thoroughfares to one another. Her attentive eyes left nothing unnoticed, the fine modern water-colour landscapes on the walls of one, the delicate inlaid cabinets in another. Then a library, with a capital billiard-table, and lastly John's den. There was something about all these rooms which seemed to show the absence of a woman. They were not untidy, but in the drawing-room was John's great microscope, with the green-shaded apparatus for lighting it; the books also from the library had been allowed to overflow into it, and encroach upon all the tables. The dining-room alone was as other people's dining-rooms, but John's own den was so very far gone in originality and strangeness of litter, that Justina felt decidedly uneasy when she saw it; it made manifest to her that her hoped-for spouse was not the manner of man whom she could expect to understand; books also here had accumulated, and stood in rows on chairs and tables and shelves; pipes were lying on the stone chimneypiece, sharing it with certain old and new, beautiful and ugly bronzes; long papers of genealogies and calculations in John's handwriting were pinned against the walls; various broken bits of Etruscan pottery stood on brackets here and there. It seemed to be the owner's habit to pin his lucubrations about the place, for here was a vocabulary of strange old Italian words, with their derivations, there a list of peculiarities and supposed discoveries in an old Norse dialect.

Emily in the meantime had noticed the absence of the twins; it was not till lunch was announced, and she went back into the dining-room that she saw them, and instantly was aware that something was amiss.

Justina advanced to them first, and the two girls, with a shyness very unusual with them, gave her their hands, and managed, but not without difficulty, to escape a kinder salutation.

And then they both came and kissed Emily, and began to do the honours of their father's table. There was something very touching to her in that instinct of good breeding which kept them attentive to Miss Fairbairn, while a sort of wistful sullenness made the rosy lips pout, and their soft grey eyes twinkle now and then with half-formed tears.

Justina exerted herself to please, and Emily sat nearly silent. She saw very plainly that from some cause or other the girls were looking with dread and dislike on Justina as a possible step-mother. The little ones were very joyous, very hospitable and friendly, but nothing could warm the cold shyness of Gladys and Barbara. They could scarcely eat anything; they had nothing to say.

It seemed as if, whatever occurred, Justina was capable of construing it into a good omen. Somebody must have suggested to these girls that their father meant to make her his second wife. What if he had done it himself? Of course, under the circumstances, her intelligence could not fail to interpret aright those downcast eyes, those reluctant answers, and the timid, uncertain manner that showed plainly they were afraid of her. They did not like the notion, of course, of what she hoped was before them. That was nothing; so, as they would not talk, she began to devote herself to the younger children, and with them she got on extremely well.

Emily's heart yearned with a painful pity that returned upon herself over the two girls. She saw in what light they regarded the thought of a stepmother. Her heart ached to think that she had not the remotest chance of ever standing in such a relation towards them. Yet, in despite of that, she was full of tender distress when she considered that if such a blissful possibility could ever draw near, the love of all these children would melt away. The elder ones would resent her presence, and teach the younger to read all the writing of her story the wrong way. They would feel her presence their division from the father whom they loved. They would brood with just that same sullen love and pouting tenderness—they would pity their father just the same, whoever wore his ring, and reigned over them in his stead.

Emily, as she hearkened to Justina's wise and kindly talk, so well considered and suitable for the part she hoped to play—Emily began to pity John herself. She wanted something so much better for him. She reflected that she would gladly be the governess there, as she could not be the wife, if that would save John from throwing himself into matrimony for his children's sake; and yet had she not thought a year ago that Justina was quite good enough for him? Ah, well! but she had not troubled herself then to learn the meaning of his voice, and look so much as once into the depths of his eyes.

Lunch was no sooner over than the children were eager to show the flowers, and all went out. Barbara and Gladys followed, and spoke when appealed to; but they were not able to control their shoulders so well as they did their tongues. Young girls, when reluctant to do any particular thing, often find their shoulders in the way. These useful, and generally graceful, portions of the human frame appear on such occasions to feel a wish to put themselves forward, as if to bear the brunt of it, and their manner is to do this edgeways.

Emily heard Justina invited to see the rabbits and all the other pets, and knew she would do so, and also manage to make the children take her over the whole place, house included. She, however, felt a shrinking from this inspection, an unwonted diffidence and shyness made her almost fancy it would be taking a liberty. Not that John would think so. Oh, no; he would never think about it.

They soon went to look at the flowers; and there was old Swan ready to exhibit and set off their good points.

"And so you had another prize, Nicholas. I congratulate you," remarked Emily.

"Well, yes, ma'am, I had another. I almost felt, if I failed, it would serve me right for trying too often. I said it was not my turn. 'Turn,' said the umpire; 'it's merit we go by, not turn, Mr. Swan,' said he."

"And poor Raby took a prize again, I hear," said Emily. "That man seems to be getting on, Swan."

"He does, ma'am; he's more weak than wicked, that man is. You can't make him hold up his head; and he's allers contradicting himself. He promised his vote last election to both sides. 'Why,' said I, 'what's the good of that, William? Folks 'll no more pay you for your words when you've eaten them than they will for your bacon.' But that man really couldn't make up his mind which side should bribe him. Still, William Raby is getting on, I'm pleased to say."

Justina had soon seen the flowers enough, and Emily could not make up her mind to inspect anything else. She therefore returned towards the library, and Barbara walked silently beside her.

As she stepped in at the open window, a sound of sobbing startled her. An oil painting, a portrait of John in his boyhood, hung against the wall. Gladys stood with her face leaning against one of the hands that hung down. Emily heard her words distinctly: "Oh, papa! Oh, papa! Oh, my father beloved!" but the instant she caught the sound of footsteps, she darted off like a frightened bird, and fled away without even looking round.

Then the twin sister turned slowly, and looked at Emily with entreating eyes, saying—

"Is it true, Mrs. Walker? Dear Mrs. Walker, is it really true?"

Emily felt cold at heart. How could she tell? John's words went for nothing; Miss Christie might have mistaken them. She did not pretend to misunderstand, but said she did not know; she had no reason to think it was true.

"But everybody says so," sighed Barbara.

"If your father has said nothing—" Emily began.

"No," she answered; her father had said nothing at all; but the mere mention of his name seemed to overcome her.

Emily sat down, talked to her, and tried to soothe her; but she had no distinct denial to give, and in five minutes Barbara, kneeling before her, was sobbing on her bosom, and bemoaning herself as if she would break her heart.

Truly the case of a step-mother is hard.

Emily leaned her cheek upon the young upturned forehead. She faltered a little as she spoke. If her father chose to marry again, had he not a right? If she loved him, surely she wanted him to be—happy.

"But she is a nasty, nasty thing," sobbed Barbara, with vehement heavings of the chest and broken words, "and—and—I am sure I hate her, and so does Gladys, and so does Johnnie too." Then her voice softened again—"Oh, father, father! I would take such care of the little ones if you wouldn't do it! and we would never, never quarrel with the governesses, or make game of them any more."

Emily drew her yet nearer to herself, and said in the stillest, most matter-of-fact tone—

"Of course you know that you are a very naughty girl, my sweet."

"Yes," said Barbara ruefully.

"And very silly too," she continued; but there was something so tender and caressing in her manner, that the words sounded like anything but a reproof.

"I don't think I am silly," said Barbara.

"Yes, you are, if you are really making yourself miserable about an idle rumour, and nothing more."

"But everybody says it is true. Why, one of Johnnie's schoolfellows, who has some friends near here, told him every one was talking of it."

"Well, my darling," said Emily with a sigh, "but even if it is true, the better you take it, the better it will be for you; and you don't want to make your father miserable?"

"No," said the poor child naïvely; "and we've been so good—so very good—since we heard it. But it is so horrid to have a step-mother! I told you papa had never said anything; but he did say once to Gladys that he felt very lonely now Grand was gone. He said that he felt the loss of mamma."

She dried her eyes and looked up as she said these words, and Emily felt a sharp pang of pity for John. He must be hard set indeed for help and love and satisfying companionship if he was choosing to suppose that he had buried such blessings as these with the wife of his youth.

"Oh!" said Barbara, with a weary sigh, "Johnnie does so hate the thought of it! He wrote us such a furious letter. What was my mother like, dear Mrs. Walker? It's so hard that we cannot remember her."

Emily looked down at Barbara's dark hair and lucid blue-grey eyes, at the narrow face and pleasant rosy mouth.

"Your mother was like you—to look at," she answered.

She felt obliged to put in those qualifying words, for Janie Mortimer had given her face to her young daughter; but the girl's passionate feelings and yearning love, and even, as it seemed, pity for her father and herself, had all come from the other side of the house.

Barbara rose when she heard this, and stood up, as if to be better seen by her who had spoken what she took for such appreciative words, and Emily felt constrained to take the dead mother's part, and say what it was best for her child to hear.

"Barbara, no one would have been less pleased than your mother at your all setting yourselves against this. Write and tell Johnnie so, will you, my dear?"

Barbara looked surprised.

"She was very judicious, very reasonable; it is not on her account at all that you need resent your father's intention—if, indeed, he has such an intention."

"But Johnnie remembers her very well," said Barbara, not at all pleased, "and she was very sweet and very delightful, and that's why he does resent it so much."

"If I am to speak of her as she was, I must say that is a state of feeling she would not have approved of, or even cared about."

"Not cared that father should love some one else!"

The astonishment expressed in the young, childlike face daunted Emily for the moment.

"She would have cared for your welfare. You had better think of her as wishing that her children should always be very dear to their father, as desirous that they should not set themselves against his wishes, and vex and displease him."

"Then I suppose I'd better give you Johnnie's letter," said Barbara, "because he is so angry—quite furious, really." She took out a letter, and put it into Emily's hand. "Will you burn it when you go home? but, Mrs. Walker, will you read it first, because then you'll see that Johnnie does love father—and dear mamma too."

Voices were heard now and steps on the gravel. Barbara took up her eyeglass, and moved forward; then, when she saw Justina, she retreated to Emily's side with a gesture of discomfiture and almost of disgust.

"Any step-mother at all," she continued, "Johnnie says, he hates the thought of; but that one— Oh!"

"What a lesson for me!" thought Emily; and she put the letter in her pocket.

"It's very rude," whispered Barbara; "but you mustn't mind that;" and with a better grace than could have been expected she allowed Justina to kiss her, and the two ladies walked back through the fields, the younger children accompanying them nearly all the way home.

CHAPTER XXVI.

MRS. BRANDON ASKS A QUESTION.

"Your baby-days flowed in a much-troubled channel;
I see you as then in your impotent strife,
A tight little bundle of wailing and flannel,
Perplexed with that newly-found fardel call'd life."
LOCKER.

JOHN MORTIMER was the last guest to make his appearance on the morning of the christening. He found the baby, who had been brought down to be admired, behaving scandalously, crying till he was crimson in the face, and declining all his aunt's loving persuasions to him to go to sleep. Emily was moving up and down the drawing-room, soothing and cherishing him in her arms, assuring him that this was his sleepy time, and shaking and patting him as is the way of those who are cunning with babies. But all was in vain. He was carried from his father's house in a storm of indignation, and from time to time he repeated his protest against things in general till the service was over.

Some of the party walked home to the house. Justina lingered, hastened, and accosted John Mortimer. But all in vain; he kept as far as possible from her, while Emily, who had gone forward, very soon found him close at her side.

"Madam," he said, "I shall have the honour of taking you in to luncheon. Did you know it?"

"No, John," she answered, laughing because he did, and feeling as if the occasion had suddenly become more festive, though she knew some explanation must be coming.

"I shall easily find an opportunity," he said, "of telling St. George what I have done. I went through the dining-room and saw the names on the plates, and I took the liberty to change one or two. You can sit by the curate at any time. In fact, I should think old friendship and a kind heart might make you prefer to sit by me. Say that they do, Mrs. Walker."

"They do," answered Emily. "But your reason, John?"

"That little creature is a match-maker. Why must she needs give me the golden head?"

"Oh, she did? Perhaps it was because she thought you would expect it."

"Expect it! *I* expect it? No; I am in the blessed case of him who expects nothing, and who therefore cannot be disappointed. I always thought you were my friends, all of you."

"So we are, John; you know we are."

"Then how can you wish such a thing for me? Emily, you cannot think how utterly tired I am of being teased about that woman—that lady. And now St. George has begun to do it. I declare, if I cannot put a stop to it in any other way, I'll do it by marrying somebody else."

"That is indeed a fearful threat, John," said Emily, "and meant, no doubt, to show that you have reached the last extremity of earnestness."

"Which is a condition you will never reach," said John, laughing, and lapsing into the old intimate fashion with her. "It is always your way to slip into things easily."

John and Emily had walked on, and believed themselves to be well in front, and out of hearing of the others; but when the right time has come for anything to be found out, what is the use of trying to keep it hidden? Justina, seeing her opportunity, went forward just as Brandon drew the rest of the party aside to look at some rather rare ferns, whose curled-up fronds, like little crosiers, were showing on the sandy bank. She drew on, and one more step would have brought her even with them, when John Mortimer uttered the words—

"If I cannot put a stop to it in any other way, I'll do it by marrying somebody else."

Justina stopped and stooped instantly, as if to gather some delicate leaves of silver-weed that grew in the sand; and Emily, who had caught her step, turned for one instant, and saw her without being perceived.

Justina knew what these words meant, and stood still arranging her leaves, to let them pass on and the others come up. Soon after which they all merged into one group. John gave his arm to Mrs. Henfrey, and Emily, falling behind, began to consider how much Justina had heard, and what she would do.

Now Dorothea had said in the easiest way possible to Justina, "I shall ask our new clergyman to take Emily in to luncheon, and Mr. Mortimer to take you." Justina knew now that the game was up; she was not quick of perception, but neither was she vacillating. When once she had decided on any course, she never had the discomfort of wishing afterwards that she had done otherwise. There was undoubtedly a rumour going about to the effect that John Mortimer liked her, and was "coming forward." No one knew better than herself and her mother how this rumour had been wafted on, and how little there was in it. "Yet," she reflected, "it was my best chance. It was necessary to put it into his head somehow to think about me in such a light; but that others have thought too much and said too much, it might have succeeded. What I should like best now," she further considered, pondering slowly over the words in her mind, "would be to have people say that I have refused him."

She had reached this point when Emily joined her

walking silently beside her, that she might not appear companionless. Emily was full of pity for her, in spite of the lightening of her own heart. People who have nothing to hope best know what a lifting of the cloud it is to have also nothing to fear.

The poetical temperament of Emily's mind made her frequently change places with others, and, indeed, become in thought those others—fears, feelings, and all.

"What are you crying for, Emily?" her mother had once said to her, when she was a little child.

"I'm not Emily now," she answered; "I'm the poor little owl, and I can't help crying because that cruel Smokey barked at me and frightened me, and pulled several of my best feathers out."

And now, just the same, Emily was Justina, and such thoughts as Justina might be supposed to be thinking passed through Emily's mind somewhat in this way:—

"No; it is not at all fair! I have been like a ninepin set up in the game of other people's lives, only to be knocked down again; and yet without me the game could not have been played. Yes; I have been made useful, for through me other people have unconsciously set him against matrimony. If they would but have let him alone"—(Oh, Justina! how can you help thinking now?)—"I could have managed it, if I might have had all the game to myself."

Next to the power of standing outside one's self, and looking at *me* as other folks see me, the most remarkable is this of (by the insight of genius and imagination) becoming *you.* The first makes one sometimes only too reasonable, too humble; the second warms the heart and enriches the soul, for it gives the charms of selfhood to beings not ourselves.

"Yet it is a happy thing for some of us," thought Emily, finishing her cogitations in her own person, "that the others are not allowed to play all the game themselves."

When Brandon got home John saw his wife quietly look at him. "Now what does that mean?" he thought; "it was something more than mere observance of his entering. Those two have means of transport for their thoughts past the significance of words. Yes, I'm right; she goes into the dining-room, and he will follow her. Have they found it out?"

All the guests were standing in a small morning-room, taking coffee; and Brandon presently walking out of the French window into the garden, came up to the dining-room outside. There was Dorothea.

"Love," she said, looking out, "what do you think? Some of these names have been changed."

"Perhaps a waft of wind floated them off the plates," said Brandon, climbing in over the window-ledge, "and the servants restored them amiss. But, Mrs. Brandon, don't you think if that baby of yours squalls again after lunch, he had better drink his own health himself somewhere else? I say, how nice you look, love!—I like that gown."

"He must come in, St. George; but do attend to business—look!"

"Whew!" exclaimed Brandon, having inspected the plates; "it must have been a very intelligent waft of wind that did this."

Two minutes after Brandon sauntered in again by the window, and John Mortimer observed the door. When Mrs. Brandon entered, she saw him standing on the rug keeping Emily in conversation. Mrs. Brandon admired Mr. Mortimer; he was tall, fair, stately, and had just such a likeness to Valentine as could not fail to be to his advantage in the opinion of any one who, remembering Valentine's smiling face, small forehead, and calm eyes, sees the same contour of countenance, with an expression at once grave and sweet; features less regular, but with a grand intellectual brow, and keen blue eyes—not so handsome as Valentine's, but with twice as direct an outlook and twice as much tenderness of feeling in them; and has enough insight to perceive the difference of character announced by these varieties in the type.

John Mortimer, who was persistently talking to Emily, felt that Brandon's eyes were upon him, and that he looked amused. He never doubted that his work had been observed, and that his wish would be respected.

"Luncheon's on the table."

"John," said Brandon instantly, "will you take in my wife?"

John obeyed. He knew she did not sit at the head of the table, so he took it and placed her on his right, while Emily and her curate were on his left. It was a very large party, but during the two minutes they had been alone together Brandon and Dorothea had altered the whole arrangement of it.

John saw that Brandon had given to him his own usual place, and had taken the bottom of the table. He thought his own way of managing that matter would have been simpler, but he was very well content, and made himself highly agreeable till there chanced to be a little cessation of the clatter of plates, and a noticeable pause in the conversation. Then Justina began to play her part.

"Mr. Mortimer," she said, leaning a little before Emily's curate, "this is not at all too late for the north of Italy, is it? I want to visit Italy."

"I should not set out so late in the year," John answered. "I should not stay even at Florence a day later than the end of May."

"Oh, don't say that!" she answered. "I have been so longing, you know, for years to go to the north of Italy, and now it seems as if there was a chance—as if my mother would consent."

"You know!" thought John. "I know nothing of the kind, how should I?"

"It really does seem now as if we might leave

England for a few months," she continued. "There is nothing at all to keep her here, if she could but think so. You saw my brother the other day?"

"Yes."

"And you thought he looked tolerably well again, did you not?"

"Yes; I think I did."

"Then," she continued persuasively, and with all serenity, several people being now very attentive to the conversation—"then, if my mother should chance to see you, Mr. Mortimer, and should consult you about this, you will not be so unfriendly to me as to tell her that it is too late. You must not, you know, Mr. Mortimer, because she thinks so much of your opinion."

This was said in some slight degree more distinctly than usual, and with the repetition of his name, that no one might doubt whom she was addressing.

It made a decided impression, but on no one so much as on himself. "What a fool I have been!" he thought; "in spite of appearances this has been very far from her thoughts, and perhaps annoyance at the ridiculous rumour is what makes her so much want to be off."

He then entered with real interest into the matter, and before luncheon was over a splendid tour had been sketched out in the Austrian Tyrol, which he proved to demonstration was far better in the summer than Italy. Justina was quite animated, and only hoped her mother would not object. It was just as well she expressed doubts and fears on that head, for Lady Fairbairn had never in her life had a hint even that her daughter was dying to go on the Continent; and Justina herself had only decided that it was well to intend such a thing, not that it would be wise or necessary to carry the intention out.

She exerted herself, keeping most careful watch and guard over her voice and smile. It was not easy for her to appear pleased when she felt piqued, and to feign a deep interest in the Austrian Tyrol, when she had not known, till that occasion, whereabouts on the map it might be found. She was becoming tired and quite flushed when the opportune entrance of the baby—that morsel of humanity with a large name—diverted every one's attention from her, and relieved her from further effort.

There is nothing so difficult as to make a good speech at a wedding or a christening without affecting somebody's feelings. Some people stand so much in fear of this, that they can hardly say anything. Others enjoy doing it, and are dreaded accordingly; for, beside the pain of having one's feelings touched, and being obliged to weep, there is the red nose that follows.

John, when he stood up to propose the health of his godson, St. George Mortimer Brandon (who luckily was sound asleep), had the unusual good-fortune to please and interest everybody (even the parents) without making any one cry.

It is the commonplaces of tenderness, and the every-day things about time and change, that are affecting; but if a speaker can add to all he touches concerning man's life, and love, and destiny, something reached down from the dominion of thought, beautiful and fresh enough to make his hearers wonder at him, and experience that elation of heart which is the universal tribute paid to all beautiful things, then they will feel deeply perhaps; but the joy of beauty will elevate them, and the mind will save the eyes from annoying tears.

Before her guests retired, Emily having lingered up-stairs with the baby, Dorothea found herself for a few minutes alone with Justina, who was very tired, but felt that her task was not quite finished. So, as she took up her bonnet and advanced to the looking-glass to put it on, she said, carelessly, "I wonder whether this colour will stand Italian sunshine."

Dorothea's fair young face was at once full of interest. Justina saw curiosity, too, but none was expressed; she only said, with the least little touch of pique, "And you never told *me* that you were wishing so much to go away."

Justina turned, and from her superior height stooped to kiss Dorothea, as if by way of apology, whereupon she added, "I had hoped, indeed, I felt sure, that you liked this place and this neighbourhood."

"What are you alluding to, dear," said Justina, though Dorothea had alluded to nothing.

But Dorothea remaining silent, Justina had to go on.

"I think (if *that* is what you mean) that no one who cares for me could wish me to undertake a very difficult task—such a very difficult task as that, and one which perhaps I am not at all fit for."

On this Dorothea betrayed a certain embarrassment, rather a painful blush tinged her soft cheek. "I would not have taken the liberty to hint at such a thing," she answered.

"She would not have liked it," thought Justina, with not unnatural surprise; for Dorothea had shown a fondness for her.

"But of course I know there has been an idea in the neighbourhood that you——"

"That I what?" asked Justina.

"Why that you might—you might undertake it."

"Oh, nonsense, dear! nonsense, all talk," said Justina; "don't believe a word of it." Her tone seemed to mean just the contrary, and Dorothea looked doubtful.

"There have been some attentions, certainly," continued Justina, turning before the glass as if to observe whether her scarf was folded to her mind. "Of course every one must have observed that! But really, dear, such a thing"—she put up her large steady hand, and fastened her veil with due care—"such a thing as that would never do. Who *could* have put it into your head to think of it?"

"She does not care for him in the least, then," thought Dorothea; "and it seems that he has cared for her. I don't think he does now, for he seemed rather pleased to sketch out that tour which will take her away from him. I like her, but even if it was base to her, I should still be glad she was not going to marry John Mortimer."

Justina was in many respects a pleasant woman. She was a good daughter, she had a very good temper, serene, never peevish; she did not forget what was due to others, she was reasonable, and, on the whole, just. She felt what a pity it was that Mr. Mortimer was so unwise. She regretted this with a sincerity not disturbed by any misgiving. Taking the deepest interest in herself, as every way worthy and desirable, she did for herself what she could, and really felt as if this was both a privilege and a duty. Something like the glow of a satisfied conscience filled her mind when she reflected that to this end she had worked, and left nothing undone, just as such a feeling rises in some minds on so reflecting about efforts made for another person. But with all her foibles, old people liked her, and her own sex liked her, for she was a comfortable person to be with; one whose good points attracted regard, and whose faults were remarkably well concealed.

With that last speech she bowled herself out of the imaginary game of ninepins, and the next stroke was made by Dorothea.

She went down to the long drawing-room, and found all her guests departed, excepting John Mortimer, who came up to take leave of her. He smiled. "I wanted to apologize," he said, taking her hand, "(it was a great liberty), for the change I made in your table."

"The change, did you say," she answered, oh so softly! "or the changes?" And then she became suddenly shy, and withdrew her hand, which he was still holding; and he, drawing himself up to his full height, stood stock still for a moment as if lost in thought and in surprise.

It was such a very slight hint to him that two ladies had been concerned, but he took it,—remembered that one of them was the sister of his host, and also that he had not been allowed to carry out his *changes* just as he had devised them. "I asked Emily's leave," he said, "to take her in."

"Oh, did you?" answered Dorothea, with what seemed involuntary interest, and then he took his leave.

"Why did I never think of this before? I don't believe there ever was such a fool in this world," he said to himself, as he mounted his horse and rode off. "Of course, if I were driven to it, Emily would be fifty times more suitable for me than that calm blond spinster. Liberty is sweet, however, and I will not do it if I can help it. The worst of it is, that Emily, of all the women of my acquaintance, is the only one who does not care one straw about me. There's no hurry—I fancy myself making her an offer, and getting laughed at for my pains." Then John Mortimer amused himself with recollections of poor Fred Walker's wooing, how ridiculous he had made himself, and how she had laughed at him, and yet, out of mere sweetness of nature, taken him. "It's not in her to be in love with any man," he reflected; "and I suppose it's not in me to be in love with any woman. So far at least we might meet on equal ground."

In the meantime, Dorothea was cosily resting on the sofa in her dressing-room, her husband was with her, and St. George Mortimer Brandon,—the latter as quiet as possible in his cot, now nobody cared whether his behaviour did him credit or not.

"Love," she said, "do you know I shouldn't

be at all surprised if John Mortimer has made Justina an offer, and she has refused him."

"*I* should be very much surprised, indeed," said Brandon, laughing; "I think highly of his good sense—and of hers, for both which reasons I feel sure, my darling, that he has not made her an offer, and she has not refused him."

"But I am almost sure he has," proceeded Dorothea, "otherwise I should be obliged to think that the kind of things she said to-day were not quite fair."

"What did she say?"

Dorothea told him.

"I do not think that amounts to much," said Brandon.

"Oh then you think he never did ask her? I hope and trust you are right."

"Why do you hope and trust, Mrs. Brandon? What can it signify to you?" Then, when she made no answer, he went on. "To be sure that would make it highly natural that he should be glad at the prospect of her absenting herself."

"I was just thinking so. Did not he speak well, St. George."

"He did; you were wishing all the time that I could speak as well!"

"Just as if you did not speak twice as well! Besides, you have a much finer voice. I like so much to hear you when you get excited."

"Ah! that is the thing. I have taken great pains to learn the art of speaking, and when to art excitement is added, I get on well enough. But John, without being excited, says, and cares nothing about them, the very things I should like to have said, but that will not perfectly reveal themselves to me till my speech is over."

"But he is not eloquent."

"No; he does not on particular occasions rise above the ordinary level of his thoughts. His every-day self suffices for what he has to do and say. But sometimes, if we two have spoken at the same meeting, and I see the speeches reported—though mine may have been most cheered—I find little in it, while he has often said perfectly things of real use to our party."

CHAPTER XXVII.

THE PLEASURES OF MEMORY.

"Pleasures of memory! O supremely blest
And justly proud beyond a poet's praise,
If the pure confines of thy tranquil breast
Contain indeed the subject of thy lays."
(Said to be by ROGERS.)

A FEW days after this Emily was coming down the lane leading to John Mortimer's house, having taken leave of Justina at the railway station. She was reading a letter just received from Valentine, signed for the first time in full, Valentine Melcombe. The young gentleman, it appeared, was quite as full of fun as ever; had been to Visp and Rifflesdorf, and other of those places—found them dull on the whole—had taken a bath. "And you may judge of the smell of the water," he went on to his sister, "when I tell you that I fell asleep after it, and dreamt I was a bad egg. I hoped I shouldn't hatch into a bad fellow. I've been here three days and seen nobody; the population (chiefly Catholic) consists of three goats, a cock and hen, and a small lake!"

Here lifting up her head as she passed by John's gate, Emily observed extraordinary signs of festivity about the place. Flags protruded from various bedroom windows, wreaths and flowers dangling at the end of long poles from others, rows of dolls dressed in their best sat in state on the lower boughs of larches, together with tinsel butterflies, frail balloons, and other gear not often seen excepting on Christmas-trees.

It was Saturday afternoon, a half-holiday; the two little boys, who were weekly pupils of a clergyman in the immediate neighbourhood, always came home at that auspicious time, and there remained till Monday morning.

From one of them Emily learned that some epidemic having broken out at Harrow, in the "house" where Johnnie was, the boys had been dispersed, and Johnnie, having been already in quarantine a fortnight, had now come home, and the place had been turned out of windows to welcome him.

"And Cray is at Mr. Brandon's," said Bertie, "but on Monday they are both to go to Mr. Tikey's with us."

Something aloft very large and black at this moment startled Emily. Johnnie, who had climbed up a tall poplar tree, and was shaking it portentously, began to let himself down apparently at the peril of his life, and the girls at the same moment coming out of the house, welcomed Emily, letting her know that their father had given them a large, *lovely* cuckoo clock to hang up in Parliament. "And you shall come and see it," they said. Emily knew this was a most unusual privilege. "Johnnie is not gone up there to look for nests," said Gladys, "but to reconnoitre the country. If we let you know what for, you won't tell?"

"Certainly not," said Emily, and she was borne off to Parliament, feeling a curiosity to see it, because John had fitted it up for the special and exclusive delectation of his young brood. It embodied his notion of what children would delight in.

An extraordinary place indeed she thought it. At least fifty feet long, and at the end farthest from the house, without carpet. A carpenter's bench, many tools, and some machines were there, shavings strewed the floor; something, evidently meant to turn out a wheel-barrow, was in course of being hewn from a solid piece of wood, by very young carpenters, and various articles of furniture by older hands were in course of concoction. "Johnnie and Cray carved this in the winter," said the girls, "and when it is done it will be a settle, and stand in the arbour where papa smokes sometimes."

At the other end of the room was spread a very handsome new Turkey carpet; a piano stood there, and a fine pair of globes; the walls were hung with maps, but also with some of the strangest pictures possible; figures chiefly, with scrolls proceeding from their mouths, on which sentences were written. A remarkable chair, very rude and clumsy, but carved all over with letters, flowers, birds, and other devices, attracted Emily's attention.

"What is that? Why, don't you see that it's a throne? Father's throne when he comes to Parliament to make a speech, or anything of that sort there. Johnnie made it, but we all carved our initials on it."

Emily inspected the chair, less to remark on the goodness of the carving than to express her approval of its spirit. Johnnie's flowers were indeed wooden, but his birds and insects, though flat and rough, were all intended to be alive. He had too much directness, and also real vitality, to carve poor dead birds hanging by the legs with torn and ruffled feathers, and showing pathetically their quenched and faded eyes; he wanted his birds to peck and his beetles to be creeping. Luckily for himself, he saw no beauty in death and misery, still less could think them ornamental.

Emily praised his wooden work, and the girls, with a sort of shy delight, questioned her: "Was it really true, then, that Miss Fairbairn was gone, and was not coming back to England for weeks and weeks?" "Yes, really true; why had they made themselves so miserable about nothing?" "Ah, you were so kind;

but, dear Mrs. Walker, you know very well how horrid it would have been to have a step-mother."

Emily sat down and looked about her. A very large slate, swung on a stand like a looking-glass, stood on the edge of the carpet. On it were written these words: "I cry, 'Jam satis,'" John's writing evidently, and of great size. She had no time, however, to learn what it meant, for, with a shout like a war-whoop, Johnnie's voice was heard below, and presently, as it were, driving his little brothers and sisters before him, Johnnie himself came blundering up-stairs at full speed with Crayshaw on his back. "Bolt it, bolt the door," panted Crayshaw; and down darted one of the girls to obey. "And you kids sit down on the floor every one of you, that you mayn't be theen below, and don't make a thound," said Johnnie, depositing Crayshaw on a couch, while Barbara began to fan him. "They're coming up the lane," were Johnnie's first words, when the whole family was seated on the floor like players at hunt the slipper. "You won't tell, Mrs. Walker?"

"Not tell what, to whom?" asked Emily.

"Why that fellow, Cray's brother, wrote to Mr. Brandon that he was coming, and should take him away. It's a shame."

"It's a shame," repeated Crayshaw, panting. "I wish the Continent had never been invented."

"Hold your tongue; if you make yourself pant they'll hear you. Hang being done good to! Why, you've been perfectly well till this day, for the last six months——"

"And should have been now," Crayshaw gasped out, "only I ran over here just after my lunch."

Emily, the only person seated on a chair, John's throne in fact, was far back in the room, and could not be seen from below. A few minutes passed away, while Crayshaw began to breathe like other people, and a certain scratching noise was heard below, upon which significant looks entreated her to be silent. She thought she would let things take their course, and sat still for a minute, when a casement was flung open below, and a shrill voice cried, "Mr. Swan, I say, here's Mr. Brandon in the stable yard, and another gentleman, and they want very particular to know where Master Johnnie is."

"I can't say I know, cookie," answered Swan.

"And," continued the same shrill voice, "if you can't tell 'em that, they'd like to know where Matthew is?"

Matthew was the coachman, and Swan's rival.

"Just as if I knew! why, he's so full of fads he won't trust anybody, and nothing ever suits him. You may tell them, if you like," he answered, not intending her to take him at his word, "that I expect he's gone to dig his own grave, for fear when he's dead they shouldn't do it to his mind."

The cook laughed and slammed the casement.

Presently, coming round to the front garden, wheels were heard grating on the gravel, and Brandon's voice shouted, "Swan, Swan, I say, is young Crayshaw here?"

"No, sir," Swan shouted in reply; "not as I know of."

Two voices were heard to parley at a distance, great excitement prevailed up in Parliament, excepting in the mind of Anastasia, whose notion of her own part in this ceremony of hiding was that she must keep her little feet very even and close together beside Johnnie's great ones; so she took no notice, though hasty footsteps were heard, and a voice spoke underneath, "Whereabout can young Mortimer be? we must find him."

"I don't know, sir," repeated Swan, still raking peaceably.

"He cannot be very far off, Swanny," said Brandon, "we saw him up the poplar-tree not a quarter of an hour ago."

"Ay, sir, I shouldn't wonder," said Swan carelessly.

"Bless you, whether their folks air rich or poor, they never think at that age what it costs to clothe 'em. I never found with my boys that they'd done climbing for crows' eggs till such time as they bought their own breeches. After that trees were nought but lumber, and crows were carrion."

"But we really must find these boys, if we can," exclaimed Brandon; "and it seems as if they had all the family with them, the place is so quiet. Where do you think they can have gone?"

"I haven't a notion, sir—maybe up to the fir-woods, maybe out to the common—they roam all about the country on half-holidays."

"Oh," said the other voice, "they may go where they please, may they?"

"Naturally so," said Swan; "they may go anywhere, sir, or do anything in reason, on a half-holiday. It would be a shame to give a pig leave to grunt, and then say he's not to grunt through his nose."

"Perhaps they're up in Parliament," observed Brandon.

"No, that they're not," Swan exclaimed; "so sure as they're there they make the roof ring."

"And the door's locked."

"Yes, the door's locked, and wherever they air they've got the key. They let nobody in, sir, but my daughter, and she goes o' mornings to sweep it out."

"Well, Swan, good day. Come on, George, we'll try the fir-wood first."

"Or perhaps they're gone to Wigfield," said the second voice.

"No, sir, I think not," said Swan. "They sent one of the little boys there on an errand, so I judge that they've no call to go again."

Yes, one of the little boys had been sent, and had no reason to be ashamed of what he had also done there on his own account.

What! though I have all sorts of good food in my

father's house, and plenty of it, shall it not still be a joy to me to buy a whole pot of plum-jam with my ninepence? Certainly it shall, and with generous ardour I shall call my younger brothers and sisters together to my little room, where in appreciative silence we shall hang over it, while I dig it out with the butt-end of my tooth-brush.

Johnnie's face grew radiant as these two went off to search the fir-wood, but nobody dared to speak or stir, for Swan was still close underneath, so close that they could hear him grumbling to himself over the laziness of a woman who had been hired to weed the walks for him, and was slowly scratching them at a good distance.

"Ay, there you go, grudging every weed you pull. The master says it ain't a woman's work—wants to raise you—you! 'Sir,' says I, 'folks can't rise o' top of parish pay.' Ay, she was a pauper, and she'd have liked to charge the parish twopence a time for suckling her own child. Now what would you have? Ain't two shillings a day handsome for scratching out half a peck of grass? You might work here for some time, too, but bless us, what's the good of saying to such as you, 'Don't stand waiting for good luck, and give the go-by to good opportunity?' Your man's just like you," he continued, using his rake with delicate skill among the flowers, while she scratched calmly on, out of hearing—" your man's just like you, idle dog! (you won't raise Phil Raby in a trice.) Why, if he was rich enough to drive his own taxed cart, he'd sooner jolt till his bones ached than get down to grease his wheels." Then a short silence, and other feet came up. "Well, Jemmy man, and what do you want?"

A small voice, in a boy's falsetto tone answered, "Please, Mr. Swan, I've brought the paper."

"Have you now, and what's the news, Jemmy, do you know?"

"Yes—coals are riz again."

"You don't say so! that's a thing to make a man thoughtful; and what else, Jemmy?"

"Why, the Governor-general's come home from India."

"Only think o' that! Well, he may come and welcome, for aught I care, Jemmy. Let the cook give warning or keep her place, it's all one to the flies in the kitchen window."

The new-comer withdrew, and Swan was presently heard to throw down his rake and go off to argue with his subordinate, whom he very soon preceded into the back garden behind the house, to the great joy of the party in Parliament, who, still sitting perfectly quiet, began to talk in low tones, Emily inquiring what they really hoped to effect by concealing themselves.

"Why, George Crayshaw," said Cray (that being his manner of designating his brother when he was not pleased with him)—"George Crayshaw is only come down here for one day, and Mr. Brandon had fully arranged that I should go to Mr. Tikey till we two return to Harrow, and now he's going to Germany, and wants me to start with him this very day—says the dry continental air may do me good. Why, I am perfectly well—perfectly."

"So it appears," said Emily.

"Look how he's grown, then," exclaimed Johnnie, who had almost left off lisping, "he hardly ever has a touch of asthma now. His brother hates trouble, so if he cannot find him he may go off by himself."

"I was just writing out my verses," Crayshaw whispered, "when I overheard Mr. Brandon saying in the garden that he expected George."

"Were you alone?" asked Gladys, hoping he had not been seen to run off.

"Was I alone? Well, there was nobody present but myself, if you call that being alone—I don't. That fellow argues so; he's so intrusive, and often makes such a noise that I can get no retirement for writing my poetry."

"What a goose you are, Cray!" said Barbara. "I wish, though, you would speak lower."

"Besides," continued Crayshaw, excusing himself to Mrs. Walker; "it's so dull being with George, he's always collecting things. The last time I saw him he was on his knees cleaning up a dingy old picture he'd just bought. Fanny stood beside him with a soapy flannel. She looked quite religious; she was so grave. I saw a red cabbage in the picture and a pot of porter, the froth extremely fine. 'I hope,' said George, very hot after his exertions, 'that when you are of age you will follow in my steps, and endow our common country with some of these priceless——' 'Common,' interrupted Mrs. Jannaway. 'Common country, do I hear aright, George Crayshaw?' (I don't love that old lady *much.*) 'George,' I said, for I pitied him for having a mother-in-law, 'when I get my money I shall pay a man to paint another old picture for you, as a companion to that. There shall be three mackerel in it, very dead indeed; they shall lie on a willow-pattern plate, while two cock-roaches that have climbed up it squint over the edge at them. There shall also be a pork-pie in it, and a brigand's hat. The composition will be splendid.' I took out my pocket-book and said, 'I'll make a mem. of it now.' So I did, and added, 'Mem.: Never to have a mother-in-law, unless her daughter is as pretty as Fanny Crayshaw.'"

The little boys were now allowed to have tools and go on with their carving, still seated on the ground. The girls took out their tatting, and talk went on.

"Mrs. Walker has just been saying that she cannot bear carving, and pictures of dead things," observed Barbara. "So, Cray, she will think you right to despise those your brother buys. And, Johnnie, she wishes to know about our pictures."

"And those great sentences too," added Emily. "What do they mean?"

"The big picture is Dover," said little Jarie, "and

that Britannia sitting on the cliff, they cut out of *Punch* and stuck on. You see she has a boot in her hand. It belongs to our Sham memory that father made for us."

"It's nearly the same as what Feinangle invented," Johnnie explained. "The vowels do not count, but all the consonants stand for figures. Miss Crampton used to make the kids so miserable. She would have them learn dates, and they could not remember them."

"Even Barbara used to cry over the dates," whispered Janie.

"You needn't have told that," said Barbara sharply.

"But at first we altered the letters so many times, that father said he would not help us, unless we made a decree that they should stay as they were for ever," said Gladys. "Johnnie had stolen the letter I, and made it stand for one. So it does still, though it is a vowel. Janie has a form of our plan. Hand it up, Janie."

Janie accordingly produced a little bag, and unfolded a paper of which this is a copy:—

JANIE MORTIMER Fecit This.

1 I. T.	2 N. B.	3 M. Y.
4 R. Q.	5 C. J. V.	6 D. S.
7 K. G.	8 H. P.	9 F. L.
	Ought W. X. Z.	

A & E & O & U dont count Youre to make up the sentense with them.

"The rule is," said Gladys, "that you make a sentence of words beginning with any one of those letters that stand for the figures you want to remember. Miss Crampton wanted us to know the dates of all Wellington's battles; of course we couldn't; we do now, though. You see Britannia's scroll has on it, 'I'll put *on* Wellington boots,' that means 1802. So we know, to begin with, that till after she put on Wellington boots, we need not trouble ourselves to remember anything particular about him."

"There's a portrait of Lord Palmerston," whispered Crayshaw, "he has a map of Belgium pasted on his breast. He says, 'I, Pam, managed this.'"

"Yes, that means the date of the independence of Belgium," said Gladys. "Johnnie made it, but father says it is not quite fair."

"The best ones," Johnnie explained, "ought not to have any extra word, and should tell you what they mean themselves. 'I hear navvies coming,' is good—it means the making of the first railway. Here are four not so good:—Magna Charta—'The Barons *extorted* this Charter,' 1215. The Reformation—'They came *out of* you, Rome,' 1534. Discovery of America—'In re *a* famous navigator,' 1492. And Waterloo — Bonaparte says it — 'Isle perfide tu *as* vaincu,' 1815."

"I have thought of one for the Reform Bill," said Emily: "get a portrait of Lord Russell, and let his scroll say, 'They've passed my bill.'"

"That is a good one, but they must not be too simple and easy, or they are forgotten," said one of the girls; "but we make them for many things besides historical events. Those are portraits, and show when people were born. There is dear Grand; 'I *owe* Grand love *and* duty.' That next one is Tennyson; 'I have won laurels.' There's Swan; Swan said he did not know whether he was born in 1813 or 1814; so Johnnie did them both. 'The principal thing's muck *as* these here *airly* tates require.'

You see the first Napoleon, looking across the Channel at Britannia with the boot: he says, 'I hate white cliffs,' which means Trafalgar; and 'I cry, Jam satis,' father has just invented for Charles, that King of Spain who was Emperor of Germany too. You can see by it that he abdicated in 1556. Miss Crampton used to wonder at our having become so clever with our dates all on a sudden. And there's one that Mr. Brandon made. You see those ships? That is a picture of Boston harbour (Cray's Boston). If you were nearer, you could see them pouring something over their sides into the water, using the harbour for a teapot. On their pennons is written, 'Tea *of* King George's *own* making.' Oh, Cray! what is that noise?" Silence, a crunching of decided step coming on fast and firmly; the faces of the party fell.

"It's all up!" sighed Crayshaw.

Somebody shook the door at the foot of the stairs; then a voice rang through the place like a silver trumpet, "Johnnie."

"Yes, father," answered Johnnie in the loud, melancholy tone not unfrequently used by a boy when he succumbs to lawful authority.

"What are you about, sir? What are you thinking of? Come down this moment, and open the door."

One of the little boys had been already dispatched down-stairs, and was turning the key. In another instant John Mortimer, coming quickly up beheld the party seated on the floor, looking very foolish, and Mrs. Walker in his throne laughing. Crayshaw got up to present himself, and take the blame on his own shoulders, and John was so much surprised to find Emily present, and perhaps aiding, that he stopped short in his inquiry how they had dared to bring him home when he was so busy, and observing the ridiculous side of the question, sat down at once, and laughed also, while she said something by way of excuse for them, and they made the best defence they could.

Emily had the little Anastasia in her arms; the child, tired of inaction, had fallen asleep, with her delicate rosy cheek leaning against Emily's fair throat.

John felt the beauty of the attitude, and perceived how Emily's presence gave completeness to the group.

Much too young to be the mother of the elder children, there was still something essentially mother-like in all her ways. His children, excepting the one asleep in her arms, were all grouped on the floor at her feet. "Just so Janie would have sat, if she had lived," he thought. "I should often have seen something like this here, as the children grew older." And while he listened to the account given by the two boys of their doings, he could not help looking at Emily, and thinking, as he had sometimes done before, that she bore, in some slight degree, a resemblance to his wife—his wife whom he had idealised a good deal lately—and who generally, in his thought, presented herself to him as she had done when, as a mere lad, he first saw her. A dark-haired and grey-eyed young woman, older than himself, as a very young man's first admiration frequently is. He felt that Emily was more graceful, had a charm of manner and a sweetness of nature that Janie had never possessed. He seldom allowed himself to admit even to his own mind that his wife had been endowed with very slight powers of loving. On that occasion, however, the fact was certainly present to his thought; "But," he cogitated, "we had no quarrels. A man may sometimes do with but little love from his wife, if he is quite sure she loves no other man more."

He started from his reverie as Crayshaw ceased to speak. "I thought you had more sense," he said, with the smile still on his mouth that had come while he mused on Emily. "And now don't flatter yourself that you are to be torn from your friends and hurled on the Continent against your will. Nothing of the sort, my boy! You have a more difficult part to play; you are to do as you please."

Crayshaw's countenance fell a little.

"Is George really angry, sir?" he asked.

"He did not seem so. He remarked that you were nearly seventeen, and that he did not specially care about this journey."

Something very like disappointment stole over Cray's face then—something of that feeling which now and then shows us that it is rather a blow to us to have, all on a sudden, what we wanted. What would we have, then? We cannot exactly tell; but it seems *that* was not it.

"Your brother thought you and Johnnie might be with me, and came to ask. I, of course, felt sure you were here. If you decide to go with him, you are to be back by six o'clock; if not, you go to Mr. Tikey on Monday. Now, my boy, I am not going to turn you out-of-doors. So adieu."

Thus saying, because Emily's little charge was awake, and she had risen and was taking leave of the girls, he brought her down-stairs, and, wishing her good-bye at his gate, went back to Wigfield, while she returned home.

This young woman, who had been accustomed to reign over most of the men about her, felt, in her newly-learned humility, a sense of elation from merely having been a little while in the presence of the man whom she loved. She reflected on his musing smile, had no thought that it concerned her, and hoped nothing better than that he might never find out how dear he was to her.

As for John Mortimer, he returned to the town, musing over some turn in political affairs that pleased him, cogitating over the contents of a bill then under discussion in Parliament, wondering whether it would get much altered before the second reading, while all the time, half unconsciously to himself, the scene in that other Parliament was present to him.

Just as a scene; nothing more. Emily sitting on his throne—his! with his smallest child nestling in her arms, so satisfied, one knew not which of the two had the most assured air of possession. Half unaware, he seemed to hear again the contented sighing of the little creature in her sleep, and Emily's low, sweet laugh when she saw his astonishment at her presence.

Then there was the young American stepping forward through a narrow sunbeam into the brown shade to meet him, with such a shamefaced, boyish air of conscious delinquency. Conscious, indeed, that he was the author of a certain commotion, but very far, assuredly, from being conscious that he, Gifford Crayshaw, by means of this schoolboy prank, was taking the decisive step towards a change in the destiny of every soul then bearing a part in it.

John Mortimer reached the town. He had rallied the boy, and made him see his folly. "A fine young fellow," he reflected, "and full of fun. I don't care how often he comes here," and so in thought he dismissed Crayshaw and his boyish escapade, to attend to more important matters.

Emily, as she went towards home, was soon overtaken by the twins, Johnnie, and Crayshaw. Opposition being now withdrawn, the latter young gentleman had discovered that he ought to go with his brother, and was moderately good-tempered about it. Johnnie Mortimer, on the other hand, was gloriously sulky, and declined to take any notice of his fellow-creatures, even when they spoke to him.

At the stepping-stones over the brook, Emily parted with the young people, receiving from Crayshaw the verses he had copied.

"Gladys had possessed them for a week, and liked them," said the young poet. "I meant one of them for a parody, but Mr. Mortimer said it was not half enough like for parody, it only amounted to a kind of honest plagiarism."

Considering the crestfallen air of the author, and

the sigh with which he parted from her and went his way to join his brother, she was rather surprised to find the sort of verses that they were. They were copied in a neat, boyish hand, and read as follows:—

SOUVENIR OF SOUTH WALES.

(A cad would thay "I thor.")

But once I saw her by the stream
  (A cad would say "I sor"),
Yet ofttimes of that once I dream,
  That once and never more.

By the fair flood she came to lean
  (Her gown was lilac print),
And dip her pitcher down between
  The stalks of water-mint.

Then shoals of little fishes fled,
  And sun-flecks danced amain,
And rings of water spread and spread
  Till all was smooth again.

I saw her somewhat towzled hair
  Reflected in the brook—
I might have seen her often there,
  Only—I didn't look.

G. C.

SONG OF THE BASEMENT STORY.

Her mean abode was but a cell;
  'Twas lonely, chill, and drear.
Her work was all her wealth, but well
  She wrought with hope and cheer.

She, envious not of great or gay,
  Slept, with unbolted doors;
Then woke, and as we Yankees say,
  "Flew round" and did her chores.

All day she worked; no lover lent
  His aid; and yet with glee
At dusk she sought her home, content,
  That beauteous Bumble Bee.

A cell it was, nor more nor less.
  But O! all's one to me
Whether you write it with an S,
  Dear girl, or with a C.

April 1st.

N.B. The motto for this ought to be, "For she was a water-rat."

CHAPTER XXVIII.

MELCOMBE.

In the pleasant orchard closes
'God bless all our gains,' say we,
But, 'May God bless all our losses,'
Better suits with our degree "
E. B. Browning.

THE shade of twilight was but just fleeting, a faint glow waxed over the eastern hills, and the great orchard of pear-trees that pressed up to one end of Melcombe House showed white as an army of shrouded ghosts in the dim solemnities of dawn. The house was closely shut up, and no one met Valentine, as, tired after a night journey, he dismissed a hired fly at the inn, and came up slowly to those grand old silent trees.

Without sunshine, white in nature is always most solemn. Here stillness was added ; not a bird was yet awake, not a leaf stirred. A faint bluish haze appeared to confuse the outlines of the trees, but as he lingered looking at them and at the house which he had now fully decided to take for his home, Mr. Melcombe saw this haze dissolve itself and retreat; there was light enough to make the paleness whiter, and to show the distinct brown trunk of each pear-tree, with the cushions of green moss at its roots. Formless whiteness and visible dusk had divided themselves into light and shade, then came a shaft of sunshine, the boughs laden with dewy blossom sparkled like snow, and in one instant the oppression of their solemnity was over, and they appeared to smile upon his approach to his home.

He had done everything he could think of, and knew not how to devise anything further, and yet this secret, if there was one, would not come forward and look him in the face. He had searched the house in the first instance for letters and papers; there were some old letters, and old papers also, but not one that did not seem to be as clear in the innocence of its meaning as possible; there was even one that set at rest doubt and fear which he had hitherto entertained. He had found no closets in the wall, no locked chambers; he had met with no mysterious silences, mysterious looks, mysterious words. Then he had gone to meet the bereaved mother, that if she had anything to say in the way of warning to him, or repentance for herself, he might lay himself out to hear it; but no, he had found her generally not willing to talk, but all she did say showed tender reverence for the dead Melcombes, and passionate grief for her boy who had been taken, as she said, before he was old enough even to estimate at its due value the prosperous and happy career he had before him. He tried Laura. Laura, though sincerely sorry for poor little Peter's death, was very sentimental; told Valentine, to his surprise, that it was mainly on her account they had wintered on the Continent, and with downcast eyes and mysterious confusion that made him tremble, at first utterly declined to tell him the reason.

When he found, therefore, that Mrs. Melcombe did not care at present to return to England, and was far better able than he was to arrange her journey when she did, he might have come home at once, but for this mystery of Laura's. And when, after cultivating his intimacy with her for nearly a month, he at last found out, beyond a doubt, that it related to a love affair which Amelia had not approved of, he felt as if everything he approached, concerning the matter of his father's letter, melted into nothingness at his touch.

He acknowledged to himself that he should have been deeply disappointed if he had discovered anything to justify this letter; and when the full, low sunlight shone upon his large comfortable old house, glorified the blossoming orchard and set off the darkness of the ancient yews, he felt a touch of that sensation, which some people think is not fancy only. Everything about him seemed familiar. The old-fashioned quaintness was a part of himself. "The very first time I saw that clean, empty coach-house," he reflected, "I felt as if I had often played in it. I almost seemed to hear other boys shouting to me. Is it true that I never let off squibs and crackers in that yard?"

He walked nearer. How cheerful it all looked, swept up with extra neatness, and made orderly for the new master's eyes!

"By-the-bye," he thought, catching sight of a heavy old outhouse door, "there is the ghost story. Having examined all realities so far as I can, I will try my hand at things unreal—for even now, though I am very grateful to Providence for such a house and such an inheritance, once show me a good reason, and over it goes, as it should have done at first, if my father could have given me one. That door seems just the sort of thing for a ghost to pass through. I'll look at the book Laura told me of, and see which door it was."

So the house being now open, and Mr. Melcombe observed by his servants (who alone were there to give him welcome), he entered, ordered breakfast, which was spread for him in the "great parlour," and having now got into the habit of making investigations, had no sooner finished his meal than he began to look at the notes he had made from what Mrs. Melcombe had told him of the ghost story.

It was a story that she had not half finished when

he recognised it—he had read it with all its particulars in a book, only with the names and localities disguised.

"Oh, yes," she answered, when he said so. "It is very well known; it has always been considered one of the best authenticated stories of its kind on record, though it was not known beyond the family and the village for several years. Augustus Melcombe, you know, was the name of the dear grandmother's only brother, her father's heir; he was her father's only son, two daughters born between died in infancy. That poor young fellow died at sea, and just at the time (as is supposed) that he expired, his wraith appeared to the old woman, Becky Maddison, then a very young girl. I am sorry to say the old woman has made a gain of this story. People often used to come to hear it, and she certainly does not always tell it exactly the same. People's inquiries, I suppose, and suggestions, have induced her to add to it; but the version I am giving you is what she first told."

Mrs. Melcombe mentioned the book in which Valentine would find it, and repeated from memory the impressive conclusion, "And this story of the young man's appearance to her had been repeatedly told by the girl before his family became alarmed at his protracted absence. It was during the long war, and the worst they feared was that he might have been taken prisoner; but more than three years after a member of the family met by accident, when some hundreds of miles away from home, a naval officer who had sailed in the ship to which this young lieutenant belonged, and heard from him, not without deep emotion, that at that very time and at that very hour the youth had died at sea."

"There is only one mistake in that version," continued Mrs. Melcombe, "and that is, that we do not know the exact time when the young man died. Cuthbert Melcombe was not told the month even, only the year."

"But surely that is a very important mistake," said Valentine.

"Yes, for those to consider who believe in supernatural stories. It is certain, however, that the girl told this story within a day or two, and told it often, so that it was known in the village. It is certain also that he was at sea, and that he never came home. And it is undoubtedly true that Cuthbert, when in London, heard this account, for he wrote his mother home a description of the whole interview, with the officer's name and ship. I have seen the letter, and read it over several times. The year of the death at sea is mentioned, but not the day. Now the day of the ghost's appearance we cannot be wrong about; it was that before the night of the great gale which did such damage in these parts, that for years it could not be forgotten."

"You have read the letter, you say?"

"Yes; it was an important one, I suppose. But I fancy that it was not read by any one but the dear grandmother till after poor Cuthbert Melcombe's sad death, and then I think the family lawyer found it among her papers when she had to inherit the estate. He may have wanted evidence, perhaps, that Augustus Melcombe was dead."

"Perhaps so," said Valentine. "It is just of the usual sort, I see, this story; a blue light hovering about the head. The ghost walked in his shroud, and she saw the seams in it."

"Yes, and then it passed through the door without opening it," added Laura, who was present. "How dear grandmother disliked the woman! She showed a sort of fear, too, of that door, which made us sure she believed the story."

"Very natural," said Mrs. Melcombe, sighing, "that she could not bear to have her misfortunes made a subject for idle talk and curiosity. I am sure I should feel keenly hurt if it was ever said that my poor innocent darling haunted the place."

"Had anything been said against him in his lifetime?" Valentine next ventured to ask. "Had he done anything which was likely to put it into people's heads to say he might be uneasy in his grave?"

"Oh no, nothing of the sort," said Laura. "And then old Becky is thought to have added circumstances to the story, so that it came from that cause to be discredited of late. It is almost forgotten now, and we never believed it at all; but it certainly is an odd coincidence that she should have told it of a man who never came back to contradict her, and who really did die, it appears, about that time."

Valentine accordingly went in the course of a few days to find old Becky Maddison. The cottage was not far from the village. Only the daughter was below, and when Valentine had told his name and errand, she went up-stairs, perhaps to prepare her mother, to whom she presently conducted him.

Valentine found her a poor bedridden creature, weak, frail, and querulous. She was in a clean and moderately comfortable bed, and when she saw him her puckered face and faded eyes began to look more intelligent and attentive, and she presently remarked on his likeness to his father.

A chair was set for him, and sitting down, he showed a sovereign in his palm, and said, "I want to hear the ghost story; tell it me as it really was, and you shall have this."

A shabby book was lying on the bed.

"Her can tell it no better'n it's told here," said the daughter.

Valentine took up the book. It was the same that he knew; the blue light and the shroud appeared in it. He put the money into her hand. "No," he said; "you shall have the money beforehand. Now, then, say what you really saw."

Old Becky clutched the gold, and said, in a weak, whimpering tone, "'Tain't often I tell it—ain't told it sin' Christmas marnin', old Madam couldn't abide to hear on't."

"Old Madam's gone," said Valentine seriously.

"Ay, her be—her wer a saint, and sings in heaven now."

"And I want to hear it."

Thereupon the old woman roused herself a little, and with the voice and manner of one repeating a lesson, told Valentine word for word the trumpery tale in the book; how she had seen Mr. Melcombe early in the morning, as she went up to the house on washing-day, to help the servants. For "Madam," a widow already, had leave to live there till he should return. He was walking in his shroud among the cherry-trees, and he looked seriously at her. She passed, but turned instantly, and he had disappeared; he must have gone right through the crack of the door.

Valentine was vexed, and yet relieved. Such a ridiculous tale could only be an invention; and yet, if she would have told it in different words, or have added anything, it might have led to some discovery —it might, at least, have shown how it came to pass that such a story had obtained credit.

"That was it, was it?" he said, feigning content. "I should like to ask you another question; perhaps your daughter will not mind going down."

With evident reluctance the daughter withdrew. Valentine shut the door, and came back to his place.

Naturally enough, he cared nothing about the story; so he approached the only thing he did care about in the matter. "I want to ask you this one thing: a ghost, you say, appeared to you—well, what do you think it was for—what did it want—what did it mean?"

Evident surprise on the part of his listener.

"It must have come for something," Valentine added, when she remained silent. "Have you never considered what?"

"Ay, sir, sure-ly. He came to let folks know he was gone."

"And that was all, you think?"

"What else could he come for?" she answered.

"Nobody has ever said, then, that it came for anything else," thought Valentine. "The poor ghost is not accused of any crime, and there is no crime known of concerning the family or place that could be imputed to him."

"You are sure you have nothing more to say to me?"

"Ne'er a word, sir, this blessed marnin', but thank you kindly."

Perhaps Valentine had never felt better pleased in his life than he did when he went down the narrow, dark stairs, after his interview with Becky Maddison. To find that without doubt she was either a fool or an impostor, was not what should have softened his heart and opened his purse for her; but he had feared to encounter her story far more than he had known himself till now that all fear was over. So when he got down to the daughter he was gracious, and generously gave her leave to come to the house for wine and any other comforts that the old woman might require. "And I shall come and see her from time to time," he added, as he went his way, for with the old woman's last word had snapped the chain that had barred the road to Melcombe. It was his. He should dispense its charity, pay its dues, and from henceforth, without fear or superstition, enjoy its revenues.

About this time something occurred at John Mortimer's house, which made people hold up their hands, and exclaim, "What next?"

It would be a difficult matter to tell that story correctly, considering how many had a hand in the telling of it, and that no two of them told it in the least degree alike; considering also that Mr. Mortimer, who certainly could have told the greater part of it, had (so far as was known) never told it at all.

Everybody said he had knocked up Swan and Mrs. Swan at six o'clock one morning, and sent the former to call up Matthew the coachman, who also lived out of the house. "And that," said Swan, when he admitted the fact to after questioners, "Matthew never will forgive me for doing. He hates to get his orders through other folks, specially through me. He allus grudges me the respect as the family can't help feeling for me. Not but that he gets his share, but he counts nothing his if it's mine too. He'd like to pluck the very summer out of my almanack, and keep it in his own little back parlour." Everybody said, also, that Mrs. Swan had made the fire that morning in Mr. Mortimer's kitchen, and that Matthew had waited on him and his four daughters at breakfast, nobody else being in the house, gentle or simple.

Gentle or simple. That was certainly true, for the governess had taken her departure two days previously.

After this, everybody said that Matthew brought the carriage round, and Mr. Mortimer put in the girls, and got in himself, telling Matthew to drive to Wigfield Hall, where Mr. Brandon, coming out to meet him with a look of surprise, he said, "Giles, we are early visitors;" and Mr. Brandon answered, "All the more welcome, John." Everybody said also that the four Miss Mortimers remained for several days with Mrs. Brandon, and very happy they seemed.

But though people knew no more, they naturally said a good deal more—they always do. Some said that Mr. Mortimer, coming home unexpectedly after a journey in the middle of the night, found the kitchen chimney on fire, and some of the servants asleep on the floor, nothing like so sober as they should have been. Others said he found a dance going on in the servants' hall, and the cook waltzing with a policeman, several gentlemen of the same craft being present. Others, again, said that when he returned he found the house not only empty, but open; that he sat down and waited, in a towering passion, till they all returned in two flys from some festivities at a public-house in Wigfield; and then, meeting them at the door, he retained the flys, and waving his hand, ordered them all off the premises; saw them very shortly depart, and locked the doors behind them. It was a comfort to be able to invent so many stories, and not necessary to make them tally, for no one could contradict them; certainly not any one of the four Miss Mortimers, for they had all been fast asleep the whole time.

Mr. Mortimer held his peace; but while staying with Mr. and Mrs. Brandon till he could reconstruct his household, he was observed at first to be out of spirits, and vastly inclined to be out of temper. He did his very best to hide this, but he could not hide a sort of look half shame, half amusement, which would now and then steal round the corners of his mouth, as if it had come out of some hiding-place to take a survey of things in general.

John Mortimer had perhaps rather prided himself on his penetration, his powers of good government, the order and respectability of his household, and other matters of that description. He had been taught in rather an ignominious fashion that he had overvalued himself in those particulars.

He was always treated by strangers whom he employed with a great deal of respect and deference; but this was mainly owing to a somewhat commanding presence and a good deal of personal dignity. When the same people got used to him, perceived the *bonhomie* of his character, his carelessness about money matters, and his easy household ways, they were sometimes known to take all the more advantage of him from having needlessly feared him at first.

He said to Giles, "It is very evident now that I must marry. I owe it to the mother of my children, and in fact to them."

Mrs. Brandon said this to Mrs. Walker when, the next day, these two ladies met, and were alone together, excepting for the presence of St. George Mortimer Brandon, which did not signify. "The house might have been robbed," she continued, "and the children burnt in their beds."

"Giles told you this afterwards?"

"Yes."

Emily looked uncomfortable. "One never knows how men may discuss matters when they are alone. I hope, if John ever asked advice of Giles, he would not——"

Here a pause.

"He would not recommend any one in particular," said Dorothea, looking down on her baby's face. "Oh no, I am certain he would not think of such a thing. Besides, the idea that he had any one to suggest has, I know, never entered his head."

This she said without looking at Emily, and in a matter-of-fact tone. If one had discovered anything, and the other was aware of it, she could still here at least feel perfectly safe. This sister of hers, even to her own husband, would never speak.

"And that was all?"

"No; Giles said he gave him various ludicrous particulars, and repeated, with such a sincere sigh, 'I must marry—it's a dire necessity!' that Giles laughed, and so did he."

"Poor John!" said Emily, "there certainly was not much in his first marriage to tempt him into a second. And so I suppose Giles encouraged him, saying, as he often does, that he had never known any happiness worth mentioning till he married."

"Yes, dear," said Dorothea, "and he answered, 'But you did not pitch yourself into matrimony like a man taking a header into a fathomless pool. You were in love, old fellow, and I am not. Why, I have not decided yet on the lady!' He cannot mean, therefore, to marry forthwith, Emily; besides, it must be the literal truth that he has not even half unconsciously a real preference for any one, or he could not have talked so openly to Giles. He does not even foresee any preference."

"But I hope to help him to a preference very soon," she thought, and added aloud, "Dear, you will stay and dine with us?"

Emily replied that she could not, she was to dine with a neighbour; and she shortly departed, in possession of the most imprudent speeches John had ever made (for he was usually most reticent), and she could not guess of course that one of his assertions time had already falsified. He *had* decided on the lady.

While the notion that he must marry had slumbered, his thought that Emily should be his wife had slumbered also; but that morning, driving towards Wigfield, he had stopped at his own house to give some orders, and then had gone up into "Parliament" to fetch out some small possessions that his twin daughters wanted. There, standing for a moment to look about him, his eyes had fallen on his throne, and instantly the image of Emily had recurred to him, and her attitude as she held his little child. To give a step-mother to his children had always been a painful thought. They might be snubbed, misrepresented to him, uncherished, unloved. But Emily! there was the tender grace of motherhood in her every action towards a little child; her yearning sense of loss found its best appeasement in the pretty exactions and artless dependence of small young creatures. No; Emily might spoil step-children if she had them, but she could not be unkind.

His cold opinion became a moderately pleased conviction. This was so much the right thing, that once contemplated, it became the only thing. He recalled her image again, as he looked at the empty throne, and he did not leave the room till he had fully decided to set her on it.

When John went back to dinner, he soon managed to introduce her name, and found those about him very willing to talk of her. It seemed so natural in that house. John recalled some of the anecdotes of her joyous girlhood for Dorothea's benefit; they laughed over them together. They all talked a good deal that evening of Emily, but this made no difference to John's intention; it was fully formed already.

So the next morning, having quite recovered his spirits, and almost forgotten what he had said three days before to his host, he remarked to himself, just as he finished dressing, "She has been a widow now rather more than a year. The sooner I do it, the better."

He sat down to cogitate. It was not yet breakfast time. "Well," he said, "she is a sweet creature. What would I have, I wonder!"

He took a little red morocco case from his pocket-book, and opened it.

"My father was exceedingly fond of her," he next said, "and nothing would have pleased him better."

His father had inherited a very fine diamond ring from his old cousin, and had been in the habit of wearing it. John, who never decked himself in jewellery of any sort, had lately taken this ring to London, and left it with his jeweller, to be altered so as to fit a lady's finger. He intended it for his future wife.

It had just been sent back to him.

Some people say, "There are no fools like old fools." It might be said with equal truth, there are no follies like the follies of a wise man.

"I cannot possibly play the part of a lover," said Mr. Mortimer, and his face actually changed its hue slightly when he spoke. "How shall I manage to give it to her!"

He looked at the splendid gem, glittering and sparkling. "And I hate insincerity," he continued. Then, having taken out the ring, he inspected it as if he wished it could help him, turning it round on the tip of his middle finger. "Trust her? I should think so! Like her? Of course I do. I'll settle on her anything Giles pleases, but I must act like a gentleman, and not pretend to any romantic feelings."

A pause.

"It's rather an odd thing," he further reflected, "that so many women as have all but asked me—so many as have actually let other women ask me for them—so many as I know I might now have almost at a week's notice, I should have taken it into my head that I must have this one, who doesn't care for me a straw. She'll laugh at me, very likely—she'll take me, though!"

Another pause.

"No, I won't have any one else, I'm determined. I'll agree to anything she demands." Here a sunbeam, and the diamonds darted forth to meet one another. The flash made him wink. "If she'll only undertake to reign and rule, and bring up the children—for she'll do it well, and love them too—I'm a very domestic fellow, I shall be fond of her. Yes, I know she'll soon wind me round her little finger." Here, remembering the sweetness of liberty, he sighed. "I'll lay the matter before her this morning. I shall not forget the respect due to her and to myself." He half laughed. "She'll soon know well enough what I'm come for; and if I stick fast, she will probably help me!" He shut up the ring. "She never has had the least touch of romance in her nature, and *she knows* that *I know* she didn't love her first husband a bit." He then looked at himself, or rather at his coat, in a long glass—it fitted to perfection. "If this crash had not brought me to the point, I might have waited till somebody else won her. There goes the breakfast bell. Well, I think I am decidedly glad on the whole."

CHAPTER XXIX.

UNHEARD-OF LIBERTIES.

"If he come not then the play is marred: it goes not forward, doth it?"

Midsummer Night's Dream.

MISS CHRISTIE GRANT, sitting with Emily at ten o'clock in the morning, heard a ring at the bell, which she thought she knew. She pricked up her head to listen, and as it ceased tinkling she bustled out of the room.

The first virtue of a companion in Miss Christie Grant's view, was to know how to be judiciously absent.

" Mr. Mortimer."

Emily was writing, when she looked up on hearing these words, and saw John Mortimer advancing. Of course she had been thinking of him, thinking with much more hope than heretofore, but also with much more pride.

When he had stood remote, the object of such an impassioned, and to her, hitherto, such an unknown love, which transformed him and everything about him, and imparted to him such an almost unbearable charm—a power to draw her nearer and nearer without knowing it, or wanting her at all—she had felt that she could die for him, but she had not hoped to live for him, and spend a happy life at his side.

She did not hope it yet, she only felt that a blissful possibility was thrown down before her, and she might take it up if she could.

She knew that this strange absorbing love, which, like some splendid flower, had opened out in her path, was the one supreme blossom of her life—that life which is all too short for the unfolding of another such. But the last few hours had taught her something more, it was now just possible that he might pretend to gather this flower—he had something to learn then before he could wear it, he must love her, or she felt that her own love would break her heart.

Emily had not one of those poverty-stricken natures which are never glad excepting for some special reason drawing them above themselves. She was naturally joyous and happy, unless under the pressure of an active sorrow that shaded her sky and quenched her sunshine. She lived in an elevated region full of love and wonder, taking kindly alike to reverence and to hope; but she was seldom excited, her feelings were not shallow enough to be easily troubled with excitement, or made fitful with agitation.

There was in her nature a suave harmony, a sweet and gracious calm, which love itself did not so much disturb as enrich and change,—love which had been born in the sacred loneliness of sorrow,—complicated with tender longing towards little children, nourished in silence, with beautiful shame and pride, and impassioned fear.

Yet it was necessary to her, even in all withdrawal from its object, even though it should be denied all expression for ever—necessary to the life that it troubled and raised, and enriched, with a vision of withheld completeness that was dimmed by the tears of her half "divine despair."

She rose and held out her hand, and when he smiled with a certain air of embarrassment, she did also. She observed that he was sensitive about the ridiculous affair which had led to his turning out his household, besides this early call made her feel, but not in a way to discompose her as if she were taken into the number of those ladies, among whom he meant to make his selection. Yes, it was as she had hoped. It warmed her to the heart to see it, but not the less was she aware of the ridiculous side of it. A vision of long-sustained conversations, set calls, and careful observations in various houses rose up before her; it was not in her nature to be unamused at the peculiar position that he had confessed to—"he had not decided on the lady." She felt that she knew more of this than he supposed, and his embarrassment making her quite at her ease, the smiles kept peeping out as with her natural grace she began to talk to him.

"Emily, you are laughing at me," he presently said, and he too laughed, felt at ease, and yielded to the charm that few men could resist, so far as to become at home and pleased with his hostess for making him so.

"Of course I am, John," she answered. "I couldn't think of being occupied with any one else just now!"

And then they began to talk discursively and, as it were, at large. John seemed to be fetching a wide compass. Emily hardly knew what he was about till suddenly she observed that he had ventured on dangerous ground, she managed to give a little twist to the conversation, but he soon brought it back again, and she half turned, and looked up at him surprised.

While she occupied herself with a favourite piece of embroidery, and was matching the silks, holding them up to the light, he had risen, and was leaning against the side of the bay window; a frequent attitude with him; for what are called "occasional" chairs are often rather frail and small for accommodating a large tall man, and drawing-room sofas are sometimes exceedingly low. In any one's eyes he would have passed for a fine man, something more (to those who could see it) than a merely handsome man, for the curves of his mouth had mastery in them, and his eyes were full of grave sweetness. Emily was always delighted with the somewhat unusual meeting in him of personal majesty, with the good-humoured easy *bonhomie* which had caused his late discomfiture. She half turned, and looked up.

"How charming she is!" he thought, as he looked down; "there will be grace and beauty into the bargain!" and he proceeded, in pursuit of what he considered sincere and gentlemanlike, to venture on the dangerous ground again, not being aware how it quaked under him.

The casual mention of some acquaintance who had lately married gave him the chance that he thought he wanted. He would be happy enough—people might in general be happy enough, he hinted, glancing from the particular instance to lay down a general proposition—"if they did not expect too much—if they were less romantic; for himself, he had not the presumption to expect more than a sincere liking—a cordial approval—such as he himself could entertain. It was the only feeling he had ever inspired, or——"

No, he did not say felt.

But he presently alluded to his late wife, and then reverting to his former speech, said, "And yet I was happy with her! I consider that I was fortunate."

"Moderate," thought Emily; "but as much as it is possible for him to say."

"And," he continued, "she has laid me under obligations that make it impossible for me ever to forget her. I feel the blessing of having our children about me. And—and also—what I owe to her on their account—I never spend a day without thinking of her."

"Poor Janie!" thought Emily, very much touched, "she did not deserve this tribute. How coldly I have often heard her talk of him!"

And then, not without a certain grave sweetness of manner that made her heart ache, alike with tender shame to think how little her dead husband had ever been accounted of, compared with this now possible future one, and with such jealousy as one may feel of a dead wife who would have cared as little for long remembrance as she had done for living affection, Emily listened, while he managed quite naturally, and by the slightest hints, to bring her also in—her past lot and opinions. She felt, rather than heard, the intention; "and he could not presume to say," he went on, "he was not sure whether a man might hope for a second marriage, which could have all the advantages of a first. Yet he thought that in any suitable marriage there might be enough benefit on both sides to make it almost equally——"

"Equally what?" Emily wondered.

John was trying to speak in a very matter-of-fact way, as merely laying down his views.

"Equally advantageous," he said at last; and not without difficulty.

"John," said Emily, rallying a little, and speaking with the least little touch of audacity,—"John, you are always fond of advancing your abstract theories. Now, I should have thought that if a man had felt any want in his first marriage, he would have tried for something more in a second, rather than have determined that there was no more to be had."

"Unless his reason assured him in more sober hours that he had had all, and given all that could in reason be expected," John answered. "I did not confess to having felt any want," he presently added. "Call this, since it pleases you, my abstract theory."

And then Emily felt that she too must speak; her dead husband deserved it of her far more than his dead wife had ever done.

"I do please," she answered; "this can be only an abstract theory to me. I knew no want of love in my marriage, only a frequent self-reproach—to think that I was unworthy, because I could not enough return it."

"A most needless self-reproach," he answered. "I venture to hope that people should never rebuke themselves because they happen to be incapable of romantic passion, or any of the follies of youthful love."

"Intended to restore my self-esteem. Shall I not soon be able to make you feel differently?" thought Emily. "You still remember Janie; you will never let her be disparaged. I think none the worse of you for that, my beloved—my hope."

He was silent till she glanced up at him again, with a sweet wistfulness, that was rather frequent with her; turning half round—for he stood at her side, not quite enough at his ease to look continually in her face—he was much surprised to find her so charming, so naïve in all her movements, and in the flitting expressions of her face.

He was pleased, too, though very much surprised, to find that she did not seem conscious of his intention (a most lovely blush had spread itself over her face when she spoke of her husband), but so far from expecting what he was just about to say, she had thrown him back in his progress more than once—she did not seem to be expecting anything. "And yet, I have said a good deal," he reflected; "I have let her know that I expect to inspire no romantic love, and do not pretend to be in love with her. I come forward admiring, trusting, and preferring her to any other woman; though I cannot come as a lover to her feet." He began to talk again. Emily was a little startled to find him in a few minutes alluding to his domestic discomforts, and his intention of standing for the borough. He had now a little red box in his hand, and when she said, "John, I wish you would not stand there," he came and sat nearly opposite to her, and showed her what was in it—his father's diamond ring. She remembered it, no doubt; he had just had the diamond reset. Emily took out the ring, and laid it in her palm. "It looks small," she said. "I should not have thought it would fit you, John."

"Will you let me try if it will fit you?" he answered; and, before she had recovered from her surprise, he had put it on her finger.

There was a very awkward pause, and then she drew it off. "You can hardly expect me," she said, and her hand trembled a little, "to accept such a very costly present." It was not her reason for returning it, but she knew not what to say.

"I would not ask it," he replied, "unless I could offer you another. I desire to make you my wife. I beg you to accept my hand."

"Accept your hand! What, now? directly? to-day?" she exclaimed almost piteously, and tears trembled on her eye-lashes.

"Yes," he answered, repeating her words with something like ardour. "Now, directly, to-day. I am sorely in want of a wife, and would fain take you home as soon as the bans would let me. Emily?"

"Why you have been taking all possible pains to let me know that you do not love me in the least, and that, as far as you foresee, you do not mean to love me," she answered, two great tears falling on his hand when he tried to take hers. "John! how dare you!"

She was not naturally passionate, but startled now into this passionate appeal, she snatched away her hand, rose in haste, and drew back from him with flashing eyes and a heaving bosom; but all too soon the short relief she had found in anger was quenched in tears that she did not try to check. She stood and wept, and he, very pale and very much discomfited, sat before her in his place.

"I beg your pardon," he presently said, not in the least aware of what this really meant. "I beg—I entreat your pardon. I scarcely thought—forgive my saying it—I scarcely thought, considering our past—

and—and—my position, as the father of a large family, that you would have consented to any wooing in the girl and boy fashion. You make me wish, for once in my life—yes, very heartily wish, that I had been less direct, less candid," he added rather bitterly. "I thought"—here Emily heard him call himself a fool—"I thought you would approve it."

"I do," she answered with a great sobbing sigh. Oh, there was nothing more for her to say; she could not entreat him now to let her teach him to love her. She felt, with a sinking heart, that if he took her words for a refusal, and by no means a gentle one, it could not be wondered at.

Presently he said, still looking amazed and pale, for he was utterly unused to a woman's tears, and as much agitated now in a man's fashion as she was in hers,

"If I have spoken earlier in your widowhood than you approve, and it displeases you, I hope you will believe that I have always thought of you as a wife to be admired above any that I ever knew."

"My husband loved me," she answered, drying her eyes, now almost calmly. She could not say she was displeased on his account, and when she looked up she saw that John Mortimer had his hat in his hand. Their interview was nearly over.

"I cannot lose you as a friend," he said, and his voice faltered.

"Oh no; no, dear John."

"And my children are so fond of you."

"I love them; I always shall."

He looked at her for a moment, doubtful whether to hold out his hand. "Forget this, Emily, and let things be as they have been heretofore between us."

"Yes," she answered, and gave him her hand.

"Good-bye," he said, and stooped to kiss it, and was gone.

She stood quite still listening, and yet listening,

till all possible chance was over of catching any longer the sound of his steps. No more tears; only a great aching emptiness. The unhoped-for chance had been hers, and she had lost it knowingly. What else could she have done?

She scarcely knew how long she remained motionless. A world and a lifetime of agitation, and thought, and passionate yearning seemed to stand between her and that brief interview, before, casting her eyes on the little velvet-covered table across which he had leaned to put it on her hand, she saw the splendid ring; sunbeams had found it out, and were playing on the diamond; he had forgotten it, and left it behind him, and there was the case on the floor. It seemed to be almost a respite.

"We are to dine with Giles and Dorothea to-day, and meet him. This morning's work, then, is not irretrievable. I can speak now to Dorothea, tell her what has occurred, and she will see that I have opportunity to return him this—and—and things may end in his loving me a little, after all. Oh, if they could—if, indeed, he had not told me he did not. He did not look in the least angry,—only surprised and vexed when I rejected him. He cares so little about me."

She took up the ring, and in course of time went with her old aunt to dine at her brother's house. She knew John was aware that he was to meet her; she was therefore deeply disturbed, though perhaps she had no right to be surprised when Dorothea said—

"We are so much disappointed! John Mortimer has sent this note to excuse himself from coming back to dinner to-day—or, indeed, coming here at all to-night. He has to go out, it seems, for two or three days."

"Ay," said Miss Christie, "that's very awkward for him." Miss Christie had built certain hopes upon that morning's visit. "It seems to me," she continued, "that John Mortimer's affairs give him twice as much trouble as they used to do."

Emily was silent; she felt that *this* was not letting things be as they had been heretofore. She took up the note. He did not affirm that he was obliged to go out. Even if he was, what should she do now? She was left in custody of the ring, and could neither see him nor write to him.

"On Sunday I shall see him. I shall have his hand for a moment; I shall give him this, after morning service."

But, no. Sunday came; the Mortimers were at church, but not their father. "Father had walked over to that little chapel-of-ease beyond Wigfield, that Grand gave the money to build," they said. "He took Johnnie with him to day."

"Yes," said Barbara, "and he promised next Sunday to take me."

"He will not meet me," thought Emily.

She waited another week, hoping she might meet him accidentally; hoping he might come to her, hoping and fearing she hardly knew what. But still John Mortimer made no sign, and she could not decide to write to him; every day that she retained the ring made it more difficult for her to return it, without breaking so the slender thread that seemed to hold her to him still. There was no promise in it of any future communication at all.

In the meantime curiosity, having been once excited about John Mortimer and his concerns, kept open eyes on him still, and soon the air was full of rumours which reached all ears but those of the two people most concerned. A likely thing, if there is the smallest evidence in the world for it, can easily get headway if nobody in authority can contradict it.

All Wigfield said that Mr. Mortimer had "proposed" to Mrs. Walker, and she had refused him. Brandon heard it with amazement, but could say nothing; Miss Christie heard it with yet more; but she, too, held her peace.

Johnnie Mortimer heard it, made furtive observations on his father, was pleased to think that he was dull, restless, pale—remembered his own letter to his sisters, and considered himself to be partly to blame. Then the twins heard it, took counsel with Johnnie, believed it also, were full of ruth and shame. "So dear papa loved Mrs. Walker, and she would not marry him. There could only be one reason; she knew she had nothing to expect but rebellion and rudeness and unkindness from them. No, papa was not at all like himself; he often sighed, and he looked as if his head ached. They had seen in the paper that he had lost a quantity of money by some shares and things; but they didn't think he cared about that, for he gave them a sovereign the next day to buy a birthday present for Janie. Father must not be made miserable on their account. What had they better do?"

Emily, in the meantime, felt her heart faint; this new trouble going down to the deepest part of her heart, woke up and raised again the half-appeased want and sorrow. Again she dreamed that she was folding her little child in her arms, and woke to find them empty. She could not stand against this, and decided, in sheer desperation, to quit the field. She would go on the Continent to Justina; rest and change would help her, and she would send back the ring, when all was arranged, by Aunt Christie.

She was still at her desk, having at last managed to write the note.

She was to start the next morning. Miss Christie was then on her way to John Mortimer with the ring, and tired with her own trouble and indecision, she was resting in a careless attitude when she heard a knock at the door.

"That tiresome *boy* again," she disrespectfully murmured, rousing up a little, and a half smile stealing out. "What am I to do with him?" She thought it was the new curate. "Why, Johnnie, is that you?" she exclaimed as Johnnie Mortimer produced himself in all his youthful awkwardness, and advanced, looking a good deal abashed.

Johnnie replied that it was a half-holiday, and so he thought he would come and call.

Emily said she was glad to see him; indeed, she felt refreshed by the sight of anything that belonged to John.

"I thought I should like to—to—in short, to come and call," repeated Johnnie, and he looked rather earnestly at his gloves, perhaps by way of occupation. They were such as a Harrow boy seldom wears, excepting on "speech day"—pale lilac. As a rule Johnnie scorned gloves. Emily observed that he was dressed with perfect propriety—like a gentleman, in fact; his hair brushed, his tie neat, his whole outer boy clean, and got up regardless of trouble and expense.

"Well, you could not have come at a better time, dear boy," said Emily, wondering what vagary he was indulging now, "for I have just got a present of a case of shells and birds from Ceylon, and you shall help me to unpack and arrange them, if you like."

"I should like to do anything you please," said Johnnie with alacrity. "That's what I meant, that's what I came to say." Thereupon he smoothed the nap on his "chimneypot" hat, and blushed furiously.

The case was set upon the floor, on a piece of matting; it had already been opened, and was filling the room with a smell of sandal-wood and camphor.

Emily had risen, and when she paused, arrested by surprise at the oddness of this speech, he added, taking to his lisp again, as if from sheer embarrassment, "Thome fellows are a great deal worse than they theem. No, I didn't mean that; I mean thome fellows are a great deal better than they theem."

"Now, Johnnie," said Emily, laughing, and remembering a late visit of apology, "if any piece of mischief has got the better of you, and your father has sent you to say you are sorry for it, I'll forgive you beforehand! What is it? Have you been rooting up my fences, or flooding my paddock?"

"It's a great deal worth than that," answered Johnnie, who by this time was kneeling beside the case, hauling out the birds and shells with more vigour than dexterity.

"Nothing to do with gunpowder, I hope," said Emily with her usual *insouciance.*

"There are the girls; I hear them coming in the carriage," exclaimed Johnnie by way of answer, while Emily was placing the shells on a table. "No, father didn't send me; he doesn't know."

"What is it, then?" she repeated, feeling more at liberty to investigate the matter, now she had been expressly told that John had nothing to do with it.

On this, instead of making a direct reply, he exclaimed, looking very red and indignant, "I told them it was no use at all my coming, and now you see it isn't. They thaid they wouldn't come unless I did. If you thought I should be rude, you might make me stop at school all the holidays, or at old Tikey's; I shouldn't thay a word."

Emily's hand was on the boy's shoulder as he knelt before the case. Surely she understood what he meant; but if so, where could he possibly have acquired the knowledge he seemed to possess? And even then he was the last person from whom she could have expected this blunt, embarrassed, promise of fealty.

The girls entered, and the two little ones. Emily met them, and while she gave each a kiss, Johnnie started up, and with a great war-whoop of defiance to his sisters, burst through the open window, and blushing hotly fled away.

Much the same thing over again. The girls were all in their best; they generally loved to parade the crofts and gardens clad in brown holland and shaded by flapping hats. The children scorned gloves and all fine clothes as much as they did the carriage; and here they were—little Hugh in his velvet suit, looking so fair and bright-haired; Anastasia dressed out in ribbons, and with a very large bouquet of hothouse flowers in her hand. The girls pushed her forward.

"It's for you," said the little girl, "and isn't it a grand one! And my love, and we're come to call."

"Thank you, my sweet," said Emily, accepting the bouquet, "I never saw such a beauty!" She was sitting on a sofa, and her young guests were all standing before her. She observed that little Hugh looked very sulky indeed. "It's extremely unfair," he presently burst out, "they made Swan cut the best flowers in the houses, and they gave them all to Nancy to give, and I haven't got *none.*"

Barbara whispered to him, trying to soothe his outraged feelings, but he kept her off with his elbow till Emily drew him near, and observed that it was not her birthday, and therefore that one present was surely enough.

Barbara replied that Hughie had brought a present, but he was very cross because it was not so pretty as Anastasia's.

"Yes, I've brought this," said Hugh, his countenance clearing a little as he opened his small gloved hand, and disclosed a very bright five-shilling piece. "It's not so pretty, though, as Nannie's."

"But it will last much longer," said Emily; "and so you meant this for me, my sweet man. I'll take care of it for you, and look at it sometimes till you want to spend it; that will be a very nice present for me, and then you can have it back."

"Papa gave it him," said Anastasia; "it's a new one. And may we go now and look at our gardens?"

Hugh appeared to be cogitating over Emily's proposal; his little grave face was the image of his father's. "You may if Mrs. Nemily says so," answered Gladys. "You always want to do what Mrs. Nemily pleases, don't you?"

"Oh yes," said the sprite, dancing round the room; and off they set into the garden.

"And so do we all," said Barbara.

Gladys was sitting at Emily's feet now, and had a little covered basket in her hand, which rustled as if it contained some living thing.

"Janie and Bertie don't know—none of the little ones know," said Barbara; "we thought we had better not tell them."

Emily did not ask what they meant; she thought she knew. It could make no difference now, yet it was inexpressibly sweet and consoling to her.

"We only said we were coming to call, and when Janie saw the bouquet she said she should send you a present too." Thereupon the basket was opened, and a small white kitten was placed on Emily's knee.

There seemed no part for her to play, but to be passive; she could not let them misunderstand; she knew John had not sent them. "We should be so glad if you came," whispered the one who held her hand. "Oh, Janie," thought Emily, "if you could only see your children now!"

"And when Johnnie wrote that, he didn't know it was you," pleaded the other.

"My darlings!" said Emily, "you must not say any more; and I have nothing to answer but that I love you all very, very much indeed."

"But we want you to love father too."

Unheard-of liberty! Emily had no answer ready; but now, as she had wondered what their mother would have felt, she wondered what John would have felt at this utter misunderstanding, this taking for granted that he loved her, and that she did not love him. A sensitive blush spread itself over her face. "Your father would not be pleased, my dears," she answered lovingly but firmly, "at your saying any more; he would think (though I am sure you do not mean it) that you were taking a great liberty."

CHAPTER XXX.

A CHAPTER OF TROUBLES.

"She's daft to refuse the laird of Cockpen."
Scotch Ballad.

AND now John Mortimer had again possession of his ring. Emily had sent it, together with a little book that she had borrowed some time previously, and the whole was so done up in stiff paper that Miss Christie Grant supposed herself to be returning the book only.

"So you gave it to John, auntie," said Emily, when Miss Christie came back, "and told him I was going out, and he read the note?"

"Yes," answered Miss Christie curtly.

"Is he looking well?" asked Emily with a faint attempt at the tone of ordinary interest.

"I should say not at all; it would be queer if he was."

"Why, Aunt Christie?"

Miss Christie Grant paused. Confidence had not been reposed in her; to have surprised Emily into it would have given her no pleasure; it would have left her always suspicious that her niece would have withheld it if she could; besides, this rumour might after all be untrue. She answered, "Because, for one thing, he has had great, at least considerable, losses."

"Yes, I know," said Emily.

"But he aye reposed great confidence in me, as a friend should."

"Yes."

"And so I would have asked him several questions if I had known how to express myself; but bonds and debentures, and, above all, preference stock, were aye great stumbling-blocks to my understanding. Men have a way of despising a woman's notions of business matters; so I contented myself with asking if it was true that he was arranging to take a partner, and whether he would have to make any pecuniary sacrifice in order to effect this? He said 'Yes;' but I've been just thinking he meant that in confidence."

"You shouldn't tell it to me then."

"And then he told me (I don't know whether that was in confidence or not), but——"

"But what?"

"But I don't want to have any reservations with my own niece's child, that was always my favourite, any more than I suppose ye would have any with me."

Miss Christie here seemed to expect an answer, and waited long enough for Emily to make one, if she was so minded; but as Emily remained silent, she presently went on.

"I made the observation that I had heard he meant to sell his late father's house; but lest he should think I attached too much importance to his losses, I just added that I knew his children were very well provided for under the will. He said 'Yes.'"

"And that was all?" asked Emily, amused at the amount of John's confidence, and pleased to find that nothing but business had been talked of.

"Yes, that was all—so far as I know there was nothing more to tell; so I just said before I came away that I was well aware my knowledge of banking was but slender, which was reason enough for my not offering any advice. Well, if anybody had told me ye could laugh because John Mortimer was less prosperous than formerly, I would not have believed it!"

Emily made haste to look grave again. It was no

secret at all that John Mortimer meant to take a partner; and as to his losses, she did not suppose they would affect his comfort much.

Johnnie Mortimer, however, on hearing of them was roused to a sense of responsibility toward his father, and as a practical proof that he and his sisters were willing to do what they could, proposed to them that they should give up half their weekly allowance of pocket-money. The twins assented with filial fervour, and Johnnie explained their views to his father, proposing that his own pony should be sold, and the money flung into the gap.

John was smoking a cigar in an arbour near the house when his heir unfolded to him these plans for retrenchment. He was surprised. The boy was so big, so clever with his lessons, and possessed so keen a sense of humour that sometimes the father forgot his actual age, and forgot that he was still simple in many respects, and more childlike than some other youths.

He did not instantly answer nor laugh (for Johnnie was exceedingly sensitive to ridicule from him); but after a pause, as if for thought, he assured his son that he was not in any want of money, and that therefore these plans, he was happy to say, were not necessary. "As you are old enough now," he added, "to take an intelligent interest in my affairs, I shall occasionally talk to you about them."

Johnnie, shoving his head hard against his father's shoulder, gave him an awkward hug. "You might depend on my never telling anybody," he said.

"I am sure of that, my boy. Your dear grandfather, a few months before his death, gave his name to an enterprise which, in my opinion, did not promise well. A good deal of money has been lost by it."

"Oh," said Johnnie, and again he reflected that, though not necessary, it would be only right and noble in him to give up his pony.

"But I dare say you think that I and mine have always lived in the enjoyment of every comfort, and of some luxuries."

"Oh, yes, father."

"Then if I tell you that I intend to continue living exactly in my present style, and that I expect to be always entitled to do so, you need perhaps hardly concern yourself to inquire how much I may hitherto have lived within my income."

Johnnie, who, quite unknown to himself, had just sustained the loss of many thousands hitherto placed to his name, replied with supreme indifference that he hoped he was not such a muff as to care about money that his father did not care about himself, and did not want. Whereupon John proceeded,—

"It is my wish, and in the course of a few years I hope that I shall be able, to retire."

"Oh," said Johnnie again, and he surprised his father to the point of making him refrain from any further communication, by adding, "And then you'll have plenty of time to rummage among those old Turanian verbs and things. But, father?"

"Yes, my boy."

John looked down into the clear eyes of the great, awkward, swarthy fellow, expecting the question, "Will this make much difference to my future prospects?" But, no, what he said was, "I should like to have a *go* at them too. And you said you would teach me Sanscrit, if ever you had leisure."

"So I did," said John, "and so I will."

To his own mind these buried roots, counted by the world so dry, proved, as it were, appetising and attractive food. How, then, should he be otherwise than pleased that his son should take delight in the thought of helping him to rake them up, and arguing with him over "the ninth meaning of a particle?" "The boy will learn to love money quite soon enough," he thought.

Johnnie then went his way. It was Saturday afternoon; he told his sisters that "it was all right," and thereupon resolving no longer to deny themselves the innocent pleasures of life, they sent little Bertram into the town for eighteenpennyworth of "rock."

"Where's the change?" he inquired, with the magisterial dignity belonging to his race, when his little brother came home.

Bertram replied with all humility that he had only been tossing up the fourpenny piece a few times for fun, when it fell into the ditch. He couldn't help it; he was very sorry.

"*Soufflez* the fourpenny piece," said Johnnie in a burst of reckless extravagance; "I forgive you this once. Produce the stuff."

He felt a lordly contempt for money just then; perhaps it was wrong, but prosperity was spoiling him. He was to retain his pony, and this amiable beast was dear to him.

In the meantine Valentine, established at Melcombe, had been enjoying the sweetness of a no less real prosperity.

From that moment, when the ghost story had melted into mist, he had flung aside all those uneasy doubts which had disturbed his first weeks of possession.

He soon surrounded himself with the luxury that was so congenial to him. All the neighbourhood called on him, and his naturally sociable temper, amiable, domestic ways, and good position enabled him, with hardly any effort, to be always among a posse of people who suited him perfectly.

There were more ladies than young men in the neighbourhood. Valentine was intimate with half-a-dozen of the former before he had been among them three weeks. He experienced the delights of feminine flattery, a thing almost new to him. Who so likely to receive it? He was eligible, he was handsome, and he was always in a good humour, for the place and the life pleased him, and all things smiled.

In a round of country gaieties, in which picnics

and archery parties bore a far larger proportion than any young man would have cared for who was less devoted to the other sex, Valentine passed much of his time, laughing and making laugh wherever he went. His jokes were bandied about from house to house, till he felt the drawback in passing for a wit. He was expected to be always funny.

But a little real fun goes a long way in a dull neighbourhood, and he had learned just so much caution from his early escapade as to be willing to hail any view concerning himself that might be a corrective of the more true and likely one that he loved to flirt.

He was quite determined, as he thought, not to get into another scrape, and perhaps a very decided intention to make, in the end, an advantageous marriage, may have grown out of the fancy that his romance in life was over.

If he thought so, it was in no very consistent fashion, for he was always the slave (for the day) of the prettiest girl in every party he went to.

It was on a Saturday that John Mortimer received his son's proposal for retrenchment; on the Wednesday succeeding it Valentine, sitting at breakfast at Melcombe, opened the following letter, and was amused by the old-fashioned formality of its opening sentence:—

"Wigfield, June 15th, 18—.

"My dear Nephew,—It is not often that I take up my pen to address you, for I know there is little need, as my niece Emily writes weekly. Frequently have I wondered what she could find to write for; indeed, it was not the way in my youth for people to waste so much time saying little or nothing—which is not my case at the present time, for your sister being gone on the Continent, it devolves upon me, that is not used to long statements, to let ye know, what ye will be very sorry to hear. I only hope it may be no worse before it is over.

"Matthew, the coachman, came running over to me on Monday morning last, and said would I come to the house, for the servants did not know what to be at, and told me that Johnnie, who had been to go back to Harrow by the eleven o'clock train, had got leave to drive the pheaton to the Junction with the four girls in it, and Bertram, who, by ill luck—if I may use such a word (meaning no irreverence)—of this dispensation of Providence, had not gone back to Mr. Tikey's that morning. So far as I can make out, he thought he should be late, and so he turned those two spirited young horses down that steep sandy lane by the wood, to cut off a corner; and whether the woodman's children ran out and frightened them, or whether he was shouting and whooping himself, poor laddie—for I heard something of both—but Barbara was just sobbing her heart away when she told it, and he aye raised the echoes wherever he went; but the horses set off, running away, tearing down that rough road. Johnnie shouted to them all to sit still, and so they did, though they were almost jolted out; and if they had been let alone, there might have been no accident; but two men sprung out of a hedge and tried to stop them, and they turned on to the common, and sped away like the wind towards home, till they came to the sand bank by the small inn, the Loving Cup, and there they upset the carriage, and when the two men got up to it Johnnie and all of them were tossed out, and the carriage was almost kicked to pieces by the horse that was not down.

"This is a long tale, Valentine, and I seem to have hardly begun it. I must take another sheet of paper. When I got to the house, you never saw such a scene. Johnnie had been brought in quite stunned, and his face greatly bruised. There were two doctors already with them. Bertram had got a broken arm; he was calling out, poor little fellow, and Nancy was severely hurt, but I was grieved to see her so quiet. Gladys seemed at first to be only bruised and limping; but she and Barbara were faint and sick with fright. Janie was not present; she had been carried into the inn; but I may as well tell ye that in her case no bones were broken, poor lamb. She is doing very well, and in a day or two is to be brought home.

"It was a very affecting scene, as ye may suppose, and my first words were, 'Who is to tell this to Mr. Mortimer?' They said your brother has already gone to fetch him and prepare him. Well, I knew everything that was in the house, and where it was kept; so I'm thankful to think I was of use, and could help the new governess and the strange servants.

"Dorothea and Mrs. Henfrey soon came in, and by the time John arrived all the invalids had been carried up-stairs, and Johnnie had begun to show signs of consciousness.

"John was as white as chalk. He was rather strange at first; he said in a commanding, peremptory way, that he wouldn't be spoken to; he wouldn't hear a word; he was not ready. Everybody stood round, till Dorothea disobeyed him; she said, 'They are all living, dear Mr. Mortimer;' and then Giles got him to sit down, and they gave him some water to drink.

"He then noticed Dr. Limpsy, who had come down, and asked if any of them were in danger, and the doctor said yes—one. So he said he prayed God it was not his eldest son; he could bear anything but that. And yet when the doctor said he had every hope that Johnnie would do well, but he had great fears for the little Anastasia, he burst into tears, poor man, and said that of all his children she would be the hardest to spare. But I need not tell ye we did not remind him of the inconsistency, and were glad to think he was not to lose the one he set his heart most upon. And after that he was perfectly himself and more composed than anybody, which is a wonder, for such a catalogue of broken bones and sprains and contusions as came to light as the doctors examined further, was enough to disturb anybody's courage. Giles sat up with Johnnie all night; indeed nobody went to bed. John was by Nancy, and in the morning they spoke hopefully of her. Johnnie's first words were about his father; he couldn't bear his father near him, because now and then he was surprised into shouting out with pain, and he wouldn't have John distressed with his noise. He was nothing like so well as we had hoped this morning; but still the doctors say there is no danger. He got a kick from the horse when he was down, and he thinks he fainted with the pain. When John came down to get a little breakfast he was very much cheered to have a better account than he had expected of Nancy, and he made the remark that ye would be sorry to hear of this; so I said I would write, which I am doing, sitting beside little Bertram, who is asleep.—I am

"Your mother's affectionate aunt,
and always affectionately yours,
"CHRISTIAN GRANT."

Valentine read the letter, and thought that if it had not been for two or three picnic parties that he had on hand, he would have gone down to his old home, to see whether he could be of use to John Mortimer. He wrote to him, and resolved to wait a day or two; but he heard nothing till after the succeeding Sunday; then a telegram came from Emily:—"Two of John's children are extremely ill. I think your presence might be useful."

Emily had come home then.

Valentine set forth at once, and reached John Mortimer's house in the afternoon. A doctor's carriage stood at the door; a strange lady—evidently a nurse—passed through the hall; people were quietly moving about, but they seemed too anxious, and too much occupied to observe him.

At last Emily came down.

"Is Johnnie worse?" asked Valentine.

"Yes; but I wanted you to help us with John. Oh, such a disaster! On the third night after the accident, just before I arrived—for Dorothea had sent for me—every one in the house was greatly tired; but Johnnie and Anastasia were both thought better; so much better that the doctors said if there was no change during the night, they should consider dear little Nancy quite out of danger. Giles and Dorothea had gone home. The nurse sent for was not come. John knew how fatigued the whole household was, and all who were sitting up. He had not been able to take any sleep himself, and he was restlessly pacing up and down in the garden, watching and listening under the open windows. It was very hot.

"He fancied about three o'clock that there had been a long silence in Anastasia's room. She was to have nourishment frequently. He stole up-stairs, found the person with her asleep from fatigue, gave the child some jelly himself, and then finding her medicine, as he supposed, ready poured out in the wine-glass, he gave it to her, and discovered almost instantly a mistake. The sad imprudence had been committed of pouring the lotion for the child's temples into a wine-glass, to save the trouble of ringing for a saucer. The child was almost out of danger before that terrible night; but when I came home there was scarcely a hope of her life, and her father was almost distracted. I mean that, though he seems perfectly calm, never loses his self-control, he is very often not able to command his attention so as to answer when they speak to him, and he cannot rest a moment. He spent the whole of last night wandering up and down the garden, leaning on St. George's arm. He cannot eat nor occupy himself, and the doctors begin to be uneasy about him. Oh, it is such a misfortune!

"And Johnnie is very ill," continued Emily, tears

glittering on her eyelashes; "but John seems to take it all with perfect composure. Everything else is swallowed up in his distress of mind for what he has unfortunately done. If the child dies, I really think he will not get over it."

Some one called Emily, and she passed up-stairs again. Valentine turned and saw John near him; he came forward, but attempted no greeting. "I thought I might be of use, John," he said, as if they had seen one another but the day before. "Is there anything I can do for you over at the town?"

Valentine was a little daunted at first at the sight of him; his face was so white and he showed so plainly the oppression that weighed down his soul by the look in his eyes; they were a little raised, and seemed as if they could not rest on anything near at hand.

Valentine repeated his words, and was relieved when John roused himself, and expressed surprise and pleasure at seeing him. He sent Valentine to one of his clerks for some papers to be signed, gave him other directions, and was evidently the better for his presence.

It was not without many strange sensations that Valentine found himself again in that room where he had spent such happy hours, and which was so connected with his recollections of his old uncle. The plunge he had taken into the sweet waters of prosperity and praise had made him oblivious of some things that now came before his thoughts again with startling distinctness; but on the whole he felt pleasure in going back to the life that he had elected to leave, and was very glad to forget John's face in doing what he could to help him.

When he returned to the house John had commenced his restless walk again. Swan was walking beside him, and he was slightly leaning his hand on the old man's shoulder, as if to steady himself.

Valentine drew near.

"And you are sure he said nothing more?" John was saying in the low inward tone of fatigue and exhaustion.

"No, sir. 'Tell Mr. Mortimer,' says he, 'that his son is considerable better,' and he told Mrs. Walker—I heard him say it—that the blessed little one was no worse, not a morsel worse."

Valentine paused and heard John speak again in that peculiar tone—"I have no hope, Swan."

"I wouldn't give up, sir, if I was you: allers hold on to hope, sir."

"I cannot stand the strain much longer," he continued, as if he had not listened, "but sometimes—my thoughts are often confused—but sometimes I feel some slight relief in prayer."

"Ay, sir," answered Swan, "the Scripture says, 'Knock, and it shall be opened to you,' and I've allers thought it was mighty easier for one that begs to go and knock there than anywhere else, for in that house the Master opens the door himself."

CHAPTER XXXI.

A WOMAN'S SYMPATHY.

" Midsummer night, not dark, not light,
  Dusk all the scented air,
I'll e'en go forth to one I love,
  And learn how he doth fare.
O the ring, the ring, my dear, for me,
  The ring was a world too fine,
I wish it had sunk in a forty-fathom sea,
  Or ever thou mad'st it mine.

" Soft falls the dew, stars tremble through,
  Where lone he sits apart,
Would I might steal his grief away
  To hide in mine own heart.
Would, would 'twere shut in yon blossom fair,
  The sorrow that bows thy head,
Then—I would gather it, to thee unaware,
  And break my heart in thy stead.

" That charmèd flower, far from thy bower,
  I'd bear the long hours through,
Thou should'st forget, and my sad breast
  The sorrows twain should rue.
O sad flower, O sad, sad ring to me.
  The ring was a world too fine;
And would it had sunk in a forty-fathom sea,
  Ere the morn that made it mine."

TEN o'clock on the succeeding night. It seemed an age to John Mortimer since Valentine had met him in the hall, a night and a day that were almost a lifetime had come between; but his thoughts were not confused now. Something awful but fresh, breaking across his distracted mind, had diverted the torrent of his despairing fear lest his child should die through his mistake, and though he had bowed down his head and wept since the unexpected loss of another, those were healing tears, for with them came for a time escape from the rending strain that was breaking him down.

A sudden noise, when all was so quiet, and some one running down the garden, had startled him.

He tried to recall it. Valentine was with him, having just come back from the town, and one of the doctors was coming up; he took him by the hand. Other people were about him before he had time to think. Some of them were in tears. No, it was not Anastasia; he recollected how they kept telling him that it was not Anastasia, and then that they wished him to leave the house, though she was still in such imminent danger—leave the house and go to the inn. He could not receive a new thought suddenly. Why should he go to the inn? He was not anxious about his little Janie; he had not seen her for two or three days, but he could not leave the house now.

And yet he saw that he must do it. He was walking among the others to a carriage in the yard. He believed nothing; it was only as they drove along that he could understand the doctor's words—a change. They had feared that there might be an internal injury; he was to remember that they had mentioned to him some symptoms which should have made him aware of their solicitude. All very slowly, very cautiously said, but till he saw his child he did not believe a word of it.

The little face looked restless and troubled. Dorothea was sitting at her side fanning her. "Dear papa's come," she said, and then the child looked gravely satisfied, and for a long time she seemed to derive a quiet satisfaction from gazing at him. Then, by slow degrees, she fell into a deep sleep. He was so thankful to see it, and yet no one comforted him with any hopeful words. And it must have been a long time, for all the west was orange when some one woke him from an exhausted doze, his first dream since his great misfortune.

All his children were well again. They were all

present but Janie. Anastasia was sitting on his knees, rosy and smiling. "Did she know," he seemed to ask her, "what her poor father had done to her?" and while he felt this peace and joy of recovering her, some one touched his arm, and the dream was gone. He started and woke. Janie, yes, little Janie was there. "Do you want me, my darling?" were his first words, before he had quite dismissed the delusive comfort of that dream.

A remarkable, a perfectly indescribable change had come over the little face, it looked so wise. "You'd better kiss me now," she said, with a wistful, quaint composure.

"Yes, my treasure."

"I can't say my prayers to-night, papa," she presently added, "I suppose you'll have to say them for me." And before he could believe that he must part with her she was gone.

Little Janie, his little Janie. As he sat in the dusk that night he repeated her name many, many times, and sometimes added that she was his favourite child, the only one who in character and mind resembled her mother.

She was a quaint, methodical little creature. She had kept an account-book, and he had found it, with all its pretty, and now most pathetic little entries. He had put it in his breast-pocket, and his hand sought it every few minutes as he sat in the long dusk of the midsummer night. This was the first gap in his healthy, beautiful family. He felt it keenly, but a man who has six children left does not break his heart when he has to give one of them back to God.

No; but he was aware that his heart was breaking, and that now and then there came intervals in his sleepless nights and days when he did not feel at all or think at all. Sometimes for a few minutes he could not see. After these intervals of dull, amazed quiescence, when he was stupid and cold even to the heart, there were terrible times when he seemed to rouse himself to almost preternatural consciousness of the things about him, when the despair of the situation roused up like a tiger, and took hold of him and shook him body and mind.

It was true, quite true, his carelessness (but then he had been so worn out with watching), his fatal mistake, his heartless mistake (and yet he would almost have given his own life for his children) had brought him down to this slough of despond. There was no hope, the doctors never told him of any, and he knew he could not bear this much longer.

There are times when some of us, left alone to pull out again our past, and look at it in the light of a present, made remorseless and cruel with the energy that comes of pain, are determined to blame ourselves not only for the present misfortune, but to go back and back, and see in everything that has gone wrong with us how, but for our own fault, perversity, cowardice, stupidity, we might have escaped almost all the ills under which we now groan.

How far are we right at such times? Most of us have passed through them, and how much harder misfortune is to bear when complicated with the bitterness of self-reproach and self-scorn!

It was not dark. John Mortimer remembered that this was Midsummer night. A few stars were out; the moon, like a little golden keel, had gone down. Quantities of white roses were out all over the place. He saw them as faint, milky globes of whiteness in the dusk.

There were lights in the opened rooms up-stairs. It was very hot; sometimes he saw the nurses passing about. Presently he saw Emily. She was to be one of the watchers that night with Anastasia.

The little creature a day or two after her accident, finding fault with every one about her, and scarcely conscious that her own pain was to blame because they could not please her, had peevishly complained that she wanted Mrs. Nemily. Mrs. Nemily was a kind lady, and could tell her much prettier stories, and not give her such nasty things to drink.

Emily was instantly made aware of this, but when she arrived her little charge was past noticing any one. And yet Emily was full of hope. Impassioned and confiding prayer sustained her courage. She had always loved the little one keenly, and desired now with indescribable longing that her father might be spared the anguish of parting with her thus.

Yes, there was Emily; John Mortimer saw her move toward the window, and derived some faint comfort from the knowledge that she would be with Anastasia for the night.

Lovely, pale, and calm, he saw and blessed her, but she could not see him; and as she retired she too was added to the measure of his self-reproaches. He had lost her, and that also he had but himself to thank for; he himself, and no other, was to blame for it all.

He loved her. Oh yes, he had soon found out that he loved her! Fool! to have believed that in the early prime of his life the deepest passions of humanity were never to wake up again and assert themselves, because for the moment they had fallen into a noonday sleep. Fool, doubly fool, to have prided himself on the thought that this was so; and more than all a fool, to have let his scorn of love appear and justify itself to such a woman as Emily. Lovely and loving, what had he asked of her? which was to be done without the reward of his love. To bring up for him another woman's children, to manage a troublesome household, to let him have leisure and leave to go away from her from time to time, that he might pursue his literary tastes and his political destiny, to be responsible, to be contented, and to be lost, name and ambition, in him and his.

All this had flashed across his mind, and amazed

him with his own folly, before he reached the town on the morning that he left her. But that was nothing to the knowledge that so soon followed, the discovery that he loved her. For the first time in his life it seemed to be his part in creation to look up, and not to look down. He wrestled with himself, and fought with all his power against this hopeless passion; wondered whether he had done his cause irretrievable mischief by speaking too soon, as well as by speaking amiss; seldom hoped at all, for he had been refused even with indignation; and never was less able to withdraw his thoughts from Emily, even for a moment, than when he felt most strongly that there was no chance for him at all.

Still they went on and on now, his thoughts of her; they gave poignancy to all his other pain. The place, the arbour where he sat, had become familiar to him of late. He had become used to wander and pace the garden at night some time before this accident. Hour after hour, night after night, he had gone over the matter; he had hardly decided to go back to her, and implore her to give him a chance of retrieving his deplored mistake, when she sent him back his ring, and early the next morning was gone.

That was all his own fault, and but for it he now thought he should not have been so unobservant of things about him. Could he, but for such weary nights of sleepless wandering and watching, have let his darling boy drive those young horses, filling the carriage so full of his brothers and sisters that there was no room for any beside him whose hands were strong enough to hold them in? He was not sure. His clearer thought would not consent to admit that he could have foreseen the danger, and yet he had been so accustomed to hold things in hand, and keep them safe and secure, that he could hardly suppose they would not, but for his own state of mind, have been managed better.

It was midnight now; he had no intention of

coming indoors, or taking any rest, and his thoughts went on and on. When the misfortune came, it was still his own perturbation of mind, which had worn and fretted him so that he could not meet it as he might have done. This woman, whom he loved as it seemed to him man had never loved before, had taken herself out of his reach, and another man would win her. How could he live out the rest of his days? What should he do?

It was because that trouble, heaped upon the other, had made it hard to give his mind to the situation, that he had not forced himself to take rest, and what sleep he could, instead of wasting his powers in restless watching, till his overwrought faculties and jaded eyes had led him to the fearful moment when he had all but killed his own child.

Emily had scarcely spoken to him since her arrival. All her thoughts were for her little favourite. Perhaps even, she saw little in this fatal carelessness at all out of keeping with his character, as she had lately thought of it. No, his best chances in this life were all brought to an end; the whole thing was irretrievable.

"Is that Valentine?" he asked as some one approached.

"Yes, it is past one o'clock. I am going to bed; I suppose you will too."

"No," he answered in the dull inward voice now become habitual with him. "Why should I come in? Val, you know where my will is?"

"Yes," said Valentine, distressed to hear him say it.

"If you and Giles have to act, you will find everything in order."

"What is to be done for him?" thought Valentine. "Oh for a woman to talk to him now!—I cannot." He took to one of the commonplaces of admonition instead: "Dear John, you must try and submit yourself to the will of God."

"You have no need to tell me of that," he answered

with the same dimness of speech. "I do not rebel, but I cannot bear it. I mean," he continued, with the calmest tone of conviction, "that this is killing me."

"If only the child might be taken," thought Valentine, "he would get over it. It is the long suspense that distracts him."

"They want you to come in and eat something," he urged, "there is supper spread in the dining-room."

"No, I cannot."

He meant, "I cannot rise from my seat." Valentine supposed him only to say as usual that he could not eat.

"My mind wanders," he presently added, in the same low dull tone; and then repeated what he had said to his old gardener, "But sometimes I find relief in prayer."

Valentine went in rather hastily; he was alarmed not so much at the words as at his own sudden conviction that there was a good deal in them. They might be true. He must find some one to console, to talk to him, some one that could exercise influence over him. He knew of no one but Emily who would be likely to know what to say to him, and he hung about on the stairs, watching for her, hoping she would come out of little Anastasia's room; but all was so quiet, that he hoped the little sufferer might be asleep, and he dared not run the least risk of waking her.

It was now two o'clock.

John Mortimer saw some one holding aside a dark dress, and moving down the rose-covered alley towards him. It was not dark, and yet everything looked dim and confused. The morning star was up, it seemed to tremble more than usual; he knew he should not see it set, it would go out in its place, because the dawn came so early.

He knew it was Emily. "Only one thing could

have brought her," he said in his dull tone, and aloud. "The end is come."

But no, she was at his side. Oh what a sweet tone! So clear and thrilling, and not sad.

"The darling is just as usual, and I have brought you some coffee; drink it, dear John, and then come in and take some rest."

"No," he answered in a low tone, husky and despairing.

She made out that he was sitting on the wooden bench his boys had carved for him. It had only been placed there a few days, and was finished with an elbow, on which he was leaning his arm. It was too low to give him much support. She came to his side, the few trembling stars in the sky gave scarcely any light. Standing thus, and looking at the same view that was before him, she saw the lighted windows of the children, Johnnie's, little Bertram's, and Anastasia's. Three or four stars trembling near the horizon were southing fast. One especially bright and flickering was about, it was evident, in a few minutes to set; as far as she could see, John was gazing at it. She hoped he was not linking with it any thought of the little tender life so likely also to set. She spoke to him again in tones of gentle entreaty, "Take this cup, dear John."

"I cannot," he answered.

"Cannot!" she said, and she stooped nearer, but the dimness hid his face.

"No; and something within me seems to be failing."

There was that in the trembling frame and altered voice that impressed her strangely. What was failing? Had the springs of life been so strained by suffering that there was danger lest they should break?

Emily did not know; but everything seemed to change for her at that moment. It was little to her that he should discover her love for him now; but he would not, or, if he did, he was past caring, and he had been almost forgotten by those about him, though his danger was as great as that of any. He had been left to endure alone. She lifted the cup to his lips, and thought of nothing, and felt nothing, but the one supreme desire to console and strengthen.

"She will die, Emily," he found voice enough to say when the cup was empty; "and I cannot survive her."

"Yes, you can; but I hope she will not die, dear John. Why should she live so long, to die after all?"

She leaned toward him, and, putting her arms about him, supported his head on her shoulder, and held it there with her hand. At least that once her love demanded of her that she should draw near. *She* should not die; perhaps there was a long life before her; perhaps this might be the only moment she might have to look back to, when she had consoled and satisfied her unheeded heart.

"Have you so soon forgotten hope?" she said as she withdrew her arms.

"I thought I had."

"They always say she is not worse; not to be worse is to be better."

"They never say that, and I shall not forgive myself."

"No?" she exclaimed, and sighed. There was, indeed, so little hope, and if the child died, what might not be feared for the father? "That is because, though you seem a reverent and sincere Christian, you do not believe with enough reality that the coming life is so much sweeter, happier, better, than this. Few of us can. If you did, this tragedy could not fold itself down so darkly over your head. You could not bring yourself almost to the point of dying of pity and self-blame, because your child is perhaps to taste immortal happiness the sooner for your deplored mistake. Oh! men and women are different."

"You do not think you could have outlived a misfortune so irreparable?"

"I do think so. And yet this is sad; sometimes I cannot bear to think of it. Often I can find in my heart to wish that I might have handed that glass in your stead. Even if it had broken my heart, I stand alone; no other lives depend on me for well-being, and perhaps for well-doing. Cannot you think of this, dear John, and try to bear it and overlive it for their sakes? Look, day begins to dawn, and the morning star flickers. Come in; cannot you rise?"

"I suppose not; I have tried. You will not go?"

"Yes; I may be wanted."

"You have no resentments, Emily?"

"Oh no," she answered, understanding him.

"Then give me one kiss."

"Yes." She stooped again toward him and gave it. "You are going to live, John, and serve and love God, and even thank Him in the end, whatever happens."

"You are helping me to live," he answered.

It seemed impossible to him to say a single word more, and she went back towards the house again, moving more quickly as she drew near, because the sound of wheels was audible. As for him, he watched in the solemn dawn her retiring figure with unutterable regret. His other despair, who had talked to him of hope and consoled him with a simple directness of tender humanity, given him a kiss because he asked it. He had often wanted a woman's caressing affection before, and gone without it. It promised nothing, he thought; he perceived that it was the extremity she saw in the situation that had prompted it. When she next met him she would not, he knew, be ashamed of her kiss. If she thought about it, she would be aware that he understood her, and would not presume on it.

The spots of milky whiteness resolved themselves again into blush roses; hundreds and hundreds of them scented the air. Overhead hung long wreaths of honeysuckle ; colours began to show themselves ; purple iris and tree peony started out in detached patches from the shade; birds began to be restless ; here and there one fluttered forth with a few sudden, imperfect notes; and the cold curd-like creases in the sky took on faint lines of gold. And there was Emily—Emily coming down the garden again, and Giles Brandon with her. Something in both their faces gave him courage to speak.

"St. George, you are not come merely to help me in. I heard wheels."

Emily had moved a step forward ; it was light enough now to show her face distinctly. The doctors had both paid a visit; they came together, she told him.

"It was very good of them; they are more than considerate," he answered, sure that the news could not be bad.

"They both saw Anastasia, and they agreed that there was a decided improvement."

"I thank God."

With the aid of hope and a strong arm he managed to get up and stagger towards the house; but having once reached his room, it was several days before he could leave it or rise, though every message told of slow improvement.

A strange week followed the return of hope. The weeds in the garden began to take courage after long persecution, while Mr. Swan might frequently be seen reading aloud by Johnnie's bedside, sometimes the Bible, sometimes the newspaper, Master A. J. Mortimer deriving in his intervals of ease a grave satisfaction from the old man's peculiar style and his quaint remarks.

"I'm allers a comfort to them boys," Swan was heard to remark in the middle of the night, when

Valentine, who was refreshing himself with a short walk in the dark, chanced to be near him as he came on with his wife.

"And how do you get on, Maria?"

"Why, things seem going wrong, somehow. There's that new nurse feels herself unwell, and the jelly's melted, and Miss Christie was cross."

"That's awkward; but they're trifles. When the mud's up to your neck, you needn't trouble yourself because you've lost your pattens. You want a night's rest, my dear."

"Ay, I do; and don't you worrit, Swan, over Matthew being so *ugly* with you."

"Certainly not," said Swan. "He's turned more civil too. Said he to me this morning, 'Misfortunes in this life is what we all hev to expect. They ought not to surprise us,' said he; 'they never surprise me, nor nothing does.' It's true too. And he's allers for making a sensible observation, as he thinks (that shows what a fool he is). No, if he was to meet a man with three heads, he wouldn't own as he was surprised; he'd merely say, 'You must find this here dispensation very expensive in hats.'"

CHAPTER XXXII.

MR. BRANDON IS MADE THE SUBJECT OF AN HONOURABLE COMPARISON.

JOHN MORTIMER, thanks to a strong frame and an excellent constitution, was soon able to rise. He stood by his little Janie when she was laid in the grave, and felt, when he could think about it, how completely he and his had been spared the natural sorrow they would have suffered by the overshadowing gloom of greater misfortunes.

There was no mother to make lamentation. It was above all things needful to keep up Johnnie's spirits, and not discourage him. He had gone through a harder struggle for his life than his father knew of; but the sight of his pinched features and bright, anxious eyes began only now to produce their natural effect. John always came into his room with a serene countenance, and if he could not command his voice so as to speak steadily and cheerfully, he sat near him, and was silent.

There was little sign of mourning about the place. Never did a beautiful little promising life slip away so unobserved. Anastasia did not even know that her companion was gone. She was still not out of danger, and she wanted a world of watching and comforting and amusing.

They all wanted that. John, as he passed from room to room, strangely grateful for the care and kindness that had come into his house almost unbidden, was sometimes relieved himself in listening to the talk that went on.

Only two of his children were quite unhurt; these were Barbara (and she found quite enough occupation in waiting on her twin-sister) and little Hugh, who sometimes wandered about after his father almost as disconsolate as himself, and sometimes helped to amuse Bertram, showing him pictures, while Miss Christie told him tales. Master Bertram Mortimer, having reached the ripe age of nine years, had come to the conclusion that it was *muffish*—like a *cad*, like a girl—to cry. So when his broken arm and other grievances got beyond his power of endurance, he used to call out instead, while his tender-hearted little brother did the crying for him, stuffing his bright head into the pillows and sobbing as if his heart would break.

On one of these occasions John drew the child away and took him down-stairs. "I'm crying about Janie too," he said, creeping into his father's arms to be consoled, and not knowing the comfort this touch of natural sorrow had imparted to an over-strained heart.

The weather was unusually hot for the time of year, the doors and windows stood open, so that John could pass about as he pleased; he judged by the tone of voice in which each one spoke whether things were going well or not. After he had sent little Hugh to bed that evening he went up-stairs and sat in a staircase window, in full view of Johnnie's room. Swan was talking by the boy's bedside, while Johnnie seemed well content to listen. Little notice was taken when he appeared, and the discourse went on with quiet gravity, and that air of conviction which Swan always imparted to his words.

"Ay, sir, Mr. Fergus will have it that the cottagers are obstinate because they wont try for the easy things as he wants them to. The common garden stuff they show has allers been disgraceful, and yet, sometimes they interfere with him and take a prize for flowers. 'That shows they know their own business,' says I; 'it don't follow that because my parrot can talk, my dog's obstinate because he won't learn his letters.' 'Mr. Swan,' says he, 'you're so smothered in illustrations, there's no argufying with you.' Master Johnnie, you was to drink your beef tea by this time."

"Not just yet. I hate it. Tell me the rest about Fergus."

"'Well,' he said, 'I mean no disrespect to you, Mr. Swan.' 'No?' says I. 'No,' said he, 'but you and I air that high among the competitors that if we didn't try against one another we could allers hev it our own way. Now, if you'll not show your piccatees this time, I'll promise you not to bring forrard so much as one pelagonium.'"

"The cheat!" exclaimed Johnnie. "Why we have none worth mentioning, and the piccatees are splendid, Swanny."

"That's it, sir. He'd like me to keep out of his way, and then, however hard it might be on the other gardeners, he'd have all the county prizes thrown open to the cottagers, that's to say, those he doesn't want himself. He's allers for being generous with what's not his. He said as much to me as that he wished this could be managed. He thought it would be handy for us, and good for the poor likewise. 'That,' I says, 'would be much the same as if a one-legged man should steal a pair of boots, and think to make it a righteous action by giving away the one he didn't want in charity.' As he was so fond of illustrations, I thought I'd give him enough of them. 'Mr. Swan,' says he, rather hot, 'this here is very plain speaking.' 'I paid for my pipe myself,' says I, 'and I shall smoke it which side my mouth I please.' So now you know why we quarrelled, sir. It's the talk of all the country round, and well it may be, for there's nobody fit to hold a candle to us two, and all the other gardeners know it."

"I'll drink the stuff now," said Johnnie. "Father, is that you?"

"Yes, my dearest boy."

"You can't think how well I feel to-night, father. Swanny, go down and have some supper, and mind you come again."

"Ay, to be sure, Mr. Johnnie."

"You're not going to sit up to-night, my good old friend," said John, passing into the room.

"Well, no, sir, Mr. Johnnie hev cheated the doctor to that extent that he's not to hev anybody by him this night, the nurse is to come in and give him a look pretty frequent, and that's all."

John came and sat by his boy, took his thin hand, and kissed him.

"It's a lark, having old Swanny," said the young invalid, "he's been reading me a review of Mr. Brandon's book. He told Val that Smiles at the post office had read it, and didn't think much of it, but that it showed Mr. Brandon had a kind heart. 'And so he has,' said Swan, 'and he couldn't hide that if he wished to. Why, he's as good as a knife that has pared onions, sir,—everything it touches relishes of 'em.'"

"You had better not repeat that to Mr. Brandon," said John, "he is rather touchy about his book. It has been very unfavourably reviewed."

"But Swan intended a compliment," answered Johnnie, "and he loves onions. I often see him at his tea, eating slices of them with the bread and butter. You are better now, dear father, are you not?"

"Yes, my boy. What made you think there was anything specially the matter with me?"

"Oh, I knew you must be dreadfully miserable, for you could hardly take any notice even of me."

A small shrill voice, thin and silvery, was heard across the passage.

"Nancy often talks now," said Johnnie; "she spoke several times this morning."

John rose softly and moved towards it.

"And what did the robin say then," it asked.

Emily's clear voice answered, "The robin said, 'No, my wings are too short, I cannot fly over the sea, but I can stop here and be very happy all the winter, for I've got a warm little scarlet waistcoat.' Then the nightingale said, 'What does winter mean? I never heard of such a thing. Is it nice to eat?"

"That was very silly of the nightingale," answered the little voice. The father thought it the sweetest and most consoling sound he had ever heard in his life. "But tell the story," it went on peremptorily in spite of its weakness, "and then did the robin tell him about the snow?"

"Oh yes; he said, 'Sometimes such a number of little cold white feathers fall down from the place where the sun and moon live, that they cover up all the nice seeds and berries, so that we can find hardly anything to eat. But,' the robin went on, 'we don't care very much about that. Do you see that large nest, a very great nest indeed, with a red top to it?' 'Yes,' the nightingale said he did. 'A nice little girl lives there,' said the robin. 'Her name is Nancy. Whenever the cold feathers come, she gives us such a number of crumbs.'"

"Father, look at me," said the little creature, catching sight of her father. "Come and look at me, I'm so grand." She turned her small white face on the pillow as he entered, and was all unconscious both how long it was since she had set her eyes on him, and the cause. Emily had been dressing a number of tiny dolls for her, with gauzy wings, and gay robes; they were pinned about the white curtains of her bed. "My little fairies," she said faintly; "tell it, Mrs. Nemily."

"The fairies are come to see if Nancy wants anything," said Emily. "Nancy is the little Queen. She is very much better this evening, dear John." John knelt by the child to bring her small face close to his, and blessed her; he had borne the strain of many miserable hours without a tear, but the sound of this tender little voice completely overpowered him.

Emily was the only person about him who was naturally and ardently hopeful, but she scarcely ever left the child. He was devoured by anxiety himself, but he learned during the next two days to bless the elastic spirits of youth, and could move about among his other children pleased to see them smile and sometimes to hear them laugh. They were all getting better; Valentine took care they should not want for amusement, and Crayshaw, who, to do him justice, had not yet heard of little Janie's death or of Nancy's extremely precarious state, did not fail to write often, and bestow upon them all the nonsense he could think of. After his short sojourn in Germany, he had been sent back to Harrow, and there finding letters from the Mortimers awaiting him, had answered one of them as follows:—

LINES COMPOSED ON RECEIVING A PORTRAIT OF GLADYS WITH BLOB IN HER ARMS.

I gazed, and O with what a burst
 Of pride, this heart was striving!
His tongue was out! that touched me first.
 My pup! and art thou thriving?

I sniffed one sniff, I wept one weep
 (But checked myself, however),
And then I spake, my words went deep,
 Those words were, "Well, I never."

Tyrants avaunt! henceforth to me
 Whose Harrow'd heart beats faster,
The coach shall as the coachman be,
 And Butler count as master.

That maiden's nose, that puppy's eyes,
 Which I this happy day saw,
They've touched the manliest chords that rise
 I' the breast of Gifford Crayshaw.

John Mortimer was pleased when he saw his girls laughing over this effusion, but anxiety still weighed heavily on his soul—he did not live on any hope of his own, rather on Emily's hope and on a kiss.

He perceived how completely but for his father's companionship he had all his life been alone. It would have been out of all nature that such a man falling in love thus unaware should have loved moderately. All the fresh fancies of impassioned tenderness and doubt and fear, all the devotion and fealty that youth wastes often and almost forgets, woke up in his heart to full life at once, unworn and unsoiled. The strongest natures go down deepest among the hidden roots of feeling, and into the silent wells of thought.

It had not seemed unnatural heretofore to stand alone, but now he longed for something to lean upon, for a look from Emily's eyes, a touch from her hand.

But she vouchsafed him nothing. She was not so unconscious of the kiss she had bestowed as he had believed she would be; perhaps this was because he had mistaken its meaning and motive. It stood in his eyes as the expression of forgiveness and pity,—he never knew that it was full of regretful renunciation, and the hopelessness of a heart misunderstood.

But now the duties of life began to press upon him, old grey-headed clerks came about the place with messages, young ones brought letters to be signed. It was a relief to be able to turn, if only for a moment, to these matters, for the strain was great: little Nancy sometimes better, sometimes worse, was still spoken of as in a precarious state.

Every one in the house was delighted, when one morning he found it absolutely necessary to go into the town. Valentine drove him in, and all his children rejoiced, it seemed like an acknowledgment that they were really better.

Johnnie ate a large breakfast and called to Swan soon after to bring him up the first ripe bunch of grapes—he had himself propped up to eat them and to look out of the window at the garden.

"What a jolly bunch!" he exclaimed when Swan appeared with it.

"Ay, sir, I only wish Fergus could see it! The Marchioness sent yesterday to inquire,—sent the little young ladies. I haven't seen such a turn-out in our lane since last election time. Mr. Smithers said they were a sight to be seen, dressed up so handsome. 'Now then,' says he, 'you see the great need and use of our noble aristocracy. Markis is a credit to it, laying out as he does in the town he is connected with. Yes, they were a sight.' Mr. Smithers was the 'pink' Wigfield draper. 'Ay, ay,' says I, 'who should go fine if not the peahen's daughters?'"

"Everybody seems to have sent to inquire," said Johnnie ungraciously. "I hate to hear their wheels. I always think it is the doctor's carriage."

"Old Lady Fairbairn came too," proceeded Swan, "and Miss Justina. The old lady has only that one daughter left single, as I hear; she has got all the others married."

Johnnie made a grimace, and pleased himself with remembering how Valentine, in telling him of that call, had irreverently said, "Old Mother Fairbairn ought to be called the Judicious Hooker."

Johnnie was sincerely sorry these acquaintances had returned; so was Emily. Had she not given John a positive denial to his suit? Who could be surprised now if he turned to her rival?

It was afternoon when John Mortimer came in. The house was very quiet, and a little flag hung out of Nancy's window, showing that the child was asleep. He therefore approached quietly, entered the library, and feeling very tired and disquieted, sat down among his books. He took one down, and did not know how long he might have been trying to occupy himself with it, when he heard the rustle of a silk dress, and Dorothea stood in the open window. She looked just a little hurried and shy. "Oh, Mr. Mortimer," she began, "Emily sent her love to you, and——"

"Emily sent her love to me?" he exclaimed almost involuntarily, "sent her love? are you sure?"

Dorothea, thus checked in her message, drew back and blushed—had she made herself very ridiculous? would Emily be displeased? His eyes seemed to entreat her for an answer. She faltered, not without exceeding surprise, at the state of things thus betrayed, and at his indifference to her observation. "I suppose she did. I thought all this family sent love to one another." Thus while she hesitated, and he seemed still to wait for her further recollection, she noticed the strange elation of hope and joy that illumined his face.

"I don't think I could have invented it," she said.

"Ah, well," he answered, "I see you cannot be sure; but let me hear it again, since it possibly might have been said. 'Emily sent her love,' you began——"

"And she is sitting with Nancy, but she wanted you to know as soon as you came in that the doctors have paid another visit together, and they both agreed that Nancy might now be considered quite out of danger."

"Oh, I thank God!" he exclaimed.

Emily had sent her love to him to tell him this. He felt that she might have done, it was not impossible, it reminded him of her kiss. He had been weighed down so heavily, with a burden that he was never unconscious of for a moment, a load of agonized pity for his little darling's pain, and of endless self-reproach; that the first thing he was aware of when it was suddenly lifted off and flung away was, that his thoughts were all abroad. It was much too soon yet to be glad. He was like a ship floated off the rock it had struck on, a rock like to have been its ruin, but yet which had kept it steady. It was drifting now, and not answering to the helm.

He could not speak or stir, he hardly seemed to breathe.

A slight sound, the rustling of Dorothea's gown as she quietly withdrew, recalled him a little to himself, he locked himself in and went back to his place.

He was not in the least able to think, yet tears were raining down on his hands before he knew that they were his tears, and that, as they fell, his heart long daunted and crushed with pain, beat more freely, and tasted once more the rapture of peace and thankfulness. Presently he was on his knees. Saved this once, the almost despairing soul which had faintly spoken to God, "I do not rebel," was passionate now in the fervour of thankful devotion. The rapture of this respite, this return to common blessings, was almost too ecstatic to be borne.

It was nearly dusk before he could show himself to his children; when he stole up-stairs to look at his little Nancy she was again asleep. "Mrs. Walker had gone back to her own house for the night," the nurse said, "but she had promised to come back after breakfast."

That night Emily slept exquisitely. The luxury of a long peaceful interval, free from anxiety and responsibility, was delightful to her. She came down very late, and after her breakfast sauntered into the drawing-room, looking fresh as a white blush rose, lovely and content; next to the joy of possession stands, to such as she was, the good of doing good, and being necessary to the objects of their love.

A little tired still, she was sitting idly on a sofa, more wistfully sweet and gravely glad than usual, when suddenly John Mortimer appeared, walking quickly through her garden.

"He was sure to come and thank me," she said simply, and half aloud. "I knew he would sooner or later," and she said and thought no more.

But as he advanced, and she saw his face, she remembered her kiss, hoped that he did not, and blushing beautifully, rose and came a step or two forward to meet him. "None but good news, I hope," she said.

"No, they are all better, thank God; and my little Nancy also. Emily, how can I ever thank you? My obligation is too deep for words."

"Who could help wishing to be of use under such circumstances? Am I not enough thanked by seeing you all better?"

"I hardly know how I could have presumed to intrude here and disturb you and—and trouble you with such things as I can say—when you are come home for an interval of rest and quiet. Emily, if I had lost her, poor little girl, I never could have lifted up my head again. It was hard on that blameless little life, to be placed in such peril; but I suffered more than she did. Did you sometimes think so? did you sometimes feel for me when you were watching her day and night, night and day?"

"Yes, John, I did."

"I hoped so."

"But now that the greatest part of the sorrow is over, fold it up and put it away, lay it at the feet of the Saviour; it is his, for He has felt it too." When she saw his hands, that they had become white and thin, and that he was hollow-eyed, she felt a sharp pang of pity. "It is time now for you to think of yourself," she said.

"No," he answered, with a gesture of distaste. "The less of that the better. I am utterly and for ever out of my own good graces. I will not forgive myself, and I cannot forget—have I only one mistake to deplore? I have covered myself with disgrace," he continued, with infinite self-scorn; "even you with your half divine pity cannot excuse me there."

"Cannot I?" she answered with a sweet wistfulness, that was almost tender. .

He set his teeth as if in a passion against himself, a flash came from the blue eyes, and his Saxon complexion showed the blood through almost to the roots of the hair. "I have covered myself with disgrace—I am the most unmanly fool that ever breathed—I hate myself!" He started up and paced the room, as if he felt choked, whilst she looked on amazed for the moment, and not yet aware what this meant.

"John!" she exclaimed.

"I suppose you thought I had forgotten to despise myself," he went on in a tone rather less defiant. "When that night I asked you for a kiss—I had not, nothing of the kind—I thought my mind would go, or my breath would leave me before the morning. Surely that would have been so but for you. But if I have lived through this for good ends, one at least has been that I have learned my place in creation—and yours. I have seen more than once since that you have felt vexed with yourself for the form your compassion took then. I deserve that you should think I misunderstood, but I did not. I came to tell you so. It should have been above all things my care not to offend the good angel so necessary in my house during those hours of my misfortune. But I am destined never to be right—never. I let you divine all too easily the secret I should have kept—my love, my passion. It was my own fault, to betray it was to dismiss you. Well, I have done that also."

Emily drew a long breath, put her hand to her delicate throat, and turning away hastily moved into the window, and gazed out with wide-opened eyes. Her face suffused with a pale tint of carnation was too full of unbelieving joy to be shown to him yet. He had made a mistake, though not precisely the mistake he supposed. He was destined, so long as he lived, never to have it explained. It was a mistake which made all things right again, made the past recede, and appear a dream, and supplied a sweet reason for all the wifely duty, all the long fealty and impassioned love she was to bestow on him ever after.

It was strange, even to her, who was so well accustomed to the unreasoning, exaggerated rhapsody of a lover, to hear him; his rage against himself, his entire hopelessness; and as for her, she knew not how to stop him, or how to help him; she could but listen and wonder.

Nature helped him, however; for a waft of summer wind coming in at that moment, swung the rose-branches that clustered round the window, and flung some of their white petals on her head. Something else stirred, she felt a slight movement behind her, and a little startled, turned involuntarily to look, and to see her cap—the widow's delicate cap—wafted along the carpet by the air, and settling at John Mortimer's feet.

He lifted it up, and she stood mute while she saw him fold it together with a man's awkwardness, but with something of reverence too; then, as if he did not know what else to do with it, he laid it on the table before an opened miniature of Fred Walker.

After a moment's consideration she saw him close this miniature, folding its little doors together.

"That, because I want to ask a favour of you," he said.

"What is it?" she asked, and blushed beautifully.

"You gave me a kiss, let me also bestow one—one parting kiss—and I will go."

He was about to go then, he meant to consider himself dismissed. She could not speak, and he came up to her, she gave him her hand, and he stooped and kissed her.

Something in her eyes, or perhaps the blush on her face, encouraged him to take her for a moment into his arms. He was extremely pale, but when she lifted her face from his breast a strange gleam of hope and wonder flashed out of his eyes.

She had never looked so lovely in her life, her face suffused with a soft carnation, her lucid grey-blue eyes full of sweet entreaty. Nevertheless, she spoke in a tone of the quietest indifference—a sort of pensive wistfulness habitual with her.

"You can go if you please," she said, "but you had much better not."

"No!" he exclaimed.

"No," she repeated. "Because, John—because I love you."

CHAPTER XXXIII.

THE TRUE GHOST STORY.

Horatio.—"Look, my lord, it comes!"
HAMLET THE DANE.

VALENTINE was at Melcombe again. He had begun several improvements about the place which called for time, and would cost money. It was not without misgiving that he had consented to enter on the first of them.

There was still in his mind, as he believed, a reservation. He would give up the property if he ever saw fit cause.

Now, if he began to tie himself by engaging in expensive enterprises, or by undertaking responsibilities, it might be impossible to do this.

Therefore he held off for some little time.

He fell into his first enterprise almost unawares, he got out of his reluctant shrinking from it afterwards by a curious sophistry. "While this estate is virtually mine," he thought, "it is undoubtedly my duty to be a good steward of it. If, in the course of providence, I am shown that I am to give it up, no doubt I shall also be shown how to proceed about these minor matters."

He had learnt from his uncle the doctrine of a particular providence, but had not received with it his uncle's habit of earnest waiting on providence, and straightforward desire to follow wherever he believed it to lead.

Valentine came almost at once under the influence of the vicar, Mr. Craik, the man who had always seen something so more than commonly mysterious about the ways of God to men. Mr. Craik wanted Valentine to restore the old church, by which he meant to pull it almost to pieces, to raise the roof, to clear away the quaint old oaken galleries, to push out a long chancel, and to put in some painted windows, literally such, pictures of glass, things done at Munich.

When Valentine, always facile, had begun to consider this matter, a drawing of the building, as it was to look when restored, was made, in order to stir up his zeal, and make him long for a parish church that would do him and the vicar credit. He beheld it, and forthwith vowed, with uncivil directness, that he would rather build the vicar a *crack church* to his mind, in the middle of the village, than help in having that dear old place mauled and tampered with.

Mr. Craik no sooner heard this than he began to talk about a site.

He was a good man, had learned to be meek, so that when he was after anything desirable he might be able to take a rebuff, and not mind it.

In the pleasant summer evenings he often came to see Valentine, and while the latter sauntered about with a cigar, he would carve faces on a stick with his knife, walking beside him. He had given up smoking, because he wanted the poor also to give it up, as an expensive luxury, and one that led to drinking. Valentine respected him, was sure the scent of a cigar was still very pleasant to his nostrils, and knew he could well have afforded to smoke himself. That was one reason why he let himself be persuaded in the matter of the site (people never are persuaded by any reason worth mentioning). Another reason was, that Mr. Craik had become a teetotaller, "for you know, old fellow, that gives me such a *pull* in persuading the drunkards;" a third reason was, that there was a bit of land in the middle of the village, just the thing for a site, and worth nothing, covered with stones and thistles. Mr. Craik said he should have such a much better congregation, he felt sure, if the church was not in such an extremely inconvenient out-of-the-way place; that aged saint, who was gone, had often regretted the inconvenience for the people.

Valentine at last gave him the site. Mr. Craik remarked on what a comfort it would have been to the aged saint if she could have known what a good churchman her heir would prove himself.

But Valentine was not at all what Mr. Craik meant by a good churchman. Such religious opinions and feelings as had influence over him, had come from the evangelical school. His old father and uncle had been very religious men, and of that type, almost as a matter of course. In their early day evangelical religion had been as the river of God —the one channel in which higher thought and fervent feeling ran.

Valentine had respected their religion, had seen that it was real, that it made them contented, happy, able to face death with something more than hope, able to acquiesce in the wonderful reservations of God with men, the more able on account of them to look on this life as the childhood of the next, and to wait for knowledge patiently. But yet, of all the forms taken by religious feeling, Valentine considered it the most inconvenient; of all the views of Christianity, the most difficult to satisfy.

He told the vicar he did not see why his grandmother was to be called a saint because she had gone through great misfortunes, and because it had pleased her to be *trundled* to church, on all Sundays and saints' days, besides attending to the other ordinances of the church and the sacraments.

When he was mildly admonished that a site seemed

to presuppose a church, he assented, and with one great plunge, during which he distinctly felt, both that his position as landlord was not to be defended, and that this good use of the money might make things more secure, he gave a promise to build one—felt a twinge of compunction, and a glow of generosity, but blushed hotly when Mr. Craik observed that the old church, being put in decent repair, and chiefly used for marriages and for the burial service, it might perhaps be a pleasing testimony, a filial act, to dedicate the new one to St. Elizabeth. "Simply in reverend recollection, you know, Melcombe, of that having been—been your grandmother's name."

"No, I shouldn't like it," said Valentine abruptly. Mr. Craik was not sure whether his evident shrinking was due to some low-church scruple as to any dedication at all, or whether the name of the sainted Elizabeth had startled him by reminding him of self-renunciation and a self-denial even to the death, of all that in this world we love and long for. This Elizabeth, his grandmother, might have been a saintly old woman in her conversation, her patience, her piety, for anything Valentine knew to the contrary, but he had hold now of all her accounts; he knew from them, and from investigations made among the tenants, that she had held a hard grip of her possessions, had sometimes driven shrewd bargains, and even up to her extreme old age had often shown herself rather more than a match for some of those about her. Things to be done by others she had seen to with vigilance, things to be done by herself she had shown a masterly power of leaving undone. Her property had considerably increased during her term of possession, though in ordinary charity a good deal had been given away. All was in order, and her heir whom she had never seen was reaping the fruits of her judgment and her savings; but whether she ought to be called a saint he rather doubted.

He had returned to Melcombe, not without shrewd

suspicions that his cousin was soon to be his brother-in-law. A letter following closely on his steps had confirmed them. Some time in September he expected a summons to be present at the wedding; he wished after that to travel for several months, so he allowed Mr. Craik to persuade him that his good intentions ought not to be put off, and he made arrangements for the commencement of the new church at once.

It was to cost about three thousand pounds, a large sum; but the payment was to be spread over three or four years, and Valentine, at present, had few other claims. He had, for instance, no poor relations, at least he thought not; but he had scarcely given his word for the building of the church when he received a letter from Mrs. Peter Melcombe—"an ugly name," thought Valentine. "Mrs. Valentine Melcombe will sound much better. Oh, I suppose the young woman will be Mrs. Melcombe, though." Mrs. Peter Melcombe let Valentine know that she and Laura had returned to England, and would now gladly accept his invitation, given in the spring, to come and stay a few weeks with him whenever this should be the case.

"I have always considered Laura a sacred trust," continued the good lady. "My poor dear Peter, having left her to me—my means are by no means large—and I am just now feeling it my duty to consider a certain very kind and very flattering offer. I am not at all sure that a marriage with one whom I could esteem might not help me to bear better the sorrow of my loss in my dear child; but I have decided nothing. Laura has actually only five hundred pounds of her own, and that, I need not say, leaves her as dependent on me as if she was a daughter."

"Now look here," exclaimed Valentine, laying the letter down flat on the table, and holding it there with his hand—"now look here, this is serious. You are going to bring that simpleton Laura to me, and you would like to leave her here, would you? Preposterous! She cannot live with me! Besides, I am such a fool myself, that if I was shut up with her long, I should certainly marry her. Take a little time, Val, and consider.

> 'Wilt thou brave?
> Or wilt thou bribe?
> Or wilt thou cheat the kelpie?'

Let me see. Laura is my own cousin, and the only Melcombe. Now, if Craik had any sense of gratitude —but he hasn't—it seems so natural, 'I built you a church, you marry my cousin. Do I hear you say you won't? You'd better think twice about that. I'd let you take a large slice of the turnip-field into your back garden. Turnips, I need hardly add, you'd have *ad lib.* (very wholesome vegetables), and you'd have all that capital substantial furniture now lying useless in these attics, and an excellent family mangle out of the messuage or tenement called the laundry—the wedding breakfast for nothing. I think you give in, Craik?' Yes; we shake hands—he has tears in his eyes. 'Now, Laura, what have you got to say?' '*He has sandy hair.*' 'Of course he has, the true Saxon colour. Go down on your knees, miss, and thank heaven fasting for a good man's love (Shakespeare).' '*And he has great red hands.*' 'Surely they had better be red than green—celestial rosy red, love's proper hue.' Good gracious! here he is."

"Ah, Craik! is that you? How goes it?"

One of Mr. Craik's gifts was that he could sigh better than almost anybody; whenever he was going to speak of anything as darkly mysterious, his sigh was enough to convince any but the most hardened. He *fetched* a sigh then (that is the right expression) —he fetched it up from the very bottom of his heart, and then he began to unfold his grievances to Valentine, how some of his best school-girls had tittered at church, how some of his favourite boys had got drunk, how some of the farmers had not attended morning service for a month, and how two women, regular attendants, had, notwithstanding, quarrelled to that degree that they had come to blows, and one of them had given the other a black eye, and old Becky Maddison is ill, he concluded. "I've been reading to her to-day. I don't know what to think about administering the Holy Communion to her while she persists in that lie."

"Do you mean the ghost story?" asked Valentine.

"Yes."

"It may have been a lie when she first told it; but in her extreme old age she may have utterly forgotten its first invention. It may possibly not be now a conscious lie, or, on the other hand, it may be true that she did see something."

"Your grandmother always considered that it was a lie, and a very cruel lie."

"How so? She accused no one of anything."

"No, but she made people talk. She set about a rumour that the place was haunted, and for some years the family could hardly get a servant to live with them."

"Poor old soul!" thought Valentine. "I suppose it would be wrong to try and bribe her to deny it. I wish she would though."

"I think," said Mr. Craik, an air of relief coming over his face—"I think I shall tell her that I regard it in the light you indicated."

Soon after that he went away. It was evening, the distant hills, when Valentine sauntered forth, were of an intense solid blue, gloomy and pure, behind them lay wedges of cloud edged with gold, all appeared still, unchanging, and there was a warm balmy scent of clover and country crops brooding over the place.

Valentine sauntered on through the peaceful old churchyard, and over the brow of the little hill. What a delightful evening view! A long hollow, with two clear pools (called in those parts meres) in it, narrow, and running side by side, the evening star and crescent moon, little more than a gold line, reflected in one of them. The reed warbler was beginning to sing, and little landrails were creeping out of the green sedges, the lilies were closing and letting themselves down. There was something so delightful, so calm, that Valentine felt his heart elevated by it. The peace of nature seems a type of the rest of God. It reminds man of that deep awful leisure in which his Maker dwells, taking thought for, and having, as we express it, time, to bless and think upon his creatures.

Valentine watched the gold in the sky, and the primrose-tinted depths beyond. He was thankful for his delightful home; he felt a good impulse in him, urging that he must do his duty in this his day and generation; he seemed to respond to it, hoped the new church would be of use in the neighbourhood, and felt that, even if it cost him some sacrifice, Laura must be provided for; either he must settle on her something that she could live on, or he must promise her a marriage portion.

As for himself, he was a good young fellow, better than many, and when he went on to think of himself, he saw, in his vision of his own future, nothing worse than an almost impossibly pretty girl as his bride, one with whom he was to take a specially long and agreeable wedding tour; and some time after that he supposed himself to see two or three jolly little boys rolling about on the grass, the Melcombes of the future, and with them and their mother he saw himself respected and happy. Sauntering on still, he came past Becky Maddison's cottage, a pleasant abode, thatched, whitewashed, and covered with jasmine, but too close to the mere. "I will talk to that poor old soul again, and see if I can make anything of her. I am sure Craik is mistaken about her."

"She fails fast," said the daughter, when accosted by Valentine; and she took him up-stairs to see her mother. He first made himself welcome by giving her a handsome alms, and then inquired about her health.

The daughter had gone down of her own accord. "I'n bin very bad with my *sparms*," meaning spasms, she answered in a plaintive voice. Valentine saw a very great change in her, the last sunset's afterglow fell upon her face, it was sunk and hollow, yet she spoke in clear tones, full of complaint, but not feeble. "And I'n almost done wi' this world."

"Mr. Craik comes to see you, I know; he told me to-day that you were ill."

"Parson were always hard on I."

"Because he doesn't believe the ghost story."

"Ay, told me so this blessed marnin'; and who be he? wanted I to own 'twas a lie, and take the blessed sacrament, and make a good end. 'Sir,' says I, 'Mr. Martimer believed it, that's Mr. Melcombe now—and so 'e did, sir.'"

"No, I didn't," said Valentine.

"No?" she exclaimed, in a high piping tone.

"No, I say. I thought you had either invented it—made it up, I mean—or else dreamed it. I do not wish to be hard on you, but I want to remind you how you said you had almost done with this world."

"Why did 'e goo away, and never tell I what 'e thought?" she interrupted.

Valentine took no notice, but went on. "And the parson feels uneasy about you, and so do I. I wish you would try to forget what is written down in the book, and try to remember what you really saw; you must have been quite a young girl then. Well, tell me how you got up very early in the morning, almost before it was light, and tell what you saw, however much it was, or however little; and if you are not quite sure on the whole that you saw anything at all, tell that, and you will have a right to hope that you shall be forgiven."

"I'n can't put it in fine words."

"No, and there is no need."

"Would 'e believe it, if I told it as true as I could?"

"Yes, I would."

"I will, then, as I hope to be saved."

"I mean to stand your friend, whatever you say, and I know how hard it is to own a lie.'

"Ay, that it be, and God knows I'n told a many."

"Well, I ask you, then, as in the sight of God, is this one of them?"

"No, sir. It ain't."

"What! you did see a ghost?"

"Ay, I did."

Valentine concealed his disappointment as well as he could, and went on.

"You told me the orchard of pear-trees and cherry-trees was all in blossom, as white as snow. Now don't you think, as it was so very early, almost at dawn, that what you saw really might have been a young cherry-tree standing all in white, but that you, being frightened, took it for a ghost?"

"The sperit didn't walk in white," she answered; "I never said it was in white."

"Why, my good woman, you said it was in a shroud!"

"Ay, I told the gentleman when he took it down, the ghost were wrapped up in a cloak, a long cloak, and he said that were a shroud."

"But don't you know what a shroud is?' exclaimed Valentine, a good deal surprised. "What is the dress called hereabout, that a man is buried in?"

"His buryin' gown. 'Tis only a sperit, a ghost, that walks in a shroud. I'n told that oft enough, I *should* know." She spoke in a querulous tone, as one having reasonable cause for complaint.

"Well," said Valentine, after a pause, "if the shroud was not white, what colour was it?"

"Mid have been black for aught I know, 'twere

afore sunrise; but it mid have been a dark blue, and I think 'twas. There were a grete wash up at the house that marnin', and I were coming to help. A sight of cherry-trees grow all about the door, and as I came round the corner there it stood with its hand on the latch, and its eyes very serious."

"What did it look like?"

"It looked like Mr. Cuthbert Martimer, and it stared at I, and then I saw it were Mr. Melcombe."

"Were you near it?"

"Ay, sir."

"Well, what next?"

"I dropped a curtsey."

"Good heavens!" exclaimed Valentine, turning cold. "What, curtsey to a ghost, a spirit?"

"Ay, I did, and passed on, and that very instant I turned, and it were gone."

Valentine's voice faltered as he asked the next question. "You were not frightened?"

"No, sir, because I hadn't got in my head yet that 'twere a sperit. When I got in, I said, 'I'n seen him.' 'You fool,' says Mary Carfoil, that was cook then, 'your head,' says she, 'is for ever running on the men folks. He's a thousand mile off,' says she, 'in the Indies, and the family heerd on him a week agoo.' 'I did see him,' says I. 'Goo along about your business,' says she, 'and light the copper. It were Mr. Cuthbert 'e saw, got up by-times to shoot rooks. Lucky enough,' says she, 'that Mr. Melcombe be away.'"

"Why was it lucky?"

"Because they'd both set their eyes on the same face—they had. It's hard to cry shame on the dead, but they had. And *she's* dead too. Neither on 'em meant any good to her. They had words about her. She'd have nought to say to Mr. Cuthbert then."

Valentine groaned.

"No, nor she wouldn't after I'n seen the ghost, nor

till every soul said he was dead and drowned, and the letter come from London town."

"There must have been others beside you," said Valentine, sharply, "other people passing in and out of the laundry door. Why did no one see him but you—see it but you?"

"It were not the laundry door, sir, 'twere the door in the garden wall, close by the grete pear-tree, as it went in at; Madam shut up that door for ever so many years—'e can't mistake it."

"Ah!"

"That's the place, sir."

"And who was fool enough first to call it a ghost?" cried Valentine almost fiercely. "No, no, I mean," he continued faltering—"I don't know what I mean," and he dropped his face into his hands, and groaned. "I always thought it was the yard door."

"No, sir."

"And so when he disappeared, and was no more seen, you thought you had seen his ghost?"

"Ay, sir, we all knowed it then, sure enough; Madam seemed to know't from the first. When they told her I'n seen Mr. Melcombe, she fell in a grete faint, and wrung her hands, and went in another faint, and cried out he were dead; but the sperit never walked any more, folks said it came for a token to I, 'her did ought to look for death by-times,' said they."

"That's all, is it?"

"Ay, sir, that be all."

"I believe you this time."

"'E may, sir, and God bless 'e."

CHAPTER XXXIV.

VALENTINE AND LAURA.

"The flower out of reach is dedicate to God."
Tamil Proverb.

SOME one passing Valentine as he walked home in the gloaming, started, and hurried on. "He came up so still-like," she said, afterwards, "that I e'en took him for a sperit, he being a Melcombe, and they having a way of *walking*."

She did not speak without book, for old Madam Melcombe was already said to haunt the churchyard. Not as a being in human guise, but as a white, wide-winged bird, perfectly noiseless in its movements, skimming the grass much as owls do, but having a plaintive voice like that of a little child.

Late in the night again, when all the stars were out sparkling in a moonless sky, and the household should long have been asleep, the same fancy or fear recurred. Two housemaids woke suddenly, and felt as if there was a moaning somewhere outside. They had been sleeping in the heat with their window open, and they looked out and saw a dark shadow moving in the garden, moving away from the house, and seeming to make as if it wrung its hands. After this, still peering out into the starlight, they lost sight of it; but they fancied that they heard it sigh, and then it stood a dark column in their sight, and seemed to fall upon the bed of lilies, and there lie till they were afraid to look any longer, and they shut their window and crept again into their beds.

But the lilies? It might have been true that they saw somewhat, but if a spirit had haunted the dark garden that night, surely no trace of its sojourn would have remained on the bed of lilies; yet in the morning many, very many of their fragrant leaves were crushed and broken, as if in truth some houseless or despairing being had crouched there.

The housemaids told their tale next morning, and it was instantly whispered in the house that the ghost had come again. The maids shook with fear as they went about, even in broad daylight. The gardener alone was incredulous, and made game of the matter.

"Hang the ghost!" said he; but then he came from the eastern counties, and had no reverence for the old family "fetch." "Hang the ghost! why shouldn't that shadow have been the brown pony? Ain't he out at grass, and didn't I find the garden-door ajar this morning? He came in, I'll be bound." Then the gardener shouldered his spade, and finding a number of footmarks all over the place, specially about the bed of lilies, and certainly not those of a pony, he carefully obliterated them, and held his peace. Shaking his head when alone, and muttering, "They're a queer lot, these Melcombes—who'd have expected this now! If the dead ones don't walk, the live ones do. Restless, that's what it is. Restless, too much to eat, I should say, and too little to do. When the missis comes we shall have more sensible doings, and I wish the missis had never left us, that I do."

Mrs. Peter Melcombe, thus welcomed back again in the gardener's mind, was then driving up to the door of Melcombe House, and Valentine was stepping out to receive her.

It was natural that she should feel agitated, and Valentine accosted her so seriously as to increase her emotion. She had been able to recover her usually equable spirits after the loss of her child, it was only on particular occasions that she now gave way to tears. She was by no means of their number who love to make a parade of grief; on the contrary, emotion was painful to her, and she thankfully avoided it when she could.

She retired with Laura, and after a reasonable time recovered herself, taking care to go at once into the room where her darling had slept, and where he had played, that she might not again be overcome.

"I have dreaded this inexpressibly," she said, sobbing, to Laura, who was following her with real sympathy.

"Valentine was very odd," answered Laura; "you would, I am sure, have got over your return quite calmly, if he had been less solemn. Surely, Amelia dear, he is altered."

"He was oppressed, no doubt, at sight of me; he felt for me."

Laura said no more, but several times during that first day she made wondering observations. She looked in vain for the light-hearted companionable young fellow with whom she had become intimate in cousinly fashion, and whom she had fully hoped to consult about a certain affair of her own. She saw an air of oppressive bitterness and absence of mind that discouraged her greatly. "There is no mistaking his expression of countenance," she thought; "he must have been disappointed in love."

"Laura," exclaimed Mrs. Melcombe, when the two ladies, having left the dining-room, were alone together in the old grandmother's favourite parlour, now used as a drawing-room—"Laura, what can this mean? Is he dyspeptic? Is he hypochondriacal? I declare, if Mr. Craik had not been invited to meet us, I hardly see how we could have got through the dinner: he is very odd."

"And surely the conversation was odd too," said Laura. "How they did talk about old Becky Maddison and her death this afternoon! How fervently he expressed his gladness that Mr. Craik had seen her to-day, and had administered the sacrament to her! I suppose you observed Valentine's hesitation when you asked if he believed her story?"

"Yes; I felt for the moment as if I had no patience with him, and I asked because I wanted to bring him to reason. He can hardly wish to own before sensible people that he does believe it; and if he does not, he must know that she was an impostor, poor old creature." Then she repeated, "He is very odd," and Laura said—

"But we know but little of him. It may be his way to have fits of melancholy now and then. How handsome he is!"

Amelia admitted this; adding, "And he looks better without that perpetual smile. He had an illness, I think, two years ago; but he certainly appears to be perfectly well now. It cannot be his health that fails him."

There was the same surprise next morning. Valentine seemed to be making an effort to entertain them, but he frequently lapsed into silence and thought. No jokes, good or bad, were forthcoming. Mrs. Melcombe felt that if she had not received such a warm and pressing invitation to come to visit Melcombe, she must have now supposed herself to be unwelcome. She took out some work, and sat in the room where they had breakfasted, hoping to find an opportunity to converse with him on her own plans and prospects; while Laura, led by her affectionate feelings, put on her hat and sauntered down the garden—to the lily-bed of course, and there she stood some time, thinking of her dear old grandmother. She was not altogether pleased with its appearance, and she stooped to gather out a weed here and there.

Presently Valentine came down the garden. He was lost in thought, and when he saw Laura he started and seemed troubled. "What can you be about, Laura dear?" he said.

He had made up his mind that she had a pecuniary claim on him, and therefore he purposely addressed her with the affection of a relative. He felt that this would make it easier for her to admit this convenient claim.

"What am I about?" answered Laura. "Why, Valentine, I was just picking off some of these leaves, which appear to have been broken. The bed looks almost as if some—some creature had been lying on it."

"Does it?" said Valentine, and he sighed, and stood beside her while she continued her self-imposed task.

"These lilies, you know," she remarked, "have great attractions for us."

"Yes," said Valentine, and sighed again.

"How he shivers!" thought Laura. "You cannot think," she said, rising from her task and looking about her, "how it touches my feelings to come back to the old place."

"You like it then, Laura?"

"Like it! I love it, and everything belonging to it."

"Including me!" exclaimed Valentine, rallying for the moment and laughing.

Laura looked up and laughed too, but without answering. Before there was time for that, she had seen the light of his smile die out, and the gloom settle down again. A sort of amazement seemed to be growing under his eyelids; his thought, whatever it was, had gradually returned upon him, and he was struck by it with a new surprise.

"Valentine!" she exclaimed.

"Yes," he answered steadily and gravely, and then roused himself to add, "Come out from under the shadow of this wall. The garden is all gloomy here in the morning; it makes me shiver. I want to speak to you," he continued, when they had passed through the door in the wall, and were walking on the lawn before the house.

"And I to you," she replied. "It was kind of you to ask us to come here."

"I suppose Mrs. Melcombe has decided to marry again," he began.

"Yes, but she would like to tell you about that herself."

"All right. I consider, Laura dear, that you have much more claim upon me than upon her."

"Do you, Valentine, do you?"

As they walked down into the orchard, Laura shed a few agitated tears; then she sat down on a grassy bank, and while Valentine, leaning against the trunk of a pear-tree, looked down upon her, she said—

"Then I wish you would help me, Valentine. The devotion that I have inspired, if I could only meet it as it deserves—" And then she went on in a tone of apology, "And it is only help that I want, for I have five hundred pounds of my own, if I could but get at it."

"Where is the devotion?" exclaimed Valentine, suddenly rallying. "Let me only catch hold of that devotion, and I'll soon have it down on its knees, and old Craik's large red hands hovering over it and you, while he matches it as the Church directs to a devotion more than worthy of it, as I will the five hundred pounds with another."

"Ah, but you can't," said Laura, laughing also, "because he's in America; and, besides, you don't know all."

"Oh, he's in America, is he?"

"Yes; at least I suppose he's on the high seas by this time, or he will be very shortly, for he's going up to New York."

"*Up* to New York! Where does he hang out then when he's at home?"

"At Santo Domingo."

"That at least shows his original mind. Not black, of course? Not descended from the woman who 'suddenly married a Quaker?'"

"Oh no, Valentine—an Englishman."

"An Englishman and live at Santo Domingo! Well, I should as soon have expected him to live in the planetary spaces. It would be much more roomy there, and convenient too, though to be sure a planet coming up might butt at him now and then."

"It is rather a large island," said Laura. "But, Valentine——"

"Well."

"He speaks Spanish very well. He is comfortably off."

"His speciality, no doubt, is the sugar-cane. Well, I shall consider him very mean if he doesn't let me have my sugar cheap, in return for my kindness."

"You are sure you are going to be kind then."

"Yes, if he is a good fellow."

"He is a good fellow, and I am not worthy of him, for I behaved shamefully to him. He has written me a very gentlemanly letter, and he said, with perfect straightforwardness, that he did at one time believe himself to have quite got over his attachment to me, but—but he had been a good deal alone, had found time to think, and, in short, it had come on again; and he hoped he was now able to offer me not only a very agreeable home, but a husband more worthy of me. That's a mistake, for I behaved ill to him, and he well, and always well, to me. In short, he begged me to come over to New York in September: he is obliged to be there on business himself at that time. He said, taking the chances, and in the hope of my coming, he would name the very line of steamers I ought to come by; and if I could but agree to it, he would meet me and marry me, and take me back with him."

"Somehow, Laura, I seem to gather that you do not consider him quite your equal."

"No, I suppose, as I am a Melcombe—"

"A Melcombe!" repeated Valentine with bitter scorn. "A Melcombe!" Laura felt the colour rush over her face with astonishment. She knew rather than saw that the little glimpse she had had of his own self was gone again; but before she could decide how to go on, he said, with impatience and irritation, "I beg your pardon; you were going to say——"

"That he is in a fairly good position now," she proceeded, quoting her lover's language; "and he has hopes that the head of the firm, who is a foreigner, will take him into partnership soon. Besides, as his future home is in America (and mine, if I marry him), what signifies his descent?"

"No," murmured Valentine with a sigh. "'The gardener Adam and his wife' (Tennyson)."

"And," proceeded Laura, "nothing can be more perfectly irreproachable than his people are—more excellent, honest, and respectable."

"Whew!" cried Valentine with a bitter laugh, "that is a great deal to say of any family. Well, Laura, if you're sure they won't mind demeaning themselves by an alliance with us——"

"Nonsense, Valentine; I wish you would not be so odd," interrupted Laura.

"I have nothing to say against it."

"Thank you, dear Valentine; and nobody else has a right to say anything, for you are the head of the family. It was very odd that you should have pitched upon that particular line to quote."

"Humph! And as I have something of my own, more than three thousand pounds in fact——"

"And Melcombe," exclaimed Laura.

"Ah, yes, I forgot. But I was going to say that you, being the only other Melcombe, you know, and you and I liking one another, I wish to act a brotherly part by you; and therefore, when you have bought yourself a handsome trousseau and a piano, and everything a lady ought to have, and your passage is paid for, I wish to make up whatever is left of your five hundred pounds to a thousand, that you may not go almost portionless to your husband."

"I am sure, dear Valentine, he does not expect anything of the sort," exclaimed Laura faintly, but with such a glow of pleasure in her face as cheated Valentine for the moment into gladness and cordiality.

"Depend upon it, he will be pleased notwithstanding to find you even a better bargain than he expected." Laura took Valentine's hand when he said this, and laid it against her cheek. "What's his name, Laura?"

"His name is Swan."

Thereupon the whole story came out, told from Laura's point of view, but with moderate fairness.

Valentine was surprised; but when he had seen the letters and discovered that the usually vacillating Laura had quite made up her mind to sail to New York, he determined that his help and sanction should enable her to do so in the most desirable and respectable fashion. Besides, how convenient for him, and how speedy a release from all responsibility about her! Of course he remembered this, and when Laura heard him call her lover "Don Josef," she thought it a delightful and romantic name.

But Mrs. Peter Melcombe was angry when Laura told her that Joseph had written again, and that Valentine knew all and meant to help her. She burst into tears. "Considering all I have suffered," she said, in consequence of that young man's behaviour, I wonder you have not more feeling than to have anything to say to him. Humanly speaking, he is the cause of all my misfortunes; but for him, I might have been mistress of Melcombe still, and my poor darling, my only delight, might have been well and happy."

Laura made no reply, but she repeated the conversation afterwards to Valentine with hesitating compunction, and a humble hope that he would put a more favourable construction on her conduct than Amelia had done.

"Humanly speaking," repeated Valentine with bitterness. "I suppose, then, she wishes to insinuate that God ordained the child's death, and she had nothing to do with it?"

"She behaved with beautiful submission," urged Laura.

"I dare say! but the child had been given over to her absolute control, and she actually had a warning sent to her, so that she knew that it was running a risk to take him into heat, and hurry, and to unwholesome food. She chose to run the risk. She is a foolish, heartless woman. If she says anything to me, I shall tell her that I think so."

"I feel all the more bitter about it," he muttered to himself, "because I have done the same thing."

But Mrs. Melcombe said nothing, she contented herself with having made Laura uncomfortable by her tears, and as the days and weeks of her visit at Melcombe went on she naturally cared less about the matter, for she had her own approaching marriage to think of, and on the whole it was not unpleasant to her to be for ever set free from any duty toward her sister-in-law.

Valentine, though he often amazed Laura by his fits of melancholy, never forgot to be kind and considerate to her; he had long patience with her little affectations, and the elaborate excuses she made about all sorts of unimportant matters. She found herself, for the first time in her life, with a man of whom she could exact attendance, and whom she could keep generally occupied with her affairs. She took delighted advantage of this state of things, insomuch that before she was finally escorted to Liverpool and seen off, people in the neighbourhood, remarking on his being constantly with her, and observing his only too evident depression, thought he must have formed an attachment to her; it was universally reported that young Mr. Melcombe was breaking his heart for that silly Laura; and when, on his return, he seemed no longer to care for society, the thing was considered to be proved.

It was the last week in October when he reached Wigfield, to be present at his sister's wedding. All the woods were in brown and gold, and the still dry October summer was not yet over. John's children were all well again, and little Anastasia came to meet him in the garden, using a small crutch, of which she was extremely proud, "It was such a pretty one, and bound with pink leather!" Her face was still pinched and pale, but the nurse who followed her about gave a very good account of her, it was confidently expected that in two or three months she would walk as well as ever. "A thing to be greatly wished," said the nurse, "for Mr. Mortimer makes himself quite a slave to her, and Mrs. Walker spoils her."

Valentine found all his family either excited or fully occupied, and yet he was soon aware that a certain indefinable change in himself was only the more conspicuous for his fitful attempts to conceal it.

As to whether he was ill, whether unhappy, or whether displeased, they could not agree among themselves, only, as by one consent, they forbore to question him; but while he vainly tried to be his old self, they vainly tried to treat him in the old fashion.

He thought his brother seemed, with almost studied care, to avoid all reference to Melcombe. There was, indeed, little that they could talk about. One would not mention his estate, the other his wife, and as for his book, this having been a great failure, and an expensive one, was also a sore subject. Almost all they said when alone concerned the coming marriage, which pleased them both, and a yachting tour.

"I thought you had settled into a domestic character, St. George?" said Valentine.

"So did I, but Tom Graham, Dorothea's brother, is not going on well, he is tired of a sea life, and has left his uncle, as he says, for awhile. So as the old man longs for Dorothea, I have agreed to take her and the child, and go for a tour of a few months with him to the Mediterranean. It is no risk for the little chap, as his nurse, Mrs. Brand, feels more at home at sea than on shore.

On the morning of the wedding Valentine sauntered down from his sister's house to John Mortimer's garden. Emily had Dorothea with her, and Giles was to give her away. She was agitated, and she made him feel more so than usual; a wedding at which Brandon and Dorothea were to be present would at any time have made him feel in a somewhat ridiculous position, but just then he was roused by the thought of it from those ideas and speculations in the presence of which he ever dwelt, so that, on the whole, though it excited it refreshed him.

He was generally most at ease among the children; he saw some of them, and Swan holding forth to them in his most pragmatical style. Swan was dressed in his best suit, but he had a spade in his hand. Valentine joined them, and threw himself on a seat close by. He meant to take the first opportunity he could find for having a talk with Swan, but while he waited he lost himself again, and appeared to see what went on as if it was a shifting dream that meant nothing; his eyes were upon the children, and his ears received expostulation and entreaty: at last his name roused him.

"And what Mr. Melcombe will think on you it's clean past my wits to find out. Dressed up so beautiful, all in your velvets and things, and buckles in your shoes, and going to see your pa married, and won't be satisfied unless I'll dig out this here nasty speckled beast of a snake."

"But you're so unfair," exclaimed Bertram. "We told you if you'd let us conjure it, there would be no snake."

"What's it all about?" said Valentine, rousing himself and remarking some little forked sticks held by the boys.

"Why, it's an adder down that hole," cried one.

"And it's a charm we've got for conjuring him," quoth the other. "And we only want Swanny to dig, and then if the charm is only a sham charm, the adder will come out."

"I should have thought he was a sight better wheer he is," said Swan. "But you've been so masterful and obstinate, Master Bertie, since you broke your arm!"

"It's not at all kind of you to disappoint us on father's wedding-day."

"Well, Mr. Melcombe shall judge. If he says, 'Charm it,' charm you shall; for he knows children's feelings as well as grown folks's. There never was anybody that was so like everybody else."

"It's conjuring, I tell you, cousin Val. Did you never see a conjuror pull out yards and yards of shavings from his mouth, and then roll them up till they were as small as a pea, and swallow them? This is conjuring too. We say, 'Underneath this hazelin mote;' that's the forked-stick, you know; and while we say it the adder is obliged to roll himself up tighter and tighter, just like those shavings, till he is quite gone."

"*I* can't swallow that!" exclaimed Valentine. "Well, off then."

"But I won't have the stick poked down his hole!" cried Swan, while Hugh shouted down his defiance—

"'Underneath this hazelin mote
There's a braggerty worm with a speckled throat,
Now!
Nine double hath he.'

That means he's got nine rings."

"Well, I shall allers say I'm surprised at such nonsense. What do you think he cares for it all?"

"Why, we told you it would make him twist himself up to nothing. Go on, Hughie. It's very useful to be able to get rid of snakes."

"'Now from nine double to eight double,
And from eight double to seven double,
And from seven double to six double,
And from six double to five double,
And from five double to four double,
And from four double to three double.'

(He's getting very tight now!)

'And from three double to two double,
And from two double to one double,
Now!
No double hath he.'

There, now he's gone, doubled up to nothing. Now dig, Swanny, and you'll see he's gone."

"It's only an old Cornish charm," said Valentine. "I often heard it when I was a boy."

"I call it heathenish!" exclaimed Mr. Swan. "What do folks want with a charm when they've got a spade to chop the beast's head off with?"

"But as he's gone, Swan," observed Valentine, "of course you cannot dig him out; so you need not trouble yourself to dig at all."

"Oh, but that's not fair. We want, in case he's there, to see him."

"No, no," said Swan dogmatically; "I never heard of such a thing as having the same chance twice over. I said if you'd sit on that bench, all on you, I'd dig him out, if he was there. You wouldn't; you thought you'd a charm worth two of that work, and so you've said your charm."

"Well, we'll come and sit upon the bench to-morrow. then, and you'll dig him."

"That'll be as I please. I've no call to make any promises," said Swan, looking wise.

The only observer felt a deep conviction that the children would never see that snake, and slight and ridiculous as the incident was, Swan's last speech sunk deeply into Valentine's heart, and served to increase his dejection. "And yet," he repeated to himself, "I fully hope, when I've given up all, that I shall have my chance—the same chance over again. I hope, please God, to prove that very soon; for now Laura's gone, I'm bound to Melcombe no longer than it takes me to pack up my clothes and the few things I brought with me."

CHAPTER XXXV.

A VISIT TO MELCOMBE.

"Fairest fair, best of good,
Too high for hope that stood;
White star of womanhood shining apart
O my liege lady,
And O my one lady,
And O my loved lady, come down to my heart.

"Reach me life's wine and gold,
What is man's best all told,
If thou thyself withhold, sweet, from thy throne?
O my liege lady,
And O my loved lady,
And O my heart's lady, come, reign there alone."

AFTERWARDS while Valentine stood in the church, though his eyes and his surface thoughts were occupied with the approaching ceremony, still in devouter and more hopeful fashion than he had found possible of late, he repeated, "Please God, when I have given up all, as my poor father would wish, I shall have my chance over again. I'll work, like my betters, and take not a stick or a clod away from that Melcombe."

The guests were arriving. John Mortimer had been standing at the altar-rails, his three sons with him. Several members of the family grouped themselves right and left of him. This was to be the quietest of weddings. And Miss Christie Grant thought what a pity that was; for a grander man than the bridegroom or handsomer little fellows than his two younger sons it would be hard to find. "He's just majestic," she whispered to Mrs. Henfrey.

"Never did I see him look so handsome or so content, and there's hardly anybody to see him. Ay, here they come." Miss Christie seldom saw anything to admire in her own sex. Valentine looked down the aisle; his sister was coming, and John Mortimer's twin-daughters, her only bridesmaids, behind her.

The children behaved very well, though it was said afterwards that a transaction took place at that moment between Bertie and Hugh, in the course of which several large scarlet-runner beans were exchanged for some acorns; also that when John Mortimer moved down the aisle to meet his bride little Anastasia, seizing Mrs. Henfrey's gown to steady herself, thrust out her crutch toward Valentine, that he might have the privilege of again admiring it.

The peculiarity of this wedding, distinguishing it from others where love is, was the measureless contentment of the future step-children. "Nothing new in this family," observed Mrs. 'Henfrey. "When Emily's mother came here, all her children took to my father directly, and loved him as if he had been their own."

Emily had been married from her brother's house, Valentine's old home, and in the dining-room there was spread a wedding breakfast. The room looked nearly as it had done when Valentine should have appeared to be a bridegroom himself; but he did not know this so well as Dorothea did; yet he felt exceedingly sheepish, and was only consoled by observing that she also was a good deal out of countenance, and scarcely knew whether to blush or to smile when she spoke to him or met his eyes.

So the ceremony of the breakfast well over, and John Mortimer and his wife departed, Valentine was very glad to take leave of his family and walk across the fields with Johnnie. He did this partly to while away the time before his train started, partly to see Swan, who, with Mrs. Swan in gorgeous array, was found walking about the garden, her husband showing her the plants and flowers, and enlarging on their perfections.

"But how can I find time for it, even on this noble occasion, Mr. Melcombe, my wife's just been saying, is a wonder, for that long new conservatory all down the front of the house will take a sight of filling—filled it shall be, and with the best, for if ever there was a lady as deserved the best, it's Mrs. John Mortimer. I'm sorry now I burnt so many of my seedlings."

"Burnt them, Nicholàs?"

"Why yes, sir," said Mrs. Swan, "when he used to be sitting up with Mr. Johnnie, he had plenty of time to think, and he did it."

Johnnie being not yet so strong as before his accident, now went into the house to rest, and Swan proceeded to explain matters.

"It seems, sir, that the new mistress said some time ago, that if there was a conservatory along the front of the house, the rooms could be entered from it, and need not be thoroughfares; so Mr. John Mortimer built one, for he prizes every word she ever said. Now he had allers allowed me to sell for my own benefit such of my seedlings as we couldn't use ourselves. And Fergus sent, when the children were ill, and made me a handsome bid for them. But there air things as can't be made fair and square anyhow. The farrier has no right to charge me so high for shoeing my horse that I'm forced to sell him my horse to pay his bill; but he has a right to say he won't shoe him at all. Well, I reckoned as a fair price wouldn't do for me, and an unfair price I was above asking, so I flung the seedlings on my pea-sticks, and made a bon-fire on 'em."

"You did! I think that was waste, Swan. I think it was wrong."

"No, sir, I think not; for, as I said, some things won't pay at any figure. Their soil's better than ours. He meant to bribe me, and so beat me, and bring me down through my own plants. But would it pay a man to insure his brig that was not seaworthy (though he was to get £50,000 if she went down) provided he had to sail in her himself? Better by half break her up in the harbour, and have a dry burial for his corpse when his time was come, and mourners to follow, decent and comfortable. Now it's reason that if I'd known of this here new conservatory, and the new lad I'm to have to help me, I'd have kept them."

"Mrs. Swan," said Valentine, observing that she was moving away, "if it's agreeable to you, I'll come in shortly and take a cup of tea with you."

Mrs. Swan expressed herself pleased, and Swan marched off after her to get ready some cuttings which he was very desirous to send to the gardener at Melcombe.

"How Swanny talks!" said Barbara, who had now returned with her sisters in the carriage, and joined Valentine; "he is so proud when his wife has her best things on, her silk gown and her grand shawl; she only wears them at flower shows and great days like this because she's a Methodist."

Mrs. Swan, in fact, consented out of wifely affection to oblige her husband by wearing this worldly array when he specially desired it, but she always sighed more than usual, and behaved with even more sobriety and gravity then, as if to show that the utmost splendour of the world as represented by the satinet gown and a Paisley shawl could not make her forget that she was mortal, or puff up her heart with unbecoming pride.

Valentine, when a young boy, had often taken tea with Mrs. Swan, generally by invitation, when radishes and fruit were added to the buttered muffins.

On this occasion she gave him brown bread and butter, and some delicate young onions, together with a cake, baked in honour of Mr. Mortimer's wedding. Valentine thought it was only due to her that she should be told something concerning Joseph's wedding. A man's mother does not often care to hear of her son's love for another woman, but Valentine expected to please Mrs. Swan on this occasion.

"Like old times to see you, sir," she said, "ain't it, Nicholas?"

Then Valentine, seated at his ease, told his story, and was aware before it was half over that Swan was attempting to feign a surprise he did not feel, and that Mrs. Swan was endeavouring to keep within due bounds her expression of the surprise she did feel.

"Bless my heart!" she exclaimed, "you take this very easy, Nicholas."

Then Mr. Swan said, looking rather foolish, "Well, Maria, there's many more wonderful things in this world to hear on than to hear that a young man have fell in love with a young woman."

Mrs. Swan gasped. "Our Joey!" she exclaimed; "and what will Mr. Mortimer think?"

Valentine sat, composed, and almost impassive.

"You think she likes our boy, sir?"

"I am sure of it."

"How is he ever to maintain her as she'll expect!"

"She has a thousand pounds of her own; that will help him. I have written to him that he must settle it on her."

Here Mrs. Swan's added surprise made her thoughtful.

"She is a good, modest, virtuous young lady, as I've heerd," said Swan, looking pointedly at Valentine, as if to admonish him that the mother would like to have this confirmed.

"Yes," answered Valentine, with great decision; "she is all that and more, she is very affectionate, and has a good temper."

"Well," said Swan, drawing a deep breath, "all I have to observe is, that wives were made afore coats of mail, though coats of female would be more to the purpose here" (he meant coats of arms), "and," continued the gardener, with that chivalrous feeling which lies at the very core of gentlemanhood, "I'm not going to disparage my son, my Joey, that would be to disparage her *chice.* If she thinks he's ekal to be her husband, she'll respect him as a wife should. Why, bless you, Maria, my dear, if you come to that, there's hardly a young man alive that's ekal to his young wife, whether she be gentle or simple. They're clean above us, most on 'em. But he can rise; Joseph can rise if she'll help him."

"My word!" repeated Mrs. Swan several times over; and then added slowly, "It'll be an awk'ard thing for Swan if Mr. Mortimer should take offence about this."

Valentine was perfectly aware that something either in his manner, or his account of his own part in the matter, had much surprised them; also he thought that their poor place and preferment in this world seemed to them to be menaced by it. He did what he could to dissipate any such thoughts, and added a request that until they heard from Joseph that he was actually married nothing might be said about the matter. This request was very welcome to Mrs. Swan. It seemed to put off an eventful day, which she was not ready for even in imagination.

"Swan," said Valentine, "when he had taken leave of his hostess, this is no news to you."

"No, sir, Joseph told me all about it afore he sailed, and how he thought he'd got over it. Mr. Mortimer knows, as you're aware. Well, lastly, Joseph wrote again and told me he was fairly breaking his heart about her, and he should try his chance once more. You see, sir, his ways and fashions and hers are not alike. It would not have answered here—but there they'd both have to learn perfectly new ways and manners, and speak to their feller creatures in a new language. There's hardly another Englishman for her to measure him with, and not one

English lady to let her know she should have made a better match."

"Mr. Mortimer knows?"

"Ay, sir."

"And you never told your wife?"

"No, she has a good deal to hear, Mr. Valentine, besides that, and I thought I'd tell it her all at once."

Valentine saw that he was expected to ask a question here.

"What, Swanny, is something else coming off then?"

"Ay, sir; you see, Mr. Melcombe, I'm lost here, I'm ekal to something better, Mr. Mortimer knows it as well as I do. He's said as much to me more than once. What he'll do without me I'm sure I don't know, but I know well enough he'll never get such another."

"No, I don't suppose he will."

"There ain't such a gardener going—not for his weight in gold. But I'm off in the spring. I've done a'most all but break it to my wife. It's Joseph that's helping me, and for hindrance I've got a Methodist chapel and a boarded floor. There's boarded floors to her kitchen, and back kitchen, as Mr. Mortimer put in for her, because she was so rheumatic, they air what she chiefly vally's the place for. But at some of them small West India islands there's a fine opening, Joey says, for a man with a headpiece as can cultivate, and knows what crops require, and I ought to go. I'm only sixty-one or thereabouts. You'll not say anything about it, sir," he continued, as the twins, who were in the garden, came towards Valentine.

They brought him in triumph to the schoolroom, which was decorated, and full of the wedding presents the children had made for their father and the dear mamma.

"And you'll remember," said Bertram, "how you promised us—promised us *with all your might*, that we should come to Melcombe."

"Yes, all of us," proceeded Anastasia; "he said the little ones too."

"So you should have done, you poor darlings, but for that accident," said Valentine.

"And we were to see the pears and apples gathered, and have such fun. Do you know that you're a sort of uncle now to us?"

"What sort? The right sort?"

"Yes, and now when shall we come?"

"I am afraid I shall be away all the winter."

"In the spring, then, and father and the dear mamma."

"It's a long time till the spring," said Valentine, with a sigh; "but if I am at Melcombe then——"

"You'll have us?"

"Yes."

"Then let it be in the Easter holidays," said Johnnie, "that I may come too."

"All right," said Valentine, and he took leave of them, and departed in one of their father's carriages for the Junction, muttering as he looked back at the house, "No, you'll never see Melcombe, youngsters. I shall be at the other end of the earth, perhaps, by that time."

"Oh, what a long time to wait!" quoth the younger Mortimers; "five months and a half to Easter — twenty-three weeks — twenty-three times seven—what a lot of days! Now, if we were going to sea, as the Brandon baby is, we shouldn't mind waiting. What a pity that such a treat should come to a little stupid thing that does nothing but sputter and crow instead of to us! Such a waste of pleasure." They had never heard of "the irony of fate," but in their youthful manner they felt it then.

So St. George Mortimer Brandon was borne off to the *Curlew*, and there, indifferent to the glory of sunsets, or the splendour of bays and harbours, he occupied his time in cutting several teeth, in learning to seize everything that came near him, and in finding out towards the end of the time how to throw or drop his toys overboard. He was even observed on a calm day to watch these waifs as they floated off, and was confidently believed to recognise them as his own property, while in such language as he knew, which was not syllabic, he talked and scolded at them, as if, in spite of facts, he meant to charge them with being down there entirely through their own perversity.

There is nothing so unreasonable as infancy, excepting the maturer stages of life.

His parents thought all this deeply interesting. So did the old uncle, who put down the name of St. George Mortimer Brandon for a large legacy, and was treated by the legatee with such distinguishing preference as seemed to suggest that he must know what he was about, and have an eye already to his own interests.

Four months and a half. The Mortimers did not find them so long in passing as in anticipation, and whether they were long or short to their father and his new wife, they did not think of considering. Only a sense of harmony and peace appeared to brood over the place, and they felt the sweetness of it, though they never found out its name. There was more freedom than of yore. Small persons taken with a sudden wish to go down and see what father and mamma were about could do so; one would go tapping about with a little crutch, another would curl himself up at the end of the room, and never seem at all in the way. The new feminine element had great fascinations for them, they made pictures for Emily, and brought her flowers, liking to have a kiss in return, and to feel the softness of her velvet gown.

The taller young people, instead of their former tasteless array, wore delightfully pretty frocks and hats, and had other charming decorations chosen for them. They began to love the memory of their dead mother. What could she not have been to them if she had lived, when only a step-mother was so sweet and so dear and so kind? And mamma had said to them long before she had thought of marrying father, that their mother would have greatly wished them to please their father's wife, and love her if they could. Nothing was so natural as to do both, but it was nice, to be sure, that she would have approved.

It was not long after John Mortimer and his wife returned from their very short wedding tour that they had a letter from Valentine, and he had spoken so confidently of his intended absence in the south of Europe during the later autumn and the whole winter, that they were surprised to find he had not yet started, and surprised also at the excessive annoyance, the unreasonable annoyance he expressed at having been detained to be a witness at some trial of no great importance. The trial had not come on so soon as it should have done, and he was kept lingering on at this dull, melancholy Melcombe, till he was almost moped to death.

Emily folded up this letter with a sensation of pain and disappointment. She had hoped that prosperity would do so much for Valentine, and wondered to find him dissatisfied and restless, when all that life can yield was within his reach.

His next letter showed that he meant to stay at Melcombe all the winter. He complained no more; but from that time, instead of stuffing his letters with jokes, good and bad, he made them grave and short, and Emily was driven to the conclusion that rumour must be right, the rumour which declared that young Mr. Melcombe was breaking his heart for that pretty, foolish Laura.

At last the Easter holidays arrived, Johnnie came home, and forthwith Emily received a letter from Valentine with the long-promised invitation. The cherry orchards were in blossom, the pear-trees were nearly out; he wanted his sister and John Mortimer to come, and bring the whole tribe of children, and make a long stay with him. Some extraordinary things were packed up as presents for cousin Val, an old and much-loved leader, and Emily allowed more pets and more toys to accompany the cavalcade than anybody else would have thought it possible to get into two carriages. The little crutch, happily, was no longer wanted.

All the country was white with blossom when Valentine met his guests at the door of Melcombe House. It was late in the afternoon. Emily thought her brother looked thin, but the children rushing round him, and taking possession of him, soon made her forget that, and the unwelcome thought of Laura, for she saw his almost boyish delight in his young guests, and they made him sit down, and closed him in, thrusting up, with tyrannous generosity, cages of young starlings, all for him, and demanding that a room, safe from cats, should immediately be set aside for them. Then two restless, yelping puppies were proudly brought forward, hugged in their owner's arms. Emily, who loved a stir, and a joyous chattering, felt her spirits rise. Her marriage had drawn the families yet nearer together, and for the rest of that evening she pleased herself with the thought.

The next morning she wanted to see this beautiful house and garden. Valentine was showman, and the whole family accompanied her, wandering among the great white pear-trees, and the dark yews, then going into the stable-yard, to see the strange, old out-buildings, with doors of heavy, ancient oak, and then on to the glen.

Valentine did not seem to care about his beautiful house, he rather disparaged it.

"You're not to say, 'it's well enough,' when it's beautiful," observed Anastasia.

Then with what was considered by the elder portion of the party to be a pretty specimen of childish sagacity, Hugh admonished his little sister—

"But he mustn't praise his own things; that's not good manners. He talks in this way to make us think that he's not conceited; but he really knows in his heart that they're very handsome."

"Is he grander than father, mamma dear?" asked Anastasia.

"I don't think so, my sweet," answered Emily laughing. "I see you are not too grand, Val, to use your father's old repeater."

"No," said Valentine, who had been consulting rather a shabby old watch, and who now excused himself for leaving the party on the ground of an appointment that he had made. "This, and a likeness of him that I have in the house, are among the things I most value."

What did the appointment matter to them?

John noticed that he walked as if weary, or reluctant perhaps to leave them. He was the only person who noticed anything, for you must understand that the place was full of nests. All sorts of birds built there, even herons; and to stand at the brink of the glen, and actually see them—look down on to the glossy backs of the brooding mothers, and count the nests—wealth incalculable of eggs, and that of all sorts,—to do this, and not to be sure yet whether you shall ever finger them, is a sensation for a boy that, as Mr. Weller said, "is more easier conceived than described."

And so Valentine went in. There were two appointments for him to keep, one with his doctor, one with his lawyer. The first told him he had unduly tired himself, and should lie down. So lying down, in his grandmother's favourite sitting-room, he received the second, but could decide on nothing, because he had not yet found opportunity to consult the person principally concerned.

So after the man of law had departed, Valentine continued to lie quietly on the sofa for perhaps an hour; he closed his eyes, and had almost the air of a man who is trying to gather strength for something that he has to do.

Children's voices roused him at last. Emily was moving up the garden towards the house, leaning on John's arm; the two younger children were with them, all the others having dispersed themselves about the place.

Valentine sat up to gaze, and as their faces got nearer a sudden anguish, that was not envy, overcame him.

It was not so much the splendour of manly prime and strength that struck him with the contrast to himself, not so much even the sight of love, as of hope, and spring, and bloom, that were more than he could bear. How sufficient to themselves they seemed! How charming Emily was! A woman destined to inspire a life-long love seldom shows much consciousness of it. "I never saw a fellow so deeply in love with his wife," thought Valentine. "Surely she knows it. What are you saying to her, John?" They had stopped under the great fruit-trees near the garden-door. John bent down one of the blossom-laden boughs, and she, fair, and almost pale, stood in the delicate white shadow looking at it.

Beautiful manhood and womanhood! beautiful childhood, and health, and peace! Valentine laid himself down again and shut his eyes.

Emily had betrayed a little anxiety about him that morning. He was very thin, she said; he must take care of himself.

"Oh, yes," he had answered, "I shall do that. I have been very unwell, but I am better now." And then he had noticed that John looked at him uneasily, and seemed disturbed when he coughed. He thought that as they stood under the fruit-trees John had caught sight of him.

"I knew he would come up as soon as he found opportunity, and here he is," thought Valentine, not moving from his place, but simply lifting up his head as John entered. "What have you done with Emily?" he asked.

"Emily is gone up to her dressing-room. She means to hear the children read."

"Ah," exclaimed Valentine, with a sudden laugh of good-humoured raillery, "of all womankind, John, you have evidently secured the pearl, the 'one entire and perfect chrysolite.' You know you think so."

"Yes," answered John gravely, "but don't put me off, my dear fellow."

"What do you want? What do you mean?" said Valentine, for John sitting down near him, held out his hand. "Oh, nonsense; I'm all right." But he put his own into it, and let John with his other hand push up the sleeve of his coat.

"Too thin by half, isn't it?" he said, affecting indifference, as John gravely relinquished it; "but I am so mummied up in flannels that it doesn't show much."

"My dear fellow," John Mortimer repeated.

"Yes, I have been long unwell, but now I have leave to start in one week, John. I'm to take a sea voyage. You told me you could only stay here a few days, and there is a great deal that ought to be done while you are here. Don't look so dismayed, the doctors give me every hope that I shall be all right again."

"I devoutly hope so——"

"There's nothing to drive the blood from your manly visage," Valentine said lightly, then went on, "There is one thing that I ought not to have neglected so long, and if I were in the best health possible I still ought to do it, before I take a long sea voyage." He spoke now almost with irritation, as if he longed to leave the subject of his health and was urgent to talk of business matters. John Mortimer, with as much indifference as he could assume, tried to meet his wishes.

"You have been in possession of this estate almost

a year," he said, "so I hope, indeed I assume, that the making of a will is not what you have neglected?"

"But it is."

Rather an awkward thing this to be said to the heir-at-law. He paused for a moment, then remarked, "I met just now, driving away from your door, the very man who read to us our grandmother's will."

"I have been telling him that he shall make one for me forthwith."

"When I consider that you have many claims," said John, "and consider further that your property is all land, I wonder at your——"

"My neglect. Yes, I knew you would say so."

"When shall this be done then?"

"To-morrow."

Then Valentine began to talk of other matters, and he expressed, with a directness certainly not called for, his regret that John Mortimer should have made the sacrifices he had acknowledged to, in order eventually to withdraw his name and interest altogether from his banking affairs.

John was evidently surprised, but he took Valentine's remarks good-humouredly.

"I know you have had losses," continued Valentine. "But now you have got a partner, and——"

"It's all settled," said John, declining to argue the question.

"You fully mean to retire from probable riches to a moderate competence?"

"Quite; I have, as you say, made great sacrifices in order to do so."

"I rather wonder at you," Valentine added; "there was no great risk, hardly any, in fact."

"I do not at all repent my choice," said John with a smile in his eyes that showed Valentine how useless it was to say more. John was amused, surprised, but not moved at all from his determination. He thought proper to add, "My father, as you know, left two thousand pounds each to every one of my children."

"And he gave the same sum to me," Valentine broke in. "You said my property was all land, but it is not. And so, John, you will no longer be a rich man."

"I shall be able to live just as I do at present," answered John Mortimer, calmly turning him round to his own duty. "And you have relatives who are decidedly poor. Then one of your sisters has married a curate without a shilling, or any seeming chance of preferment; and your brother, to whom you owe so much, has cramped his resources very much for the sake of his mother's family. Of course, when I married Emily, I insisted on repaying him the one thousand pounds he had made over to her on her first marriage, but——"

"Giles is very fairly off," interrupted Valentine, "and some day no doubt his wife will have a good fortune."

"I thought the old man had settled eight thousand pounds on her."

"He made a settlement on her when she was to marry me, and he signed it. But that settlement was of no use when she married St. George."

"Had he the imprudence, then, to leave everything to chance?"

"Even so. But, John, St. George will never have a single acre of Melcombe."

CHAPTER XXXVI.

A PRIVATE CONSULTATION.

"Remove from me the way of lying . . . I have chosen the **way of truth.**"—PSALM cxix. 29, 30.

"WHY, you young rogues, you make your father blush for your appetites," said John Mortimer to his boys, when he saw Valentine at the head of the table, serving out great slices of roast beef at a luncheon which was also to be early dinner for the children.

Valentine had placed Emily at the other end of the table. "Take my place, John," he now said laughing, "I always was a most wretched carver."

"No, love, no," pleaded Emily to her husband in a quick low tone of entreaty, and John, just in time to check himself in the act of rising, turned the large dish toward him instead, and began to carve it, making as if he had not heard Valentine's request. But Valentine having taken some wine and rested for a few moments, after the slight exertion, which had proved too much for his strength, looked at his sister till she raised her eyes to meet his, smiled, and murmured to her across the table, "You daughter of England, 'I perceive that in many things you are too superstitious.'"

Emily had nothing to say in reply. She had made involuntary betrayal of her thought. She shrank from seeing her husband in her brother's place, because she was anxious about, afraid for, this same brother.

She had even now and then a foreboding fear lest ere long she should see John there for good. But to think so, was to take a good deal for granted, and now Valentine chose to show her that he had understood her feeling perfectly.

She would fain not have spoken, but she could not now amend her words. "Never was any one freer from superstition than he," she thought, "but after all, in spite of what John tells me of his doctor's opinion, and how the voyage is to restore him, why must I conceal an anxiety so natural and so plainly called for? I will not. I shall speak. I shall try to break down his reserve; give him all the comfort and counsel I can, and get him to open his mind to me in the view of a possible change."

Emily was to take a drive at four o'clock, her husband and her brother with her.

In the meantime Valentine told her he was going to be busy, and John had promised to help him. "An hour and a half," he sighed, as he mounted the stairs with John to his old grandmother's sitting-room, "an hour and a half, time enough and too much. I'll have it out, and get it over."

"Now then," said John Mortimer, seating himself before a writing-table, "tell me, my dear fellow, what it is that I can do to help you?"

He did not find his position easy. Valentine had let him know pointedly that he should not leave the estate to his half brother. All was in his own power, yet John Mortimer might have been considered the rightful heir. What so natural and likely as that it should be left to him? John did not even feign to his own mind that he was indifferent about this, he had all the usual liking for an old family place or possession. He thought it probable that Valentine meant it to come to him, and wanted to consult with him as to some burdens to be laid on the land for the benefit of his mother's family.

If Valentine's death in early youth had been but

a remote contingency, the matter could have been very easily discussed, but hour by hour John Mortimer felt less assured that the poor young fellow's own hopeful view was the true one.

Valentine had extended himself again on the sofa. "I want you presently to read some letters," he said; "they are in that desk, standing before you."

John opened it, and in the act of turning it towards him his eyes wandered to the garden, and then to the lovely country beyond; they seemed for the moment to be arrested by its beauty, and his hand paused.

"What a landscape!" he said, "and how you have improved the place, Val! I did not half do it justice the last time I came here."

"I hate it," said Valentine with irritation, "and everything belonging to it."

John looked at him with scarcely any surprise.

"That is only because you have got out of health since you came here; you have not been able to enjoy life. But you are better, you know. You are assured that you have good hope of coming back recovered. I devoutly trust you may. Forget any morbid feelings that may have oppressed you. The place is not to blame. Well, and these letters—I only see two. Are they all?"

"Yes. But, John, you can see that I am not very strong."

"Yes, indeed," said John with an involuntary sigh.

"Well, then, I want you to be considerate. I mean," he added, when he perceived that he had now considerably astonished John Mortimer—"I mean that when you have read them, I want you to take some little time to think before you speak to me at all."

"Why, this is in my uncle's handwriting!" exclaimed John.

"Yes," answered Valentine, and he turned away as he still reclined, that he might not see the reader, "so it is."

Silence then—silence for a longer time than it could have taken to read that letter. Valentine heard deep breathing from time to time, and the rustling of pages turned and turned again. At last, when there was still silence, he moved on the sofa and looked at his cousin.

John was astonished, as was evident, and mystified; but more than that, he was indignant and exceedingly alarmed.

Valentine had asked him to be considerate. His temper was slightly hasty; but he was bearing the request in mind, and controlling it, though his heightened colour and flashing eyes showed that he suffered keenly from a baffling sense of shame and impending disgrace. These feelings, however, were subsiding, and as they retired his astonishment seemed to grow, and his hand trembled when he folded up the letter for the last time and laid it down.

He took up the second letter, which was addressed to his grandmother, and read it through.

It set forth that the writer, Cuthbert Melcombe, being then in London, had heard that morning the particulars of his young uncle's death at sea, had heard it from one of the young man's brother officers, and felt that he ought to detail them to his mother; he then went on to relate certain commonplace incidents of a lingering illness and death at sea.

After this he proceeded to inform his mother that he had bought for her in Leadenhall Street the silver forks she had wished for, and was about to pack them up, and send them (with this letter enclosed in the parcel) by coach to Hereford, where his mother then was.

"Why did you show me this?" said John in a low, husky tone. "There is nothing in it."

"I found it," Valentine replied, "carefully laid by itself in a desk, as being evidently of consequence."

"We know that all the other Melcombes died peaceably in their beds," John answered; "and it shows (what I had been actually almost driven to doubt) that this poor young fellow did also. There is no real evidence, however, that the letter was written in London; it bears no post-mark."

"No," said Valentine; "how could there be? It came in a parcel. THE LETTER, John, will tell you nothing."

"I don't like it," John Mortimer answered. "There is a singular formality about the narrative;" and before he laid it down he lifted it slightly, and, as it seemed half unconsciously, towards the light, and then his countenance changed, and he said beneath his breath, "Oh, that's it, is it!"

Valentine started from the sofa.

"What have you found?" he cried out, and, coming behind John, he also looked through the paper, and saw in the substance of it a water-mark, showing when it had been pressed. Eighteen hundred and seven was the date. But this letter was elaborately dated from some hotel in London, 1804. "A lie! and come to light at last!" he said in an awe-struck whisper. "It has deceived many innocent people. It has harboured here a long time."

"Now, wait a minute," answered John. "Stop—no more. You asked me to be considerate to you. Be also considerate to me. If, in case of your death, there is left on earth no wrong for me to right, I desire you to be silent for ever."

He took Valentine by the arm and helped him to the sofa, for he was trembling with excitement and surprise.

"There is no wrong that can be righted now," Valentine presently found voice enough to say; "there never has been from the first, unless I am mistaken."

"Then I depend on your love for me and mine—your own family—to be silent in life, and silent after death. See that no such letters as these are left behind you."

"I have searched the whole place, and there is not another letter—not one line. You may well depend on me. I will be silent."

John stood lost in thought and amazement; he read Daniel Mortimer's letter again, folded it reverently, and pressed it between his hands. "Well, I am grateful to him," Valentine heard him whisper, and he sank into thought again.

"Our fathers were perfectly blameless," said Valentine.

John roused himself then. "Evidently, thank God! And now these two letters—they concern no one but ourselves." He approached the grate; a fire was burning in it. He lifted off the coals, making a hollow bed in its centre. "You will let me burn them now, of course?"

"Yes," said Valentine; "but not together."

"No; you are right," John answered, and he took old Daniel Mortimer's letter and laid it into the place he had prepared, covering it with the glowing cinders, then with the poker he pushed the other between the lower bars, and he and Valentine watched it till every atom was consumed.

There was no more for him to tell; John Mortimer thought he knew enough. Valentine felt what a relief this was, but also that John's amazement by no means subsided. He was trying hard to be gentle, to be moderately calm; he resolutely forbore from any comment on Valentine's conduct; but he could not help expressing his deep regret that the matter should have been confided to any one—even to Brandon—and finding, perhaps, that his horror and indignation were getting the better of him, he suddenly started up, and declared that he would walk about in the gallery for awhile. "For," he said pointedly to Valentine, "as you were remarking to me this morning, there is a good deal that ought to be done at once," and out he dashed into the fresh spring air, and strode about in the long wooden gallery, with a vigour and vehemence that did not promise much for the quietness of their coming discussion.

Ten minutes, twenty minutes, went by—almost half an hour—before John Mortimer came in again.

Valentine looked up and saw, as John shut himself in, that he looked almost as calm as usual, and that his face had regained its customary hue.

"My difficulty, of course, is Emily," he said. "If this had occurred a year ago it would have been simpler." Valentine wondered what he meant; but he presently added in a tone, however, as of one changing the subject, "Well, my dear fellow, you were going to have a talk with me, you know, about the making of your will. You remarked that you possessed two thousand pounds."

Valentine wondered at his coolness, he spoke so completely as usual.

"And what would you have me do with that?" he answered with a certain directness and docility that made John Mortimer pause; he perceived that whatever he proposed would be done.

"I think if you left a thousand pounds to the old aunt who brought your mother up, and has a very scanty pittance, it would be worthy of your kindly nature, and no more than her due."

"Well, John, I'll do it. And the other thousand?"

"Louisa has married a rich man's son, and I have made a handsome settlement on Emily, but your sister Lizzie has nothing."

"I will leave her the other thousand; and—and now, John, there is the estate—there is Melcombe. I thought you had a right to know that there had been a disadvantage as regarded my inheritance of it, but you are perfectly——" He hesitated for a word.

John turned his sentence rather differently for him, and went on with it. "But you feel that I am perfectly entitled to give you my opinion?"

"Certainly."

"I advise that you leave it for a county hospital."

"John!"

"Unconditionally and for ever, for," John went on calmly and almost gently, "we are here a very long way from the county town, where the only hospital worth anything is situated. This house has, on two stories, a corridor running completely through it, and is otherwise so built that it would require little alteration for such a purpose. The revenue from the land would go a good way towards supporting it. Therefore, as I said before——" Then pausing, when he observed the effect of his words on Valentine, he hesitated, and instead of going on, said, "I am very sorry, my dear Valentine."

"This is a shock to me," said Valentine. "It shows me so plainly that you would not have acted as I have done, if you had been in my place."

As he seemed to wait for an answer, John said, with more decided gentleness, "I suppose it does;" and went on in a tone half apology, half persuasion, "But you will see your lawyer to-morrow, and, using all discretion, direct him as I propose."

"Yes. Nothing at all is to go to you then?"

"I should like to have this portrait of your father; and, Val, I wish to assure you most sincerely that I do not judge your conduct. I have no opinion to give upon it."

"I have a good right to tell you now, that I have for some months fully intended to give up the place."

"Well, I am glad of that."

"I hope to recover, and then to work, living abroad, the better to conceal matters. I had quite decided, John; and yet what you have done is a shock to me. I feel that I am judged by it. I told you in the autumn that I meant to go away; I did. But though I took the estate so easily, so almost inevitably, I could not get away from it, though I wished and tried."

"But you can now. If you want money, of course you will look to me to help you. And so you could not manage to go?"

"No. So long as I was well and in high spirits I never meant to go; but one night I got a great shock, and walking home afterwards by the mere, I felt the mist strike to my very marrow. I have never been well since. I had no heart to recover; but when I might have got away I was detained by that trumpery trial till I was so ill that I could not safely travel; but now, John, I am ready, and you cannot imagine how I long to be off, and, please God, begin a better life, and serve Him as my old father did. I have three hundred pounds of honest money in hand, besides the two thousand your father gave me. But, John, Emily is my favourite sister."

"There!" said John, "I was afraid this would come."

"If I *should* die young—if she *should* find that I have left every shilling and every acre away from you and her, two of the people I love most, and thrown it into the hands of strangers, I could not bear to know that she would think meanly of my good sense and my affection after I am gone."

John was silent.

"For," continued Valentine, "no one feels more keenly than she does that it is not charity, not a good work, in a man to leave from his own family what he does not want and can no longer use, thinking that it is just as acceptable to God as if he had given it in his lifetime, when he liked it, enjoyed it—when, in short, it was his own."

"You alienate it with no such thoughts."

"Oh, no, God forbid! But she will think I must have done. There is hardly any one living who cares for me as much as she does. It would be very distressing for me to die, knowing she would think me a fanatic, or a fellow with no affection."

"I was afraid you would think of this."

"You will say something to her, John. All will depend on you. She will be so hurt, so astonished that I should have done such a thing that she will never open her lips about it to you. I know her, and, and——"

John seemed to feel this appeal very keenly: he could not look Valentine in the face. "I acknowledge," he muttered, "that this is hard."

"But you will say *something* to her?"

"If you can think of anything in the world that would not be better left unsaid—if you can think of any one thing that for the sake of her love and sorrow, and my peace and your own memory, should not be left to the silence you deprecate—then tell me what it is."

Neither spoke for some time after that. At last the poor young fellow said, with something like a sob, "Then you meant *that* when you mentioned Emily?"

"Yes, I did. I felt how hard it was. I feel it much more now I know you are going to divest yourself of any profit during your life." He had been looking at Valentine anxiously and intently. The large eyes, too bright for health; the sharp, finely-cut features and pallid forehead. Suddenly turning, he caught sight of himself in the glass, and stood arrested by a momentary surprise. Very little accustomed to consider his own appearance, for he had but a small share of personal vanity, he was all the more astonished thus to observe the contrast. The fine hues of health, the clear calm of the eyes, the wide shoulders and grand manly frame. This sudden irresistible consciousness of what a world of life and strength there was in him, had just the opposite effect of what seemed the natural one. "Perhaps he may survive us both," he thought. "Who can tell?"

"But it seems to me," he continued aloud, "that we have talked as if it was more than likely that Emily and I were to have some knowledge and consciousness of this will of yours; and yet the vicissitudes of life and the surprises of death ought to place them almost outside our thoughts of probability. I hope to see you some day as grey-headed as your father was. *I* hope it indeed! it may well be the case, and I not be here to see."

Valentine, always hopeful, was very much cheered by this speech. He did not know how John's thought had been turned in this direction by a strong sense of that very improbability which he wanted to leave out of the question.

They remained some time in silence together after this—John lost in thought, Valentine much the better for having relieved his mind. Then Emily came to the door ready for her drive, and looking very sweet and serene.

"Come, you have been talking long enough. John, how grave you look! I could not forbear to let you know that some letters have arrived. St. George and Dorothea are at home again, and the baby can almost walk alone. But, Val, it seems that you have been inviting young Crayshaw here?"

"I have taken that liberty, madam," said Valentine. "Have you anything to say against it?"

Emily smiled, but made no answer.

"That boy and I suit each other uncommonly well," continued Valentine. "Our correspondence, though I say it, would be worth publishing—stuck as full of jokes as a pincushion should be of pins. It often amused me when I was ill. But his brother is going to take him home."

"Ah, home to America!" said Emily, betraying to neither John nor Valentine the pleasure this news gave her.

John was silent, still deeply pondering the unwelcome surprise of the afternoon. Valentine was refreshed by her presence, and at finding his avowal over.

"And so," continued Valentine, "he wrote to me

and asked if I would have him for two days before he left. He knew that you would all be here, and he wanted to take leave."

"He is a droll young fellow," said Emily. "Johnnie will miss his 'chum.' One of the letters was from him. He is to be here in an hour, and Johnnie has started off to meet him, with Bertie and one of the girls."

The other of the girls, namely, Gladys, had betrayed just a little shyness, and had left his young allies to go and fetch Crayshaw without her. Emily meeting her in the corridor as she came up-stairs, had stopped and given her a cordial kiss.

"She is so very young," thought the warm-hearted step-mother. "She will soon forget it."

She took Gladys with her, and after their short drive managed that they should be together when young Crayshaw appeared; and she helped her through a certain embarrassment and inclination to contradict herself while answering his reproachful inquiries respecting Blob, his dog.

"Father would not let us bring him," said Barbara, confirming the assurance of the others on that head.

"I have a great mind to go back all the way round by Wigfield to take leave of him," said Crayshaw. "You think I don't love that dog? All I know is, then, that I called him out of his kennel the last time I left him—woke him from his balmy slumber, and kissed him."

"Oh, yes, we know all about that," observed Barbara. "It was quite dusk, mamma, and Johnnie had stuck up the kitchenmaid's great mop, leaning against the roof of Blob's kennel, where he often sits when he is sulky. We all went to see the fun, and Cray thrust his face into it. It looked just like Blob's head."

"I'm sure I don't know what A. J. Mortimer could see of a military nature in that tender incident," said Crayshaw, with great mildness. "I did not expect, after our long friendship, to have a Latin verse written upon me, and called 'The Blunderbuss.'"

Crayshaw had grown into a handsome young fellow, and looked old for his years, and manly, though he was short. He had quite lost his former air of delicate health, and, though sorry to part with the young Mortimers, could not conceal a certain exultation in the thought of leaving school, and returning to his native country.

"Scroggins has been growing faster than ever," he said, half-enviously. "Whenever he gets from under my eyes he takes advantage of it to run up."

Emily remonstrated. "I don't like to hear you call Johnnie 'Scroggins.'"

"Oh, that's only my poetical way; the old poets frequently did it. 'Lines to his Mistress, Eliza Wheeler, under the name of Amaryllis.' You often see that kind of thing. In the same way I write to my chum, A. J. Mortimer, under the name of Scroggins. 'Scroggins, of vertuous father vertuous son.' I think it sounds extremely well."

Valentine was very well pleased the next afternoon to find himself sitting among a posse of young Mortimers and Crayshaw, under the great pear and apple trees, the latter just coming out to join their blossom to that of their more forward neighbours. It was his nature to laugh and make laugh, and his character to love youth, his own being peculiarly youthful. His usual frame of mind was repentant and humble, and he was very grateful for the apparent removal of illness. He was soon to be well, and hope and joy woke up in his heart, and came forth to meet the spring.

John Mortimer and Emily sat near enough, without joining the group, to catch the conversation, when they chose to listen. John was peculiarly grave and silent, and Emily was touched for the supposed cause. Valentine was the only relation left who had lived in his presence. She knew he had almost a brother's affection and partial preference for him. She knew that he had doubts and fears as to his health, and she thought of nothing more as the cause of his silence and gravity.

She made some remark as to Valentine's obvious improvement that morning; in fact, his spirits were lightened, and that alone was enough to refresh him. Things were making progress also in the direction he wished; his berth was secured, his courier was engaged, and some of his packing was done.

By degrees the mere satisfaction of Emily's presence made it easier for John, Mortimer to accept the consolation of her hope. He began to think that Valentine might yet do well, and the burnt letters receded into the background of his thoughts. Why, indeed, unless his cousin died, need he ever allow them to trouble him again?

Valentine looked from time to time at John and at Emily, and considered also the situation, thinking, "He loves her so, his contentment with her is so supreme, that nothing of dead and done crime or misery will hang about his thoughts long. He will get away, and in absence forget it, as I shall. I'll take a long look, though, now, at these high gables, with the sunshine on them, and at those strange casements, and these white trees. I know I shall never regret them, but I shall wish to remember what they were like."

He looked long and earnestly at the place and at the group. The faces of some were as grave as their father's.

Little Hugh, having a great matter to decide, could hear and see nothing that passed. What should he give Crayshaw for a keepsake? The best thing he had was his great big plank, that he had meant to make into a see-saw. It was such a beauty! Cray loved carpentering. Now, the question was—Cray would like it, no doubt, but would the ship take it over? How could it be packed?

Next to him sat Gladys, and what she felt and thought she hardly knew herself. A certain link was to be snapped asunder, which, like some growing tendril, had spread itself over and seemed to unite two adjacent trees.

Cray was in very high spirits at the thought of going home. She felt she might be dull when he was gone.

She had read his letter to Johnnie; there was in it only a very slight allusion to her. She had told him how the German governess had begun one to her, "Girl of my heart." He had not answered, but he showed thus that he had read her anecdote.

His letter to Johnnie ran as follows :—

"AUGUSTUS JOHN OF MY HEART,—When I heard I was going home to America, I heaved up one of the largest sighs that ever burst from a young-manly bosom. I'm better now, thank you. In short, I feel that if I were to be deprived of the fun of the voyage, it would blight a youth of heretofore unusual promise.

"George Crayshaw, when he saw my dismay at the notion of leaving this little island (into which, though you should penetrate to the very centre, you could never escape the salt taste of the sea-air on your lips), said he was ashamed of me. The next day, when I was furious because he declared that we couldn't sail for three weeks on account of packing the rubbish he has collected, he said so again. There is a great want of variety in that citizen," &c.

Gladys was roused from her cogitations by hearing Valentine say—

"Sitting with your back to Barbara! You'll have to take some lessons in manners before you go where they think that 'the proper study of mankind is *wo*man.'"

"It was I who moved behind him," said Barbara, "to get out of the sun."

Crayshaw replied with a sweet smile and exceeding mildness of tone—

"Yes, I must begin to overhaul my manners at once. I must look out for an advertisement that reads something like this :—

"'The undersigned begs to thank his friends and the public for their continued patronage, and gives notice that gentlemen of neglected education can take lessons of him as usual on his own premises, at eightpence an hour, on the art of making offers to the fair sex. N.B.—This course paid in advance.

"'Dummy ladies provided as large as life. Every gentleman brings a clean white pocket-handkerchief, and goes down on his own knees when he learns this exercise. Fancy styles extra.

"'Signed,

"'VALENTINE MELCOMBE.

"'References exchanged.'"

"You impudent young dog!" exclaimed Valentine, delighted with this sally, and not at all sorry that Mr. and Mrs. Mortimer were out of hearing—they having risen and strolled down to a lower portion of the orchard.

Valentine was seated on a low garden-chair, and his young guests were grouped about him on a Persian carpet which had been spread there. Gladys was roused from her reverie by seeing Valentine snatch a piece of paper from Crayshaw—peals of laughter following his pretended reading of it.

"They actually think, those two, of having their poems printed," Barbara had been saying.

"It would only cost about £30," said Crayshaw, excusing himself, "and Mrs. Mortimer promised to subscribe for twenty copies. Why, Lord Byron did it. If he wrote better Latin verse than Scroggins does, where is it?"

"The first one, then," said Barbara, "ought to be

Johnnie's parody that he did in the holidays. Mamma gave him a title for it, 'Ode on a Distant Prospect of leaving Harrow School.' "

Then it was that Valentine snatched the paper.

"Most of them are quite serious," Crayshaw here remarked.

"Ah, so this is the list of them," said Valentine, pretending to read :—

" 'POEMS BY TWO SCHOOLBOYS.

" ONE.—'Lines written on a late Auspicious Occasion' (I do so like that word auspicious), 'and presented to my new step-uncle-in-law, with a smile and a tear.' I'll read them :—

> 'Respecting thee with all my might,
> Thy virtues thus I sing.' "

"It's a story!" shouted Johnnie, interrupting him. "I don't respect you a bit, and I never wrote it."

"Two," proceeded Valentine, " 'The Whisper, by a Lisper,' and 'The Stick of Chocolate, a Reverie.' Now, do you mean to tell me that you did not write these?"

"No, I didn't! you know I didn't!"

"FOUR," Valentine went on, " 'The City of the Skunk, an Ode.' Now, Cray, it is of no use your saying you did not write this, for you sent me a copy, and told me that was the poetical name for Chicago."

"Well," said Crayshaw, "I tried that subject because Mr. Mortimer said something about the true sustenance of the poetic life coming from the race and the soil to which the poet belonged; but George was so savage when I showed it to him that I felt obliged to burn it."

"FIVE.—'To Mrs. M. of M.,'" continued Valentine. "It seems to be a song :—

> 'Oh, clear as candles newly snuffed
> Are those round orbs of thine.' "

"It's false," exclaimed Crayshaw; "Mrs. Melcombe indeed! She's fat, she's three times too old for me."

"Why did you write it, then?" persisted Valentine. "I think this line,—

'Lovely as waxwork is thy brow,'

does you great credit. But what avails it! She is now another's. I got her wedding cards this morning. She is married to one Josiah Fothergill, and he lives in Warwick Square.

"SIX—'The Black Eye, a Study from Life.'"'

"But their things are not all fun, cousin Val," said Gladys, observing, not without pleasure, that Crayshaw was a little put out at Valentine's joke about Mrs. Melcombe. "Cray is going to be a real poet now, and some of his things are very serious indeed."

"This looks very serious," Valentine broke in; "perhaps it is one of them: 'Thoughts on Futurity, coupling with it the name of my Whiskers.'"

"There's his ode to Sincerity," proceeded Gladys; "I am sure you would like that."

"For we tell so many stories, you know," remarked Barbara; "say so many things that we don't mean. Cray thinks we ought not."

"For instance," said Johnnie, "sometimes when people write that they are coming to see us, we answer that we are delighted, when in reality we wish that they were at the bottom of the sea."

"No, no," answered Valentine, in a deprecatory tone; "don't say at the bottom, that sounds unkind. I'm sure I never wished anybody more than half-way down."

Two or three days after this a grand early dinner took place at Melcombe. All the small Mortimers were present, and a number of remarkable keepsakes were bestowed afterwards on Crayshaw by way of dessert. After this, while Mr. and Mrs. John Mortimer sat together in the house the party adjourned to the orchard, and Crayshaw presently appeared with a small box in which had hitherto been concealed his own gifts of like nature. Among them were two gold lockets, one for each of the twins.

"I helped him to choose them," said Johnnie, "and he borrowed the money of his brother."

"There's nothing in them," observed Barbara. "It would be much more romantic if we put in a lock of Cray's hair."

"I thought of that," quoth the donor, "but I knew very well that the first new friend you had, you would turn it out and put his in, just as both of you turned my photograph out of those pretty frames, and put in Prince Leopold after he had passed through the town. You are to wear these lockets."

"Oh yes," said Barbara, "and how pretty they are with their little gold chains!"

"Cray, if you will give me a lock of your hair, I promise not to take it out," said Gladys.

She produced a little pair of scissors, and as he sat at her feet, cut off a small curl, and between them they put it in. A certain wistfulness was in her youthful face, but no one noticed it.

"I shouldn't wonder," she remarked, "if you never came back any more."

"Oh yes, I shall," he answered in a tone of equal conviction and carelessness.

"Why? you have no friends at all but us."

"No, I haven't," he answered, and looked up at her as she stood knitting, and leaning against a tree.

"Of course you'll come," exclaimed Johnnie, "you're coming for your wedding tour. Your wife will make you; you're going to be married as soon as you're of age, old fellow."

Then Crayshaw, blushing hotly, essayed to hi. Johnnie, who forthwith started up and was pursued by him with many a whoop and shout, in a wild circling chase among the trees. At length, finding he was not to be caught, Crayshaw returned a good deal heated, and Johnnie followed smiling blandly, and flung himself on the grass breathing hard.

"Well, I'm glad you two are not going to finish up your friendship with another fight," said Valentine.

"He's always prophesying something horrid about me," exclaimed Crayshaw. "Why am I to be married any more than he is, I should like to know? If I do, you'll certainly have to give up that visit to California, that Mr. Mortimer almost promised you should make with me. Gladys, I suppose he would not let you and Barbara come too?"

"Oh no. I am sure he would not."

"What fun we might have!"

"Yes."

"I don't see if you were a family man, why it shouldn't be done," said Johnnie, returning to the charge, "but if you won't marry, even to oblige your oldest friends, why you won't."

"Time's up," said Valentine, looking at his watch, "and there's my dog-cart coming round to the door."

The youth rose then with a sigh, took leave of Valentine, and reluctantly turned towards the house, all the young Mortimers following. They were rather late for the train, so that the parting was hurried, and poor little Gladys as she gazed after the dog-cart, while Johnnie drove and Crayshaw looked back, felt a great aching pain at her heart, and thought she should never forget him.

But perhaps she did.

The young Mortimers were to leave Melcombe themselves the next day, and Valentine was to accompany them home, sleeping one night at their father's house by way of breaking his journey, and seeing his family before he started on his voyage.

He was left alone, and watched his guests as their receding figures were lost among the blossoming trees. He felt strangely weak that afternoon, but he was happy. The lightness of heart that comes of giving up some wrong or undesirable course of action (one that he thought wrong) might long have been his, but he had not hitherto been able to get away from the scene of it.

To-morrow he was to depart. Oh, glad to-morrow!

He laid himself back in his seat, and looked at the blue hills, and listened to the sweet remote voices of the children, let apple-blossoms drop all over him, peered through great brown boughs at the empty sky, and lost himself in a sea of thought which seemed almost as new to him and as fathomless as that was.

Not often does a man pass his whole life before him and deliberately criticize himself, his actions and his way.

If he does, it is seldom when he would appear to an outsider to have most reasonable occasion; rather during some pause when body and mind both are still.

The soul does not always recognise itself as a guest seated within this frame; sometimes it appears to escape and look at the human life it has led, as if from without. It seems to become absorbed into the august stream of being; to see that fragment *itself*, without self-love, and as the great all of mankind would regard it if laid open to them.

It perceives the inevitable verdict. Thus and thus have I done. They will judge me rightly, that thus and thus I am.

If a man is reasonable and sees things as they were, he does not often fix on some particular act for which to blame himself when he deplores the past, for at times of clear vision, the soul escapes from the bondage of incident. It gets away from the region of particulars, and knows itself by nature even better than by deed. There is a common thought that beggars sympathy in almost every shallow mind. It seldom finds deliberate expression. Perhaps it may be stated thus :—

The greatness of the good derived from it, makes the greatness of the fault.

A man tells a great lie, and saves his character by it. No wonder it weighs on his conscience ever after. And yet perhaps he has told countless lies, both before and since, told them out of mere carelessness, or from petty spite or for small advantages, and utterly forgotten them. Now which of these, looked at by the judge, is the great offender? Is the one lie he repents of the most wicked, or are those that with small temptation he flung about daily, and so made that one notable lie easy?

Was it strange that Valentine, looking back, should not with any special keenness of pain have rued his mistake in taking Melcombe?

No. That was a part of himself. It arose naturally out of his character, which, but for that one action, he felt he never might have fully known.

So weak, so longing for pleasure and ease, so faintly conscious of any noble desire for good, so wrapped up in a sense as of the remoteness of God, how could it be otherwise?

If a man is a Christian, he derives often in such thoughts a healing consciousness of the Fatherhood and Humanity of God. He perceives that he was most to be pitied and least to be judged, not while he stood, but when he fell. There is no intention of including here hardened crimes of dishonesty, and cruelty, and violence, only those pathetic descents which the ingrain faults and original frailty of our nature make so easy, and which life and the world are so arranged as to punish even after a loving God forgives.

"These faults," he may say, "they seem to live, though I shall die. They are mine, though I lose all else beside. Where can I lay them down, where lose them? Is there any healing to be found other than in His sympathy, His forgiveness who made our nature one with His to raise it to Himself?"

The world is not little. Life is not mean. It spreads itself in aspiration, it has possession through its hope. It inhabits all remoteness that the eye can reach; it inherits all sweetness that the ear can prove; always bereaved of the whole, it yet looks for a whole; always clasping its little part, it believes in the remainder. Sometimes, too often, like a bird it gets tangled in a net which notwithstanding it knew of. It must fly with broken wings ever after. Or, worse, it is tempted to descend, as the geni into the vase, for a little while, when sealed down at once unaware, it must lie in the dark so long, that it perhaps denies the light in heaven for lack of seeing it.

If those who have the most satisfying lot that life can give are to breathe freely, they must get through, and on, and out of it.

Not because it is too small for us, but too great, it bears so many down. On the whole that vast mass of us which inherits its narrowest portion, tethered, and that on the world's barest slope, does best.

The rich and the free have a choice, they often choose amiss. Yet no choice can (excepting for this world) be irretrievable; and that same being for whom the great life of the world proved too much, learns often in the loss of everything, what his utmost gain was not ordained to teach.

He wanted all, and at last he can take that all, without which nothing can make him content. He perceives, and his heart makes answer to, the yearning Fatherhood above; he recognises the wonderful upward drawing with love and fear.

> "This is God!
> He moves me so, to take of Him what lacks;
> My want is God's desire to give; He yearns
> To add Himself to life, and so for aye
> Make it enough."

CHAPTER XXXVII.

HIS VISITOR.

"The fairy woman maketh moan,
 'Well-a-day, and well-a-day,
Forsooth I brought thee one rose, one,
 And thou didst cast my rose away.'
Hark! Oh hark, she mourneth yet,
 'One good ship—the good ship sailed,
One bright star, at last it set,
 One, one chance, forsooth it failed.'

"'Clear thy dusk hair from thy veiled eyes,
 Show thy face as thee beseems,
For yet is starlight in the skies,
 Weird woman piteous through my dreams.
'Nay,' she mourns, 'forsooth not now,
 Veiled I sit for evermore,
Rose is shed, and charmèd prow
 Shall not touch the charmèd shore.

"There thy sons that were to be,
 Thy small gamesome children play;
There all loves that men foresee
 Straight as wands enrich the way.
Dove-eyed, fair, with me they wonn
 Where enthroned I reign a queen,
In the lovely realms foregone,
 In the lives that might have been."

THAT glad to-morrow for Valentine never came. At the time when he should have reached Wigfield, a letter summoned his brother to Melcombe.

Emily and John Mortimer had delayed their return, for Valentine, whether from excitement at the hope of setting off, or from the progress of his disease, had been attacked, while sitting out of doors, with such sudden prostration of strength that he was not got back again to the house without the greatest difficulty. They opened a wide window of the "great parlour," laid him on a couch, and then for some hours it seemed doubtful whether he would rally.

He was very calm and quiet about it, did not at all give up hope, but assented when his sister said, "May I write to St. George to côme to you?" and sent a message in the letter, asking his brother to bring his wife and child.

He seemed to be much better when they arrived, and for two or three days made good progress towards recovery; but the doctors would not hear of his attempting to begin his journey, or even of his rising from the bed which had been brought down for him into the wide, old-fashioned parlour.

And so it came to pass that Brandon found himself alone about midnight with Valentine, after a very comfortable day of little pain or discomposure. All the old intimacy had returned now, and more than the old familiar affection. Giles was full of hope, which was all the stronger because Valentine did not himself manifest that unreasonable hopefulness which in a consumptive patient often increases as strength declines.

His will was signed, and in his brother's keeping; all his affairs were settled.

"I know," he had said to his brother, "that I have entirely brought this illness on myself. I was perfectly well. I often think that if I had never come here I should have been so still. I had my choice; I had my way. But if I recover, as there seems still reason to think I may, I hope it will be to lead a higher and happier life. Perhaps even some day, though always repenting it, I may be able to look back on this fault and its punishment of illness and despondency with a thankful heart. It showed me myself. I foresee, I almost possess such a feeling already. It seems to have been God's way of bringing me near to Him. Sometimes I feel as if I could not have done without it."

Valentine said these words before he fell asleep that night, and Giles, as he sat by him, was impressed by them, and pondered on them. So young a man seldom escapes from the bonds of his own reticence, when speaking of his past life, his faults, and his religious feelings. This was not like Valentine. He was changed, but that, considering what he had undergone, did not surprise a man who could hope and believe anything of him, so much as did his open, uncompromising way of speaking about such a change.

"And yet it seems strange," Valentine added, after a pause, "that we should be allowed, for want of knowing just a little more, to throw ourselves away."

"We could hardly believe that it was in us, any of us, to throw ourselves away," Brandon answered, "if we were always warned to the point of prevention."

Valentine sighed. "I suppose we cannot have it both ways. If God, because man is such a sinner, so overruled and overawed him that no crime could be committed, he would be half-unconscious of the sin in his nature, and would look up no more either for renewal or forgiveness. Men obliged to abstain from evil could not feel that their nature was lower than their conduct. When I have wished, Giles, as I often have done lately, that I could have my time over again, I have felt consoled, in knowing this could not be, to recollect how on the consciousness of the fault is founded the conscious longing for pardon. But I will tell you more of all this to-morrow," he added; and soon after that he fell asleep.

A nurse was to have watched with him that night, but Brandon could not sleep, and he desired that she would rest in an adjacent room till he called her. In the meantime, never more hopeful since he had first seen Valentine on reaching Melcombe, he continued to sit by his bed, frequently repeating that he would go up-stairs shortly, but not able to do it.

At one o'clock Valentine woke, and Brandon, half excusing himself for being still there, said he could not sleep, and liked better to wake in that room than anywhere else.

Valentine was very wakeful now, and restless; he took some nourishment, and then wanted to talk. All sorts of reminiscences of his childhood and early youth seemed to be present with him. He could not be still, and at length Brandon proposed to read to him, and brought the lamp near, hoping to read him to sleep.

There was but one book to be read to a sick man in the dead of the night, when all the world was asleep, and great gulfs of darkness lurked in the corners of the room.

Giles read, and felt that Valentine was gradually growing calmer. He almost thought he might be asleep, when he said—

"St. George, there's no air in this room."

"You must not have the windows open," answered Brandon.

"Read me those last words again, then," said Valentine, "and let me look out; it's so dark here."

Brandon read, "The fulness of Him that filleth all in all."

Valentine asked to have the curtain drawn back, and for more than an hour continued gazing out at the great full moon now rapidly southing, and at the lofty pear-trees, so ghostly white, showering down their blossom in the night. Brandon also sat looking now at the scene, now at him, till the welcome rest of another sleep came to him; and the moon went down, leaving their shaded lamp to lighten the space near it, and gleam on the gilding of quaint old cabinets and mirrors, and frames containing portraits of dead Melcombes, not one of whom either of these brothers had ever seen.

Brandon sat deep in thought, and glad to hear Valentine breathing so quietly, when the first solemn approaches of dawn appeared in the east; and as he turned to notice the change, Valentine woke, and gazed out also among the ghostly trees.

"There he is," said Valentine, in his usual tone of voice.

"Who is?" asked Brandon.

"My father—don't you see him walking among the trees? He came to see my uncle—I told you so!"

Brandon was inexpressibly startled. He leaned neared, and looked into Valentine's wide-open eyes, in which was no sign of fear or wonder.

"Why, you are half asleep, you have been dreaming," he presently said, in a reassuring tone. "Wake up, now; see how fast the morning dawns."

Valentine made him no answer, but he looked as usual. There was nothing to bespeak increased illness till he spoke again, faintly and fast—

"Dorothea—did he bring Dorothea?"

Giles then perceived with alarm that he was not conscious of his presence—took no notice of his answer. He leaned down with sudden and eager affright, and heard Valentine murmur—

"I thought he would have let me kiss her once before I went away."

Brandon started from his knees by Valentine's bed as this last faint utterance reached him, and rushed up-stairs to his wife's room with all the speed he could command.

Oh, so fast asleep! her long hair loose on the pillow. How fair she looked, and how serene, in her dimpled, child-like beauty!

"Love, love!—wake up, love! I want you, Dorothea."

She opened her startled eyes, and turned with a mother's instinct to glance at her little child, who was asleep beside her, looking scarcely more innocent than herself.

"Love, make haste! Valentine is very ill. I want you to come to him. Where's your dressing-gown?—why here. Are you awake now? What is it, do you ask? Oh, I cannot tell—but I fear, I fear."

He rushed down-stairs again, and was supporting Valentine's head with his arm when Dorothea appeared, and stopped for one instant in the doorway, arrested by some solemn words. Could it be Valentine that spoke? There was a change in his voice that startled her, and as she came on her face was full of tender and awe-struck wonder.

"The fulness of Him," he said, "that filleth all in all."

Brandon looked up, and in the solemn dawn beheld her advancing in her long white drapery, and with her fair hair falling about her face. She looked like one of those angels that men behold in their dreams.

Valentine's eyes were slowly closing.

"Kiss him, my life!" said Brandon, and she came on, and kneeling beside him put her sweet mouth to his.

Valentine did not have that kiss!

THE END.

MESSRS. ROBERTS BROTHERS

HAVE JUST PUBLISHED:

By the Author of "Christian Art and Symbolism."

OUR SKETCHING CLUB: Letters and Studies on

Landscape Art. With an authorized Reproduction of the Lessons and Woodcuts in Professor Ruskin's "Elements of Drawing." By R. ST. JOHN TYRWHITT. 8vo. $2.50.

This book is in the form of a narrative, and is the doings of a supposed Sketching Club, their letters, talks, and essays on various art subjects, — nearly all practical ones, — such as would be likely to be exchanged between fairly good critics and well-educated men and women. It is a handsome 8vo volume, with numerous illustrations.

By the Author of "The Intellectual Life."

HARRY BLOUNT: Passages in a Boy's Life on Land and

Sea. By PHILIP GILBERT HAMERTON. With Frontispiece Illustration. 16mo. $1.50.

Mr. Hamerton has successfully accomplished a difficult task, and "his book for boys reaches the standard of a first-rate one," says the *London Academy;* and the *Spectator* says, "Harry Blount is a fine fellow, and we are glad to see him safely through his perils."

By the Author of "The Old Masters" and "Modern Painters."

MUSICAL COMPOSERS AND THEIR WORKS.

By SARAH TYTLER. 16mo. $2.00.

"Distinctively gossipy and very entertaining. Lovers of music, who read for entertainment, will heartily enjoy these bright and minute sketches of the great composers; in point of readableness they are not surpassed by any similar sketches in recent literature," says *The* (Boston) *Literary World.*

PARAGRAPH HISTORY OF THE UNITED

STATES, from the Discovery of the Continent to the Present Time, with Brief Notes on Contemporaneous Events. By EDWARD ABBOTT. Square 18mo, flexible cloth covers. 50 cents.

A pocket *vade mecum* of great value at this interesting period. It will be published on the Centennial Anniversary of the Battle of Lexington and Concord.

THROUGH THE YEAR. By Rev. H. N. POWERS,

D D., Rector of St. John's Church, Chicago. 16mo. $1.50.

A collection of serious and religious papers suited to the seasons of Nature and of the Church.

A SHEAF OF PAPERS. By THOMAS G. APPLETON.

16mo. $1.50.

Bostonians in particular, and lovers of good things in literature in general, will be glad that the author of these Papers, the rich and ripened fruits of his intellectual labors, has been induced to gather them into a Sheaf for publication. A few of them only have been previously printed.

MADAME RÉCAMIER AND HER FRIENDS.

From the French of Madame LENORMANT, by the translator of "Memoirs and Correspondence of Madame Récamier." 16mo. $1.50.

Madame Lenormant's previous volume contained the memoirs of Madame Récamier, and the correspondence of her friends. The present volume is the complement of the first, and contains her Friendships and her Private Correspondence.

THE DEFENCE OF GUENEVERE AND OTHER

POEMS. By WILLIAM MORRIS. Crown 8vo. $2.00.

The author of "The Earthly Paradise" has been induced to reprint his earlier poems, now for a long time out of print. The volume was never published here, and is therefore entirely unknown to the numerous admirers of Mr. Morris's poetry in America.

FREEDOM AND FELLOWSHIP IN RELIGION.

A Collection of Essays and Addresses. Edited by a Committee of The Free Religious Association. 16mo. $2.00.

Jean Ingelows Prose Story Books.

In 5 vols. 16mo, uniformly bound.

STUDIES FOR STORIES FROM GIRLS' LIVES. Illustrated, Price, $1.25.

"A rare source of delight for all who can find pleasure in really good works of prose fiction. . . . They are prose poems, carefully meditated, and exquisitely touched in by a teacher ready to sympathize with every joy and sorrow."—*Athenæum.*

STORIES TOLD TO A CHILD Illustrated. Price, $1.25.
STORIES TOLD TO A CHILD. Second Series. Illustrated. Price, $1.25.

"This is one of the most charming juvenile books ever laid on our table. Jean Ingelow, the noble English poet, second only to Mrs. Browning, bends easily and gracefully from the heights of thought and fine imagination to commune with the minds and hearts of children; to sympathize with their little joys and sorrows; to feel for their temptations. She is a safe guide for the little pilgrims; for her paths, though 'paths of pleasantness,' lead straight upward."—*Grace Greenwood in "The Little Pilgrim."*

A SISTER'S BYE-HOURS. Illustrated. Price, $1.25.

"Seven short stories of domestic life by one of the most popular of the young authors of the day,—an author who has her heart in what she writes,—Jean Ingelow. And there is heart in these stories, and healthy moral lessons, too. They are written in the author's most graceful and affecting style, will be read with real pleasure, and, when read, will leave more than momentary impressions.' —*Brooklyn Union.*

MOPSA THE FAIRY. A Story. With Eight Illustrations · Price, $1.25.

"Miss Ingelow is, to our mind, the most charming of all living writers for children, and 'Mopsa' alone ought to give her a kind of pre-emptive right to the love and gratitude of our young folks. It requires genius to conceive a purely imaginary work which must of necessity deal with the supernatural, without running into a mere riot of fantastic absurdity; but genius Miss Ingelow has, and the story of Jack is as careless and joyous, but as delicate, as a picture of childhood.

"The young people should be grateful to Jean Ingelow and those other noble writers, who, in our day, have taken upon themselves the task of supplying them with literature, if for no other reason, that these writers have saved them from the ineffable didacticism which, till within the last few years, was considered the only food fit for the youthful mind."—*Eclectic.*

Sold everywhere Mailed, postpaid, by the Publishers.

ROBERTS BROTHERS, BOSTON.

Seven Times One. — Exultation.

There's no dew left on the daisies and clover,
There's no rain left in heaven:
I've said my "seven times" over and over,
Seven times one are seven.

THE WRITINGS

OF

JEAN INGELOW.

Poems.

LIBRARY EDITION. 2 vols. 16mo. Price $3 00

BLUE AND GOLD EDITION. 2 vols. 32mo. Price 2.50

CABINET EDITION. 1 vol. 18mo. Price 2 25

ILLUSTRATED EDITION. Square 8vo. Price 7.50

DIAMOND EDITION. 1 vol. square 18mo. Price 1.50

RED LINE EDITION. 1 vol. square 12mo. Price 3.75

SONGS OF SEVEN. Illustrated. 8vo. Price 2.50

SONGS OF SEVEN. Cheap illustrated edition. 16mo. Illuminated paper cover. Price 20 cents; cloth, neat, price . 0.30

Miss Ingelow's New Poems.

THE MONITIONS OF THE UNSEEN, AND POEMS OF LOVE AND CHILDHOOD. With 12 superb illustrations. 1 vol. 16mo. Cloth, neat. Price 1.50

Prose.

STUDIES FOR STORIES, FROM GIRLS' LIVES. Price . . . 1.25

STORIES TOLD TO A CHILD. First and second series. Each 1.25

A SISTER'S BYE-HOURS. Price 1.25

MOPSA THE FAIRY. Price 1.25

POOR MATT; or, The Clouded Intellect. Price 0.60

OFF THE SKELLIGS. A novel. Price 1.75

FATED TO BE FREE. A novel. Price 1.75

These editions of Miss Ingelow's Poetical and Prose Writings are the only authorized American Editions, and are issued with her sanction, by her Publishers,

ROBERTS BROTHERS,

BOSTON.

www.ingramcontent.com/pod-product-compliance
Lightning Source LLC
LaVergne TN
LVHW021316110826
845150LV00003B/590

* 9 7 8 1 4 2 5 5 5 7 3 3 1 *